Drawing Card

Drawing Card

A Baseball Novel

Dorothy Seymour Mills

McFarland & Company, Inc., Publishers

Jefferson, North Carolina, and London

LIBRARY OF CONGRESS CATALOGUING-IN-PUBLICATION DATA

Mills, Dorothy Seymour.
    Drawing card : a baseball novel / Dorothy Seymour Mills.
      p.   cm.

    ISBN 978-0-7864-6814-0
    softcover : acid free paper ∞

    1. Women baseball players—Fiction.   2. Baseball stories.
I. Title.
PS3613.I5676D73 2012
813'.6—dc23   2012009885

BRITISH LIBRARY CATALOGUING DATA ARE AVAILABLE

Cover art: Bill Knapp, "Annie on the Mound," 2011, oil on board
12½" x 17½" (www.billknappart.com)

Manufactured in the United States of America

McFarland & Company, Inc., Publishers
  Box 611, Jefferson, North Carolina 28640
    www.mcfarlandpub.com

Prologue

"I DON'T UNDERSTAND, GRAN. These stories are about you?"

Annie, standing at the other end of the kitchen, busied herself by occasionally stirring the sauce as she made the salad. Reluctantly, she replied to the young man with the scrapbook in his lap. "They're about something I did long ago. Want some more wine? Your mom and dad should be here any minute. We're eating here instead of in the dining room, so please set the table."

"Where's Gina?"

"It's her day off. You know I enjoy cooking."

"Gran, why didn't you ever tell us about this? How long did you play ball? I never even knew you liked athletics."

"You just don't remember, Tommy," she smiled as came out from behind the counter and handed him the salad bowl. He put down the scrapbook and accepted the bowl. "We played catch when you were growing up," she went on. "We played croquet in the front yard..."

"Croquet, sure, but that's a sissy game compared with baseball." He laid out the silverware and napkins but soon picked up the album again.

"Swimming, skating, backyard basketball... We did those things together. I remember when your Aunt Isabel took your father horseback riding..."

"Okay. We enjoyed those things, but it's hardly the same as facing another team in competitive baseball games. Listen, Gran, were you pretty good at it? It sounds like it, from these newspaper clippings. How was the competition? And what does 'Collinwood Cardinals' mean?"

Cindy Smith tapped on the door and opened it, calling out, "Hi, it's me. That smells so good, Ma! I brought ice cream. Johnny is parking the car..." She bent to hug her. "What's that you've got, Tommy?"

"Listen, Mom, I want you to look at this album I found in Gran's cabinet with those recipes you told me to look for. It's an old scrapbook from

1

the 1920s and '30s with clippings about Gran playing baseball. Did you know about this?"

But Cindy, shaking her head, was putting the ice cream in the freezer. "I smell real spaghetti sauce. Gina's not here?"

Annie intervened, "Tommy, don't pester your mom. You forgot to put the salad bowls on."

"I think I saw it once, long ago," Cindy murmured, glancing at it. "I've sort of forgotten... Johnny, do you remember this scrapbook?"

John Smith Junior walked in, his limp hardly noticeable, and kissed his mother on the cheek. He shook his graying blonde head at Cindy and turned back to his mother, who was still stirring the sauce. "I never get such good spaghetti at home as yours, Ma. Sometimes it's hell being married to a Slovenian." He looked slyly at his wife, whose frown meant she was pretending to be angry. "Is that garlic bread I smell? When do we eat?" He snitched a small hot pepper from a platter of antipasto.

"Wash up, everyone. It's ready."

"Now Tommy, simmer down." When he grinned, John revealed the wrinkles at the corners of his eyes, and he looked more like his mother. "Your grandma isn't the type to sue."

"Dad, I'm telling you, she has a good case. A big business organization discriminated against her."

"Tommy," said his mother as she passed a cup of coffee to her husband. "We're proud of you for passing the bar exams and getting promoted, but surely this is something outside your field of expertise."

"Not really. It's information available to everyone. It's been eleven years since Title Nine was passed—you know, the law saying girls and women can't be excluded from any sports they want to play in college. It also prevents colleges from getting any public money if they don't give their female students the same sports program opportunities as the men. That's why Sis has such solid support for her college basketball team."

John Junior set his cup down and reached for another anise-flavored cookie. "Tommy, what does your Gran's experience in baseball have to do with the new college law?"

Tommy made a face that seemed to mean "Maybe nothing."

"Exactly." Anna Cardello Smith sat back with satisfaction. Her son had, as usual, put his finger on the issue. "Tommy, you know I never attended college—I married too early. After your grandpa died and your dad was born, I took some courses, but that's all. Of course, your grandpa Smith graduated from Western Reserve and played sports there. Pass the cream, please."

"Yes, but the element of discrimination is still present in this case," Tommy insisted. "I seem to remember that some people were successful when they tried suing for discrimination that took place long ago. Maybe I'll check it out." He finished the last of his ice cream.

Annie shook her head in disapproval. "I'd rather you didn't."

John Junior sat back and raised his eyebrows, pursing his lips the way his mother did. After a pause, he tried to speak about the issue in more general terms. "Employment discrimination in Organized Baseball? I never heard of it."

"Well, maybe not, but... Listen," Tommy went on. "Title Seven of the 1964 Civil Rights Act prohibits employment discrimination on the basis of race, sex, national origin, or religion. Of course," he went on, beginning to recall relevant facts, "you're supposed to try administrative remedies first, before instituting a suit. But since Judge Landis is dead—"

"The guy who was the baseball commissioner?"

"Yes. Gran said he was the commissioner in the 1930s. He died in the forties."

"Ma, what about Judge Landis?" John Junior became more interested.

She waited, realizing he would not leave it alone, then replied reluctantly, "Well, he nullified my contract."

"What contract?"

"The one that Joe Cambria got me to sign."

"Cambria. Wasn't he a scout? He signed you to a baseball contract?"

"Yes. But it's too late to do anything about it now. I'm going to clear up. Cindy, will you bring—"

"What club? Ma, what club did you sign with?"

Annie, holding the tray of garlic bread, turned. "His own. At that time, Cambria ran the Albany Club. It was in the International League."

"Well, I'll be darned. I didn't realize that. You signed with a club in Organized Baseball, and Landis nullified your contract because you're a female?"

"Yes. But it was a long time ago."

"Maybe Tommy has an idea here. Let's take a look at that scrapbook. And how about the contract, Ma? Do you still have it?"

"Somewhere... Now, let me do my work." She walked into the kitchen, where Cindy had already brought some leftovers.

Leftovers, she thought. I'm a leftover, too. Left over from an earlier time, when girls and women who wanted to play baseball were taunted and teased, harassed and vilified. Even by other girls and women. Even after the success of the women's league of the forties. But it all means nothing now. Best to forget about the whole thing. This is a *Cold Case* file that won't bear reopening.

Annie avoided further questions about baseball.

That night, as they got ready for bed at home in Shaker Heights, Cindy asked her husband, "Do you get the feeling that your mom doesn't want us to know any more about her baseball experience?"

"I think she's hiding something from us. I've never seen her so secretive, even defensive. I wonder what it is. I wish my father were still alive. Maybe he'd know." He removed his leg brace and began rubbing his game leg.

In her own living room, Annie was sitting there brooding in the dark. She was remembering a backyard picnic that took place at the home of Elwood "Pinky" Crane and his wife Phyllis. It turned out to be an unpleasant occasion.

Pinky, so-called because he blushed easily, wore a heavy blue cotton apron and stood unsteadily at the backyard grill. Inside, at the cocktail table, he had already enjoyed several gin martinis but had since graduated to Leisy's, Cleveland's own popular beer. Pinky flipped burgers with abandon, and the chef's hat Phyllis had bought him tipped jauntily to one side.

Phyllis and her kitchen helper were bringing big bowls of potato salad and macaroni salad to the trestle table when the conversation among those standing around it with their drinks turned to baseball and Cleveland's terrible team.

"Remember when we had Colavito?" Pinky asked. "We haven't had a decent year since."

Annie found herself nodding in agreement. "I remember June of 1959, when he hit four homers in one game."

Her comment was ignored.

"What we need on the team is some stars," said "Flash" Gordon Wade.

"Some really good players like Barry Bonds, George Brett, Ken Griffey," threw in Stu Sherwin.

"Yes," said Phyllis. "Or Albert Belle."

"Mike Piazza," suggested Parmely Blanford. Parmely's wife was out of town, so he was drinking more than usual, trying to keep up with Pinky.

"Listen," said Pinky, piling burgers on a platter. "We could use anybody. Anybody at all would be better than what we've got." His face was reddening.

"He'd better serve those burgers soon," Phyllis murmured to Annie.

"Yeah," Stu's wife Thea responded to Pinky's complaint. "We'll take the Bad News Bears."

"Or even a woman player," Pinky added with a grin.

Annie looked up from where she sat on a bench. "There've been some good woman players," she commented. "I played myself, as a young woman, with a successful baseball team."

"You mean softball," Pinky remarked, gingerly approaching the trestle table and the crowd around it with his platter of burgers.

"No, I mean baseball."

Flash flicked his eyes at Parmely, but neither said anything. Both of them had known Annie for a long time but only recently became re-acquainted with her as a widow.

Pinky carefully and successfully put the plate of burgers down on the table and removed his cooking mitt. "Why would a girl want to play base-ball?" He reached for another bottle of Leisy's among those cooling in the metal bucket, but it slipped out of his hand. Flash retrieved it for him and pulled off the cap.

Annie paused briefly before replying, "That's like saying, 'Why would a man want to cook?'"

In the long pause that followed, Pinky lowered his chin, flushed darker, then retorted, "Are you calling me feminine?"

Annie smiled. "Only if you're calling me masculine." She crossed her legs, letting her skirt slide up to her thigh, then broadened her smile. The women laughed, helping defuse the situation, and some sat down at the table on one of the two benches.

Pinky began to relax. "I suppose you're right. Let women play baseball, if they think they can." He grinned ruefully. "Once a female mechanic fixed my car. Afterwards, it actually ran better!"

Phyllis began putting burgers and spoonfuls of salad on the children's plates and bringing them to the low table set aside for them, so the children stopped playing and fighting, beginning to gather around the food.

Annie grew silent, thinking: Parmely and Flash know that I played baseball well but said nothing to support me. Nothing.

Thea Sherwin, a historian who taught at Western Reserve, helped repair the conversation by spinning out the thread about crossed-over gender roles. "Now that we have female airline pilots and surgeons and even astronauts, it seems foolish to assign males and females any particular roles."

"You sound like a sociologist, Thea; I thought you were a historian," Phyllis contributed.

Thea ignored that as she served herself some salad. "I've been wondering what Peter is going to be when he grows up. His favorite activity is knocking down his sister's block towers." She stopped. "I know: Destruction engineer!"

Giggles started. Phyllis added, "I think Courtney's going to be a professional scissors duller. She's always cutting up stuff that isn't meant to be cut with scissors, like her father's favorite ties. Pass the mustard."

They can keep nattering on and on about nothing, thought Annie. They'll never say anything in support of a professional female baseball player.

For the rest of that evening, she spoke only when spoken to.

Still brooding in her dark living room, she thought, well, at least I evened things up for myself.

She rose and went upstairs. She had a lot to remember.

PART ONE:
ANNIE PLAYS THE GAME

1

"Papa?"

"What, Anna? Did you finish your homework, my little girl?"

"Yes, Papa. But I want to ask you something."

"Of course, Anna." Giovanni Cardello took the cigar from his mouth and put down his copy of *La Voce del Popolo Italiano*, Voice of the Italian People, the locally-published paper that presented its news for Clevelanders in both English and Italian.

He saw the concerned look on her face, her pursed lips. "What could be bothering my little girl?" Giovanni, comfortable in his living room chair, felt that he must be concerned for his daughter.

"Papa, the *Cleveland Plain Dealer* today says a girl named Margaret Gisolo—an Italian name, isn't it?—she played for an American Legion baseball team last year, did you know? But this year, the American Legion says from now on, girls can't play on American Legion ball teams. Just because they're girls. Is that fair?"

"Well, maybe not fair, little girl, but maybe it's best. Girls are different from boys. They're not as tough."

"But I'm tough enough for my team, Papa. Gennaro likes me to play with his team. I'm a good pitcher. And—"

"Now don't get all excited, Anna. You're only fourteen."

"Fifteen."

"You'll change later on. Then you won't want to play any more." Giovanni felt sure of his judgments. His confidence showed on his face.

"I *will*. I *will* want to play. Papa, I want to ask you something else."

Giovanni's expression changed, but Annie went on.

"Papa, today's *Cleveland News* says Thomas Edison—you know, the man who invented the light bulb—he and other men held a contest to find the brightest boy in America. Every state picked one boy to compete, and Mr. Edison, along with Mr. Ford, and Mr. Eastman, and Mr. Firestone, and Mr. Lindbergh, they decided that a Wyoming boy was the brightest. Papa, I want to ask you this: Why didn't they hold a contest for the brightest girl in America?"

Giovanni Cardello's jaw dropped. "Why... Why, I don't know. I suppose that... I suppose they thought finding the brightest boy was more important."

Annie stared at him for a moment. Her mouth opened a little, then closed. She dropped her eyes to the floor, then looked up again. After a few moments, she went on, "One more thing, Papa. Remember when you told me about the Sons of Italy? The club you belong to."

"It's more than a club, Anna." Here was an opportunity for Giovanni to hold forth on the virtues of the institution. He sat up straighter and took a strong breath. "It's a lodge, a place where we can get together with other *paesani* here in Cleveland, to talk the old language and sing the old songs..."

"I know, Papa. But remember the paper you showed me that told what the Sons of Italy stand for?"

"Of course. We have our life insurance through the Lodge, and—"

"No, I mean what the Lodge *stands* for."

Giovanni shifted in his chair. He raised and lowered his eyebrows. Am I being challenged? By my own daughter? He thought. Then he took another breath and began, "Well, it stands for equality of opportunity. The words on the paper say 'equality that gives the benefits of human association to everyone.'"

"No discrimination, you said."

"Of course not. We stand together because we want to be sure that Italian American culture is respected here. Same as the Slovenian Americans. Don't they have their *Slovenska Dom*? Don't the German Americans have their *Deutscher Verein*? The Czechs, they have their *Sokol* on Clark Avenue. Even the Bohemians have a hall, over on Broadway. For us, the Italian Americans, having the Lodge is a way of getting together to make sure that Italian Americans receive their measure of respect."

"*All* Italian Americans? All of them should have equality of opportunity?"

"Of course. We are proud *Siciliani* and *Napolitani*..."

"Then why didn't the Sons of Italy complain when the American Legion said Margaret Gisolo couldn't play?"

Taken aback, Giovanni put his cigar in the ashtray and explained, "Now, Anna, playing a game is not the same as getting a job."

"Why isn't it, Papa? You always said I should think of school as my job, and I should think of American clubs I belong to as my job, too. Like the Girl Scouts. You said I should treat them seriously, that they're important. Isn't playing in American Legion baseball important?"

Giovanni hesitated. "Not the way a real grownup job is important."

Annie paused, turned sideways, waited a few moments, then turned back. "Papa, how did you get your job?"

"By knowing other *Italiani*," he said proudly, "the ones who were contractors. A few even came from Sicily, the way I did. We *paesani* stick together."

"They hired you because you're a *paisano*?" Now she was kneeling in front of him, her face near his.

"Well, also because I'm a good worker." Giovanni's lip trembled. He was beginning to feel uncomfortable with this close questioning.

"Papa, are you equal to the Slovenian Americans and the German Americans? Are we equal to them?"

He drew back. "Of course."

"Then why do you need to depend on *paesani* to get jobs?"

His mouth opened and closed. "Well, now. *Depend*. That's a strong word. *Depend*. I don't *depend* on them. Not really *depend*. Just... Take advantage of knowing them." He began to stroke his moustache.

"But if we're all equal, and we all have equal opportunity, why do you need *paesani*? Why do the Slovenians and the Germans need their clubs?"

Giovanni was stumped. He could not think of an answer. He knew only that he was beginning to get annoyed. His opinions and declarations were being questioned. That meant his authority was being questioned, the way it was when his daughter started to play baseball.

Giovanni's nostrils twitched, and his eyes shifted around.

After a moment, he said, "Anna, you are stepping beyond the bounds. These are not matters for a girl to consider. Leave them to the grownups."

Annie was still for about twenty seconds. Her eyelids lowered, and her lips pursed. "Okay, Papa," she said meekly, and turned away.

But Giovanni didn't forget. And neither did Annie.

Annie's mother Bianca, listening from the kitchen, took note of this exchange, realizing there was a fundamental difference between the attitudes of her husband and her daughter. She asked herself, now, where do I stand on this matter? I know only that such differences make me uncomfortable.

The next day, in talking to Yolanda, her closest friend, over coffee in the small Cardello house, she brought up the subject. "I cannot be disloyal to my husband," she said, bringing to the table a plate of anise-flavored cookies. "But I also see my daughter's point of view: Why should the girls be kept from playing their favorite game? Can it be that harmful, Yolanda? I want Anna to grow up to be a lady, yes, not unruly like my boys. But children must play."

Yolanda shrugged. To her, another topic was more important. "Your boys, Bianca: Are they still mixed up with those hoodlums, the Lonardos and the Porrellos?"

Bianca looked down at her cup. I might as well say it, she thought. "Yes, and it tears my heart. If only the Boiardi food company hadn't moved out of Cleveland! My boys might still have good jobs there." Bianca's mouth turned down. "They only went with those gangsters because they lost their jobs. But now that Hector Boiardi has opened a restaurant here, perhaps my boys still have a chance with the company..."

"Bianca. You know better. Now that your boys have had a taste of the big money that they can get doing illegal things, they will never go back. Prohibition has made it too easy for boys to make big money. They think they are big shots. They will never change."

"Never say never! I cannot believe that. I will not." But then her tears came.

The money in Annie Cardello's purse made her feel important, so her posture as she walked toward the beautiful building occupied by the Society for Savings in downtown Cleveland reflected her pride. As she stepped toward the entrance inside the granite pillars of the arcade, she glanced admiringly at the decorative ironwork around the door.

I feel important here, she thought. I can put the money I earned all by myself into this important Cleveland bank—a place where important people put theirs. I'm just as good as they are, for I make money, too.

Annie had saved a full ten dollars over the last month, despite giving her parents five dollars a week for room and board. Her father's work hours had been cut, so her five dollars a week meant a lot in 1930. She felt pleased with herself for having a job, in these times when some families had lost their income, and she was proud and happy to have a bank account.

John E. Smith noticed her right away, from his position at a corner desk behind a metal barrier, where he passed on loans and helped set bank policy.

A beautiful girl with stately bearing. She walks well. Graceful, but also athletic. She probably rides bicycles and goes skating and likes horses, as I do. Those dark, dramatic eyes, and all that dark hair. Not tall, but nicely formed. Simply dressed. Nothing fancy—no jewelry. She has taste.

John realized that he was staring, so he lowered his eyes; instead, he listened to her soft voice as she spoke to the teller.

How can I bring myself to her attention? I've got to meet this girl.

She finished with the teller. Stepping past the gold-topped pillars and stained-glass windows set in pink marble walls, she walked over to the stand that patrons used for recording transactions in their personal records. Above it, framing her body for John, spread a rather garish-looking mural in medieval style. As she picked up a pen, he stood up and approached her. "Finding everything you need, miss?"

Surprised, she looked up at him with dark Mediterranean eyes. "Yes, thanks."

"Good. Very good. Glad you came in. We appreciate your business."

"You're welcome," she replied, taking him literally. Then she thought: Would this large and important bank really appreciate my ten dollars? The Society for Savings must have thousands of dollars... No, millions of dollars.

She looked at the speaker more closely and realized he was simply an attractive young fellow who wanted to talk to a young woman. Her mouth started to turn up at the corners.

He probably approaches only the young girls and pays no attention to the old ones or to the men. Maybe he's a masher. I'd better get out of here.

She completed the recording of her transaction as he stood there watching her, rocking back on his heels. Hurriedly, she picked up her purse, dislodging a deposit slip from the stand. It fell to the floor, and they both started toward it, bumping shoulders.

"Sorry."

"Sorry."

She let him pick it up and offer it: "Do you need this?"

"No, thanks. Goodbye."

"Goodbye. Nice talking to you."

He watched her leave, then went to the teller. "Is that young woman a regular patron?"

"Yes, Mr. Smith. Is anything wrong?"

"No. But I'd like her name, please. And her address." He was thinking: I can see now that she may not be a member of Cleveland society, as I thought. I wonder how she'd fit in with my crowd. I'll bet she could handle it. She has personal dignity. Pride. Probably is proud of her heritage. Greek? Italian? A dark, Mediterranean kind of beauty.

Walking back to his desk staring at the slip of paper bearing the name "Anna Cardello" and her address in the blue-collar Collinwood section, he thought of his family and how hard it might be for the Smiths to accept the notion of his seeing such a girl.

My father, he thought, would probably classify her with the anarchists Sacco and Vanzetti. This is probably something I shouldn't pursue.

"Good morning, Patrolman Osowski." Annie always greeted the policeman standing at the corner of Euclid and East Ninth Street, seemingly guarding the Statler Hotel from invasion by the army of modest-appearing workers on their way to their jobs.

"Good morning, Miss Cardello." Sam Osowski touched his hat for the pretty young seamstress going to work at Halle Brothers Company. "A little early this morning, aren't you?"

"Yes, I need to get something done for a customer. Bye."

"Goodbye, Miss."

Jodhpurs, thought Annie, sitting at her table in the alterations department. What exaggerated pants! I prefer my baseball uniform.

First cutting out the pattern and using the electric pinking machine on the material, she then stitched the pants so that they would fit tightly across the customer's knees and ankles, yet bulge out widely at the hips. Made-to-measure jodhpurs were items of clothing featured at Halle's Department Store, and if necessary the women in the alterations department could create them from scratch for the buyer.

"How's it coming, Anna?" The supervisor approached.

"Fine, Miss Ziska. The jodhpurs will be ready for the customer's three o-clock fitting."

"Good. That's Miss Smith, isn't it?"

"Yes. Miss Isabel Smith."

"Lovely girl. Good family. One of the city's finest."

Annie didn't reply, thinking to herself: I have a good family, too. What's so good about Miss Smith's family, besides being rich enough to afford horseback riding? Miss Ziska, not being a member of one of these fine families, seems to defer to them anyway, even when such deference doesn't seem necessary. Probably wishes she were a Smith herself. Well, I'm a Cardello, and I'm not ashamed of it. In the back of her mind rankled the question: Was Miss Isabel Smith related to John Smith, the banker? It seemed likely. They're surely on the same social level. I wonder what she'll be like.

Just then "Mr. Sam" entered the Women's Alterations room. A short, quiet, almost shy man, Samuel H. Halle made an unlikely-looking owner of the company, one of the two founding brothers of the Halle Brothers Company. He often visited the various departments of the store, smiled at the employees, greeted them, even inquired after their well-being when he'd heard they had personal problems. He stopped to talk to Miss Ziska, smiling his sweet smile, then running his hand over his nearly-bald head.

Sam Halle was sixty. The other Halle brother had retired to his hobbies, so Sam remained in charge but was grooming a promising young son to take over. He nodded pleasantly to the employees in the room.

Remembering that one girl, an Italian immigrant named Giulia, was new, Mr. Sam walked over to her. "How are you coming along with your English, Giulia?" Sam Halle spoke to everyone as though they were equals. He expected to be treated like a friend because he considered his employees part of his extended family.

Embarrassed by being singled out by the "big boss," Giulia blushed and managed only "Good. Good, thank you."

"I'm glad to hear it, Giulia."

"Giulia is doing all right," Emma Ziska threw in. "How are your flying lessons coming along, Mr. Sam?"

"Not ready to solo yet, Emma, but maybe next month. If I continue to do well I'm going to get myself a Stearman. I'll take you for a ride, if you like."

"No! No, thanks, Mr. Sam. I like to stay on the ground."

He nodded and smiled, then got serious. "Let's talk in your office, Emma."

When they emerged, they both looked grim. After Sam Halle left, Emma Ziska asked for everyone's attention and made her announcement.

"All employees are being asked to work fewer hours. For the first time, Halle's has lost money. Nobody will be fired. In order to retrench, the alterations department will be closed on Mondays, so we will all lose one day's pay."

Disappointment showed in the faces of the women who worked in Ladies' Alterations. They glanced at each other, thinking their own thoughts, knowing that their personal goals were compromised, their lives made more difficult.

Sixteen dollars a week was little enough, Annie thought. Now she would get less.

It came to her mind: I won't be able to visit the Society for Savings as often as before.

2

"ONCE," JOJO SRENIC BEGAN, "when I was at summer camp in Pennsylvania..." She was lounging on the grass with the other girls, reminiscing. The fans were starting to arrive, but the game wouldn't start for fifteen minutes.

"You got to go to summer camp?" Annie felt a twinge of jealousy.

"Sure. My parents let me go for a week to this place called Pine Tree Camp, in the Pocono Mountains, and—"

Katy said admiringly, "Wow. You sure are lucky. Your parents rich?"

"Nah. My aunt paid for it. She's got dough, or at least her husband does. Anyway, it was at a place called Pocono Pines, and the field even had a grandstand. It was great. When we weren't playing ball, we got to watch. We had a whole league of teams."

"All girls?"

"Yep. It was a girls' camp."

"Never get to see any boys? How boring." Katy touched her wavy blonde hair and looked around Humphreys' Field to see if any fellows she knew had arrived.

"Anyway, as I was saying, our team was the best. The Speedy Maroons. And we won the pennant."

"Pennant? What was it like?"

Jojo explained, "Just a triangle of yellow felt on a stick. It had a symbol of a green pine tree on it. We didn't get to keep it, just hold onto it and display it during the party."

"Party?"

"Yeah, we celebrated with free ice cream."

Katy was curious: "No boys at the party, either?"

"Oh, Katy, you're boy-crazy... That camp is where I learned to bat like Ty Cobb, with my hands spread wide apart on the bat."

"What else was spread wide apart?"

Jojo jumped up and went at Katy with raised fists, but Katy ran away. Annie tackled Jojo, who fell and had to suffer Annie's sitting on her back. She finally squirmed away and sat up.

Katy, figuring she was safe, returned. It was her turn to brag. "Once I saw a big field in New York, so big that three girls' games could play at the same time."

"G'wan."

"No, honest. It was when my grandfather took us there. I was little, about five, but boy, was that something to see. The players all wore middy blouses with red or blue ties, depending on which team they were on, and dark blue baggy bloomers... Where's my new mask? It's a Wilson. I just got it." Her voice rose, and she looked around at the group of girls gathering for the game. "Who took it?" She stood there belligerently, hands on hips. "I'm not gonna catch without it."

"You left it behind that tree," Annie pointed out. "Calm down."

"Don't mind her," Jojo explained to the others. "She's used to people stealing from her."

"Did you hear that the Bloomer Girls are coming to town?"

"Aw, there's lots of teams named Bloomer Girls. There's the Western Bloomer Girls and the New York Bloomers and the Boston Bloomers..."

"Well, the New York team is the best."

"Why would any team want to give themselves a name like Bloomers? Besides, those pants could hardly be uglier."

"Yeah, but the pants were named after a woman whose last name was Bloomer, so—"

"I hate that elastic they put in bloomers. We have to wear those things to gym class, and the elastic hurts my legs. Makes red marks..."

Then came the call from Maggie Schmidt, the coach: "Time to warm up, Card!"

So Annie Cardello got ready to pitch, and her audience started talking about her.

"She's a skinny little thing. Sure she can do the job?"

"She's got a pitch something like Christy Mathewson's fadeaway It breaks in and down. Wait till you see it. She can throw pretty fast, too."

"Well, let's see it. The girls from the Westinghouse factory have a reputation for heavy hitting... Why, that was a drop ball. The batter was looking for it in the wrong place."

"Didn't I tell you she was good? I saw her pitch against a mixed team from Massillon, and she—"

"Wow! See that? She got the batter out on another drop ball."

"That's her change of pace. Kind of a slow drop."

"She sure surprised that batter."

A tall young woman in pigtails stepped up and wiped her hands on the letter W at the front of her uniform, then took up the bat and made two practice swings before going into a sort of batting crouch.

"This girl gets on base." The speaker omitted to reveal that he was a stringer for the *Cleveland News* and attended as many industrial games he could, even those of the women, so he could send in news items to the sports department.

"C'mon McPherson!" A small W embroidered on the pocket of the fan's shirt showed that McPherson's backer came from Westinghouse. "Show what you can do!" A contingent of Westinghouse fans applauded.

And McPherson obliged, hitting the second pitch into the space between short and second.

The third Westinghouse batter, Bartunek, smiled expectantly as she got ready to bat. Annie, annoyed by the batter's confidence, determined to fool her. She began with a low, slow pitch that curved so much that it had the batter making a futile reach. Then, starting out by reaching to her right, Annie pitched a sort of crossfire, which came at Bartunek at an unexpected angle and confused her completely. Annie's third pitch was all speed, and Bartunek slashed at it but missed.

A roar from the crowd greeted Annie as she walked to the plaid blanket that served as a bench for the Collinwood Cardinals. Clapping ensued, and Annie grinned as her teammates tapped her on the back. Coach Maggie nodded her approval.

"Why, she's even got a fastball. It's no Rube Walberg speeder, but it's good."

The Cardinals batted rather weakly at first. Srenic tried to redeem herself after being unable to catch McPherson's hit but struck out on three Westinghouse pitches. Ethel O'Rourke, a seamstress at the Kaynee Company, manufacturer of boys' clothes, earned a walk, but Florrie Morgenstern, who worked at the National Carbon Company, couldn't send her on despite a hard-hit ball; it went straight to the Westinghouse first basewoman.

After that, the Westinghouse girls began to hit. Seemingly catching on to Annie's style, they managed two hits in the second inning, although neither of the hitters scored. Annie decided she'd have to bear down harder and, at Jojo Srenic's sign, threw a few knucklers.

She'd learned the pitch by watching a crack semipro pitcher in the Cleveland Amateur Association, a fellow named Wilbur Schardt, who played on the champion White Motor Company team and had once pitched for Brooklyn in the National League. Annie had boldly accosted him after a game of the White Motors versus the Telling-Belle Vernon Dairy, both men's teams in the Cleveland Baseball Federation, and got him to show her how to throw a knuckleball.

"Lord," came a rhetorical question, "Has she got a spitter, too?"

The third inning proved to be the big one for the Collinwood Cardinals. Jojo Srenic, a textile worker who loved coming to bat, hit a three-bagger, but nobody else was on base yet. Pretty Katy Reiner, who sewed blouses, followed her by hitting the pitch almost directly to a Westinghouse fielder who nearly caught the ball but couldn't quite manage it. So Jojo scored, and Katy reached second. Up came Hattie Steuben, a heavy Germanic blond who operated electric sewing machines for Kaynee and lived on nearby Arcade Avenue. Hattie hit at the same outfielder that Katy had buffaloed and brought home Katy, reaching second herself. Two to nothing, one on base, and nobody out! The Collinwood Cardinals were jumping and clapping, and so were some of the fans.

Edith Pratt, a machine worker for Standard Parts Company, was next. Trying too hard, she struck out on four pitches. One out. Then it was Annie's turn, with Hattie Steuben still on second.

Hoots and hollers for and against Annie failed to rattle her, and she hit the first pitch behind third base, where the Westinghouse fielder stuck out her hand too late, so the ball had to be chased while Annie reached second and Hattie rushed to third.

It was Florrie Morgenstern's turn. She was hit on the arm by the Westinghouse pitcher so went to first. Annie jumped around at second, and Hattie pretended to consider stealing home. Polly Barghosian, the tallest girl on the team, finally brought both Hattie and Annie home with a three-base hit behind first base into right field. Florrie moved to second.

The Collinwood Cardinals' eighth player, Effa Hrdlicka, a fast runner, knew Coach Maggie would want her to get Polly and Florrie home in any way possible. She decided on a bunt, laying down a perfect dribble in front of the pitcher that took so many seconds to collect that Polly was able to score and Effa got to first, but Florrie was tagged out. Two out, one on. The Westinghouse pitcher got the next batter out, so Effa was left on base, but the Cardinals had the game.

That's all Annie's team could manage, but it was enough—for a while. Her pitching dominated the next several innings. The Westinghouse girls got a few hits, but nobody scored until the eighth inning when tall Emily McPherson started what she hoped would be a rally with a three-base hit, and Mary Bartunek, a men's clothing worker, followed her with a hit to right that drove in McPherson. Annie began depending on the knuckler, which fooled the next two Westinghouse batters and left Bartunek on base unable to score. Annie's fans were cheering this display of pitching virtuosity.

The Collinwood Cardinals wrapped it up in the ninth. Hattie Steuben, who already had a two-base hit to her credit in the game, hit another one. Then Edith Pratt, who was still in high school and who had managed to do exactly nothing so far, suddenly blossomed, hitting a Westinghouse fastball to right. Through a head-first slide that galvanized her team, she managed to get to second base, sending Hattie Steuben home.

The crowd that sat around Humphrey's Field on newspapers or small folding seats knew it was Annie's turn and began to call out encouragement: "C'mon, Card!"

"Let's see what the lady twirler can do at bat!"

"Aw, she's the pitcher. You can't expect her to drive in that run."

"Listen, you guys, I bet you both a quarter that she brings that runner home." The woman offering the bet worked for the Grennan Cake Company and had seen Annie in action against the Grennan girls' team.

Chatter and cries of encouragement died down as the Card focused on the pitch to come. She knew the runner would be ready.

Maggie would want me to lay down the bunt. Got to tap it just right to put it out of reach of the infielders...

The windup. The pitch, a fast one, low and outside.

Easy to reach! At the last moment Card's arms extended the bat for the bunt. A solid click meant contact, and the ball dribbled away toward short as she took off for first as fast as she could go, the fans watching her legs spin around.

"Look at her go! She'll make it!"

The Westinghouse shortstop had found the ball and moved into position to throw it to the catcher at home. Meanwhile, the first basewoman tried to block Annie from touching the bag, but Annie slid under her and knocked her off balance, then jumped up and down to try to attract a throw there instead of at home. Her gyrations were just enough to put the worried shortstop off her throw, and it went wide enough of the catcher to require a leaping, reaching catch. Edith Pratt, not the fastest runner, got home anyway.

Clapping and shouting followed. "She's tough, that Card."

"Fast, too," said the woman reaching for the quarters she had won.

The Westinghouse pitcher tried to calm herself as Annie made fake darts toward second. Florrie Morgenstern came up and got a base hit off the rattled pitcher while Annie raced to second and beat the throw there. From then on, it was a cakewalk for the Collinwood Cardinals. Polly Barghosian drew a walk, and then the hit-and-run was on: Effa Hrdlicka bunted, and Annie ran home although Polly was caught in a run-down and young Effa fell, suffering an injury. About a dozen cinders embedded themselves in her forearm. Humphrey's Field was hardly a smooth, finished diamond.

The umpire, a fat man named Myron Valencic, who sat on a small folding chair, stopped the game, ruling that the Collinwood Cardinals had won. Maggie Schmidt went to her first aid kit and scraped out the cinders while the others gathered around Effa for support.

"Aw, what kind of game was that?" a fan hollered. "Called on account of injury?"

Annie heard it and turned on him in anger. "We had the game won," she called.

Umpire Valencic got up slowly from his tiny seat and said loudly, "The game is over. The Collinwood Cardinals won, 8 to 1." Valencic, who lived on nearby Corsica Avenue and boosted local teams with his free umpiring, stared down the few critics of his work.

A woman hollered, "Hurrah for the Collinwood Cardinals!" Clapping ensued.

"That lady twirler knows how to play," called the young stringer, rising from the grass and dusting himself off. A fan seated nearby, a man who still wore his suitcoat, remarked, "Splendid work indeed."

"Aw, she's tricky. All those motions she made on first base—what kind of playing is that?"

Card turned, anger in her dark eyes, her lips pursing, but she restrained herself and didn't reply. Marching back to Maggie, she announced, "I got 'em."

The coach tapped her on the shoulder and said, "Good going, girl. Just take care of that arm. You're our Drawing Card."

"Thanks, Maggie."

Jojo and Katy ran up to Annie for hugs, patted her on the shoulder, and shouted, "You're the Card!"

Fans were still talking. "What a record she has! That's her tenth win."
"Good going, Card!"

Card hugged her teammates back. "Thanks, Jojo. You did swell, Katy."

Katy Reiner bent her blond head toward the pitcher's black pigtails and put her hands on Annie's shoulders. "You pitched a good game, practically a no-hitter." As the catcher for the only pitcher on the team, Katy knew Card's moods as well as her style of pitching.

As the girls began to wind down, Annie reminded Katy, "Let's get going. Jojo is always ready fast."

After a few moments to respond to the greetings of regular fans, who were picking up their blankets and newspapers before leaving the field, Annie sat down on the grass and began to take off her spikes. The girls would leave Humphreys' Field carrying their spiked shoes but wearing their uniforms—there was no place to change. They were lucky, as Maggie kept reminding them, that the Humphreys, who owned the field just across the boulevard from Euclid Beach Park, as well as the Park itself, didn't mind ball teams using it.

Can't lollygag around congratulating ourselves, Annie thought; got to get home. We all have to work tomorrow

"Did you see that scout out there?" asked Edith as she pulled off her spikes.

"He was watching you, Card," added the coach. Maggie Schmidt was a tall, imposing woman. Placing her hands on her hips, she looked at her pitcher, a slight figure in a dusty uniform. "He was taking notes." Maggie raised her left eyebrow and permitted herself a small smile.

Annie looked up hopefully. She knew she was a good pitcher. Some of the other players were older and had more power—they were stronger and taller. But Annie was determined, highly skilled, and usually successful.

"He must have read about you in the Cleveland papers," added Florrie. "I wish he'd read about me, too." But Florrie knew that pitchers, not fielders, attracted the attention.

"Are you saying that a woman pitcher has a chance with a team in the real minors?" The Card stood at rigid attention.

Maggie strode to the one short bench and sat down. "Why not? Didn't you ever hear that the Cleveland team once considered Alta Weiss, back before the war?"

Florrie snorted. "You know that was just a joke the newsmen were pulling, Maggie. They were pretending she had a chance."

"Sure, they were making news for themselves," commented Hattie, another outfielder, as she put her glove in a bag for carrying home. "That's what newspapermen do. My uncle said so."

Maggie turned, annoyed. "Who's your uncle? God? I wish you wouldn't always quote men as if they were oracles, Hattie. Listen, Card. One of these days a good female player is going to make it. Mae Arbaugh is doing awfully well. So is Jackie Mitchell. A rumor's going around that Joe Engel wants her for Chattanooga."

"No kidding?" Card was alert. If these other women had a chance, she might, too. After all, her three-year record was tops against local independents and teams in Cleveland's organized industrial leagues. Playing baseball, even with only grudging approval from her father, made her happy, and she kept working at improving.

"Well, now that I've hooked on with your team, Maggie, maybe I'll get some real attention."

"Yeah, practically nobody heard of you while you played with Richman Brothers Clothing," Edith threw in, "even when you were beating that crack women's team from General Electric at Nela Park. Gosh, Nela Park has a great team."

"Well, Nela Park also has beautiful grounds and a rec program. My team had a little flat spot next to the plant, and we could play only during lunch hour."

"So that's why you're so skinny," Hattie commented. "No lunch."

"Katy," said Maggie, crooking her finger at the catcher, "How many programs did you sell? We won't be traveling next weekend without money." Maggie needed to find out whether the team, which depended on contributions, took in enough through solicitations by the prettiest team member, Katy Reiner, who was sent into the audience before the game to sell programs at a quarter each. The programs were prepared free by Hattie's father, in his small print shop. To sell them, Katy had to thread her way through fans seated on newspapers or blankets around the field, although a few had folding seats.

"Almost twenty dollars worth," smiled Katy, who knew how to ingratiate herself with male fans. They loved to greet her with refrains from the song made popular during the war: "K-K-K-Katy, beautiful Katy, you're the only G-G-G-Girl that I adore!"

"Good. We'll be able to play the Chicago Stars next weekend."

"Yeah, if Katy can pry herself away from Joe, her latest boyfriend," said Hattie, only half-kidding.

Katy grinned coyly, then said, "I threw him over already. I'm considering somebody else now."

Moans from some of the other players.

Maggie rolled her eyes and smiled ruefully. Lord, deliver me from this simpering child who thinks mainly of powder puffs and men. Oh well, on the field she knows how to handle the Card, and she gets her share of hits, too.

"Say, Ethel," Katy called over to her teammate, "Don't you come from Chicago? Got any family there? You might see them next weekend." Katy thought she'd turn attention away from herself by mentioning Ethel O'Rourke's Chicago connection.

Ethel looked up sullenly. "Never mind that, you meanie," and she walked away from them.

Surprised, Katy wondered what she had said wrong.

As Annie ambled with Katy and Jojo toward Lake Shore Boulevard, where her two friends could board the streetcar, she enlightened Katy about Ethel's reaction. "Ethel does come from Chicago, Katy. But she comes from the Chicago Home for Girls. You know, a home for delinquents. It's where she learned to play ball."

"Oh. No wonder she thought I was being mean. So bad girls play ball, too?"

Jojo laughed. "And college girls. The woman who taught Ethel was a college grad, a woman from the University of Wisconsin who started the team at the Home. Ethel played there for four years before ... uh, graduating and coming to Cleveland to live with an aunt."

"Listen," said the Card as they reached the streetcar stop, "I can hear the screams from the Roller Coaster at Euclid Beach Park. When are we going to the Beach again?"

"It's gotta be two weeks from Sunday, if there's no game that day." Jojo moved the cloth bag with her spikes from one arm to the other as she took out her nickel for the streetcar ride.

"Gosh, we sure had fun last time on the Thriller! Say, next time let's go on that new ride, the Flying Turns, where you practically stand on your head." Annie Cardello was always game for the biggest thrills of all.

"I prefer the Carousel," announced Katy as they turned to watch the streetcar approach. "There's something graceful about riding those wooden horses slowly up and down, in time to music, while the whole platform moves in circles. And those chariots with carvings are so pretty..."

"Huh. That's for kiddies," Annie pronounced. "I want to try the Dodgem."

"Hitting other little cars with your own?" queried Jojo. "You must be feeling aggressive."

"Or we could go on the one called Over the Falls."

Katy was having none of that. "And get my hair splashed with water? No thanks. A boy took me on that once..."

The others laughed: Katy and her dates. Jojo suggested, "Well, how about going on the Whip? I'm getting tired of three rides in a row on the Thriller."

Annie started walking and waving goodbye to the others as they boarded the car. "Well, you were the one who said that the fellow taking tickets was handsome..."

Maggie Schmidt was still sitting there alone on the little folding bench after all the players had left, but she stood up as she saw a man walking toward her.

3

"Do you think the Lonardos are suspicious, Angelo?"

"Naw. We been playing cards and talking business with them for a week, haven't we? And nothing's happened, has it? Don't worry. It'll all work out. I ain't got six brothers for nothing. I'm sick of being a corporal for Joe Lonardo and his stupid brother John."

Angelo Porrello spoke to the others with his usual "in-charge" demeanor. Holding their playing cards, they sat around a table in the back room of the Porrello Barber Shop on Woodland Avenue.

"We sure made money while Big Joe Lonardo was in Sicily visiting his mother. An extra five thou every week for six months. Great." Prohibition worked fine for small-time hoodlums like the Lonardos and Porrellos. For them the depression meant nothing.

"Well, who wouldn't make money? Joe's brother John is no leader. Joe was crazy to leave stupid John in charge. He let it all slip right through his fingers. We just picked it up."

"They keep trying to persuade us to return their lost clientele to them. Don't they see that's not gonna work?"

"Well, today's the day. Today we're gonna persuade them otherwise."

"Everything's ready?"

"As soon as they come in, it's gonna happen. All of Cleveland's corn sugar business is gonna be ours. For good. We're cornering the market. No liquor is gonna be made in Cleveland without our corn sugar."

"Angelo, you're amazing," Rick Cardello felt a bit confused, but he was sure everything would become clear soon. "Say, how'd you get in with the Lonardos in the first place?"

"You ask too many questions, Rick. Wait till you get made. Besides, the Lonardos aren't any better than we are. Who are they? Nothing. My brothers and them was friends back in Sicily." Angelo used the spittoon, then went on. "We all worked in the sulphur mines there. A hell-hole on the south coast. What are the Lonardos? Nothing. Besides, I got more brothers than Joe Lonardo."

Along with the other card players, Rick Cardello laughed nervously. He was about to be in on something big. For the first time. But he wasn't sure what it was.

The rear door of the shop opened, and to Rick's surprise, shooting started immediately. As soon as the first gun went off, Angelo dived under the table. Rick followed suit. When it was all over, the two Lonardos who had walked confidently into the room lay there dead.

Angelo emerged, dusted himself off, and said, "So! Guess who's the new corn sugar baron?"

Sirens came closer, but Angelo Porrello sat down confidently and lit a cigar. Rick, staring and shaken, left by the back door.

John Smith looked up from the craps table at the elegant Harvard Club. "Was that someone knocking at the door?"

Parmely was gathering up his winnings. "Nonsense. Nobody knocks on the Harvard Club door. Men who want to gamble here just walk in, don't they?"

The pounding continued. Shimmy Patton was summoning his bouncers as he walked slowly toward the door of his exclusive gambling joint. About five hundred patrons stirred and muttered.

John and Parmely, noticing with dismay that two of Shimmy's bouncers carried machine guns, began to think of leaving.

The dealers, warily eyeing the door and the bouncers, were starting to pack up.

Shimmy Patton, one of the owners of the club, shouted warnings against the invaders that if they tried to enter they would have their heads knocked off.

That gave pause to the group at the door, headed by the County Prosecutor Frank Cullitan, who immediately sent for his boss, Eliot Ness, the new Cleveland Safety Director. Ness had been put in charge of both police and firemen in order to crack down on gangsters and their association with crooked police.

"It can't be the Cleveland law," said Parmely. "After all, the club is technically in Maple Heights, where the law never bothers us."

Stuffing cash in his pockets, John replied, "I hear shouting. Maybe that over-zealous judge, Lousy Lausche, got the Cleveland police to harass us."

"That's what we get for letting immigrants into our city," Parmely groused. "Let's go out the back way. There goes Creepy Karpis. We'll follow him." John and Parmely didn't realize that the FBI wanted Karpis as a suspect in several murders and two kidnappings; to them he was just a gambler like the rest.

"Probably, Shimmy forgot to pay off enough police officers."

"Never mind. There's always the Mounds Club. I think it's even more plush. Free drinks, too. Or maybe we should just go to the Girlie Show." He looked meaningfully at Parmely, who smiled.

The bouncers stood there uncertainly. Patton himself had retreated and was moving with many of his patrons to rear exits, the men in tuxedos donning overcoats as they went, the women covering their gowns and diamonds with fur coats. Limousines, expensive cars, and trucks pulled away full of frustrated gamblers.

By the time Ness, Cullitan, a group of policemen, and some reporters decided to enter the front door, few gamblers and less gambling equipment remained. Some deputies, trailed by reporters, pushed past the surly bouncers, who seemed unsure what their response should be.

Photographer Byron Filkins of the *Cleveland Press*, spotting what seemed to him like the familiar face of a notorious gambler, flashed his camera at him and was immediately pushed backward onto the floor. Byron, a small man, had trouble getting up, whereupon Webb Seeley, a husky reporter for a rival paper, the *News*, hit the gambler in the face, laying him out on top of a craps table. Nothing else occurred except that the customers, desiring not to see their names and pictures in a newspaper, left.

Nobody was arrested, and the Harvard Club reopened within a week. So many Cleveland policemen were being paid off by gangsters that the law could not control the city's crime. Ness had been hired in 1935 to change this situation, and he was warming to the task.

Hulda Schaefer ran up the steps of the Cardello home on Pythias Avenue and knocked on the frame of the screen door, at the same time calling out "Mr. Cardello! Mr. Cardello?" Her voice carried all through the small house.

Giovanni got up from the supper table and walked to the front door. "What, Hulda?"

"Mr. Cardello, your son Rick wants you to come to the restaurant. You and Mrs. Cardello."

"In trouble again."

By then Bianca had reached the door, too. "I'm not going into that place. A beer joint. It's not for good women."

"In the garden, Mrs. Cardello. He said to meet him in the garden." She meant the outdoor tables, in the *Biergarten*, surrounded by a low fence and connected to Jack's Place but accessible through a separate entrance.

"We are going," said her husband.

As she removed her apron Bianca muttered, "We must get our own telephone." Then she directed, "Annie, clear the table while we're gone."

At the Biergarten down the street, Giovanni sat down opposite his son Rick and ordered a mug of beer. He preferred a good red wine, but Jack's Place didn't cater to Italian tastes. "What now, Ricardo? What kind of trouble are you in? And why give so much pain to your mother by mixing with those crooked *Siciliani*?"

Colored lights shone directly on Rick's handsome young face and shiny dark hair. "The Porrello brothers were arrested," he said, playing with a pretzel. "They're sure they'll get off. But it might happen to me next."

"God help us!"

"*Calma*, Bianca. I won't let anything happen to your son. You, Rick, come home for a few days. Where is Dominic? Is he involved?"

"Nah. Dom's out of town. Las Vegas."

"What did you do?"

"Nothing. I was just there when it happened."

"What happened?"

"The Lonardo brothers got shot, two of them. Killed, in the Porrello barber shop."

"Who did it?"

"Don't ask me that, Papa."

"Did *you*?"

Rick shook his head. "No. But since I was there, the police might pick me up for questioning."

"The police." Bianca shrank back. "I don't want them coming to my home."

"Then I won't be able to come there. I'll go back to Woodland Avenue. That's where I belong, anyway." Actually, he thought, I can go and stay for a while with one of the vaudeville girls I know. But then what?

Bianca looked stricken, then bowed her head. "Those bums. You have to mix with those bums."

"It's where the money is, Mama. And they're powerful men. Angelo Porrello is gonna be the head of the Cleveland Mafia. He's invited Mafia men from Chicago and New York and Florida to a big meeting at the Statler. They're gonna set him up as the head of the Cleveland LCN."

"What's LCN?"

"*La Cosa Nostra*." Our Thing.

Bianca was close to tears. "I don't understand all this. Especially about 'Our Thing.' I'm going home."

"I want to see my sister."

"I don't want her mixed up in this."

"Just for a minute."

Giovanni looked at his wife. She gave in.

"Good morning, Patrolman Osowski."

"Good morning, Miss Cardello. How are you today?"

"Just fine, and yourself?"

"Very well, thanks. I hope your day is a good one."

"And yours."

Sam Osowski, who regularly stood on the corner of Euclid Avenue and Ninth Street at this hour, let his eyes follow her slight figure until he was distracted by the approach of a stream of impressively large autos approaching the Statler Hotel. Even Annie Cardello, who hated being late for work, turned to look at them.

Men dressed in expensive suits, white spats, and sparkling jewelry alighted from their cars and approached the hotel, walking as though they were important. They carried expensive-looking matched leather luggage. Annie noticed velvet on the collars of some overcoats.

Overcoats, in this warm weather?

The travelers moved and looked around arrogantly. Some smoked cigars.

Wonder what this convention is, thought the patrolman. Maybe I'll check the hotel register.

Annie Cardello thought she recognized the men as Italian, or Italian American. Several were short and stocky. About twenty of them streamed in.

Why, Annie thought, this is it! This is the Mafia conference Rick told me about.

She watched at a distance, noticing that Patrolman Osowski had just disappeared into the hotel, too. Perhaps, she thought, perhaps there is something I can do. Especially since Rick isn't with them.

She began walking slowly toward the hotel entrance. Sam Osowski came out of the building, putting his pencil in his pocket as he headed for his patrol car.

"I know who they are, Patrolman Osowski."

He stopped in his tracks, eyebrows raised. "Friends of yours?"

"No, no. Mafia. Did you get the names?"

"Sure. Copied them from the register."

"Tilocco? The Porrellos? Mangano, Giunta, Mirabella? Profaci?"

"Those are sure on the list. How'd you know?"

"I heard. Tell your boss they're Mafia, mostly from out of town."

"Sure will. Thanks, Miss. Gotta get to Central Station."

Giovanni Cardello read aloud from the *Cleveland Plain Dealer*: "Joe Profaci of the Brooklyn Mafia had hardly walked into the lobby of the Statler and greeted Vince Mangano, founder of the Gambino family, when the police closed in and arrested them both. The gangsters didn't even have time to start their meeting."

"Not Ricardo? Not Dominic?" Bianca's voice trembled.

"No, they're not mentioned. It says here the men were heading for a fancy breakfast in a private room. They had to pay their hotel bills before the police led them out of the hotel by the rear door."

Annie's eyes shone. She put down the dish she was drying and picked up another, trying not to let a smile pick up the ends of her mouth.

"It says the Porrellos got their family and friends to raise money for bonds to get the gangsters out of jail. They did it by putting up their houses as collateral."

Bianca, putting the leftover food away in the ice box, said softly, "I wonder where my two sons are, and if they're safe."

"They're safe, Mama."

"What do you know about this, child?" Giovanni put in.

"Rick told me they would be okay. I believe him."

"Where are you going, girl?"

"Out to play baseball, Mama, on Gennaro's team. See you later!" And out she ran, joyfully.

Brookside Park echoed with the cries and cheers of the spectators seated on the grass all over the hills around the diamond in this natural hollow, a big bowl surrounded by gentle hills, because the Collinwood Cardinals were beating a crack women's industrial team from the White Motors Company. Men from White Motor could compete in a city league connected with the National Baseball Federation, but not women players. The Federation didn't accept women. But White Motors Company had the pull to reserve Brookside Park when their girls' team played.

"Today the independent girls are really showing up the White Motors," grinned Parmely Blanford. His friend John Smith and a younger pal, Gordon Wade, seemed riveted by the action. "You like looking at those girls, don't you, Gordon?"

"Aw, they're okay," said Gordon. At sixteen he was just getting interested in girls and took a lot of kidding.

John didn't reply. He seemed fixated on one of the pitchers. Finally he muttered, "I think I know that girl. The one pitching for the Collinwood Cardinals."

"The pitcher? You know the Drawing Card? How could you ever meet such a girl? She's an Italian." Parmely didn't know any Italians.

"In the bank. She's a patron. Anna Cardello."

"Oh, some immigrants put their money in the Society for Savings? How interesting."

"Immigrants have money, too, Parmely. Anyway, I doubt if she's an immigrant. Her English is as good as yours or mine."

"Ah! You've already talked to her! Congratulations. What about? Spaghetti? Not Italian opera, I'll wager."

"Don't be so stuck up, Parmely. She's nice."

Parmely glanced at John ironically, then looked away at the crowd, so John went on.

"She saves money. She lives in one of the second-generation districts, up only a notch from the shotgun houses and the sixes-and-eights built for immigrants."

"Heavens."

"Think about it, Parmely: We need these people, we founders. So we live where the founders of the city live, in Euclid Avenue mansions with the Mark Hannas, the Myron T. Herricks, the Samuel H. Mathers... We're founders, yes, but you know we all depend on families like hers."

Parmely wiped the sweat from his forehead with a white linen handkerchief. "Why, John, I do believe you've fallen for a little Italian. Is her family in the Mafia?"

Screams and cheers prevented John from making a sharp reply. The Collinwood Cardinals had beaten the White Motors team two to one, and the winners were jumping and hugging.

John stood up and watched Anna Cardello accept the congratulations of teammates and fans. Even in those ridiculous knickers and cap, he thought, she looked lovely.

Parmely had been considering John's remarks. "You know, John, you may have something there."

"You mean about the immigrants being the foundation of the city? After all, leaders need followers. You know Cleveland is called the Western Reserve, Connecticut's outpost in the wilderness, the representative of New England civilization in this area. We're Connecticut's remote vanguard." John was feeling expansive, so he summoned his powers of eloquence. "We civilized people, descended from New Englanders, established the factories and businesses out here in the Reserve, but immigrants provide the work force for them. Without the immigrants, our businesses wouldn't flourish. Of course, in some ways we in the hinterlands have outshone Connecticut."

"No, I didn't mean that. I meant that this is a good place to look over the young women, to find a really young and inexperienced girl, if you know what I mean. The girls display their charms; we pick one, a really young one who hasn't yet—well, you know. We might even marry one."

John sat back. "I hadn't thought of that. You're right. Here's a place to find a virgin."

Parmeley smiled. "You got it." The inexperienced Gordon looked at them with respect.

4

JOHN TURNED AGAIN TO WATCHING Anna Cardello as she moved off the field. He got up and started walking toward her. That exotic Mediterranean beauty! he thought to himself. Besides, she's young and impressionable.

It took John a half-hour of persuasion to convince Annie to spend the Fourth of July at Euclid Beach with him and his friends. "We're just going to walk around, go on some rides, maybe swim, maybe dance, get something to eat, and of course watch the fireworks in the evening."

Annie kept looking down at the ground, glancing at him, then gazing elsewhere, a frown on her face, giving excuses like "I don't really know you," or "My father doesn't know you," or "I don't go swimming much. I don't dance much."

She was conscious of Katy in the background, checking out the man she was talking to. Why me? thought Annie. Katy's the pretty one. Probably just because he has a contact with me: He saw me in his bank.

"Don't you celebrate the Fourth at Euclid Beach? You live so near by."

So he knew where she lived. Well, he would have access to the bank's records.

"Well, yes, my family usually goes over there after dark with blankets, to sit on the beach and watch the fireworks. After all, the show is free..."

Of course, John thought. Since the Wall Street crash, people without his own family's resources took as much advantage of free entertainment as they could.

"Don't you go over to Euclid Beach in the daytime?"

"Sometimes. On a Sunday."

"What do you like to do there?"

"I like to wander through the Penny Arcade, or just walk on the sand next to the water. Sometimes I watch that fountain in the middle of the swimming pool. My girlfriends and I go on some of the rides, and we listen to the organ music at the Carousel."

"How about the Pavilion? Really good orchestras play there." By now they were walking away from the crowd.

"Mostly, we just watch; dancing there costs money. The fellows I know don't have much to spare. If we stay into the evening we go up to the balcony of the Pavilion to watch the dancers and listen to the music. Sometimes we buy popcorn balls or taffy kisses..."

She blushed at having said such an intimate word. I wonder: Does this rich fellow want kisses from me? What could that come to? Nothing, she thought.

And in her mind she visualized someone laughing at her, laughing heartily: It was the laugh she had heard many times at Euclid Beach, the recorded guffaws that seemed to emanate from the huge dummy called Laughing Sal, a dummy standing behind glass, shaking and holding her stomach as the loud, deep laugh played, and played, and played.

Olga Kunesh sat glumly in the Halle lunchroom thinking about the cut in pay that less work meant for her family. Olga lived with her mother and brother on the West Side. Since Annie was sitting there, too, Olga thought out loud: "I wish my brother wasn't too sick to work. How about you, Annie? Are you going to get by? Say, where's your book? Aren't you going to read for a while?"

"I'm doing okay. I think I can still pay my parents the same amount for room and board. My book? I left it in my locker. I'm going to the Downstairs Store to look for a dress. I've got a date." She couldn't help letting the thrill show on her face.

"A date? With that jumper, Gennaro?" Olga referred to a fellow who pursued Annie relentlessly, a young man who worked on the shiny maroon delivery vans owned by the Halle Brothers Company. Gennaro's job was to jump out of the van with a package, run to the door of the house, ring the bell, call out "Halle's!" and make the delivery, then run back to the van and jump in to prepare for the next one.

"No. Somebody I just met. Tell you more later," she said, rising to leave after only a few bites so that she could hurry to the elevator and ride to the store's basement to search for a bargain.

"Wait!" called Olga. "Are you going to the auditorium right after work? That radio columnist, Dorothy Fuldheim, is speaking, and Mrs. Schindler is handing out free tickets. Did you get yours?"

"Not going this time. Saw Fuldheim already; she arrived this morning and is staying across the street at the Statler. Gotta get going and find a new dress."

Annie straightened the black dress she wore. The uniform was required for female store employees, although she hated wearing it. "This thing makes me look as though I'm going to a funeral," she once told Olga. Like most Halle employees, she kept the uniform in her locker and wore it only in the store, preferring to wear her own everyday clothes to and from work. For special-occasion clothes, when she could afford it she shopped in Halle's bargain basement, euphemistically called the Downstairs Store.

As she passed the racks of blouses, long gowns, and party frocks, she started thinking of John Smith.

I wonder what color he likes.

Her eye settled on a green dress, something more stylish than she had ever owned. Small pleats started at the hip and gave a graceful flare to the skirt. The top, she realized, was actually a separate jacket—nice to put on when the evening turned cool.

I've never owned a green dress... What am I thinking of? Am I really trying to attract a rich fellow named John Smith? Me, the daughter of an Italian immigrant? Do these matches really happen?

Then she remember Mr. Sam Halle, a rich Jewish man.

Mr. Sam, who established the Halle dynasty, had married an Irish working girl named Blanche Murphy.

Annie felt lucky to live on Cleveland's Pythias Avenue. Pythias was the second street, after Damon, from Lake Shore Boulevard and Euclid Beach, the popular amusement park owned by the Humphrey family. Not only could she walk home from baseball games at Humphreys' Field, she could get to the Beach in five minutes.

Looking behind her now, as she walked home from a game in which she pitched a two-hitter and won with a sacrifice bunt, she savored the view of the famous arched entrance to Euclid Beach between two miniature towers, the arch bearing the park's name and the reassuring sign: OPEN FOR THE SEASON. To Annie, this arch was like a shrine. Entrance to the Beach was free, and whenever she felt she had the time she loved to go there and just walk around to enjoy the sights.

Annie's neighborhood, the Collinwood District of Cleveland, was a homey section of town where second-generation Americans lived. Their forebears had settled there around the turn of the century after emigrating from Europe. The grownups, mostly blue-collar, worked in Cleveland industry and business.

As Annie approached Damon and Pythias Avenues, she remembered that in school she discovered that Damon and Pythias were the names of ancient Greek friends, and she wondered if Greeks had ever lived on these streets. Now the residents included German-speaking and Italian-speaking families, some that spoke Slovenian, and one Russian family, along with several who knew only English. The kids all played together.

Walking past Jack's Place, operated by German Americans named Schaefer on the corner of Damon, she got a whiff of the beer that was already being served there, at four in the afternoon. A waiter was setting the outside tables in the attached *Biergarten* strung with wires bearing colored lights that would later be glowing to give the area a fairyland appearance. Annie could hear the familiar sound of Jack Graney's nasal voice describing a game the Indians were playing from several homes as she walked by. Every few minutes, the crowd roared in approval or moaned in disappointment.

The snug little home of the Cardellos, like others on Pythias Avenue, featured a tiny front porch for evening socializing and for greeting passers-by. As she approached, getting hungrier by the minute, Annie realized that a shiny Ford she had noticed when turning the corner was actually parked in front of her own house and that her father, along with her uncle Paolo, who lived on Damon, sat on the porch swing, talking. Standing in front of them was another man. Annie could glimpse her mother standing just inside the screen door, watching.

Unexpected company, and someone who owned an automobile.

"Anna," called her father, "come here and meet Mr. Cambria. He's a *paisano*. Born in Messina, Sicily. Mr. Cambria owns the Albany, New York, International League Baseball Club."

Then it came to Annie: Maybe I'm about to get help from a *paisano*.

Annie felt nervous. Waiting at the entrance to Euclid Beach Park, with its famous two-towered archway, she saw them approach—in an automobile! Two automobiles! One green, one blue.

I should have known they wouldn't take the streetcar. They must own their own autos.

John Smith was driving the big green car, and next to him sat his younger friend, the one named Gordon. John's other friend Parmely drove the blue car. She had met them both briefly at Brookside Park. But now with Parmely was a girl that Annie assumed was Parmely's date.

Gordon was getting out. He nodded a greeting as John called, "Hop in, Annie! We'll park over there somewhere." Gordon moved to the back seat of the car, and Annie saw that she was expected to sit in front. "Don't look at Gordon; he doesn't have a girl yet." Predictably, Gordon blushed.

Am I John's girl? Already? Annie wondered.

"How do you like my Reo? It's evidently the right color—it matches your dress."

From the last remark, Annie figured out that the word "Reo" referred to his car, so she replied, "It's very comfortable."

"Parmely prefers his Cord sedan. I think it's a bit ostentatious." She tried to look as though she knew what "ostentatious" meant.

At the car park, John took Annie's elbow and moved her toward Parmely's date, a girl who suddenly looked familiar. "I want you to meet my sister," he said. As the girl approached, Annie stopped.

Just a short time ago I fitted her with the jodhpurs I sewed "to order" for her at Halle's, she thought. Annie swallowed, her throat suddenly dry.

The dismay showed in her face, but nobody seemed to notice, least of all Isabel. "Why, how nice! We've met, at Halle's. Hello, Annie."

"Hello. Hello, Parmely."

I'm supposed to call Miss Smith by her first name now? I feel so awkward, Annie thought.

John took Annie's seeming lack of enthusiasm for shyness and started suggesting activities to oil the machinery of sociability. "Let's start out with the Rocket Ships. I haven't tried them yet."

"I like the ride called Over the Falls," Gordon contributed. "Let's go on that one, too."

"Isabel, what's your choice?" Parmely deferred to his date.

"Laff in the Dark," Isabel grinned. Gordon snickered, for he knew that meant she was daring Parmely to steal a kiss in the tunnel that the boat rode through. Parmely took her arm and smiled at her with mock lasciviousness, raising and lowering his eyebrows. She laughed.

"Let's get some popcorn balls first," John said as they approached the stand where the sticky confection was made. "Do you like them, Annie?"

"I love them."

"How about the loganberry juice at that stand over there?"

"Never tried it."

"Well, you must."

The big silvery tubes called Rocket Ships were suspended on cables from a central pole and flew around it with ever-increasing distance as their angle from the pole increased. The illusion of suspension in space and the sensation of flying were exhilarating. Parmely and Isabel sat in another Rocket Ship.

John watched the delight on Annie's face. Gordon sat behind them, hollering, "Yippee! I'm flying!"

Recalling a popular comic strip, Annie turned around and said to the shouting boy, "You're Flash Gordon!" And Flash was his name for the rest of the day.

Annie kept one hand on the cellophane bag of four popcorn balls and the other hand on her straw hat. "Take your hat off," John asked. His arm rested on the back of the double seat.

She looked at him in surprise." My hair will get all blown to pieces."

"I like your hair—all those waves in it." He was looking at her as if he wanted to get even closer.

She thought for a while, then finally removed her hat. "My brothers say my hair is Fudge Rippled."

He laughed but kept his eyes on her. Then the Rocket Ships slowed. "Let's go to Crosby's, everyone." John called out. He helped Annie climb out and added, "I like your dress. Where did you get it?"

"Halle's." She omitted the words "Downstairs Store."

Why did I do that? She thought. He must already know that I don't have much money.

Isabel overheard and came up to say how lucky Annie was to be at Halle's. "Don't you just love their model rooms?" Surprised, Annie found that they both liked to examine the elegant antiques and reproductions in the home furnishings department, especially the period rooms. They began walking next to each other.

"Do you like the ones designed for Georgian brick mansions?" Isabel asked. "Or the ones that look as though they come from French chateaux? The Van Sweringens like the French styling."

"The French rooms are so formal. I really prefer the Elizabethan rooms: You know, with those plain Gothic chests, the old refectory table, the Windsor chairs—I've learned a lot by asking questions about them." She was happy that she had bothered to find out what a refectory was.

"Indeed you have," Isabel replied, pleasantly surprised.

Annie looked directly at Isabel and said clearly, "I don't know the Van Swearens, or whatever you called them."

"I don't either. I've just heard my mother talk about their preferences. And since they're such taste-setters, people listen to their opinions. The Van Sweringens are the brothers who are building the Terminal Tower downtown on Public Square."

"Oh."

"What'll you have?" Annie had never eaten at Crosby's. The most expensive refreshments she'd had when visiting the Beach was a soda from a nearby stand. Her parents, when planning to stay for several hours, always packed a lunch for eating at one of the picnic tables. John suggested steak and potatoes, but Annie said she preferred fish. She found the cafeteria-style restaurant easy to negotiate, so she began to get comfortable.

It was at the Pavilion, when they were dancing to mellow orchestra music, that John asked if her parents were coming to the fireworks in the evening so that he could meet them.

Oh no, Annie thought, not so soon! Meeting my parents is serious. And he won't think much of them—they aren't educated people. They even speak with an accent.

"Why so silent, Annie?" He was holding her in his arms, and it was a sensation she wasn't used to.

"I'm enjoying this so much. I seldom get to dance here." After all, it cost ten cents a ticket to dance on the floor of the Pavilion, and the young fellows she knew, like Gennaro, invited her on cheaper dates, like picnics. "Let's not spoil it."

"Spoil it? How could ... well, never mind. We'll talk about that later." And he began holding her closer.

"Watch it, John!" called Parmely as he swooped by with Isabel. "Remember the enforcers!" John recalled that the Beach employed "enforcers" to be sure none of the dancers moved in a way considered vulgar. He had seen a fellow named Ted ejected from the dance floor for movements unacceptable to the management. So he loosened his grasp.

She thought, maybe he's angry with me. How am I going to tell him that I'm leaving town?

As they climbed to the balcony to find seats, John brought up another subject. "My parents are throwing a shindig for my twenty-first. It's two weeks from today. I want you to come." She looked away. "What's the matter? Don't you want to come? I guarantee that you'll have fun. Everyone does. My mother and sister organize the best games..."

"I won't be here. I'm going away," she said despondently.

"Away? Where? You mean, on vacation? Can you change the dates? I really want you to be at my party. "

"I've signed a contract. I can't get out of it."

"A contract? To do what?"

"To play baseball. In Albany, New York. I leave in two days."

Annie stood glumly in front of the church, trying to enjoy herself at an annual Italian festival she usually liked. But today she liked nothing.

Over a small paper plate of cavatelli, she looked up and saw him. He was walking straight toward her, looking pleased.

Flattered, she raised her head and let her eyes meet his.

"You didn't go!" he said to her, his face glowing. "You're still here! Hello, Annie."

She put down her plate and tried to finish chewing.

He glanced at her mother. "Hello, Mrs. Cardello; we met at the Beach on the Fourth of July."

"Yes," Bianca nodded politely. "Hello, Mr...."

"Smith. Call me John."

"My husband's name, too. Giovanni in Italian. You like Italian food?"

As he nodded, Annie cut in. "What are you doing at this festival?"

"My sister and I often come to the Feast of the Assumption. We both like the food booths. I enjoy the games of chance. And we watch the procession."

"You don't go to Holy Rosary Church."

"No, I'm not Catholic, but this festival is a nice affair, especially the procession, which is certainly a Cleveland spectacle worth seeing. My sister had to leave—"

"Spectacle?" Bianca thought that word sounded negative.

John looked embarrassed. "I mean, it's interesting to see. People are so devoted, and the statues they carry—they're striking."

Annie nodded encouragingly, but Bianca was silent, then murmured something about joining her friend Yolanda and moved away

"Annie, I never expected to see you again."

"What did you say? It's so noisy here."

"Come over to the side... Now, let's talk. Didn't you go to Albany? You stayed here after all?" She shook her head, but he went on, not catching the warning signals flashing from her eyes. "I'm so glad you're back. You know,

I wanted to take you to hear Duke Ellington at the RKO Palace, and the Indians are in town, playing Philadelphia... Did you give up baseball? Are you working somewhere? What are you doing tonight?"

"Say, Rick, who's that skinny blond guy talking to your sister?"

"Gennaro! Are you jealous?" Rick Cardello picked up and examined a small piece of religious jewelry offered for sale at the booth in front of him.

"I thought maybe I could take her out this evening, now that I have a car. I don't see her much since she left Halle's. I guess she got a pretty good job when she went back to Richman's."

"Well, you couldn't expect Halle's to hold her job open after she left, not in these times. Besides, she's baseball-crazy, and Richman's has a good team."

"I know. And that stonecutter, James Broggini, he's always running after her..." Gennaro pointed his head at a fellow at the edge of the crowd who couldn't seem to take his eyes off Annie.

Suddenly Rick put down the rosary he was considering buying. "I'm leaving. Tell my mother I had to go."

"What's wrong?"

"I just got a signal that the police are on their way. They'll probably want to question me... Listen, Gennaro. Tell my sister something for me. Say I had to execute the plan. I'm going to need her help."

"The plan? What plan?"

"She'll know. Just tell her."

Gennaro kept looking over at Annie, but she was still talking to that thin, well-dressed, rich-looking guy.

Annie was listening to John, but suddenly she interrupted him. "Over there, look! It's George DeTore—and I think that's Sal Gliatto with him!"

He looked at her questioningly.

"They're with the Cleveland Indians. George DeTore is an infielder. And Sal is a pitcher. Like me."

His eyes moved back and forth between the ballplayers and Annie. "How do you know them?"

"I don't, but a friend pointed them out to me once. They're Italian... I'd love to play with the Cleveland Indians some day."

He looked at her. "Come on, Annie. You know that's impossible."

She raised her chin, and her eyes flashed anger. "Why? Because you don't think I'm good enough?"

"You know that's not the reason. Women just don't play in the big leagues."

Still angry: "Does that mean they never will?" She turned to look again at the two players, who had stopped at a table where a woman was selling homemade pastries. "I think it will happen one day. Maybe I'm the one to make it happen."

"Annie, to begin with, you're too small and delicate to go through what these guys do. And can you imagine how they would razz you? Maybe even hurt you? Surely you've read in the papers about the mean things players do to new teammates. How do you think they'd treat a girl?"

"Somebody has to be the first. Maybe it'll be me. It has to be someone who's determined. Why did Jackie Mitchell do nothing about it after Commissioner Landis voided her contract with the Chattanooga team?"

"Jackie who? I never heard of him."

"Her. The commissioner of baseball said Chattanooga couldn't hire her for the team because she was a woman." Now Annie had really fired herself up. She dashed her paper plate into a trash container. "Jackie had to find independent men's teams to travel and play ball with."

"Annie, Annie. Think for a minute. Please give up this idea you have about baseball. Marry me instead."

"What?"

"Oh, I didn't mean to say that, not now. I wanted to wait for some romantic moment. But could you think about it? Please?"

Annie remained silent, her eyes moving around the churchyard as if she were bewildered, torn, confused by all the chatter of the festival.

Then the solution to her family problem came to her.

She thought, I know how to save Rick.

"Now sit back and relax with your wine, dear." John felt generous and expansive. The chatter in the restaurant stayed low, the way he liked it. "Since you seem set on a Mediterranean cruise for our honeymoon, I've brought this brochure for you: It's about the Italian ship *Rex*. Isn't it beautiful? It operates out of Genoa. From there we can travel to Rome, Florence, and Venice. They're the most romantic cities. Then, if you're still determined to visit Sicily, the home of your parents, we can take an island cruise with the Greek line, Epirotiki, before heading back to Genoa and picking up either the *Rex* or the *Roma* for the return trip..."

"John, I know nothing about ships." She handed the brochure back to him. "I just want to get to Italy. And Sicily. Let's get there as directly as possible. You select something and let me know ... Greek line? I thought Sicily was part of Italy."

"It is. And we could get from mainland Italy to Sicily quickly, by ferry across the straits of Messina, but it's not a comfortable trip. I suggest a cruise ship that will stop in Palermo, Syracuse, maybe the Greek temples at Agrigento—"

"Greek temples. You mean the Greeks once lived in Sicily?" She picked up her glass for a sip.

"Of course. My dear, you know so little of your own history ... I mean, of the country of your origin. The Greeks settled Sicily before the Romans did. The ancient Greek temples at Agrigento are famous. The city used to have a Greek name, Akragas. And of course the Arabs once conquered Sicily, and so did various European groups. Sicily is a conglomeration of nationalities, a colorful, if backward, place to visit."

"You make it sound ... quite a jumble."

"Yes, well, it is. And in fact it's not always safe. The officials all expect bribes, and there's a lot of thuggery. Perhaps we should take an organized tour when we get there."

She sipped her marsala, pretending to look at the photos of famous and not-so-famous entertainers mounted all over the walls of the restaurant. "I think I would feel better if I had someone from my family along."

"Someone? Who?"

"My brother Rick. He's been wanting to visit Sicily."

"Why, you don't mean ... your brother should accompany us on our honeymoon?"

"He wouldn't get in the way. He'd keep his own company; that's the kind of person he is. A loner. He wouldn't even travel first class. We would be on our own, until we reached Sicily. I think I'd like to have him with me there. And he would want it kept quiet that he will be on our ship."

John sat back in his seat and finished his scotch and water in one gulp. This will be a strange honeymoon, he thought. That's what I get for selecting someone unusual for a wife.

"All right, if that's what you want," he said. "Now let's order." He signaled the waiter. "I'm glad we came to Otto Moser's restaurant; it's so close to the Hanna Theatre, where we're going to see a play. Some time I must take you downstairs to Otto's Cheese Cellar."

She looked startled. "The Cellar?"

"It's an old tunnel under the street between Otto Moser's and the vaudeville house across the way. The performers began using it to reach the restaurant so they could get something quick to eat privately between acts. Like cheese and crackers. Now Otto serves all the vaudeville performers there. It's a sort of basement connecting the two buildings."

Annie already knew of this Cheese Cellar, for as the waiter approached their table, Rick sat below them in a dark corner of the basement, listening to the footsteps overhead. In the evening he would receive a phone call from his sister letting him know whether her plan was successful. Across from him at a square cheese table sat Sally, a vaudeville performer in a black spangled dress.

Upstairs at Otto Moser's, Annie sat up straighter and looked around the room with pleasure and gratification. John thought he had never seen her so vibrantly happy. Her exotic Mediterranean looks pleased him.

I have made her content, John thought. I think we will have a good marriage after all. All it takes is giving in to her whims. Then she will take care of mine. He started picturing the moment when he could to pin her to the bed by her hair.

She spoke again, tentatively. "Will this trip cost a lot of money?"

"I have a lot."

"From your parents, you mean."

"No!" He seemed annoyed. "I've recently come into a considerable sum of my own. And ... I've quit my job. I won't need to work any more." He sat up straighter, a satisfied look on his face.

After a silence, she merely replied, "Oh," thinking: Evidently, this is not my business. He's decided that all finances will be under his control. Everything else, too. I'm just a ... hanger-on, a person of no consequence that he will squire around. Well, what did I expect?

Later, at the Hanna Theatre, Annie found herself inside a garishly-decorated enclosure with gold-painted carvings and what looked like a mural of half-naked figures dancing in a meadow. "What is all that?" she asked John.

"It's supposed to represent ancient Greeks—at least, as conceived by the Italian who decorated this theatre. He wanted to pay tribute to ancient Greek playwrights by painting that mural. If you could see them from here you'd find the names of Aeschylus and Euripides engraved on the ceiling near the proscenium arch."

Annie felt intimidated by John's knowledge and his easy familiarity with cultural topics. She stared unseeing at the green-and-gold damask curtain, thinking about how much reading and study she had ahead of her. She frowned, considering the gap between her knowledge of the world and John's.

He continued, "Perhaps when we reach Sicily you'd like to take a side trip to Sardinia. The official language there is Catalan, the same as in Andorra..." He chatted on, largely to himself, describing Andorra as "a tiny country between Spain and France with almost no government, an almost medieval principality but nevertheless stable financially, a good place to hide money..."

Bored, she began thinking of her situation. What have I let myself in for? Why does he really want me? Maybe just for sex. Sometimes when he looks at me, I think he's seeing under my dress.

The play presented at the Hanna Theatre that evening was one she could never remember afterward. Instead, her head filled with contrasting scenes from her past in Collinwood, scenes she was about to abandon for an entirely different life.

The images and the sound track in her mind were of men playing bocci ball in their vests; women in black headscarves shopping for vegetables at the market; children running to Mrs. Mather's settlement house to learn English and baseball; the ragman crying "Paper! Rags!" as he drove his horse and cart along the narrow streets; the sound of foot-pumped sewing machines coming from the small houses as women tried to bring in extra money with home-sewn piecework; the thrill of receiving a penny for candy from the iceman or a pat on the head from the milkman, scenes from her childhood that jarred with the opulence she was being introduced to.

Then came the memory of a moment when she felt proud of her heritage: It happened one Columbus Day, when a place in Cleveland was set aside for honoring famous Italians. Papa took her and Rick—Dom was sick that day—to the opening of the Italian Garden in Rockefeller Park, a beautiful open space in the city with a fountain and a sculpture of the poet Virgil set against a stone retaining wall.

That day, tablets honoring other Italians were set into the wall. She remembered the name Michelangelo, an artist, and Verdi, a musician, and Marconi, an inventor. She had heard of them in school. It was Virgil's birthday, she was told. The two-thousand-year anniversary of his birth. Papa's fraternal society sent him and two other men to be a part of the big crowd that applauded when the bust of Virgil was unveiled.

A band played, and they all had to listen to interminable speeches, one from the Italian Consul—he had a title, Count something-or-other. She stood there as straight and tall as she could in her best dress, the white communion dress her mother had made. She felt the aura of importance like a vapor surrounding her.

I am part of this, she thought that day. Part of a two-thousand-year tradition of creativity for which Italians are recognized, not just part of an immigrant family trying to adjust to a new country. Maybe I'll be important some day, too. An important Italian girl...

Then she realized that not one of the Italians being honored that day was a woman.

5

THE MORNING WEDDING TOOK PLACE at the fashionable Cleveland venue on Public Square called the Old Stone Church. Soft light shone in through biblically-inspired Tiffany glass windows. Annie went through with the ceremony blank-faced and thinking only of where she was, not what she was doing.

Afterwards, the newlywed Mr. and Mrs. Smith took the train to New York and stayed at the Waldorf Astoria for their first night together. Annie's mother had told her what to expect, so she submitted to John's penetration despite the discomfort, hoping that eventually she would learn to like the sex act, which seemed to continue forever, until the bed was wet with blood and other fluids.

Life on the ship held different experiences, however. Each afternoon, John announced that it was "time for a siesta," taking her to their stateroom and fondling her, after which he led her through other routines that she realized were designed not to satisfy her but to employ her services. He would unzip his pants and announce, "Come over here. Kneel down in front of me." And he would direct her in performing an act she felt to be degrading and distasteful. Or he would pin her onto the bed so that she could not escape. Too often she burst into tears.

I suppose this is what wives do, she thought. But I feel more like a prostitute.

Even in bed at night, he expected her to perform most of the sexual activity. "Get on top of me," he would direct. "I don't want to get all sweaty. Now go up and down. Slowly. Now faster." And when he had climaxed, he would turn away.

Annie lay there thinking that obviously John Smith was used to being serviced. She hadn't expected this. It was not the romantic ideal that the movies had presented to Annie: A mythological state in which the worshipped woman became the recipient of tender ministrations that would lead her to desire sex. Annie realized that she knew little about married life. When she had the opportunity, she revealed to her brother Rick that she did not care for her experiences so far.

One morning, meeting Rick in the second-class lounge at 11:00 for coffee, she declared, "I'm getting off the ship when you do."

"No! You can't. I received a message. I will be met when I reach Licata, and I must be alone. Annie, I'm sorry I got you into this. But I can do nothing for you now."

She sat there quietly. Finally she replied, "I will manage. He is just using me. But we are using him, too."

"Perhaps you will have a good life. At least you are rich now."

She looked at him. "Yes. At least I am rich."

With the handles of their *stirratore* over their arms, the nighttime miners of Licata walked into the tunnel carrying their spades just as evening approached. Only the new miner known here as Ricardu had no idea what lay in store.

As he approached the dark entrance of the sulfur mine, Rick thought: The inside couldn't smell as bad or look as frightening as the outside. Those piles of burning earth—burning to extract the sulfur—bore the awful odor of rotten eggs through the air and into the nostrils of the approaching workers with their woven baskets. The smoldering, smelly piles of ore-filled earth, their reddish light outlined against the darkening sky, created what looked like a scene from hell.

It suddenly came to him: He was standing in a picture describing a poem by Dante, whose poetry he had to study at St. Jerome's School. No wonder Dante was inspired to describe hell by viewing a Sicilian sulfur mine. Fire and brimstone—another name for sulfur. If I believed in the devil, I'd say he must live here.

Then they were inside the hot tunnel, a dark, dirty space. The only light came from some bare bulbs strung on wires. "Here," said Vincenzo. "You can start digging here. Aim for the ore, Ricardu." Vincenzo used Rick's name in its Sicilian form. "The ore is yellow; see it? Fill your basket before bringing it outside, or the boss will be mad. Mussolini's fascists have taken over the mines now. His men have placed spies everywhere, so..."

Rick nodded. Vincenzo began to work, and his strong muscles rippled in the dim light.

The smell wasn't so bad inside the tunnel, but the heat and darkness bothered Rick. And he was wary of the few boards and props meant to support the ceiling.

Soon his mind began to wander. Why did I agree to come here? I wonder if the American law would really be so hard on me if I'd stayed. After
all, I just happened to be there during the shooting. I didn't take part in it.
Now that I've run away, I'm no better than a fugitive.

"Listen, Vincenzo. I've got to go. Where do I ...?"

"Try down there, to your left. *Gir' a sinistra.*"

Rick walked down a tunnel connected to the main dig. He was just
about to take it out when he realized that he wasn't alone. Ahead of him in
the darkness were two figures. Slowly he made out one person bent over the
other, moving, pushing... The one on top was giving it to the other one.
Having sex in the mine.

He backed out. "Listen, Vincenzo. Somebody's down there. Two of
them. They're ... you know." He moved his right forefinger into the circle
made by his left thumb and forefinger.

"Oh. Try the small tunnel on the other side instead." Vincenzo pointed.

Turning to go, Rick stopped and asked. "Why do they allow girls in the
mine?"

Shrugging in the age-old gesture, and letting the corners of his mouth
turn down, Vincenzo effectively conveyed the meaning: That's how things
are; what can we do? To his body movements he added the words, "Some
men and boys have strong needs, you know? And some girls don't mind."

Just then the two workers came out of the side tunnel and brushed
past. The boy was breathing hard, and even in the dim light Rick could see
the girl's red face. They dragged their empty baskets behind them.

They're no more than fifteen, thought Rick. Well, how can I judge
them? I, myself, at that age...

Sweating profusely, he stripped off his shirt. He tried to get back to
work and to think instead of the sardines wrapped in bread and the ripe
figs in his pockets for *pranzu.*

Then a very small boy, no older than five, walked by. Consternation.

"Vincenzo. That *picciriddu.* What's he doing here?"

"That's the *caruso.*"

"What? Someone named after the singer?"

Vincenzo smiled. His teeth looked very white in the dim light. "Just a
boy helper. The *carusi* carry loads up to the top. Listen, Ricardu. I forgot to
warn you. Beware of a guy named Ninu. They call him *Manazza*, Big Hands.
Don't cross him." Vincenzo moved away down the tunnel.

Rick nodded and went back to hacking away at the sulfur with his spade. I see I have a lot to learn here. At least they all use the same dialect I heard at home.

A passing miner, swaying with his load, bumped Rick, who dropped his spade and twisted his wrist, then turned in anger.

"*Scusatimi*," muttered the miner politely. Then, more threateningly, "But you stick out too far. Stay closer to the wall."

"How can I do that?" Rick replied angrily. "I need space to do this work."

The miner put down his heavy load, and then Rick saw his huge hands, which suddenly darted to Rick's throat.

"*Ah!*" called Rick as loudly as he could, at the same time trying to push the miner away.

Vincenzo was there in a moment. "Manazza! Let him go, he is new and knows nothing. He will do better, I swear."

Slowly the hands loosened, and Rick grabbed onto the tunnel wall in his weakness.

Vincenzo patted the irritated miner on his back. The big hands picked up the load. The miner, still glaring, walked away.

"Now, Ricardu. You learn. Do not talk back to Manazza." He handed Rick his spade. "*Eccu.*"

"I don't know why I agreed to come here." Rick rubbed his neck.

"I thought you killed a man—that you were *un assassinu.*"

"No. That Cleveland Mafia man ... *U visti ammazzari.* I saw him killed. Actually, two men."

"Surely you cannot be jailed for that."

"I was there, with the killers, so the police will think I helped. I was told that after a while, they will forget. But I wonder how long a while is."

The South Sicilian town of Licata, dominated by an impressive church and a convent, perched on the slope of a mountain. The walk home from the mine in early morning light was tiring.

After Rick had washed up in Vincenzo's cottage, where he had a bed, the two ate polenta fried in olive oil by Vin's grandmother. They slept in the heat of the day until late afternoon, although sometimes Vin rose early and disappeared for a while. Rick soon realized that Vincenzo was visiting his girlfriend. When Vin's grandmother came in again to do the laundry, they went to a nearby tavern to eat freshly-caught *tunnu* and some pasta cooked with wild fennel. As they sat back and began to sip marsala, the entertainment began.

A wild-looking woman in a swingy skirt moved her *tammureddu* to the front of her body and began her song, shaking the instrument to the rhythm of a mournful *canzune*. Her skirt seemed to be made of a thousand strings attached to a wide fabric belt, and it swayed seductively as she moved. Her heavy black hair framed a bony face with thick lips and half-closed black eyes.

Looks like a Saracen, Rick thought.

Behind her a short man with a generous nose and a shaggy head began blowing into a *friscalettu*. The flute added a penetrating harmony to the woman's primitive lament.

Rick felt strangely moved. It must be my Sicilian heritage stirring in my blood, he thought. This music makes me feel passion. Desire. Perhaps even love.

"*Bedda*," he murmured to Vincenzo, using the dialect word for "beautiful" and continuing to stare at the wild woman.

"You want her?"

"Is she *disponibbili?*"

"I will speak to her. Her husband plays the *friscalettu*, but..." And he made the ancient hand gesture of horns, extending forefinger and little finger from a closed fist. Rick knew that it meant "he is cuckolded."

"After all," Vincenzo added, "How could she resist you? A fine young fellow like you—an American, too." Rick knew that was just Sicilian flattery, but he wanted to believe it.

Two afternoons later Rick couldn't sleep; he had too much to think about. "Stella is pregnant," Vincenzo had revealed, speaking of his mistress. "She's going to move in with me and Grandmother. There will no longer be room for you in my cottage. I will try to make other arrangements."

While Rick thought about that, Vincenzo went on to explain. "Stella's husband kicked her out." At Rick's inquiring look, he went on, "He was working in Rome for a year, so Stella was not supposed to become pregnant. He beat her up. She is coming here to live."

"Didn't you say she had other children? Are they coming, too?"

"No." A scornful look appeared on his face. "Why should I take them? They are not mine." He shook his head, and a shock of his thick black hair dropped over his forehead. He scraped it back. Stretching, he flexed his sinewy muscles.

"The husband will raise them?"

His eyes narrowed. "They are just reminders to him of her and her infidelity. Stella's mother will take them."

"You will marry Stella?"

"Marry?" Another shrug and grimace. Then he flexed his muscles. "I don't know. I will see if she can be a good woman." He picked up a cigarette and lit it. "The husband says he is sending to Rome for his girlfriend. But I doubt if she will like it here." He drew on the cigarette. "I wonder if she is good-looking." He discarded the cigarette and lay down on his bed.

Rick lay there and thought about this. Wives, girlfriends, children... They all seem just peripheral to the men. Even mothers and grandmothers are there only to pick up the pieces of broken relationships.

Then he remembered another story Vin had told him about a miner named Luigi, who was crazy about a young girl in the village, but she refused to even look at him. Finally, he went to her house at night, threw a bag over her head, and kidnapped her, taking her to his cottage and tying her to his bed.

"Isn't kidnapping a crime in Sicily?"

"Sure. But Luigi finally convinced her to stay, and they were married. The police dropped the charges against him. That's the way some fellows get their wives here."

Can't sleep now, Rick thought, so he got up and decided to go for a walk on the beach. Fog streamed over the river banks, but he found the air refreshing.

As he approached the River Salso, he thought he saw someone running on the other bank. Then he realized it was a young woman, perhaps barely into her teens. Or maybe she was just thin and short. Why would a woman be running like that? Was she pursued? Or perhaps she was *una strega*, a witch, bound on some sinister errand.

"*Bon giornu!*" he called in the dialect. She just glanced at him and continued.

He saw that she was wearing a very short dress, like a slip, with thin straps holding it up. Her short curls bobbed as she ran. He began to run, too.

At the bridge he came up to her and was emboldened to run alongside. "Why do you run?"

"I like running."

"Who are you?"

"The runner."

"Why?" But she would say no more. He decided that she was running just because she enjoyed it.

He tired before she did. "When will I see you again?"

"On the flag."

That made no sense to him. He dropped away from the path and turned back.

While walking to the mine later that day, he asked Vincenzo about her.

"You have met the three-legged woman. She is given that name because she runs so fast. They say she must have a third leg. I have never seen her third leg, but I would like to." They laughed. "Some say she lives just outside the village. Others say she is only a ghost."

"Why did she say I would see her on the flag?"

"Did you never see the flag of Sicily?"

"I didn't know Sicily had one. I thought the Italian flag—"

"We prefer our own. The *trinacra*. The triangle. Symbol of our country, our island, which is three-cornered." He made a three-cornered shape with both thumbs and forefingers. "Its three capes—in the northeast, the southeast, and the west—form a triangular island. The name *trinacra* comes from the name of an ancient symbol called a triskelion or triskel—something with three points. On our flag the three-pointed object is a three-legged woman. The Greeks called our country Trinakrias. The Romans said Trinacrium. It means the same."

"I never knew that."

"I have a banner at home. I'll show you."

"Will it help me get to know the three-legged woman?" Vincenzo only smiled.

"What did the Greeks have to do with Sicily? I thought Sicily was Italian."

"Not at first. It was settled by Greeks; then the Romans took over. A lot of other invaders followed. The *Francisci* we hated the most—"

"The French? They took over the country?"

"And the Muslims. And earlier than that, even Germans."

"I can't believe it. I thought Sicilians were Sicilians."

Vincenzo spat. He changed his basket to the other arm. "We Sicilians are a mixture of our aborigines and our invaders. A wonderful mixture. We absorbed them all. We learned not to let any invaders into our hearts." He stopped walking and pounded his chest dramatically, then went on. "That's how *gli amici* started—what you call the Mafia. We call them *gli amici*, The Friends. We had to find ways to sabotage invaders, to keep Sicily for ourselves. Sicily is Our Thing. *Cosa nostra.* Forming The Friends was our way of controlling our own destiny even when invaders had taken over. The Fascists under Mussolini believe they have destroyed the Mafia. They are wrong."

Rick was silent. He pushed aside a wandering goat that was in the way. Obviously, Vincenzo is a member of the Mafia. That's why he is always calling them *gli amici*. The Friends. And he must have been told to befriend me here. But he is silent about that. So I must be, as well.

An old man passed by wearing a flat-topped cap and driving a garishly-painted donkey cart laden with smelly seaweed. He glanced at them briefly just as Vin looked at him. He moved on when Vin looked away.

Rick and Vin resumed their walk to the mine. Other miners were gathering in the dusk, nodding their greetings. Vincenzo continued quietly. "The Friends protect us. We protect The Friends." He paused, then continued: "That's why you are safe here."

I wonder, thought Rick. But as the others gathered, he began to feel himself a member of the quiet group of miners now marching together to the mine. He realized that he thought differently about the Mafia.

Then he thought again about the *trinacra*. And the three-legged woman came to mind.

Maybe I can stay with her, he thought. Women, it seems, are made for the convenience of men.

They reached the mine and gathered their tools. "Vin," Rick began, "does the three-legged woman need a man?"

Vincenzo shrugged, using his characteristic gesture.

"I have just had a change of plans," Vincenzo told Rick. "I am going to Catania, on the east coast. For perhaps a weekend."

"Oh? Do you know someone there?" Rick set down his stirratore.

"Yes," Vin replied mysteriously.

"What's in Catania?" Rick knew Catania was up the coast. Then he realized that his sister and her new husband were staying just north of there, at Taormina, not far from Mount Aetna. Those towns were on the way to Messina, where he had taken the train south, using money John Smith had given him.

Vin replied, "There is something I need to do."

That night Vin left to hitch a ride from a truck driver delivering a load of fish inland to Caltanissetta. From there he caught a train to Catania, then hitched another ride northwards in a produce truck.

Standing on the balcony and looking down at the water, John had his back to Annie, but he turned and said, "It's unclear to me why you don't like it here. What's wrong with it? The San Domenico has one of the top hotel ratings in the civilized world." His thin, aristocratic face showed disdain.

Annie faced him, trying to explain. The bright sun behind him shone into his bedroom of their suite at the Albergo San Domenico Palace in Taormina. "I'm uncomfortable with so much empty luxury. All this elaborate art work and the carvings, all this plush furniture, old tapestries, such high ceilings and such thick red rugs—it's all display. Surface wealth. No warmth or depth. It feels cold, sterile, inhuman. It smells of age. It has nothing to do with people, with life. Even the servants are distant and cool. It's as if the whole thing were born of tragedy."

He smiled. "You seem to be trying to understand what decadence is, my dear. You just don't appreciate it yet. You should learn to. When a wealthy family bought this wonderful old building from a religious order, members of the family spent years collecting objects of classic beauty to furnish it and to add some modern splendor. This hotel—in fact, the whole of Sicily—is the result of multiple layers of ancient civilizations piling on top of each other, with some of the early layers deteriorating. It may seem cold and unfeeling to you, but it has the same kind of aristocratic beauty that you have. Come into the sunshine."

Decadence, she thought. It's a word that seems to fit him, too. She realized that his thin lips, when pressed together, made him look scornful and cruel. I wonder if he has some dark secret, she thought. Or maybe I'm just thinking of his rough style of sex.

"I like looking at you in that white dress; it offsets your dark skin and bushy black hair." Walking to her and taking her hands, he drew her onto the small balcony, where red petunias basked in the sun. He stood with his back to the iron railing. Down below—way, way down below—sparkled the blue ocean.

It's as blue as Carter's Ink, she thought. Anyone who dropped into it would surely stain his skin that color. She looked at him and imagined him turning blue.

The hotel, perched high on a rocky promontory, stood on a narrow shelf of land. A pool, formal gardens, and dining terraces lush with bougainvillea were laid out on the shelf.

"I don't like looking out there at the water; it's frightening. But if I go to the other side of the building and look west, I'll just see the top of Mount Etna. Clouds cover the rest. The top seems to hang there in the sky, menacing everything and everyone below. The man at the hotel desk said the volcano could erupt again any time, but nobody seems to care. They live with it as they live with Mussolini's control. Yesterday you told me Etna has been releasing sulfur gas and lava every month for thousands of years."

"My dear, the Sicilians are used to living with an active volcano."

She began pacing. "I'm not comfortable in this country. It's like a covered cooking pot full of tomato sauce with the heat turned too high."

"We're perfectly safe here. Try to relax and enjoy it. Shall we just go to bed for a while?"

Annie was silent for a few moments. She felt sore from the night's sexual activities, and her shoulders ached from the way he had handled her.

I'm not interested in more of the same, she thought, and I'll ignore his suggestion.

Looking out at the water, she went on, "I noticed all those poor people we saw from the train windows, and I wonder what they think of places like this. Or of Mussolini's men marching around so arrogantly. You don't seem to notice the contrast between rich and poor in this country, the contrast between power and lack of it. The servants here, dressed in their tuxedos and bowing all the time, look like puppets. And that manager, with those glasses perched on the end of his nose so that he can look over them at us..."

Glancing down, Annie, suddenly wary of her distance to the ground, grasped the wrought iron railing with both hands. John covered one hand with his. "I've had enough travel," she continued. "I want to go home. Besides, I like places that seem homey and cozy. This is such an artificial style of life; there's nothing real about it. Being here is like being in a play at the Hanna Theatre." She turned to him. "Let's go back to Cleveland. To the house in Bratenahl that we fixed up just before we left. I think I could be comfortable there." She rubbed one aching shoulder, thinking, perhaps if I were back in familiar surroundings, I could think of a way out of this unwanted marriage.

"My dear, we just got here a few days ago. The Ohio house can wait for a while. Try to appreciate this wonderful place, where many famous people have enjoyed staying. If you don't want to rest, let's go down to lunch."

She was thinking: I shouldn't have done this. Rick might have managed some other way. How hurt my parents were when we were married where John's family insisted: At the Old Stone Church on Public Square instead of in our parish church. The Smiths worshipped where the Mathers and the Severances and other prominent Clevelanders do, so of course the Old Stone Church is the fashionable place for people to marry. And why did I marry in the first place? Not for myself; for someone else. I sacrificed my future for my brother.

Their well-appointed table in the lofty dining room was positioned near a wall bearing a gold-framed painting of a man embracing a half-dressed woman who was bent backwards in a grotesque position. The wall behind the painting bore gold carvings and old tapestries. Above their table sparkled a glittering chandelier; it looked like melting ice. An elderly couple at another table sipped white wine and looked around them haughtily. Flashes from many diamonds came from the rings on the woman's arthritic fingers.

John ordered. An attentive waiter brought them a dish of sea urchins, which Annie refused; she asked for pasta with fresh sardines (*pasta chi sardu*), an entrée that her mother sometimes served. Here it arrived in a bowl trimmed with gold, offered to her by a small, stiff server wearing white gloves. She took a deep breath. Then she began eating.

This time it was John's turn to broach a subject. "I can't get over your brother deciding to leave us when we reached Rome," John began. "Was he really so anxious to see his friend in Sicily that he couldn't even visit Venice and Florence?"

She shrugged. "I think he would not have liked Venice, anyway. That gambling house you took me to by boat, in that other palace... I think he would be as bored as I was. I don't understand how you can take part in gambling."

"Sorry it didn't suit you. Gambling is just entertainment, an ancient way of having fun."

She thought to herself: Fun for rich people. Throwing their money away. Will I ever adjust to being married to a rich man?

Annie felt more at ease at street level, in the town of Taormina, when they went downstairs and out for a walk. Women in dark clothes shopped for the vegetables and fruit displayed bountifully in the stalls. Children ran and played in the park. People walked leisurely in and out of the shops and churches. Old men sat around watching the action. "This seems like more natural living," she remarked. "But the old women: They sit facing the small houses, with their backs to the street. Why do they do that?"

"A tour guide once told me that their behavior is a remnant of the time when the Arabs ran the country. Muslim women weren't supposed to be interested in what's happening or to show their faces to the world. The Sicilians have kept some of this view of women with their emphasis on modesty and religiosity. But it may stem from an even older occupation of the island—by ancient Greece. That was long before the birth of Christ." He tucked her hand under his arm. "The Greek men kept close control of their women, preventing them from taking part in anything important, like governing the country, or even participating in the famous Olympic Games."

"Women couldn't be Olympic athletes?"

"Evidently not."

"That sounds familiar."

Annie thought to herself: In America we can play at being athletes, but as soon as we get serious, we're blocked from proceeding to the next step.

Restless, she pulled her hand away. "Let's go and see the old outdoor theatre you mentioned. First I'll stop at the post office to mail a card to my parents."

From Taormina's main square they followed directions on a sign and walked up a nearby hill. At the crest, they looked down into a huge stadium with stone seats, the rows arranged on the side of the hill to rise gradually from the stage below, so that everyone would have a good view of the play. It's like the new Municipal Stadium in Cleveland, she thought. Massive. I read that Judge Landis came to the opening of the Stadium. Judge Landis. The man who ruined my life.

But this stadium: "Is this Greek? Or Roman?"

"It opened during the time the Greeks were settling the island, around 500 B.C. The Greek playwrights presented their work here. Later, after the coming of the Romans, it was used for Roman plays."

Annie sat down on one of the low stone seats warm from the Sicilian sunshine. "Maybe some of my ancestors sat here. My parents came from a nearby town called Mineo, famous for its fruit orchards."

"I'm glad you feel the connection." He looked at her. "Maybe some of your ancestors stayed at the Hotel San Domenico, or lived there when it housed religious orders."

"I doubt it. I come from simple stock. Simple but athletic, I'm told. I once learned of a distant relative of my grandmother's who tried to run in the 1896 Olympics but wasn't allowed to because of being a woman, so she ran the course herself, in advance of the race. She was said to be crazy. Maybe the whole Revithi family was crazy." She looked at him and permitted herself a small smile. "Women who want to do unusual things are considered crazy."

"Not you." He put his arm around her. "You're just ... different. That's what attracted me to you. I notice that you still like to get up very early, before I wake up, to go outside for a walk. I would rather you didn't go out alone, at least in this country."

"I stay on the Corso, within sight of the hotel. I feel safe enough."

Except (she avoided saying) that I feel I am being watched.

On the way back through the center of town, Annie saw a painted cart with an image that interested her. The design showed three shapely legs that formed a sort of triangle, the hips connected in the center by a woman's face. "What does that design mean?" she asked John.

"I have no idea. You could ask the owner of the cart, but nobody is there now."

As they walked toward the hotel along the Corso, the town's main boulevard, a man approached. He kept staring at Annie. A strikingly hand-some man, she thought, very muscular, with thick dark hair worn leonine fashion. Not one of those rich men staying at the hotel. A laborer, evidently, from his clothing—blue cotton pants and a jerkin that revealed most of his chest and his strong arms. He permitted some of his hair to fall carelessly over his forehead. His black eyes narrowed as he walked toward them; then he lowered his gaze and let his eyes rise again as he examined Annie's body. She flushed, but she realized that she liked being appreciated by this man. She liked his confident swagger, his air of being part of this place.

That is a real Sicilian, she thought.

John's face dropped in annoyance. "What a forward fellow. Imperti-nent," he said just after the man passed. Ignoring John's mutter, the stranger then turned partly around in order to examine Annie from the back before continuing on.

"He is certainly bold," said John, turning away from the man. "Why, he's going over to that painted cart. Well, we aren't going to ask about that symbol now." He took Annie's arm possessively and steered her toward the hotel.

She could not stop thinking about the laborer with the muscular body and the way his eyes examined her. She took a deep breath in order to calm down.

She did not see him again until the next day.

She had risen early, as she always did, to leave their elaborate suite, where John slept in his own room (a rich person's habit, she learned), and to walk through the long, deserted halls toward an elevator that would take her down to the main exit so that she could enjoy a brisk walk on the Corso before breakfast.

The halls were quiet; nobody here rose early. Suddenly the man stepped out from behind a heavy plush curtain and stood right in front of her. She took in her breath.

Standing before her, he looked into her eyes boldly and said, in strongly accented English, "You are a real Sicilian woman."

"Why, no," she replied, "I'm an American."

"Sicilian," he insisted. "You need a Sicilian man, not that weak boy who is with you." He moved so close that she could smell his sweat.

"How did you get in here?" Her breath began coming fast.

"Back door. The cleaner let me in. He is one of us. I needed to see you. I needed to tell you that I can take care of your problem."

"Problem?"

"That fellow you have married. You do not want him any more. You have used him to take care of Ricardu. Now let me take care of you."

Her eyes opened wide. "You come from my brother?"

"I come from Licata. I knew you were here and that you needed me."

She drew in a breath: I should not have confided my doubts and disappointments to Rick.

The man went on: "I was with Ricardu in Licata, but he does not know I am here." He took her arm and drew her into the thick curtain with him. "I will handle everything." He put one strong arm around her. "Then you and I will be together."

Annie's eyes widened. She felt weak and a little dizzy. Good heavens, she thought, I am so attracted to this bold stranger. I feel something for him that I never felt for anyone. Certainly not for John. And ... does he mean by "problem" what I think he does?

"I'm not sure ... what you mean."

"I will take care of everything," he growled. "When will your husband get up?"

"Not until nine. He keeps banker's hours."

"All right. Come back to his room at nine-fifteen."

He looked deep into her eyes, then left, and she sat on one of the hall benches to gather strength and collect her mind. Her hand moved up to her flushed face as she reviewed over and over what had happened—how she had permitted it to happen—and surmised what was about to happen next.

Then she walked slowly to the elevator. Downstairs, she went as far as the front door, then turned around and, instead of going outside for a walk, sat on a hotel terrace overlooking the Corso and drank coffee. She was so distracted that she forgot to ask for sugar. The strong, bitter brew seemed to suit her mood.

At nine she put down her cup and went to the elevator. After reaching her floor, she walked slowly and nervously toward their suite. At ten after nine she was inside. She left the door unlocked and began to move, step by step, toward John's room.

6

CABLE TO MR. AND MRS. EMMET SMITH, Cleveland, Ohio

Something terrible has happened. Your son John, my husband, has accidentally been killed. He fell off the balcony of our suite at the Hotel Domenico Palace in Taormina, Italy. I had just returned from an early morning walk when I heard him shout, but by then it was too late. He was leaning over the balcony as I entered the room and lost his balance as he turned to welcome me. I believe he just leaned over the railing too far. He liked to lean out as he looked at the view of the Ionian Sea. I saw him go over, and his body struck the terrace many floors below. This was an awful moment for me.

The management here has been kind, but I'm sure you know how excitable these people can be. They did a lot of rushing around and waving their arms. They want to be sure they will not be blamed. Finally, the police came with an ambulance, and John's body was taken away.

I am trying to make the necessary arrangements and will cable you again tomorrow.

Anna C. Smith

Cable to Mr. and Mrs. Emmet Smith, Cleveland, Ohio

Thank you for your reply. I was so sorry to learn of Mrs. Smith's sudden and serious illness. I hope she recovers.

No, you do not need to come here. I am arranging to have John's remains shipped home so that he can be interred in Lake View Cemetery where all the Smiths are buried. I knew you would want that. I will send John's effects to our home in Bratenahl.

As soon as I know when I am arriving in Cleveland, I will ask you to arrange for church services and the viewing at the funeral home of your choice.

Since I have never traveled alone, the manager here has helped me locate a responsible person who will act as escort and servant on the trip home. This person will also assist me with everything that needs to be done with the government and the immigration service.

Please telephone my parents. Tell them what happened but assure them that I am all right and that my brother Richard is staying in Italy for now.

Anna C. Smith

Among John's things she found his travelers' checks, the bankbooks for two large accounts, an envelope full of Italian money, and return tickets for the train trip to Genoa and the crossing to New York on the *Rex*. Vincenzo, she decided, would occupy the cabin that had been reserved for her brother Rick.

With the advice of the hotel manager, she cabled one of the banks for permission to cash a sizable check in Rome so that she would have enough money to cover stops in the capital as well as in Genoa and New York.

Realizing she needed to appear the grieving widow, Annie hired a local dressmaker named Rosa to sew three black dresses and a dark traveling suit. Rosa told her that in Italy she must wear long sleeves and a black veil, at least outside the hotel. A black veil! She felt foolish in it, but at least it satisfied local convention. The black dresses made her think of the black uniform required at Halle's.

In uniform again, she thought. I'd rather have my baseball uniform. But what's the use of playing baseball, anyway? As soon as we get to be good enough to play professional ball, we're struck down. I was the Drawing Card, that's what I was. For a while. The Drawing Card who could go nowhere, my future blocked. The only thing I drew was a man whose help I needed. For a while.

Rosa, while sewing for Annie, found a suitable outfit for Vincenzo: A blue canvas uniform with brass buttons and a visored cap, in which he looked something like a policeman, although Rosa called him *Marinaru* (Seaman). He named himself Annie's personal assistant. In public he politely called her "Missus."

Annie quickly tired of the uniform and had him fitted for two fine business suits—what the British called lounge suits—along with an evening outfit for use on the ship. He stayed at a room in the town but reported to her each morning.

The manager extended her stay in the hotel while the sewing was done and while Vincenzo, with the manager's help, dealt with the local mortician, the Italian government, and American Immigration. She signed official papers, many of them written in Italian; Vincenzo assured her that they accurately reflected what she wanted and needed—and what he needed: Passage to America. He told her that after he had helped her get resettled in her Cleveland home, he would depart for Chicago, where he had a connection.

Finally, all was ready for their departure. While Vincenzo was helping her to pack the last few things, she broke down. "All this is so terrible," she said through her tears. "How did I allow it to happen? Why? I have committed a mortal sin."

He held her and said, "It was your husband who sinned. He just wanted a pretty young wife, someone who seemed to him ... different, or maybe exotic. So he chose you, and you were flattered at the attention of a rich man. You know that the two of you did not share deep love and should never have been together. You were too different." He smoothed back the hair from her forehead. "It is best this way. Sicily has solved your problem. Sicily is a great force of nature."

She wanted to believe him. She did believe him. Moreover, she began thinking that perhaps after their return he could solve another problem for her.

Two hours after they left Taormina, Etna released more sulfur dioxide into the atmosphere, and the town was dusted with warm ashes.

In Licata, Rick was still in bed one afternoon when Stella walked in on him. He sat up, then pulled the coverlet around his waist—it seemed that nobody in Sicily wore pajamas. She stood over him, looking at his bare chest.

Stella's low-cut blouse and tight skirt revealed every curve of her ample body. Her long, straight brown hair curled seductively where it touched her shoulders; her full lips attracted him.

"Stella. Where is Vincenzo? He didn't get home from Catania. And I haven't seen Nana."

She sat on the edge of his bed. "Vincenzo is not returning. He has left for America."

Rick's eyes opened wider. I am stuck here, he thought. I might have to stay here for years. Vincenzo was my lifeline.

She knew what he was thinking and put her hand on his arm. "Don't worry. The Friends will take care of you. Everything will be all right."

"How do you know that?"

Her hand tightened on his arm. "I received a message. You will learn when it is safe to return to your homeland. Meanwhile, relax. All is well. And I am here. I will stay with you."

Rick was surprised but grateful. She smiled and reached out to touch his shoulder. Then she leaned toward him. He accepted the offer. Later, she prepared for him a pasta dish, along with a *caponata* made of eggplant and fat olives that was redolent of clove, onion, and vinegar, sticky with raisins and somehow tasting of unsweetened cocoa. He no longer worried about Vin's return, or even his own.

It happened the evening Annie and Vincenzo reached Rome. In the taxi to the hotel, Annie sat as far as possible from Vincenzo, realizing the strong attraction between them and wanting to avoid or postpone contact.

After unpacking, they went out for food. Annie wanted to see the famous Spanish Steps, which she had missed before, but when they got there, the Steps seemed fairly straightforward. "What's Spanish about them? These steps look like any other steps."

"I don't know. But over there is a small restaurant; let's try it." To enter the restaurant, which was below street level, they had to use a stairway, and Vincenzo extended his hand to support her elbow.

She shook it off. "I can walk down a set of stairs by myself."

He thought to himself: She let the porter help her down the train steps, but she is afraid to let me touch her.

Inside, Annie pushed up her veil, then passed Vincenzo an envelope full of Italian money. "You pay," she said. They ordered a pasta dish and Chianti, and they sat there quietly in the simple room where chatting groups of Italians were eating.

"Only six tables; this is a small restaurant."

"Yes, it's homey." Annie liked the friendliness of the server, who was obviously the owner as well—he walked around the room in a flashy striped vest, exuding sociability and beaming at his customers.

When the food came, Vincenzo began to twirl his spaghettini around his fork, but Annie cut hers before spooning it up. They noticed each other's different styles of eating and smiled. Then her leg inadvertently touched his. She pulled away. He looked into her eyes and saw that she had felt the same electricity. He saw her chest heaving.

They finished eating quickly and left.

At the hotel he silently followed her into her room and watched as she removed her dress. Then he began undressing, still watching her unsnap her garters and slide off her stockings.

When they were both ready, she threw her arms around him, pressing her bare chest against his. They came together violently.

The crossing became a real honeymoon for Annie.

Just before boarding the ship in Genoa, she changed Vincenzo's name to Vincent, upgraded his status from assistant to companion, and asked him to discard the blue uniform so that he could be seen with her as a social equal. As Vincent del Vecchio, he joined her each evening at the ship's dining table in a tuxedo—not John's but one that had been made for Vincenzo's huskier figure.

Annie passed him off as her Sicilian cousin, and he practiced his heavily-accented English on the other passengers, using a borrowed phrasebook that proved, hilariously, to offer only British English: "Put the trunk in the boot. Wear your Wellingtons." After the evening meal, he stayed with her in her cabin until the early hours of the morning. She learned about passion; it was a revelation to her, and it kept her from dwelling on what had happened in the Hotel San Domenico Palace.

She began to fear losing him when she took up her new life in Cleveland. Why did he have to go to Chicago? she asked.

"It is best, *Cara*. I do not fit into your world there. I will be back to your city to visit you as often as possible. Let us just enjoy this time together. When we reach Cleveland, we must be more ... circumspect."

It was not until the last day at sea that Annie experienced morning sickness. She knew then that she was going to bear John's child.

Cleveland seemed different, almost a foreign place. The kitchen of her parents' home seemed small and dull. Her world had changed, and Annie's point of view had changed with it.

"Dominic," said Papa, "he telephones us once a month, all the way from Las Vegas. He says he is doing fine. What is he doing? He says he is working in the entertainment industry. What does that mean? Nothing. His boss is a man named Lucky. I hope he is really lucky. When Dominic phones, your Mama cries. 'When are you coming home?' she wants to know. He never says."

"Have another anise cookie, Anna," urged Bianca. "He says he has a girlfriend there. What is a girlfriend? A girlfriend is not a wife." Bianca sighed. "And Ricardo. When will he come home? How long is he staying in Sicily?"

"Someone will let him know when it is safe. He will be back." She leaned over the pretty blue-lined basket where the baby slept and touched his soft cheek.

"Anna, when are you going to get a man, a real Italian man? So many nice Italian men ask about you in church, or at the socials."

"Mama, I'm not ready to think of another man."

"So who is this man who drove you here? Why do we not meet him?"

"He is just a servant, Mama. A helper. He will be back to pick me up at three. Soon I will have a license to drive my own car... Mama, I want you and Papa to come over for Christmas."

"Not there. Not in that house. Your Papa and I are not comfortable there. It looks like a ... a museum, not a home. And I am not used to having a cook and a cleaner around. And a nurse."

"They are only part-time helpers, Mama. Please."

Bianca shook her head. Giovanni merely looked unhappy ... and unwell. Annie knew that the doctor had told him to watch his blood pressure. His life in America had not turned out as he would have liked. But in Annie's honor he was wearing his twenty-five dollar suit from Rosenblum's.

Annie sighed. "Then let me take you and Papa to a restaurant for dinner."

"Anna, we do not eat in restaurants," replied Giovanni. "We eat at home, good home-made Italian food. You come here for Christmas. Your mother will make cannoli and Sicilian tiramisu and other good things. Christmas we have with family. Your Uncle Paolo and his family will be here. Young Tony has lost his job, and him with a wife and new baby." He sipped coffee. "I do not understand why we have a Depression. I give thanks in my prayers that I still have a job, even though I work fewer hours. The radio, on Station WGAR, says nearly a third of Cleveland's workers are out of work."

Annie knew she was in a privileged position, being protected from the depression by the Smith money. The Smiths had granted her a large and regular allowance—because she was the mother of their grandson.

Lunch with Katy and Jojo at Stouffer's was a little awkward. Annie knew they felt she was different now and that they were unsure whether she was still interested in knowing them.

"The team pretty much broke up when you left, Card. You were our biggest draw," Katy admitted, even though she knew she was prettier. "Some of the girls went to other teams, but some just gave up playing. Florrie got married to some German from the West Side, and Edith moved back to Chicago to look for a job. Maggie is trying to put together another team for next year from the remnants of our team with some younger players who want to hook up with a heavier club."

"You wouldn't be interested in playing, would you?" Jojo asked earnestly.

Annie pursed her lips. "Not really. I've kind of lost interest since that rejection from the International League. I can't forget what Judge Landis did to me; so I'm pretty much soured on baseball. I've taken on this new volunteer work for the Alta House Settlement on Murray Hill, and I'm in the Junior League and the Women's City Club."

Dear Cousin Anna,

Here I am in Chicago, where I have made contact with the people who can help me get ahead. The person in charge, a man from Brooklyn named Capone, has just been convicted of income tax evasion and will soon go to prison. But he is being replaced by a Sicilian named Nitti, who has just returned from serving time for the same offense.

Everyone expects the ban on hard liquor to be lifted in maybe a year or two, so the organization is expanding into different fields, and I will still have a position here.

I haven't forgotten the job you asked me to do, and I am investigating ways to do it.

Thank you for helping me to get to the United States. I will come and see you in the spring.

Since my English writing is not yet very good, this letter is written for me by a friend named Costanza.

Sincerely,

Vincent del Vecchio

After walking back and forth across her living room a few times, Vincenzo explained the difficulties he was having in solving Annie's problem. "Anna, what I know so far is that the man walks to work every morning. That sounds like an opportunity, but I cannot follow him in a car because he is already being followed by somebody else: A colored bodyguard in a big limousine. The driver stays close behind, so he will spot me if I approach. I have to find another way and another place..."

He folded his hands on his stomach. "Now can't you get rid of the baby for a while so we can ... have some time together?" He looked around her home, as if wondering where the bedroom was.

Annie lit a cigarette. "Pretty soon the nurse will take him out to the village park for a ride in his perambulator. The cook won't come in until four. What else have you found out?"

He shrugged and went on. "The man smokes Cuban cigars. I might find a way to doctor them. He takes summer vacations at a lake in another part of the state. I've got to learn where it is and how to get there. He visits various baseball parks, especially in Florida in spring, but that's too public. He goes to Arizona in winter for golf—again, too public. My best chance, I think, is that he lives in a Chicago hotel instead of in a private home because his wife doesn't like to cook or clean. She will be in the way, but the hotel might still be the best place. I will check on it."

She was silent for a few moments. "So who is Costanza?"

"The widow of a guy who used to work with me... Go ahead, answer your telephone."

"Hello. ... Yes, Isabel. ... Tomorrow? Where, the Union Club? ... Oh, the Women's City Club. Noon. All right. Bye... That was my sister-in-law. She keeps inviting me here and there. We'll lunch with her friend Kay Halle."

"Are you still involved with the Halle company?"

"No, just with the family. Members of the Halle family have become friends. I kind of like old Sam Halle—he's a lovable old guy, always thinking of the employees. You know, he recognizes the need for athletics—he let Fenn College use a vacant lot he owns on Euclid Avenue." She looked away and tapped her cigarette on a silver ashtray. "I no longer take part in athletics." She paused, then looked up at him determinedly. "I'm going to see to it that my child becomes an athlete. With my coaching, he could reach the major leagues."

She drew on her cigarette, then started again. "Sometimes I see a baseball friend, Katy Reiner, but we have little in common now. She's a supervisor for a local textile company, Joseph and Feiss. My life has changed a lot... I've learned from doctors and hospitals that my son needs a lot of attention... Still, I often go to the Shoreby Club to dine. It's right down the road—membership comes with the house—and I mix with the boating people.

"I've joined another club for riding, the one Isabel belongs to. Sometimes I go downtown to shop with Kay or with Isabel; we lunch at one of the clubs."

Silence. Vincenzo passed one hand over his head and waited. She noticed that his black hair was cut shorter, that he looked rather dapper in a dark blue striped suit. And was that the beginning of a moustache?

"A Halle employee and I are friendly, too—a clothing buyer for Halle's Specialty Shop named Mary. She and I don't travel in the same circles as Kay Halle, but sometimes Kay calls on one of us for support. I depend on Mary for selecting suitable clothes. Her taste is better than mine. As the widow of John Smith, I have to look the part. Isabel's wardrobe consists mostly of jodhpurs..."

He sat back, listening a little to her chatter and looking her over more carefully: The elaborate hairdo (had her wavy hair been straightened?), the orange-red lipstick, the sleek grey silk dress, a tiny polka-dotted scarf showing at the neck. With blonde hair, she'd look like Jean Harlow. She's changed a lot. Independence has done it.

He glanced around the comfortable living room. "You're fitting into your new position. And you look it. Why do you have a statue of a bird on your bar?"

She glanced at it. "That's a cocktail shaker. In the shape of a penguin. My sister-in-law Isabel gave it to me. I'll make you a cocktail, if you like."

"I drink red wine. But not now. Are you looking for a new husband?" She seems harder, tougher, not very friendly. Maybe depressed. And drinking wine in the morning.

She sucked on her Tareyton, then picked up her wineglass. The marsala was sticky and sweet. "After what I went through with John, then having the baby without a man around... Well, I'm not looking. Some men come calling; most of them are scared off by my attitude." She looked directly at him. "A few stay the night." She lowered her eyelids.

Then she drank and set the wineglass down. "As for the Smith family, well, except for Isabel, they don't treat me warmly. I don't know what I would have done without Isabel's kindness. My mother-in-law didn't last long after John's death, and my father-in-law does a lot of brooding. I'm sure he blames me for what happened; my presence is just a reminder of it." She smoked again. "He's right, of course. You and I are co-conspirators."

Vincenzo shrugged. "You'll get over that."

"Occasionally he comes to visit his grandson. He brings presents." She got up and walked around again, touching objects, moving them slightly. "The other Smiths keep their distance. I seldom see any of them, except perhaps at social events, like the opening of Severance Hall, the new music building out at University Circle. They greet me rather coldly. I keep busy with charitable work through the Junior League. I give money to the Italian Red Cross. Sometimes I play golf at the Country Club, though it's a boring game." She paused. "Cleveland society accepts me now that my name is Smith."

"And ... your parents?"

"We talk. Mostly on the phone." She sat down and sipped. "My mother doesn't like coming here or accepting any help from me. I bought her a mangle; she won't use it. Sometimes I take Johnny in his carriage in the car and meet her at Wade Park, where we go into the art museum and then walk around the lagoon. Or we meet at Euclid Beach. Once we went to the zoo. My father talks about retiring, but I doubt that he will, though he's not well. They keep asking when Rick is coming home. They thought he might come after Angelo Porrello's funeral. I think Dominic will never come home."

He sat forward, getting a whiff of her Chanel No. 5, and said confidentially, "Rick is in New York."

"What?"

"Mussolini's fascists are cracking down on the—" Hearing someone approach, he paused.

"Mrs. Smith, excuse me. I'm taking the baby out now. I've put him in his Limousette."

"All right, Laura. Stay in the park. And be back in two hours."

"Yes, Mrs. Smith." The girl wore a white cap and a navy blue hooded cape, at Anna's insistence, because that's what children's nurses in fashionable homes wore. The cape lifted to show a white uniform as the girl turned and went back to the entrance, where the child's carriage waited. Little John Smith slept.

Vincenzo looked at the clock on the mantel to check the time and was distracted by its flashy gold and white enamel stripes, not to mention its hands, which appeared to sparkle with diamonds. He looked back at Anna. "What kind of a fancy clock is that?"

"A Cartier. In Art Deco style. A wedding gift from the Smiths. I would never buy anything like that."

"Show me the way to your bedroom." He rose, intention in his eyes.

"And Rick?"

"He's okay. I don't know when he'll be back to Cleveland."

As usual, Laura stopped at the drinking fountain in nearby Foster Park to fill the baby's water bottle. She had no idea that another baby's diaper had been washed in that same fountain the day before. John Junior drank greedily, then started dozing.

When Vincenzo left at noon, he said only, "I'll return in a few months."
She walked to the kitchen for coffee, then made a decision.

This isn't working, she thought. He's stalling. He's not going to get the job done. I'll have to go to Chicago myself.

She picked up the phone. "I'd like a reservation on the sleeper to Chicago. Sunday night. Arrange for me to stay for a week at the Ambassador East."

That evening the baby seemed fretful, but eventually his nurse got him to sleep. Annie didn't feel like socializing at the club; she wanted to think about how to carry out her plan. She had the cook prepare something, then leave. She made a leisurely meal of a lamb chop and her favorite salad with black olives.

For a moment she stood at the window at the back of the living room, with its view of Lake Erie. Then she picked up the *Cleveland Press* but was interrupted by the nurse.

"The baby has a fever. His throat is red. He won't stop crying; I think he's sick."

Investigating, she found that the nurse was right. Concerned, she called her doctor, who was associated with the prestigious Cleveland Clinic. He arrived in a half-hour.

After examining the fretful child, Dr. Bradley said to Annie, "I'm putting the baby in the hospital. I don't want to alarm you, but he seems to have an infection. It's always possible that he is developing infantile paralysis."

Annie's hand went up to her throat. Paralysis! No. My boy is going to become an athlete.

She accompanied Dr. Bradley and the nurse to the Cleveland Hospital and insisted on sitting in a chair next to his crib throughout the night. In the morning, the baby was no better, and Bradley returned to make another examination. He reported that John Smith Junior exhibited all the symptoms of the frightening disease that was attacking so many children and young adults. He would have to stay in the hospital for observation, in an isolation ward, since the disease he suspected the child had might be contagious.

Annie went home and cancelled her trip to Chicago. Then she phoned her mother.

The next day Annie drove to Pythias Avenue and picked up her mother so that they could attend noon mass at St. John's Cathedral downtown. Annie felt unworthy to sit close to the altar, so they knelt at the back, where

Bianca exhorted her, "Pray to St. Jude, Anna. Pray to the saint of lost causes, the saint who can work miracles for those in despair."

Annie shook her head. "Mine is not a lost cause. And I look to a saint who has suffered as a woman suffers. I am thinking of Saint Olympias, the patron saint of widows, whose husband died within twenty days of their wedding. John's death was the start of all my problems."

"But Anna, think of your son, not of your dead husband."

She doesn't know what I mean, Annie thought; she'll never know. Perhaps there is nobody I can tell. Then she had another idea: "Whose feast day is today?"

"Anna, didn't you see the sign at the entrance? It said today is the feast day of Saint Anne, Mother of Mary. July 26. Do you remember her story?"

For a moment Annie thought. Then she said, "I remember. Saint Anne gave birth to Mary very late in life, then lost her when Mary disappeared into the Temple when the child was only three. I cannot lose Johnny! He's all I have. If he becomes permanently paralyzed, that's almost the same as losing him." She sighed. "I have such plans for my son!"

Annie bowed her head and thought deeply. Then she began muttering:

"I think today of sweet Saint Anne, Mother of Mary, who has given me so much: my name, my life, my earthly treasures.

> "I am sad, Lady, for your own loss.
> But today I come to you for the protection of my son.
> My desire is for your intercession with God
> so that I will not be deprived of my one joy in life:
> my little son.
>
> "Your little daughter disappeared.
> You found her again only in Heaven,
> after she became the mother of Mary,
> who gave birth to Jesus, God's son.
> How painful was your loss, the loss of your dear daughter!
>
> "Sweet Saint Anne, Mother of Mary,
> In the name of Mary,
> help me to keep my child
> so that I will not suffer the same loss.
> I ask for your womanly sympathy.
> Look down on me and see my despair

for my child's serious illness.
I implore your help.

"Sweet Saint Anne,
I am heartily sorry for my sins against God.
Although I do not merit your favor,
have mercy upon me.
Bring me your grace.
Pity me for my suffering.
I require your intercession,
for I am unworthy of approaching God myself.

"I ask only that I be allowed
To care well for my treasured son,
Who needs nurturing.
I ask nothing more for myself.
God has already given me all I need.

"Spare me this calamity!
I leave this offering of money
in the offering box that bears your name.

"Gladden my heart, sweet Saint Anne.
Do not permit the cold darkness of despair
to fall upon my life.
Think kindly upon me
and grant my desire,
in memory of your own dear child."

As she sat there, she began to think of her brother Rick, whose attitude toward religion was one he called "modern." Often he asked her, "Why do you bother with prayers? You know as well as I do that they don't work. How many prayers did our mother repeat when she gave birth to a deformed baby? Didn't it die within a week? Do you really expect miracles to happen? You know nothing can protect us from bad things happening. How about Cousin Paolo's daughter getting raped? How about the Porrellos getting killed? How about the terrible pain our grandfather suffered with cancer? Prayers might make you feel a little better, but they don't prevent suffering."

In her mind she responded: I suppose you're right. What's going to happen will happen. I say prayers only from habit. Now I have in mind doing something even worse than I've done in the past. Perhaps I'll receive even more punishment. I suppose I'll just say more prayers after that.

She rose, lit a candle, and asked her mother to lunch at Stouffer's. "It's right on Euclid Avenue, Mom, and it's not fancy."

"No, I'm not comfortable in restaurants. I'll go to your house. Fix me something there."

At the house in Bratenahl, the two women sat in the kitchen munching bread and cheese with olives. Bianca told her daughter, "You know, there are other things you can do to help your child."

Startled, Annie looked at her mother. "What would that be? Do you mean become a better woman? Or stop wanting to do things that only men are allowed to do, the way Father used to tell me?"

Bianca looked down at her lap, realizing that Annie still operated from a position of resentfulness. Then, resolving not to open that conversation, she went on. "I mean use the ancient methods that women of Sicily have always used. They carry small objects that represent what they desire. They hold those objects and think about what they want to happen."

"You mean amulets. Little carvings, little stones, little beads."

"That's what I mean. I brought you some."

Surprised, Annie said, "You really believe that works?"

"I have seen it work. Remember your great-aunt Rosaria?"

"Yes."

"She kept giving birth to stillborn babies. After this happened four times, a friend gave her a tiny statue of a rabbit and told her to carry it in her pocket, taking it out sometimes to fondle it as one would a baby. In less than a year, Rosaria gave birth to your Aunt Francesca, healthy as can be."

"That was after Rosaria left Sicily for the United States."

"Yes."

"You don't think that the reason was that Rosaria ate better here and had cleaner water than in Sicily?"

Bianca took a breath. "That could be, of course. But I have known other such happenings. I believe the little stones can be helpful. Here are some I want you to have." And from her purse she took a handful of small objects.

Annie took the objects and examined them. Some looked carved and others were shaped by nature. She saw a curious bluish stone that looked like a snail; a yellowish one that resembled a person's head, face and all; a square white one carved with the head of a horse; a tiny carved hand and wrist; a beautiful green oval stone that looked like two breasts or buttocks, and two crab-shaped stones.

The most curious was a long, thin red stone that looked something like a red pepper except that it was slightly twisted. "What's this one?"

"It's a *cornicello*, a little horn, and it's to protect a person against the Evil Eye. That's the one you should keep on your body. It is supposed to prevent anything bad from happening."

Annie took it up in her palm and began rubbing it with her fingers. Touching it felt satisfying.

That evening Annie was feeling soothed. Before dinner, she picked up the Cleveland *Plain Dealer*. On the sports page she noticed a story about a decision made by Judge Landis, the Commissioner of Baseball. Landis had been asked to rule on whether the International League could hire a convicted robber who was a good ballplayer. Landis, said the story, had ruled that the International League could hire this player on his release from Sing Sing Prison, even though he had been involved in at least five other robberies.

Annie's anger flared. A convicted robber can play baseball in the International League, Landis says, but a woman like me cannot. Just because I'm a woman.

She sat there stoking her anger. And she became more resolved.

PART TWO:
DEMETRA, 406 BCE AND 400 BCE

7

"FATHER, LOOK! This man is selling little statues of Kyniska! I want one."

Stopping at the booth and glancing at the smiling seller and his goods, Leontius frowned. "Kyniska was a Spartan woman. Shameless. Spartan girls are constantly flashing their thighs."

"But Kyniska won the four-horse chariot race." Fingering the statue, Demetra looked disappointed.

"Only by training the horses and driver. You know very well that women cannot compete in the races with men."

"Why not, Father?"

Impatient to move ahead and locate the tents of the *pornoi*—the imported prostitutes—Leontius said, "It simply isn't done."

"The Spartan girls exercise with boys..."

"Spartan girls should stay at home more. They wear excessively short dresses with no undergarments." To distract Demetra, Leontius removed some silver from a leather purse and paid the seller, who advised care in handling the statue, since the feet were rather pointed.

"Thank you, Father. But tell me again why it is that mother..." She stopped as a muscular Spartan, easily identified by his long hair and red cape, shouldered past while they were trying to re-enter the crowd. The Spartan took a few moments to examine the fourteen-year-old Demetra—obviously an upperclass Greek girl, though perhaps not from the mainland. Noting the glare on the face of Leontius, he moved on.

Leontius retained his frown until he recognized a friend and fellow citizen of Akragas in the crowd. "Epious! Greetings!"

"Ah, Leontius!" replied his friend. "And this must be your daughter. It was smart of you to bring her. The Olympic Games make a good venue for virgins to attract husbands." The girl was obviously the right age, so he looked her over for his own son, Castor, who was starting to grow a beard and thus had to begin withdrawing from his long and profitable sexual relationship with his mentor.

"You may have heard," he began, "that my young Castor has trained for the *dolichos*, the long-distance foot race." He glanced again at the small but pretty girl in her virgin's short dress and demure robe, noting her fine necklace of shiny onyx stones alternating with pink crystals, probably from Macedonia. "I shall tell him your daughter will be in the audience."

"May the great god Zeus be with your son Castor in his race," Leontius said obsequiously.

Epious nodded in gratitude. "Before Castor was born, my wife dreamed that she was giving birth to an eagle, so my son is certainly destined to be a successful athlete. He has already won six prizes in cash races throughout Greater Greece. You may know that he took the laurel crown last year in the Pythian Games and those at Delphi."

"Rejoice, Epious. The fourth day of the Games will be a great day for you and your family, as well as for our city."

Demetra's annoyance with her father's deferential language began to show on her face.

"I'll be glad when it's all over," Epious replied.

Tired of this boring conversation, Demetra started looking about. The noise of the crowd thrilled her, and she kept looking around at all the sights.

Standing in this natural hollow, a big bowl, almost a valley, surrounded by gentle hills, she felt exhilarated by the hundreds of strange people milling around, calling out to acquaintances, shouting their wares, advertising jugglers and singers. What excitement! She heard the growls of huge dogs and the chatter of monkeys. The strains of lyre music penetrated the noise, and she tried to find its source. Then she started to ask her father if he would buy her some honey cakes at the next booth, but Leontius cut her off. "Quiet, girl. Don't interrupt."

Epious was still boasting. "My older son and I have been with Castor all through his qualifying races and helped him train in Elis, just north of here, so I am anxious to see the successful conclusion of all our effort and to get back to Trinakrias and my business. It's a long sail."

As if I didn't know how long it is, thought Leontius, having himself just made the same twelve-day voyage from the same island of Trinakrias, an important Greek colony.

Leontius pursed his lips with envy. He could not compete with the boast of Epious, since his own sons showed no interest in becoming Olympic champions. Leontius thought sullenly of his eldest, besotted with a prostitute of indigenous Sicel origin; he had in fact just married the girl. And his younger son had been fined and disgraced for cheating in a wrestling match by trying to gouge out his opponent's eyes. Resentful of his friend's successful son, Leontius, knowing of the bad reputation of the wife of Epious, slyly countered by asking after her health.

Epious drew himself up. "She is well. I am sure she will locate your own spouse in the wives' compound on the other side of the river."

"No doubt. And I'm sure I'll see you … uh, soon." He meant at the tent where he planned to relax with professional women, the *pornoi*. Since wives weren't permitted to attend the Olympic Games, the husbands found the occasion one of freedom and release.

Secretly, Leontius hoped to arrange a marriage between Demetra and the son of Epious. That is, if Castor won his race. If he became a champion, the young athlete would become famous and rich enough to buy something expensive, like a luxurious home. If he lost, he would be nothing.

When the two men finally parted, Demetra, relieved, asked if she could wander around on her own for a while. Nodding, her father beckoned to the servant standing at a respectful distance and charged him with watching over Demetra. "Philon, see that my daughter meets me at high sun in front of that large food cart." Demetra smiled with pleasure as Leontius gave her some coins minted in their home city, Akragas, and moved away into the crowd. She knew that when next she saw her father, he would stink of wine.

Pushing through the crowd to see who was making music, she found a beautiful young boy with tightly curled hair and a painted face playing skillfully on the lyre. His sponsor, an older man with a bushy brown beard wearing a gracefully draped robe, collected coins from admirers. After a few moments of listening, Demetra moved on, distracted by all the other sights. Pausing for a moment at a group around a fire-eater, she heard Philon start making his usual rhyming epigrams: "If you do not learn, you may be forced to burn."

"Oh, Philon, give it up. I am learning all the time."

"Tour of the temples and holy places, lady?" asked one of the itinerant guides, moving in front to thrust his hairy face (and bad breath) into hers. He hoped to make some money off this well-dressed teenager. She shook her head and moved toward some acrobats, but a Greek Egyptian crossed in front of her, displaying many jewels and followed by a proud-looking Ethiopian slave. Then she caught sight of some dancers and changed her path. Philos began muttering again. "If you think you must dance, you may not find romance."

Ignoring her servant, she watched the dancers until behind them, where the land started to rise into hills, she caught sight of two girls tossing a ball. Pushing past a storyteller and the crowd around him, she approached the girls. "If you play at ball," muttered Philon, "you sometimes fall."

"Quiet, Philon." Raising her voice, she called to the girls, "May I play?"

The taller girl smiled. "If you do, we can play the game called Girl in the Middle."

"Good! I'm Demetra of Akragas, daughter of Leontius the factor." Handing her cloak, money, and statue of Kyniska to the servant Philon, she took her position between the two ball-tossers so that she could be the Girl in the Middle and try to intercept the ball they were throwing.

The tall girl who had given the smiling invitation said, "I'm Doryla of Gela—like you, from the island colony of Trinakrias. But your city was founded by citizens of mine. Akragas is the Western Reserve of Gela. You live in our wilderness outpost."

Demetra thought this girl from Gela sounded rather snobbish.

But Doryla went on: "My father is Timoleon. He is engaged in keeping down the aborigine Sicels and Sicani."

Demetra thought about this. Doryla identifies closely with her father. But then, we were all taught to do that. "I wonder," said Demetra, speaking her thoughts, "why we never tell who our mothers are."

A pause in the conversation.

"Do mothers engage in anything besides taking care of the home?" asked the other girl. "I'm Pippa. I come from Licata, a town not far from your city, on the same island. My father owns sulfur mines in Licata. His name is Demos."

"I would like to do something besides taking care of the home," asserted Demetra. "Wouldn't you? I'm tired of trying to be a good little virgin." She heard Philon mutter, "If you stop trying, you start dying." Again she ignored his attempts at rhymed philosophizing.

"Right now," said Doryla, "I want to play Girl in the Middle." And she began the game. As Demetra took her position between the other girls, she realized that she had said aloud what she'd been thinking for a long time: I would like to do something. Then she turned her attention to the game.

The shortest of the three, Demetra tried hard to intercept the ball, jumping as high as she could, but Doryla, obviously the leader, finally declared her out, and the two exchanged places.

"I'm a much better runner than I am a jumper," apologized Demetra as she began tossing to Pippa.

"Then why don't you take part in the girls' championship race next year? Would your father let you?"

"I'm planning to ask him. That's really why I begged to come to the Olympic Games this year—to get an idea of what it would be like to take part in the Games." Pippa threw high to Demetra, far over Doryla's head, but by backing up, Demetra managed to catch the ball—and also to back into a passer-by.

"Good catch," he commented, placing his hands on Demetra's waist.

Embarrassed, she moved out of his grasp, muttering "Sorry," while Philon the slave rose from his cross-legged position on the ground, thinking he might be needed.

"Are you coming to the wrestling event tomorrow? I'll be in it." The stranger addressed Demetra.

"I don't know...," began Demetra, still annoyed at the fellow's famil-iarity, but the other girls called to him, "We'll be there!"

He smiled for the first time, and Demetra noticed his very white teeth in a thick-lipped mouth and his penetrating eyes that, as they moved back to her, seemed to see under her dress. His hair, she saw, had been cut short at the crown but left long around the face so it could be curled tightly. Standing with hands on hips and chest thrust forward, he seemed already to be posing for his victory statue.

Since Demetra was obviously too taken aback to say anything, the man started to leave, then turned and, addressing them all, informed them that his name was Laertes, son of Dionysus. Then he turned again and stalked off toward the massage tents.

"That's the tyrant's son!" reported Doryla excitedly. "You know, the tyrant of Akragas. Your city. I'll bet he's plenty rich."

So Demetra joined the others in looking after him as he strutted away. A rich man, son of the tyrant who ruled her own city, and a champion wrestler. She noted his wide thighs, his huge upper arms, his thick neck. She decided that Laertes, son of Dionysus, was ugly.

A scream brought them to attention. The clamor centered around a wooden cart, where a woman was shouting that a boy had stolen a magic charm from her. "There he goes! Get him!" called the woman, whereupon two men chased him down, pushing several people to the ground in the process. They brought a ragged boy back to her, one holding him by the hair and the other by the arm.

"Here is your magic charm," said one, handing it to her. It looked like a phallus, the kind made for selling to charioteers to ward off evil and help a competitor win his event. The woman magic-seller grabbed the phallus and whipped the boy across the face with it. He dropped with a whimper, and the crowd dispersed. The excitement was over.

Demetra found that the joy in playing had left her. "I think I'll go for a tour of the temples," she announced. The others shrugged. Doryla began tossing the ball high and catching it herself while Pippa stood there, hands on waist, then decided, "I'll come along."

Demetra's temper had darkened, but she accepted Pippa's company and began walking toward the temple of Zeus, hoping to find the one devoted to Hera, the champion of girls. "I want to pray to Hera. If I get to run next year in the races dedicated to her, I'm sure I'll win."

"You're that good a runner?"

She nodded. "Then I'll be able to help weave the hundred-tassel girdle for Hera, to decorate her statue. I love weaving."

"Tour of the temples, young ladies?" interrupted another tour guide. He thrust his face with its large nose into Demetra's, since she seemed to be the leader. He noticed her heavy shock of wavy hair, her expensive necklace, and her athletic body.

This time Demetra acquiesced. She followed the guide through the paths, lined with statues of the gods, explaining that she wanted to visit only the temple dedicated to Hera.

When she came to a statue of Hermes, she became annoyed, remembering her father's favorite pronouncement: "Herodotus in his *Histories* tells us that the Athenians were the first to carve statues of Hermes with an erect phallus." She always reacted mentally to this declaration with the thought, "So what?" but she never dared to say that aloud.

Where, she wondered, were the statues of the ancient goddesses my mother told me about, those like Doris the lunar goddess, the three Syrens, the Muses, the Nymphs, Gaia the Great Goddess, Danu the Earth Goddess, and of course Demeter the goddess of abundance? I was named after her.

Pippa lagged behind, followed by the slave Philon. When they reached the temple, Demetra signaled to Philon for her robe, money, and statue, then told him to wait outside.

Inside the dark, quiet building, the air was cool. With the two girls facing the altar, the guide began, at Demetra's request, to describe the races dedicated to Hera. He told how girls about to take part in the Heraian races let down their hair for the race and how they dressed in short tunics with the right breast exposed. He explained that the track was shortened for them by one sixth, and that the girls were divided into three groups by age. Winners of each of the three races received crowns of olives and portions of the cow sacrificed at the final banquet.

Then he grew silent as the girls stood there, thinking their own thoughts. Pippa began looking at the murals painted on the walls and wandered over to examine one. The guide stood behind Demetra as she meditated on the race she planned to run—and win. Lifting one shoulder, she fingered her small statue of Kyniska, as if for inspiration. Her robe dropped away from the other shoulder.

Her thoughts moved on to the excitement of the morning. All this ferment, she thought, all this only for the young men. Nothing here for the girls and women. We're supposed to be the ones who cheer them on. Why, when I'm a woman I won't even be able to watch. Like the slaves, I'll be unable to enter the stadium.

She became too angry to think of Hera.

And the guide became bored. His eyes, focused on the white shoulder in front of him, became clouded over with desire. Finally, unable to resist temptation, he reached ahead to touch the soft flesh before him.

Demetra whirled. She thrust her statue of Kyniska feet-first into his flabby belly. Its edge struck his main artery, and the blood spurted as he grunted and fell to one knee. Then, not realizing he was already mortally wounded, she struck him on the head.

Pippa turned at the grunt and watched as Demetra wiped her statue on the guide's tunic. Then he collapsed.

Demetra stared at Pippa, challenging her to react. Pippa stood there, eyes wide, mouth sagging into an O, saying nothing, waiting.

Demetra said, "We are leaving now." She started back to the door. Pippa followed. Outside, Demetra handed her statue to the squatting Philon. Noting that his young mistress seemed upset, he received it without comment and omitted making one of his usual rhymes.

"I want some of those honey cakes," she announced, and began moving toward the booths.

Pippa, trying to decide whether to follow, stood there. Demetra turned back to her, looking into her face. After a moment, Pippa lowered her eyes and started after Demetra.

Philon the slave followed. He wondered where the guide was. He knew something had happened in the temple, but he dared not ask. Servants and slaves did not challenge their owners in any way. The statue felt a little slippery, so he held it tightly.

Castor stood there gasping for air, the crown on his head slipping to one side, his eyebrows beginning to channel the sweat down his cheeks. The crowd was still cheering, his father and his coach were pounding his strong back, and his older brother was grinning broadly.

Castor knew he had just become rich and famous. The nineteen other contestants were hanging their heads and slinking away; there was no prize for coming in second.

The long race of Day Four was over, and Castor, his slender legs trembling after running three miles, was exultant. He had run back and forth twenty-four times, each time negotiating the two turning posts accurately. The wide stone base of each post prevented the runners from grasping a post and swinging around it. Castor had practiced for months to be able to handle this race successfully.

Once, during the race, Charmos, Castor's closest opponent among the twenty contestants, had reached out to grasp Castor's hair to slow him down, but Castor had smacked his hand away. Now Charmos approached to congratulate the winner, but Castor sneered: "You were so slow that the judges thought you were one of the statues." Charmos frowned.

Epious proudly led his victorious son back through the tunnel and out of the stadium to the sound of more cheers. The crowd did not leave; two short foot races were to follow.

All athletes took part in their events without clothing. In the hut built for the runners, Castor's brother Polydamus washed and oiled the runner's heated skin, and Epious looked for and found the shelf with his son's tunic and robe, bringing them to Castor with pleasure.

"Now, my victorious son, it's time for you to consider a wife. How pleased all these young virgins in the crowd would be if they were chosen! I have picked one for you "

"Father, surely I need not marry right away. My lover and I—"

"No more lovers for you, my boy. It's time to grow up and take on responsibilities. You need a wife. The virgin I have chosen comes from a wealthy and successful family. The father is a friend of mine and will see to it that she obeys you."

Epious thought to himself: She had better not act like my own wife, who wanders into the arms of others.

Castor considered, lacing a sandal. "What does this virgin look like?"

"She is small but graceful and wears fine jewelry."

Polydamus added, "You can train a young wife to do anything that a lover used to do." He was thinking of the girl he had married a year ago, before beginning to help with his brother's training. "I'm eager to get back to mine." The two brothers smiled at each other.

"Let us go and eat at one of the booths, and I will watch for the girl," said Epious.

Demetra was shopping for a bronze mirror with a handle in the form of a nude girl when her father Leontius bore down upon her, walking with his friend Epious and followed by two young men. Having been in the audience with Pippa when Castor won his race, she knew with one glance what had happened: Her father had bargained her away, giving her to the victorious Castor for a few handfuls of silver.

Her back stiffened and her face reddened with anger.

Castor was looking her over. A real Greek girl, he thought, with exotic good looks.

She was thinking, now I will never get to run the girls' race next year. Only unmarried girls can take part, and by next year my father will have married me off. This is the end of my plan. My plan to do something with my life.

Her eyes moved to Castor, taking in his hard body and proud face. Then she glanced at the other young man, whom she knew to be the older brother. His softer demeanor pleased her.

Perhaps I will devise a different plan, she thought, letting her body relax into a vision of herself with the fine young fellow named Polydamus, Castor's older brother.

Unfortunately for Demetra, her reddened cheeks made her doubly attractive to Castor, who resolved then and there to accept Demetra, virgin daughter of Leontius, as his wife.

Pippa had been standing silently at the booth while Demetra examined the mirrors, but at the approach of the men she faded away into the crowd. She had come to the conclusion that visiting her father's sulfur mines in

Licata would be safer and less complicated than what she was experiencing at the Olympic Games.

Demetra, who had reclaimed from Philon her statue of Kyniska, tightened her hold on it.

I may need this statue again, she thought.

8

AFTER THE CEREMONY OF TYING the knot, Castor took Demetra home to the fine house he had bought with his Olympics award. Three servants ministered to them, removing their flowered wreaths, washing their feet, and offering trays of fruit and nuts.

Then it was time for the virgin's initiation. Demetra's mother had told her what to expect, so she submitted to Castor's penetration despite the discomfort, thinking that eventually she would learn to enjoy the sex act.

But that was not the end of her education. On afternoons when Castor was not visiting friends, he announced that it was "time for a rest," leading her to their bedroom and fondling her, after which he led her through other routines that she realized were not designed to satisfy her but to enjoy her services. He would display himself and tell her to kneel down in front of him, then direct her in performing an act she had never heard of.

I suppose this is what wives do, she thought. Wives and the *pornoi*.

Even in bed at night, he expected her to perform most of the activity. "Get on top of me," he would direct. "I don't want to get all sweaty. Now go up and down. Slowly. Now faster." And when he had climaxed, he would turn away.

Demetra lay there thinking.

She hadn't expected this. She realized that she knew little about married life. But she resolved that, when the opportunity presented, she would inform herself. She would find other men, she thought, and learn other things. Maybe invent a few things of her own.

After all, if she could not create a life around her sports skills, she could do something else.

Pippa came into the room, excited. "It's tonight," she said. "Come to the old altar this evening; it's the night of the full moon. Bring a hare, can you?"

Startled, Demetra stepped back from her weaving frame. "Tonight? Let's see now: Castor is still involved in the building of another temple—and in the constant eating at banquets that seems to accompany such projects," she said, thinking of his growing belly.

She let her hands drop from her weaving, wondering if Castor might find any problem with her attendance at the women's gathering.

"You must! We are fulfilled only when we worship our ancient goddesses in the ancient ways. We must sacrifice to the Earth Mother tonight! Tell a servant to get you the hare—"

"Mistress," interrupted the nurse. "Shall I feed the child now? He's crying." Her bright blue eyes looked concerned, and her tall, square body seemed to fill the room.

Annoyed, Demetra frowned. "Of course. And if my husband asks where I am this evening, I have gone to consult my weaving teacher."

The girl nodded, her blonde curls shaking. Making a little bow, she left.

"I swear by Hera that these big, husky slaves from the North get more stupid all the time. The men like them well enough, though."

Pippa paid no attention. "I'm off to invite the others," she said, and left.

The warp is in. Tomorrow I can start the weft. I wonder if it was wise to invite Pippa to visit us here in Akragas—Castor is entirely too interested in her—but she was helpful in putting in the warp for my new design. And having her with me makes me feel more confident that she will keep her mouth shut about what happened in that temple. I'm a constant reminder to her of the need for her to keep it secret. Besides, she and I both prefer the old goddesses like Danu and Demeter to the current Olympians. Demeter has such womanly attributes; the brimming horn of plenty she carries is an assurance of ample means to live; the stalks of grain and the poppy flowers with which we associate her mean luxury, beauty, and a full life—what we all strive for. Pippa as well. Demeter symbolizes the rebirth of life in the springtime, too. Why is dedication to Demeter considered a cult, while worship of Hera isn't? Perhaps it is outdated to remind ourselves that we have so much luxury here.

In the early evening, nine women in graceful white robes left the town square, walked through a gate in the walls, and moved south of the city, passing olive grounds and fragrant almond orchards. The scent of oleanders came to them as they passed the fresh blooms. Fields of wild celery sent wafts of their tingling odor up from the coast.

The women wore delicate wreaths of iris on their heads, and they each carried a burning torch in one hand while bearing a sacrificial animal or some fruit of the land in the other.

Soon they came to the area with the temples devoted to current gods: The building with thirty-eight columns dedicated to Heracles, especially the shrine to the great god Zeus and the imposing temple devoted to the heroes Castor and Pollux.

As they went by, Demetra thought: My husband identifies with the godly Castor because he won an Olympic race. I'll give him that; but I have found no other heroic qualities in him.

They filed past the charming and relatively small temple dedicated to Hera, standing on its own four-stepped podium.

Finally, they approached the rocky sanctuary devoted to the memory of Demeter, the goddess of death returning to life, as the dead plants of winter return to life in the spring. They trod the rough ground carefully in their thin sandals.

In the growing darkness they located the temple by watching for the sacred fig tree that grew next to it, for it was not easy to find. Instead of being constructed on platforms and high ground, like so many others, the temple to Demeter lay in a depression. It was formed from the surrounding rock. Looking beyond it, they could see the gulf of water farther below.

They descended into the low area that formed a vestibule bordered by sacred pools filled with water gushing from the rocks. The small, roofless temple consisted of walls and a sacred altar. Into the altar was carved a labyrinth, to help the souls of sacrificed animals to journey through the underworld and return along its path. Shelves on the walls bore objects to be used in the women's ceremonies.

Following ritual, the women marched solemnly through three doors cut into the walls, three of them entering each door. Each deposited her sacrificial bounty on the altar, then stepped back. Demetra, because of her name, was chosen to begin the hymn.

She recited in a singsong, chanting style:

> "I sing today of the triple goddess,
> Demeter, Dea Meter, goddess mother,

she who multiplies loaves and fishes,
she who is the source of all womanly abundance.

"Demeter lost her daughter to the lord of Hades.
when Demeter's daughter Kore
was picking the flowers of spring.

"Suddenly the earth opened,
and the lord of Hades seized her,
put her in his golden chariot,
and drove away with her.
She cried out, but no mortal heard her."

Demetra stepped back, indicating that Ianthe should continue. The younger woman picked up the thread:

"Finally did the Lady Mother Demeter
hear her daughter's cries.
She ran faster than a deer
to look all over the earth for her dear daughter."

"Demeter asked for the sun's help
and received the answer:
The great god had given the girl to Hades
for his wife."

Ianthe then stepped back, and Meta moved forward to continue the hymn.

"At once Demeter was overcome
with terror and sorrow.
She went to the cities of humans,
but secretly,
so that no one knew who she was.

"One day she came to the incense-filled house
where King Eleusis lived.
She sat down in the shade near a well.
By then she looked old
and was not to be recognized."

Meta stopped the hymn, her eyes filling with tears. As the oldest woman present, Meta's hair was already graying, so this section of the hymn was especially poignant for her. Pippa stepped forward to continue:

> "The four daughters of the house
> were coming to get water
> and to carry it home in bronze jars.
> They asked who she was
> and why she had not gone to the palace,
> where she would be welcomed.
>
> "The Lady Demeter thanked them.
> For their kindness,
> she wished the daughters vigorous husbands
> and the ability to bear children.
>
> "As for herself,
> she asked only for a house with children
> where she could care for them.
> But the daughters asked
> that she come to the palace,
> where a treasured son, their brother, born late,
> needed nurturing.
> Demeter agreed to do it."

When Pippa stepped back, Elektra continued where Pippa had left off.

> "The daughters took up their water jars
> and went to the palace,
> followed by Demeter,
> cloaked and veiled.
> The queen was seated,
> holding her young son.
>
> "As the daughters told their mother
> what they had heard,
> Demeter suddenly changed,
> seeming to grow into the goddess she was,
> filling the room with divine light.

"The king's wife
was seized with fear and respect,
asking Demeter to be seated,
to take the splendid chair she was in.
But Demeter refused,
accepting only a bare stool
covered with a fleece."

Elektra halted, so Kalypso took up the hymn.

"Demeter refused the wine offered her.
She accepted only a cup of barley water.
Then the queen offered to Demeter
the chance to raise and nourish
her small late-born son.
Demeter agreed to protect the child from harm.

"The child grew up in a godly way.
But one day the queen discovered
that the child was being fed
the food of the gods.
She was anguished,
taking the child away from Demeter,
because Demeter was making him into a god.

"Demeter was angry.
Now, she told the mother,
there would be no way for the boy to avoid death."

Kalypso stopped and moved back. Tyche took up the hymn with these
words:

"The great Demeter
pronounced a curse,
saying that humans would have war
that would last forever.

"She revealed herself as Demeter,
changing her size and appearance,

becoming young and beautiful again.
The palace was filled with light.
Demeter instructed
that a temple be built in her honor.

"Demeter stayed there,
wasting away
with yearning for her daughter.
Because of her sorrow,
Demeter would not let the earth recover.

"Spring did not come.
Oxen dragged plows through the field,
but nothing grew.
Demeter might have destroyed all humans
if Zeus the great god had not noticed."

When Tyche paused in the narrative, Akaste stepped forward.

"Zeus summoned Demeter
to the immortal gods,
but she refused,
saying she would never go to Olympus
and would never permit the harvest
until she saw her daughter.
So Zeus sent another god, Hermes, to Hades
to persuade him to give up Kore.

"Hermes rushed to Hades,
where he saw the daughter suffering
from the loss of her mother.
Hermes told Hades
that he was ordered to bring the girl back,
so that Demeter would stop destroying the earth.

"Hades sent the girl back,
But secretly,
Hades gave the daughter
a magic pomegranate to eat,
so that she would not stay away for all time.

Then his chariot and horses bore her away
to the place where Demeter waited.

"The mother rushed forward
to greet her daughter.
Demeter and Kore
gladdened each others' hearts.
And Demeter made the earth flourish again.

"But the great god Zeus declared
that from that time forth,
Kore must spend a third of each year
with her husband,
in the realms of darkness.
So for a third of each year,
winter comes,
as Demeter mourns the loss of her daughter,
And refuses to let anything grow
Until her daughter is returned,
And spring comes back to the earth."

Akaste stopped and looked at Rhodeia, the youngest girl present, who picked up the thread and ended the story with this prayer:

"Come, Lady,
splendid with your gifts
and your beautiful daughter Kore,
think kindly on us as we remember you.
In return for our song,
grant us a rich, womanly, and comfortable life."

When the hymn ended, they all stood quietly, thinking their own thoughts and making their private prayers. Demetra thought of the abundance she enjoyed as the wife of a rich man. And yet, she thought, yet I am unfulfilled. There seems no way for me to enjoy the exercise of my body in the way I used to do it with other girls. I miss running. I miss ball-tossing. I miss playing games. Married girls act different; they are expected not to play. The exercise in which married girls take part ... well, it's physical, but ... it's with men. Sometimes I feel that, like Kore, I am dwelling with my husband in the realms of darkness. Must I really have a husband? When will my spring ever come?

When she looked up and came into the present moment again, she saw that the other young women were placing their torches in wall sockets. Demetra then moved to a shelf and took hold of the sacrificial knife.

She approached the altar, with its cunningly-wrought narrow trough around the edge, where liquids could collect and run off into a pit lined with stones. The ridges of the altar's central labyrinth stood out strongly in the light of the moon.

Grasping the hare, whose legs were tied, she recited,

> "Thine, ever thine, Demeter, is the power.
> With this sacrifice
> we ask that you show us thy favor."

The hare screamed as she slit its throat, and the blood ran into the trough as the animal twitched and died.

Pippa drew forward and poured sweet wine onto all the food collected on the altar, reciting the same words. Ianthe and Akaste both came forward, and on the offerings they poured oil, the first and best pressing of the season. All came forward with their sacrifices and spoke the prayer asking for Demeter's favor.

Elektra, who offered olives from her family's farm, had also brought a fine vase. Instead of crushing it on the altar as a sacrifice, she put it on a shelf, where all could admire its special markings devoted to womanly symbols like breasts and vaginas. Also symbolized on the vase were the familiar poppies, sheaves of wheat, and the horn of plenty, all representing the abundance of Demeter, along with the flowers associated with Kore. "This vase will remind us of Demeter and her gifts," Elektra said.

Tyche produced a small woolen mat, cunningly woven of geometric patterns in black and red, with a large black cleft woven into the center, which Tyche said represented the earth split by Hades when he captured Kore. The tassels that hung from fringe decorating the edges of the mat, said Tyche, stood for the fruit of the fig tree, like the one Demeter once sat under. Lovingly, she placed the mat on a shelf next to Elektra's vase.

Gradually, the women all sat down on the stony floor to share their thoughts. Demetra began, "I wish my mother were here to experience our devotion to the goddess of abundance. She revered another earth goddess,

Dea-anu, whom she called Danu, but I know she would have appreciated our gathering here to remember the great Demeter and to ask for her continued support."

The youngest girl, Rhodeia, said, "My mother is very sick. My father seldom goes to the *pornoi*, so Mother had too many babies, and the last one nearly killed her. I ask you to pray with me that she will recover." All remained quiet for a time as Rhodeia closed her eyes, and everyone thought fervently about the woman with too many babies.

Everyone but Demetra, who interrupted their thoughts by saying, "Your mother evidently never learned about the herbs that prevent conception, especially the one with the white lacy flower, and of course the wild fennel. Both are powerful preventives. I'm surprised she didn't know."

Rhodeia's eyes widened. "Really? How did you find out?"

"From a herbalist, of course."

Each thought her private thoughts about this.

Then Akaste spoke. "My problem is different. I have lost three new babies. Each time I put on the birthing apron, the child emerges dead. What can I be doing wrong?"

Ianthe spoke. "I will make you a sacred object that should help you. It is a baby carved out of a vegetable. You should carry this baby around with you. Sometimes, take it from your pocket and pet it as you would a baby, talk to it, ask it to be born live next time."

Akaste's eyes grew round. "I have heard of this. Do you think it will work?"

"Why not try? It has helped some women. I'll carve it myself," Ianthe offered, "thinking all the while of Demeter's abundance."

"Another thing you can do," said Pippa, "is carve the blade of a sickle on a doorway. Make it curve from left to right, like a curved ceiling." Pippa showed what she meant by curving her arm over her head. "It's the sign of abundant grain, and it may protect you as you enter and exit." Akaste hesitantly lifted her arm in a curve above her head.

"You can also ask Demeter for the blessings of her name, Dea-Meter, Diameter, the roundness that includes all things," explained Tyche, the weaver of the sacred mat. "Make the round sign with your arms." She demonstrated, and others joined in.

"Eat poppy seeds," advised Kalypso. "You know how fertile the poppy is. You may become fertile with live babies."

"No, she should eat quinces," Meta pronounced. "They help fertility."

"It's not fertility we're concerned with here," Pippa pointed out. "It's live births. Why not use the twisted horn that protects against the Evil Eye? If you keep it with you and touch it from time to time, nothing can harm you."

"Avoiding funeral ceremonies is the best way," Meta added. "Don't attend any of them. I hate them anyway."

"Are you living a balanced life?" inquired Kalypso, still thinking of babies. "Imbalance annoys the gods. Hippocrates claims that displeasured gods don't cause disorders. He said every disease has some natural cause. Are you eating well?"

"I agree about the funerals," pronounced Pippa. "Death is an evil, Sappho the poet wrote; for had it been good, the gods would die. That's logical, isn't it?"

"We're getting off the subject," Demetra complained. "And I want to broach my own question: Why do we need husbands? Or even babies, for that matter? They restrict our lives."

"Have you been to see Arion? She knows all kinds of things like having live babies," suggested Kalypso, still talking of live births.

"Arion is a witch," said Meta.

"So? She knows a lot of charms. One of them helped me." Then Demetra stopped talking, feeling everyone's eyes on her.

"Helped you how?" said Pippa.

Demetra breathed a few breaths and pursed her lips. "Well, it helped me get a man I wanted."

Now they were deeply interested. Everyone knew Demetra was married. What man did she want?

"Are you going to tell us more?" asked Meta, almost humorously.

Demetra waited a bit, looking here and there, then went on. "All right. I wanted the Tyrant's son." She raised her chin. "And I got him."

A few chins dropped.

"But he's not the ruler's son any more," Tyche pointed out, "not since we deposed the Tyrant for embezzling money and brought back rule by democracy among the patricians."

Demetra just tossed her head.

"I thought it was your brother-in-law you coveted," Pippa said.

"He was easy to get. The Tyrant's son took more time. And a special charm from Arion." She looked to the side, not wanting to face them all, now that she had revealed something she hadn't expected to reveal.

Pippa was the first to break the silence that ensued. "It seems to me that you were always complaining about having a man, that your husband kept you from engaging in all the activities you used to enjoy as an unmarried girl."

"A husband is ... like a jailer. I'm more interested in having a lover. That kind of man wouldn't care if I engaged in races or ball games. A husband is confining. At least, that's the way it seems to me."

"Perhaps you should live in Sparta, where the women act so independent, they even own property and engage in business," said Tyche sarcastically. "Is that what you would like?"

"Maybe. But now that I'm married, do you think I'd be able to travel to Sparta and live there? Besides, the Spartans don't even like us."

"I know a group that hates us even more," Elektra volunteered. "The Carthaginians, who settled to the west of Akragas to trade with the aborigines. I've heard it said that they envy us because our city is so rich. Maybe you'd prefer to live with them. You might find trading to your liking."

"Send her to Athens, on mainland Greece. The women there are supposed to be pretty loose," commented Tyche.

"Now we're getting silly," volunteered Pippa, always willing to support Demetra. "Let's forget all this nonsense and think of what we came here for: To urge Demeter to protect us."

"Does anybody know how to skin a hare?" asked Kalypso, who loved eating. "I'm getting hungry. We could roast that one."

"Food is something you don't need," Tyche said.

Suddenly Pippa, who had been seated facing the water view through the south door, stood up. "I see something on the water."

"Something?"

"What? Ships don't go out to sea at night."

"I see many small dots. I think they're ships."

Akaste stood, too. "She's right. Something is approaching. Maybe ships."

Several of the women stood, and some moved to the doorway. "I see them."

"Yes, they're ships. Whose?"

"I know," said Akaste. "They're Carthaginians. They're going to invade!"

"How do you know?"

"My husband builds ships. Those are quinqueremes—three rows of oars, with about 300 men. Akragas has no ships that big. And those rams on the prow, for punching holes in enemy ships... They're Carthaginian. You know that last year the Carthaginians invaded Selinus and enslaved five thousand people. They're going to attack Akragas. We must get out of here!"

Young Rhodeia could not suppress a cry that sounded like a scream.

"We have to sound the alarm," realized Demetra. "My father-in-law and the rest of the council members are in a meeting right now; it may be that nobody is aware of this."

"Why would the Carthaginians want to invade us?" whined Rhodeia.

"Because Akragas is the richest city," said Pippa. "No time to burn our sacrifices. I wish I had never come here," she said, looking at Demetra, as if she were to blame. "I'm leaving for my home city right now!"

"May the great god Zeus save us from destruction!" prayed Rhodeia.

"I'm going home!" cried Ianthe, clinging to Rhodeia. "I want my mother."

"Who's the fastest runner?" asked Meta.

"I am," said Demetra. "I'll go to the council. The rest of you follow as you can," she said, tightening the straps of her sandals.

Akaste looked again at the water, fascinated at the way the light-colored ships moved on the dark swells. The lunar light created what seemed like swirls of liquid mercury coiling over the water.

"I'm going home to my children," announced Meta.

"I'm going to head inland," Pippa said to nobody in particular. "I might be able to make it all the way back to Licata undetected."

"Take off that white robe!" Tyche told Demetra. "You'll be seen too easily against the dark hillside." Others began to remove theirs as well, revealing short, light underdresses of thin, unbleached linen.

"Maybe we performed part of the ritual wrong," said a tearful Ianthe.

"I'm not taking off my robe," said Rhodeia.

"I'm leaving." And Demetra, in her short *chiton*, pushed past the others, but she stopped at the shelf and picked up the sacrificial knife, just in case of need.

"I can see now why she finds it so easy to get men," murmured Elektra as she saw Demeter's lithe and attractive body in its thin underdress.

"Extinguish the torches," reminded Meta. "No use guiding the invaders to shore."

Demetra began with long steps as she mounted the rocky hillside. Gaining speed as she passed the rocky area and trod softer earth, she shortened her stride and began to press harder. Her legs moved faster, then faster still as she struck flat ground. Tall statues of gods seemed to look down at her in surprise.

"Look at her! Her legs are a blur," said Akaste admiringly as she labored to get through the rocks. "She's like the goddess Demeter searching for her missing daughter. Her legs are nearly invisible, they move so fast."

By then Ianthe and Rhodeia were sobbing. They took hands and tried to hold each other up, suffering mentally.

Pippa took off determinedly on a tangent toward the north, soon disappearing entirely in the dark hills.

Kalypso, the heaviest, labored in her breathing and kept getting farther behind the others. "Perhaps I am pregnant," she muttered to herself.

Meta, the oldest, was in no condition to move fast. Her pace was merely stately.

The others straggled along as best they could, trying to keep an eye on Demetra in the far distance ahead of them. "I've never seen anyone run so fast," said Elektra. "Too bad she isn't a man; she'd surely win a race at the next Olympiad."

"Tell me again," said Tyche to Akaste, "why the Carthaginians want to invade."

"We have much wealth in gold, olives, and wheat. Why should they trade for it when they can just take it?"

Meta couldn't help complaining. "Akragas has been here for more than a hundred years. I can't believe this is the end! People from Gela established our city as their Western Reserve. I guess they just built it too far west."

"I've heard it said many times that the founders built Akragas too close to the trading post of the Carthaginians," said Tyche.

And Akaste added, "Empedocles warned us against too much softness and opulence—no military exercise, no preparedness."

"You and Empedocles are wiser than our leaders," said Meta.

"What good is a democracy if its leaders fail to protect us?" Tyche mourned.

Demetra ran on, breathing deeply and well, living in the excitement of her adventure. On her exhilarating run to the city she encountered nobody. After entering through the city gate she passed an occasional torch mounted on the outside of a building. Flames from these torches shook and flickered in the breeze created by her speed.

As she approached the council hall, a lone guard named Galen, dozing at the front of the building, began to awaken with the sound of her feet on the ground and the slight stirring of the air. Galen looked up to see a strange vision of what looked like "The Legend of the Three Magic Legs" come to life. Everyone knew the story of the man who changed himself into three legs joined together and wheeled himself away from danger.

"Kymon!" called Galen in a quavering voice to a friend sleeping in front of the weapons building. "Help me! I'm in a dream!"

Kymon grunted, but just then he was kicked in his soft leather chest armor by a port worker who had run as fast as he could from the waterfront. "Wake up! Ships on the water!"

Just then the wheeling legs passed Kymon and the port worker as well as Galen the dreaming guard, then mounted the three steps, metamorphosed into a woman in her underclothes bearing a knife red with blood, and pounded on the door, shouting, "Invasion! Raise the alarm! Open this door!"

The flabbergasted guards then saw three more half-dressed women in the distance hastening toward them and just about to enter the city gate. The first woman kept pounding and shouting until the door opened.

Incredulous faces of councilmen greeted Demetra and heard her preposterous claims, but she was quickly supported by the port worker and soon enough by those of three other women, whose statements had to be accepted, since although they were only females, they were all recognized as upperclass.

Eyeing the red knife, the startled Epious asked his daughter-in-law, "Did you kill someone?"

"Just a hare. In sacrifice to Demeter. Perhaps she will help us in this hour of need."

The roused council was moved to direct that all city gates be closed and that weapons—swords and spears—be issued to the male citizens. Even some old metal armor was found in the storehouse.

The weary women, some of them dragging white robes or sobbing uncontrollably, found their homes and alerted their families.

Demetra supported the tired Meta, who dropped onto a couch with exhaustion when she reached her house. Then Demetra went home. By then Castor had already arrived; he challenged her because of her disheveled appearance, but when he saw the red knife still in her hand, he backed away. From then on, Castor never tried to limit Demetra's activities.

It was long before the workers and slaves of the city stopped talking of the three-legged man that wheeled himself up to the door of the council and then changed into a half-dressed woman who warned the city's leaders of impending attack.

The Carthaginians jubilantly surrounded Akragas and camped outside its walls, sending frequent assault groups with spears to attack the gates.

Seven months later, the city's leaders decided that Akragas could hold out no longer against the siege of the Carthaginians. Akragas surrendered, and the Carthaginians generously allowed the citizens to depart unharmed for a small town on the east coast between Syracusai and the great mountain known as Aetna. Walking there took five days; all beasts of burden had long since died and been eaten. Many citizens failed to reach the town, collapsing and expiring on the way, since they were soft from luxurious living and weak from the limitation on the food supply caused by the siege.

Demetra, trailed by a servant carrying her baby, was one who reached the coastal town. The endurance she had developed helped her survive the ordeal. Her husband Castor and Castor's older brother, along with the brother's wife, made it only as far as Syracusai, but Demetra and her father pushed on to the designated refuge. The old man died shortly after arrival.

When the citizens of Akragas had left, the Carthaginians plundered their city of all its wealth, taking everything that could be lifted. Even the sacred temples were not immune, for the Carthaginians worshipped not Zeus and the Olympic Pantheon of gods and goddesses but a god named Ba'al and his consort, Astarte. Lately, however, a new goddess called Tanit had developed a following among them.

Tanit was a Mother Goddess. Women invoked her for fertility, and her symbols included the grape and the pomegranate. Carthaginian coins showed Tanit wearing a wreath of grain, since she was the goddess of abundance. Tanit's aid in conquering the rich city of Akragas was gratefully recognized by her worshippers.

Demetra, now a worshipper of Tanit, had fulfilled her destiny, helping save her city only to see it lost.

PART THREE:
EVENTS IN THE YEARS
1282 AND 1896

9

DEMONA LINKED HER ARM into Ninu's and grinned at him. They were taking their time as they joined the crowd walking to church for the evening service. They kept looking into each others' eyes and remembering the pleasure of their united bodies.

"Are you sorry you married me?" Ninu asked playfully.

"No," she began, flipping her long black hair around. "Of course, you're not as tall as Turiddu," she teased, "or as strong as Ziu. But..."

Ninu opened his mouth in mock dismay, then pinched her buttock.

She squealed and laughed. Others around them looked and smiled. After all, the two had been married only two weeks. They were still flirting, teasing, and squeezing.

It was Easter week of the year 1282, and the euphoria of celebrating the Risen God stirred in the hearts of the Sicilian people as they approached the Church of the Holy Spirit in Palermo for the Vespers service. They forgot their resentment of the French officials who ruled them so abusively. The cheerful crowd approaching the church grew to about forty.

The sun was just setting, and Demona could see the cross on the church's roof lit by the sunlight. She admired the building—its red roof, its arched windows fitted all around with black and white stones, and its peaceful position within the grounds of a cemetery, where she liked to walk and to run. She especially looked forward to the Vespers service because it included so much beautiful music. And now she was attending with her young husband. She kept smiling at him.

Demona was enjoying the pleasant walk in the early evening breeze—until she saw the French soldiers approach. They acted as though they intended to join the crowd on their way to church, but the way they moved showed that religion was far from their minds.

Ninu saw them, too. Drunken soldiers of the hated French regime. About a dozen of them. They swaggered and laughed and joked, all the while making fun of the native Sicilians, whom they scorned.

Ninu started to steer Demona out of their way. But one officer, Sergeant

Drouet, came directly toward them. Drouet had been watching the charming behavior of Ninu's pretty companion. Her smiles and coquetry, aimed at her new husband, had attracted him.

Drouet's moustache jerked as he stopped right in front of the pink-cheeked girl, leering at her and exhaling the local red wine. Before Demona could get out of his way, he reached out and grabbed her arm. "Come here, my beauty." She tried to pull away, but Drouet kept hold. "You don't want that weak boy..." He started to say more, but by then the furious Ninu had already pulled out his knife and was stabbing the Frenchman in the chest.

The look of surprise on Drouet's face gave way to horror as Ninu stabbed again and again. The other French soldiers began elbowing the crowd to intervene, but the townspeople, their resentment and anger with French rule rising to the surface, were already throwing stones at them, and many of the men had begun following Ninu's example and striking the soldiers with knives. The fight lasted only about five minutes, and by then all of the soldiers lay dead on the ground.

Just then the church bell rang for Vespers. In the distance the people could hear the bells of other Palermo churches begin to ring to announce the evening service.

The sound became a call to action. The people looked at each other, still enraged. Then Ziu yelled, "*Moranu li Franchiski!*" (Death to the French!) The crowd's responding roar meant only one thing: Everyone there wanted to get rid of every Frenchman in Sicily.

They began by storming into the taverns that Frenchmen usually haunted. Two men would grab each hated enemy, bring him outside, and kill him, usually with knives. As they progressed through the town of Palermo, they collected more citizens, fired up by the crowd's cries of wrath. A French soldier had tried to force himself on a Sicilian girl!

The frenzied crowd gave no quarter. Anyone encountered in the street who was suspected of being French was told to pronounced the Sicilian word for "chickpeas," the word *cicere*, correctly pronounced CHEE cheh reh. The French routinely pronounced it SEE say reh. An incorrect pronunciation became a death sentence.

When they had cleaned out all the taverns, the Sicilians broke into the homes of the French; any Sicilian woman married to a Frenchman lost her life along with her husband. Then they went on to the buildings of the religious orders, killing any foreign friars whom they decided were French.

Demona lacked a knife, but she took part by striking down enemies with a large stone held in her hand and kicking them when they were down.

Even after the crowd had massacred the entire French population of Palermo—two thousand people—its anger was not sated. By then morning had arrived, and the leaders knew that they must finish what they had started.

Ziu pointed out the obvious: "All citizens of Sicily must join us in this revolution. We have to let the people of nearby towns know what happened here, so that they can act. And they must inform the people of towns near them."

"We've got to complete the job and get rid of all the French," Ettore said.

"The only way we can do that," said Ninu, "is by sending runners. I volunteer to run to the town of Corleone."

Giovanni called out, "I will go eastward to Messina."

Ziu announced, "And I will go southeast to Caltanissetta."

Then Demona spoke: "I will run west to Trapani."

Ninu turned to her. "Demona, can you really do this?"

"Of course. You know I am a good runner."

Then others, all of them men, volunteered to run to Calatafimi, to Marsala, to other towns they knew. They began their journeys immediately.

Demona put her arms around Ninu, assuring him that she would see him again within a few weeks. Turning to consult Ziu, who knew the area well through his mother's family, she asked about the best route.

He told her, "Start by taking the Monreale road, even though it is mountainous. When you reach Monreale, ask someone at the cathedral for the road that leads through Pioppo, Borgetto, and Partinico, small settlements in the mountains. You'll find that Pioppo has many running paths, for running is popular there, so be sure to stay on the road to Partinico and don't go astray on any of those goat tracks. When you reach Partinico, take the road that leads to the coast and the town of Trappeto. Stop there for a rest, and eat some of their good fish. Then stay on the coast road as far as Castellammare del Golfo, with the medieval fortress. Contact some of the prominent families there: Martino, Marazano, Magaddino. From there, you start the last third of your journey. Ask for directions to the Greek temple of Demeter, outside of town, at Segesta. From there, travel inland toward Balata di Baida. Once you reach Erice, you're practically there. Erice is a settlement high on a hill with a good view of Trapani below."

"This is the fastest way to Trapani?"

He nodded. "It cuts off two peninsulas that would add a couple of days to your journey if you tried to stay on the coastline all the way. You have about sixty-five kilometers to travel. By the way, bring me some salt from Trapani."

"Salt?"

"Yes, just south of the town are the huge salt flats famous from the days of the Phoenicians. The people have built dazzling white mountains of salt. We could use some here."

She smiled and turned, starting a loose jogging motion southwest toward Monreale.

She decided against visiting her parents, stopping only at her own home to put bread and cheese in her pocket. She trusted that somehow she would be fed along the way.

It was not until she reached Castellammare del Golfo that Demona ran into trouble. Literally ran into it.

Down the Corso she came, not watching for people but gazing ahead at the great reddish brick fortress right on the water. Giuseppe Martino, pulling his boat from the water, backed into her path and was knocked off his feet by her speed.

"Hey! Watch where you're going!" he picked himself up and began studying her.

"Sorry! I came to report the Palermo revolt against the French. I'm headed for Trapani." She stopped to catch her breath.

Martino came closer. She caught his smell of fish—and became aware of his sweat. He was a solid man, heavily muscled. Looking into his eyes, she realized that she was attracted to him. Physically.

Attracted partly because he was looking at her with desire, and she felt herself responding.

"Who are you? A messenger from the angels?" he murmured, moving much too close to her.

"I'm ... just ... Demona. From Palermo." Then she straightened up, realizing that she was enjoying his attention. "Recently married to Ninu Licata."

"Married? Then what are you doing away from him? If you were mine, I would not let you escape. Come, I will show you our fine sandy beach."

She let herself be led along the curved harbor away from the fishing boats to a lovely beach, where he suggested—no, commanded—that she sit and rest. He sat next to her.

In the gathering twilight, Giuseppe Martino fed her steamed shellfish—the biggest shrimp she ever saw. And he wooed her so successfully that during the night that followed, she became his wholly.

Demona never reached Trapani, and she never returned to Palermo. Running along the fine sandy beach became one of her pleasures. The revolution against the French continued without her.

It took only seven centuries for her descendant, Joe Martino, to become important in America. Demona had fulfilled her destiny.

10

ANGER.

That's why I'm running. Because of anger.

Why couldn't that factory owner give me a job? I'm strong and healthy, willing to work.

There's nothing for you now, Stamata, he said. Nothing.

Nothing for me in the machine shop. I found no work in shipping, either, or at the clothing factory. Nothing for Stamata in the whole busy port of Piraeus in the year 1896. How could that be?

I'm angry enough to do something... Something that will show them. Show them I'm strong and able. So what if I'm skinny? Those people who took me in starved me. Maybe I look a little wild and crazy. So what?

After my whole family died, one by one, I was desperate to get some kind of a job, to take care of myself. But nobody wants to hire a woman with no special skills. And I'm damned if I'll sell my body the way some do.

Skubala! I told them; I'm leaving. I'll make my own way. I picked up my knife and left.

I'll show them I can do something. I can run. I might have won a prize in this Olympics they are starting up now. Reviving the ancient games, they call it. Well, they're just giving people who already have money a chance to win more money. And only men get that chance. Don't women need money?

Those people running the Olympics, they don't want to let women try for the prize. They think only men can run. That's stupid. I'll show them that women can run, too.

It's too late to apply anyway, they said. Why is it too late? The race hasn't even started yet.

Well, *my* race has started. I can run their course. It's only from Marathon to Athens. What is it, about thirty-five kilometers? I can do that. Many times I've run around the perimeter of Syros, the island where I was born.

I'm starting to puff a little. I'll slow down now.

That priest in Marathon, when I asked for his blessing on my endeavor: He scorned me, saying he would bless only "officially sanctioned athletes."

Malakas. I am just as good as "officially sanctioned athletes." Maybe I should have used my knife on him. Anyway, I will show them all.

Ships going by through the straits between here and the island of Euboea: They look pretty. I'll watch for a while, then run some more.

That magistrate in Marathon, wasn't he surprised when I told him I wanted a witness to my starting time of eight in the morning! But he finally signed the paper. Guess that showed him I was serious.

These boots I bought are getting heavy.

What are those two staring at? Haven't they ever seen a woman run?

Hey, you two! Stop looking at me.

Did you get a look at that wild-looking woman running in thick boots?

Yes. There's something tragic about her. She looks sad and angry. As if she knows that what she's doing is pointless.

Maybe she's a ghost.

Or maybe a reincarnation of Melpomene, the muse of tragedy. Didn't Melpomene wear boots?

Yes. And wasn't that a knife in her hand? Melpomene carried a knife, too. I hope...

From the *New York Times*, April 26, 1896:

An article in the today's *Athens News* reports a double homicide on a mountainous road between Marathon and Athens. Two persons, a young man and woman, who were residents of an inland village called Chalandri, were found dead of knife wounds in the bushes just west of the road at a point called Nea Makri. The two were on their way to market.

Police are investigating reports that a wild-looking woman wearing heavy boots and carrying a knife was seen in the area of the crime.

The road where the crime was committed is one of the two that were considered as the track for the Marathon race that will be part of the revived Olympic Games. The road is slightly shorter than the second one but is so mountainous that it was thought to be too difficult for runners, and the longer but flatter race through the Marathon Plain was chosen instead.

A mountain stream. Think I'll rest and wash here. Throw away these boots and my knife. There, in the deepest part of the water.

Nobody's going to stop me from doing this. Nobody is going to challenge me. Nobody's going to laugh at me. I'll show them.

I'll show them.

From the *New York Times*, April 27, 1896:

The *Athens News* reports today that this afternoon a barefoot woman in a spotted dress, giving her name as Stamata Revithi, of Piraeus, approached the
guard at the beautiful white marble Olympic Stadium in Athens and stated
that she had just run the Olympic track from the town of Marathon to Athens.
She presented a paper with her name and a village official's statement giving
her starting time from Marathon as 8:00 A.M. Upon her request, the smiling
guard wrote her finish time on the paper, signing his name.

Since she arrived at the stadium at 1:30 P.M., her running time was more than
five hours. The trial run made two days ago by a local runner named Charilaos
Vasilakos was timed at three hours and 18 minutes. When the real race is run on
May 1, the runners expect to better that time.

But according to the *Athens News*, Stamata Revithi showed satisfaction with
her accomplishment, raising her signed paper on high and shouting, "I did it! I
ran the Marathon!" When passers-by asked her reason for running the track, she
replied that she expected to get a job in Athens when prospective employers saw
proof of her accomplishment.

The race, like all other events in the Olympic Games, will be a male-only event.
The Olympic Committee has excluded women from the Games.

Stamata felt satisfaction. She had completed her intended protest. Her
name was in the newspaper for posterity. Moreover, she had fulfilled her
destiny as a successful woman athlete.

PART FOUR:
CLEVELAND EVENTS
OF 1932 AND 1936

11

SEARCHING THE AIRFIELD WITH BINOCULARS from her seat in the stands, Annie finally saw Isabel talking to a man and a woman.

That must be the couple Isabel knows, the Haizlips, Jimmy and Mae.

That man standing next to Isabel must be the pilot Jimmy Haizlip. Why, he's shorter than Isabel—hardly even five feet tall! And Mae, his wife, she's even tinier! I can't believe that these small people fly those big airplanes. Jimmy is only about my height and doesn't look strong. How in the world does little Mae Haizlip manage?

But Mae's demeanor expressed confidence. She looked around her at the noisy stands, her face showing pleasure and anticipation. Her dark hair was pinned tightly around her heart-shaped face, probably so that it would fit well under the leather helmet she carried. Checking the rest of Mae's costume, Annie noticed that she wore slacks and a V-necked tennis sweater Very casual-looking.

Annie had paid a quarter for an official program of the September 1932 Cleveland Air Races, which featured an image of a red plane flying next to a red-and-white structure called a pylon. Isabel had explained that the pilots were supposed to fly their machines around these structures. Annie looked around the airfield to locate them.

Just then Isabel, wearing jodhpurs as usual, loped toward her, smiling.

Annie grinned back at her and said, "Isabel, this seems like hazardous work."

Isabel laughed. "So is riding horses. Listen, I met someone you know. He's coming over here." She settled in her seat. "I can hardly wait for the parachute jumping contests. An Ohio woman named Shirley Rauner is going to take part."

"She's going to jump from a plane wearing a parachute?"

Isabel looked at her with an amused smile. "Yes."

"And women actually fly some of these airplanes?"

Isabel laughed. "I'm working toward a pilot's license myself. I doubt if I'll ever be as good as Mae. She sets speed records and wins money prizes."

"Competing with men?"

"Sure. There's also a separate trophy for women pilots, the Aerol Trophy, established by the president of a Cleveland company that makes shock absorbers, the ones that make it possible for planes to land on ships. Mae and three other women are competing for that trophy. Mae is going to fly the same plane as Jimmy will in his races: The Wedell-Williams Ninety-One. It's a powerful plane, owned by a New Orleans lumber manufacturer... Here comes my friend now."

I can't figure this out, Annie said to herself. Here are four women accepted in a series of races in which they will pilot dangerous flying machines in a hazardous track. If women can do something like this, why can't women play baseball?

Approaching their seats was a tall man in a tan business suit who looked somehow familiar. Those soft brown eyes, that sweet smile...

"Gennaro! It's you!" She rose and took his outstretched hand, but he pulled her toward him for a hug.

"Annie, I'd know you anywhere. You look wonderful." He looked her over, taking note of the swept-up hairdo, careful makeup, and the pale yellow dress, its matching jacket only partly hiding the thin strings holding it to her shoulders.

"You look different, Gennaro!"

"It's Jerry now, Jerry Finch. I've become the assistant to Jay Iglauer—remember him? The Halle treasurer. He's advised me on investments, as well as on my name. 'Gennaro Finocchio' seemed difficult for some of my business contacts."

Isabel kept an amused look on her face. "I met Jerry at the Hunt Club, where we both ride. He's very good."

"Did he tell you? Gennaro—Jerry and I used to play baseball together when we were young."

"It wasn't so long ago, Annie. Maybe we could renew our acquaintance."

"Why didn't you come and see me last year when ... I was widowed?"

"I wasn't sure if you wanted visits from your old friends... From your earlier life."

She agreed to have lunch in town with Jerry Finch. Her old friend Gennaro.

"I remember when I first heard of the Cleveland Athletic Club," Annie told Jerry confidentially. Sitting back in the comfortable armchair and lifting her glass, she looked around the quiet dining room, a stuffy and formal place where silent, uniformed servers padded around bearing silver trays with specialties unavailable in local A & P stores, like fresh pineapple flown in from Hawaii.

"I used to think," she continued, "that the Cleveland Athletic Club was a place for athletes, and I pictured the Cleveland Indians socializing here over Coca Cola with professional football players, golfers, and maybe a few tennis stars."

Jerry smiled warmly. "Actually, upstairs there are workout rooms, and a pool..."

"Sure, for businessmen. No athletes, though. This club is for people who have made the top rung of Cleveland's social class, either by their own efforts, like you, or ... the way I did it." She finished her martini.

"The Smiths may have helped you reach the top rung of Cleveland society, but you stay in it because of yourself. You fit in."

"I would like to have made my mark through baseball." She set down her glass and let a glum look spread over her face.

"You're still bitter about your experience with Organized Baseball. I think what happened to you has colored your entire attitude. Why don't you become active in some other branch of athletics?"

"Oh, I play a little golf, but that game has no tension. I play because I'm expected to. I like team games. Or used to... The only team I'm on now is in a league of its own: A team consisting of members of the Smith family." Jerry heard bitterness in her voice. "My father-in-law is the coach."

Jerry disregarded these remarks. "Listen, Annie. Women's softball is booming in Cleveland. A lot of companies have put teams in the Cleveland Municipal Softball Association. Some girls play a fast-pitch game that's pretty close to baseball. Even Euclid Beach Park has its own team."

"You know I wouldn't fit in with those industrial players any more. I'm different, I'm older, I'm supposed to have some dignity. And I'm the mother of a hospitalized child. What team would want me?"

"Annie, you're still very young. And because you have money, you could start your own team. I saw you at the Hunt Club picnic on the Fourth—you can still run faster than other girls. You could be a drawing card for any team."

"Why, Gennaro—I mean, Jerry—I didn't realize you were at the picnic. Why didn't you come up to me and say hello?"

"You were always surrounded by admirers. You looked great in those white shorts."

"Come to think of it, why aren't *you* still playing baseball?"

He smiled again. "I *am* playing, Saturday afternoons, with the Halle Men's Team, in the Muny Fast Pitch League."

"Well, I'm surprised. You know, on my way here to meet you, when I walked past the Hanna Building, I saw the new A.G. Spalding store there, and I admit I was tempted by the beautiful new gloves in the window. Tempted to buy one, not necessarily to use it."

"You should think more about that, Annie. Start your own team, why don't you? The Bratenahl Brats? The Smith Smart Set? The Playing Cards?"

When she laughed, he said, "You look relaxed now, more like the Annie I used to know."

"You're a treat, Jerry. And a flatterer."

"Not at all. You know how much I always admired you. I still do."

She let her eyelids rise slightly and looked at him. Why, he's serious; he'd marry me if I wanted him. But the Smiths would doubtless withdraw my allowance. No, I can't let myself be more than a little attracted to this nice fellow, this old friend. He's too good for me, anyway. He has no idea what I've done, or what I am planning to do. I could never tell him.

She decided to draw back from her friendship with Jerry, and the next time he called, she turned down his offer to meet, giving her young son's condition as an excuse.

12

"ANNIE! FINALLY YOU ANSWERED the phone. Listen, you've go to go to the Great Lakes Expo with me. It's wonderful! I'm so glad Cleveland won the right to present this fair." Isabel sounded excited. "I went on the day after it opened, and really, there's so much to see and to do! I'm going back a few more times. You must go with me. I bought passes. How about tomorrow? Your housekeeper will take care of Johnny."

"Oh, Isabel, it's so terribly hot for walking around."

"No need to walk. The organizers of the Exposition have hired college students to operate jinrickshas and those wheelchairs you use at boardwalks. Or you could use one of the small busses. But the rickshas are more fun. Please! You know you don't get out enough."

Annie sighed. "I guess you're right. What time?"

"I'll pick you up at nine."

"Isn't that awfully early?"

"Just wait till you see what's in store for you. You'll want to stay long into the night! I'm telling you, girl, 1936 is a banner year for Cleveland."

Annie laughed.

"I'll see you first thing in the morning."

"Oh, hello, Bill. We'll take these two, yours and your friend's." Isabel addressed the young man offering a ride in the ricksha.

"Annie, this is Bill Burton, son of the mayor. Bill, this is my sister-in-law, Mrs. Smith. Annie, Bill is earning money for his senior year at Bowdoin. Going to play football again, Bill?"

"Yes, ma'am. Thank you," said the polite young man as Isabel paid a dollar for each fare, to him and the fellow standing next to him.

"Now, try to keep close together, boys, so that Mrs. Smith and I can talk."

Annie found the ride jerky and uncomfortable. Besides, she felt conspicuous, especially since Isabel wore her usual jodhpurs, arrived without a hat, and seemed to be the only woman nervy enough to appear in public with bare arms.

But Isabel was reveling in the experience. Realizing that for some reason Annie felt uncomfortable, she smiled and directed, "Annie, relax and decide to have fun for a change. Look, there goes Eliot Ness."

"The new Cleveland Safety Director? I wish he was working on those terrible murders instead of fooling around here."

"He's a very social person—does a lot of drinking—but you've got to give him credit. In Chicago he put that notorious Al Capone in jail. And here he's doing pretty well on cleaning up on crime by finding corrupt police officers who protect the gangsters. Surely you've read about some of that in the papers. He closed a lot of bootleggers and even illegal gambling joints."

Annie didn't want to hear about the bootleggers; she already knew more than she wanted to know about them. "But the killers: I hate reading those stories about the torso murders going on now. How could anyone be cruel enough to dismember people's bodies and leave the pieces to be found by strangers?"

"All murders are cruel, Annie," responded Isabel. That quieted Annie. It had struck her once more that she was responsible for the death of Isabel's brother. Closing her eyes for a moment, she saw a body hurtling to a harsh death on the rocks far below. In her mind, she heard a scream, her own. Involuntarily, she put her hands over her ears.

"I'm sorry, Annie. I didn't mean to bring up the subject of death. I'm sure what happened to John must still give you great pain. I miss my brother, too, but... Look over there at the band shell. Doesn't it look like a huge, half-opened clam?"

"I like the statues on each side of it."

"They were cast by a woman, a graduate of the Cleveland School of Art. They're supposed to personify Beauty and Protection."

"Like the ancient Greek and Roman goddesses."

"Wait till you see the mural on the Marine Theater. It's fifty feet tall, and it features a female goddess called Cloris, who looks after horticulture."

"I wonder if the goddess would help Cleveland."

"Annie, don't be so naïve. Men and women invent gods and goddesses in the hope that they, or someone, or something, will look after them and protect them from harm. It doesn't work. Bad things happen anyway."

Annie almost replied, "That's what my brother Rick says," but she decided not to mention him. She wanted the Smiths to continue viewing him only as a vague, seldom-present relative, not someone to be inquired about.

"Cloris was the Greek goddess of flowers," Isabel continued, "and her Roman counterpart was Flora, the center of a Roman cult. She was said to love festivals and shows. Like this one, the Great Lakes Exposition of 1936! The horticultural building here is just wonderful."

"Isabel, we just passed Donald Gray, who designed the gardens for my home. I'd recognize that big black moustache anywhere. He didn't notice me."

"Donald created the horticultural gardens for the Exhibition. Keep watching, and you'll see absolutely everyone here. Here comes Bill Milliken!"

"Johnny mentioned that name..."

"Bill Milliken is the director of the Cleveland Museum of Art." She was waving at a distinguished-looking, serious man in a double-breasted suit, who just nodded and showed part of his balding head as he started to raise his straw hat.

"Oh. Johnny knows him from taking art lessons at the museum. He said that Milliken likes sports. He sits in the bleachers at baseball games, and he exercises by walking around the Fine Arts Building twenty-one times a day!"

"Bill is a well-rounded man. He's created a fine exhibit of world-famous paintings for the museum, to coincide with the Exhibition."

"But the museum is at least three miles away from the Exhibition grounds."

"Nevertheless, the exhibit is attracting art lovers from all around the country. I'll bet Johnny loves it."

"I'll have to find out."

After touring the Horticultural Building, Annie felt as though she had seen enough.

"Now you must see at least one more section."

"It's so hot, Isabel. Aren't you getting tired?"

"This section includes the restaurants, so we can rest by going to the Trattoria Santa Lucia in the Global Village."

"Really?"

"It features scaloppini Romano, ravioli à la Milanese, and chicken cacciatore."

"It sounds good, even if it's not Sicilian."

"What does 'cacciatore' mean?"

"Hunter style. An entree made with tomatoes."

Annie could hardly help being impressed by the section of the Great Lakes Exhibition called Streets of the World, which featured copies of streets in many European towns. Even the entrance, although it was based on a medieval-looking gate in Prague, caught her attention: It featured two archways reminiscent of the entrance she grew up with: Euclid Beach. She began to get interested.

Some of the copies of European streets came from Hungary, Poland, Germany, London, Africa, Russia, and Slovakia. Annie found them curious and colorful. The ricksha operators walked past them slowly so that their passengers could admire them.

Then they arrived at the section called the Italian Village.

As Annie's ricksha came to a stop, and she and Isabel began to look around, she experienced a sudden mental return to the main street of the town of Taormina, where she had walked with her late husband John. The markets, the scenery... Her head lowered, her eyes closed, and for a few moments she declined to dismount, feeling a bit weak.

"Annie. Are you all right? Would you prefer not to stop here? What can I do for you?" Isabel felt concerned.

"Give me a little time," Annie responded softly. So Isabel dismounted and took her sister-in-law's hand, waiting quietly for recovery.

"I think I'd rather not be here," Annie said finally.

Isabel responded, "Of course. I have a better idea."

Annie felt badly. If Isabel knew what had really happened to her brother and how guilty I am of his death, she wouldn't be so solicitous. How can I keep on pretending that John's death was merely an accident? I am a cruel person, as cruel as the torso murderer.

With Annie's guilty feeling came the tears. Isabel misunderstood their reason and became all the more thoughtful.

"I know you will never recover from what happened to you in Italy. But with time, it will become easier to bear. I'm sorry I thought of the wrong place to visit today. We'll go to a place that's entirely different."

Within a few minutes Annie seemed recovered, and Isabel directed the ricksha operators to take them to the Marine Plaza. Soon they were traveling over what seemed like a wide bridge flanked with huge statues of eagles. For a moment Annie visualized the bombastic architecture she had experienced in Rome, which was supposed to celebrate Mussolini's great empire. She tried not to look at the eagles as Isabel kept up a travelogue describing the exhibits they were passing: A Standard Drug Store, a Clark's cafeteria, and continuing straight toward the lake, the Christian Science Building, an exhibit of Western Reserve University, and a building inexplicably covered with porcelain enamel, along with a newspaper building where popular local reporters like columnists Jack Warfel and gossip reporter Winsor French received news releases and typed their commentary.

Isabel added the "inside" news that Winsor was "uninterested in women" and had become infatuated with philanthropist Leonard Hanna, heir to the Hanna millions. "Are you becoming a gossip reporter, too?" Annie asked.

Then, in the distance on the lake shore, Annie saw two ships, just as Isabel was announcing that they would dine at one of them in the Admiralty Club, an exclusive restaurant open to members only.

In order to reach the private club they had to mount an extra deck of the ship, *The Moses Cleaveland*, which had been named after the city's founder, As they reached the dining room, at a far table Annie saw Walter Halle of the Halle Brothers Department Store, with his wife Helen; Dudley Blossom, the civic leader; Vernon Stouffer, head of the restaurant chain; and Philip Mather, scion of the illustrious Mather family, which gave a lot of money to Western Reserve University. Isabel pointed out Lincoln Dickey, director of the exposition, who appeared to be a very jolly man.

Isabel, who knew everyone, waved and smiled at all as she ushered Annie to a table set with Limoge china gleaming with the most striking design: Red sailboats on black waves, which Annie learned had been created by local artist and designer Viktor Schreckengost, a friend of Eliot Ness.

Walter Halle, in a glen plaid suit, elegantly thin and sporting a tan that made him more handsome than ever, gave Annie a warm smile, while "Linc" Dickey devoted his smiles to Isabel, who responded with restraint.

Isabel offered some news of the Halles. "Did you know," she asked, "that Winston Churchill's son Randolph proposed to Kay Halle? That's why Winston came to Cleveland and visited the Halles at their home in Cleveland Heights. But Kay, although she likes Randolph immensely, decided that she doesn't want to marry anyone. She's enjoying her travel-writing career."

"Kay reminds me of you. Aren't you ever going to settle down, Isabel? I'll bet you've had as many proposals as Kay has."

"I feel settled enough, thanks." And Isabel avoided any confidences by devoting herself to the menu. Afterwards, Annie found, Isabel had more touring in mind.

"Now you must see a little of the Midway. It's a lot like a carnival, with barkers calling in people to see the exhibits." And they were off again.

Isabel ordered the ricksha operators to walk slowly so that the barkers could be heard. Before they got very far, Annie's ricksha was halted by a woman who walked up to her and asked "Annie Cardello?"

Taken aback, Annie replied, "Why do you ask?"

"I'm Valentina Petrovich. Once I got a three-base hit off you," she said proudly. "I was the catcher for the Standard Knitting Mills team when you pitched for Richman Brothers Clothing."

"Oh! I liked playing Standard. Always gave us a good game. I remember you now. Your nickname was Ruskie."

"Right! And yours was The Card." They smiled at each other. "I'm playing with a traveling team now. The Ohioettes. How about you?"

"Not playing any more."

"Too bad. We could have had another matchup. Well, so long."

"Yes. Goodbye, Valentina."

It was at the Crime Prevention Exhibit that Annie began to fall apart again.

She wasn't bothered by the World War trophies exhibited by guides in khaki uniforms wearing tropical sun hats, or even by 13 Spook Street, promising a haunted castle. But then a barker describing punishment for criminals gave listeners a brief glimpse of a show featuring animated wax figures acting out the electrocution of Bruno Hauptman for killing the Lindbergh baby. Annie was horrified.

"Why would anyone want to see such an exhibit?" she asked with her hand to her face, fear in her eyes.

"We don't have to go in, Annie..."

Just then they passed an exhibit featuring a sad-looking man identified as John Dillinger's father. He was speaking to a small gathering about his son's life of crime and how he felt powerless to prevent his son's inevitable death in a gun battle with police.

Annie announced, "I must go home. This is too much to take."

"Annie, it's only a group of exhibits about the past. How can you let it affect you so much? I didn't realize you were so sensitive."

"Nevertheless. Let's go."

Somehow, they managed to pass Eliot Ness once more at the end of the boardwalk. This time Isabel asked their drivers to wait while she spoke to him, thinking that she could reassure Annie of her safety by introducing her to the most famous man in town, one working to get rid of crooked Cleveland policemen who were protecting gangsters.

"My widowed sister-in-law" were the words Isabel used in presenting Annie to Ness. "Annie, Eliot is seeing to it that our city is safe from crime. He also organized the security for this exhibition."

Annie, gazing at the man while thinking of murder, realized that Ness was a handsome man and that he was looking at her with admiration. She acknowledged the introduction, but Ness interpreted her reserve, her languorous manner, and her almost sullen response through hooded black eyes as a sexual message. In her white low-necked silky dress and masses of heavy black hair, she appeared to him as a smoldering, sexy-looking woman looking for adventure.

As a recently-divorced man, Ness had a right to ask if he could call upon her. At first startled, she shrugged her shoulders and, without thinking of the consequences, gave her phone number. Then Ness called attention to the exhibit he had helped prepare for the occasion: "The booth features a death mask of a man dismembered by the Torso Murderer. I'm hoping that showing it here will help identify the victim and perhaps lead us to the murderer."

Annie, taken aback, thought: Why would I want to view such a morbid object? Swallowing her words, she made an excuse of having already seen more than she could possibly digest.

"You've made a conquest," Isabel reported on the way to the parking lot.

It took only three days for Ness to contact Annie. "Would you like to go to the Hollenden with me on Saturday? The Vogue Room there is good for drinks and dinner." He spoke of the restaurant at a popular downtown hotel.

"A couple I know, the Sherwins, will be with us."

Annie knew that some of the Sherwins, of the Sherwin-Williams Paint Company, had married into the Halle family, so she thought they would have something in common. "All right."

"Pick you up at seven."

The evening wasn't quite a disaster, but Annie was less than entertained. The third round of cocktails made her nervous. She knew that everyone was feeling the liquor and that Ness was getting loud. "Sure, Capone was convicted on income tax cheating instead of his more serious crimes. So what? At least I got him, and Chicago is better off. In this town the gangsters are supposed to be less important. But they sure found it easy to corrupt a lot of Cleveland policemen. The men surrounding me now can't be corrupted; they're untouchable. I just found a new man on the handball court at Fenn College; he's going to make a good policeman. Right now I'm after a gangster named Angelo Lonardo. This guy and the ones in the Mayfield Road Mob are going to get caught."

That name made Annie sit up and pay attention. If Ness was after Lonardo, was he also after Rick? So Lonardo was still wanted by the law; Rick might be as well. Refusing further drinks, she asked if she could order; the others followed suit, and soon the evening was over. Ness made no advances when he delivered her to her home; he was probably too tipsy to make a pass at her, she realized, thinking, the safety director believes he is not too tipsy to drive.

She did have a question for him, which she asked in his car on the way home: "I understand that you are starting Boys' Clubs for young fellows."

"It's one of my anti-crime efforts, yes. Keep them off the streets and keep them busy."

"What activities are offered?"

"Movies, athletic competitions, music education, hobby clubs, and social affairs."

"So when do you open your Girls' Clubs?"

There was a pause while the safety director's mind considered the idea. Finally, he thought of the answer. "Girls don't get into trouble and grow up to be criminals."

"Then why do we have institutions for delinquent girls?" He glanced at her with surprise but refrained from answering, so she went on. "Providing activities only for boys is just a convenient way of forgetting that girls are children, too."

A few months later the *Cleveland Plain Dealer* announced that Eliot Ness was about to take his third wife.

The multiple murders of Cleveland citizens during the thirties were never solved.

PART FIVE:
THE EARLY 1940s

13

CHICAGO *TRIBUNE*, October 1941:

> Baseball Commissioner Kenesaw M. Landis has been admitted to Little Traverse Hospital in Petoskey, Michigan. He became ill after a hike at Burt Lake Camp, his summer home. The cause is announced as bronchial pneumonia.

Annie found the clipping from the *Tribune* in a letter from Vincenzo that said, "I doubt if you will have to worry about your problem any more. Age and illness will probably take care of it."

Annie crumpled up the letter and cursed her luck in having a son afflicted with polio. Now that Johnny was at home and being tutored in between treatments, she seemed to have less time for herself than ever. She appeared always to be involved with the child and his needs.

When will I get this problem settled?

In mid-December, after the appalling attack on Pearl Harbor, she got a phone call. "Annie? It's me, Jerry... Jerry Finch. I know you haven't heard from me for several years, but ... I've enlisted in the Air Corps, and I'm going into training next week. May I see you before I leave?"

She relented, inviting him to dine with her at the Shoreby Club just down the street from her home, where there would be a dining room full of her acquaintances, people who would be watching them closely. Jerry would not be able to trap her into expressing any emotional feelings about him.

His striking appearance at her door surprised her. The uniform suited him well, and his face seemed lit up with joy.

Jerry was beaming with pleasure both at seeing her again and because of his decision to enter the military. He almost bounded into the foyer and grabbed her hands, starting to laugh at the expression of pleasure on her face.

"You didn't realize I might want to help out with the war effort? I've heard you're doing it."

"Yes, but not in the way you are." She smiled at him with real warmth, so he tried to keep her hands in his. "Governor Bricker has had us collecting scrap metal since June," she added, "but that's not much of anything."

"Hi! Are you Mr. Finch?" Johnny came clumping into the hallway on his brace as fast as he could. "Wow! So that's an Air Corps uniform! Wow!" He was so excited that he failed to realize that the belt of his bathrobe had come undone, and when he stepped on the end of it, he almost went down. Jerry kept him from falling. The sitter rushed forward to help.

"I'm all right..."

"Mrs. Armbruster, this is Jerry Finch. Johnny, say goodnight to Mr. Finch. It's past your bedtime. You can have your Ovaltine first."

"Aw, gee. Okay, Mom. Goodnight, Mr. Finch. You sure look great in that uniform. Will you be flying a big plane? Are you going to bomb the Germans? Or the Japs?"

"It's too early to say, Johnny. I'll send you a postcard."

"Gee, thanks, Mr. Finch! Goodnight. 'Night, Mom."

Annie turned to swing her white cape over her shoulders and pick up her purse. That gave her a moment to compose herself and resolve all over again not to become involved with Jerry, who was standing there looking at her with delight and ... perhaps something more.

"The Club is just down the street and around the corner," she announced. "Let's take my car. I have a parking spot there."

Sitting next to her while she drove gave Jerry the opportunity of continuing to enjoy looking at her.

"You're making me nervous, Jerry."

"Oh, sorry."

"Tell me something about your new activities."

"I'd better not. I might get carried away and say too much. You know, Loose Lips Sink Ships, that kind of thing. Anyway, I think of it as important work."

"That sounds mysterious. I wish I could do some important work, something that would really help the war effort."

"Just write to me. That will keep my spirits up."

When they walked into the clubhouse, several diners at nearby tables turned to stare. One couple waved, and a blonde in a strapless white gown called out, "Come on over, Ann, and bring your handsome soldier."

"He's not a soldier, he's an airman, but we'll come over anyway."

"So, Airman, what is your name? How did you meet Ann?" The blonde indicated that he should sit next to her.

Annie sat down there instead, so Jerry pulled out a chair next to Annie. Before introducing him, she signaled to a waiter and said, "Let's get some drinks here first."

"Well, hurry up, we're two rounds ahead of you."

Over gin martinis, Annie introduced Connie and Gerald Bingham to Airman Jerry Finch and said she and Jerry grew up together. Connie reached around Annie to shake his hand; her husband looked pained and loosened the neckline of his shirt. Across the table sat a thin, long-faced fellow with graying hair, Willoughby Harding, who seemed to converse only in rhymes, opening with "I am the Chairman/you are the Airman." Annie explained that Will was the chairman of the club and the retired president of a local bank. Will added, "No lady seems to hanker for an old retired banker."

Connie Bingham demurred, reaching across to him: "Now, Will, I often hanker for you."

"Yes, but are you a lady?" countered her husband. Amid embarrassed laughter, Annie announced that after their cocktails she and Jerry would dine at a table for two, since they had a lot of catching up to do over dinner. "But thanks for inviting us for drinks."

On the way to their own table, Annie stopped twice more to make introductions. Jerry decided that the members of the club either were bored sophisticates or were pretending to be. He was glad he and Annie were to dine alone. The band was playing *Stardust*, and it made him feel romantic. Annie seemed uninterested in anything except the menu.

"What are courgettes?" Jerry asked.

"Zucchini."

The steaks were awfully rare, Jerry thought, but rare steak seemed to be the popular and desirable entrée. He ate the edges, all the while wishing for lasagna. "It's good you found a way to get away from those people. How can you...? Well, it's your life. I noticed you didn't mention that we played baseball together."

"That part of my life is over. They wouldn't understand it anyway. Jerry, are you happy?"

"Happy? I never thought about it. I guess I am. At least I'm happy that I chose to enlist."

"How about your folks? And your sister Mary? What do they think of your enlisting?"

"My father seems proud of me. He's taking a defense job at Jack & Heinz. My mother, well, she's worried about me, of course; that's the way mothers are. And Mary says she can't see how she'll get along without me. But she will; she loves her new job as a nurse. She's great with sick people."

"A nurse... That's wonderful. I wish I had a real job."

"You could get one, Annie. It would be good for you—give you something to think about besides Johnny. He seems to be coming along well. Why don't you look around for something challenging that gets you out of the house more?"

"I've been helping the Red Cross move to its new quarters in an old mansion on Euclid Avenue. But now the city is opening a Stage Door Canteen on Playhouse Square, and I've been asked to help entertain servicemen there. It seems that volunteer work is all I'm fit for."

"Nothing's wrong with volunteer work; I'm sure it's greatly needed."

Willoughby Grant appeared suddenly at their table, wavering and smelling strongly of gin. He put his hand on Annie's arm and intoned, "I stop to ask if you perchance/around the room would like to dance."

She was already shaking her head, but before she could say anything, Jerry had thought of the right kind of answer: "Dance alone, if you prefer. With me, perhaps, but not with her."

Although Will's eyes were dim, he caught the implication. As insulted as Jerry had intended for him to be, he removed his hand, thrust his chin forward, drew himself up. Intending to wheel about dramatically, he began tipping sideways. Jerry was ready and caught his arm, steering him back to his table and advising him to have some dinner.

Connie rose and took Will's other arm. She leaned toward Jerry and kissed him on the cheek, murmuring, "If you get bored with your dinner partner, come back."

Sitting down again, Jerry pushed back his plate. "I don't think much of these people, Annie. Let's go for a drive."

"Jerry, it's starting to snow."

"Then let's just go back to your house. Could we have our coffee there?"

The Christmas lights on the tree had switched on, and the house looked inviting as Annie drove up to the front entrance.

"Those white flakes on your black hair..."

She shook them off and unlocked the door. Dropping her cape and bag in the foyer, Annie called out to the sitter just emerging from her small suite off the kitchen. "Mrs. Armbruster, you can leave now. Is everything all right?"

"Yes, Johnny is fine, Mrs. Smith. He listened to The Lone Ranger and fell asleep around nine-thirty. I'll go now."

"Could I take you home?" Jerry volunteered.

"Thank you, but my car is parked next to the garage, and I don't have far to go."

In the kitchen, while Annie fussed with the coffee and put Christmas cookies on a plate, Jerry hovered over her. "Please, Jerry, sit down."

"I'm going to be thinking of you a lot, Annie."

She brought cups and saucers but did not reply.

"Annie," he said earnestly. "Is there any way I can make you see that you and I were meant for each other? Think of the good times we had growing up in the old neighborhood, and how we both worked on the school newspaper together and played ball together. Remember when we had that bowling league?" And then, more softly, "Think of what good friends we've been for so long. Couldn't it be something more?" He put his hand on hers.

She withdrew it. "I'm sorry, Jerry. Everything is different now. The Smiths expect certain behavior of me, at least in public, and I must satisfy them. Besides, I ... have plans. Personal plans."

"I see. Plans that don't include me."

"I ... can't help it, Jerry. There are things I need to do. I wouldn't want to involve you in them." Now I've said too much, she thought.

"Involve me? Is there something I could do for you? Now I wish I hadn't enlisted right away. If I can do something, anything, please tell me."

"Not at all. There are things I have to do myself. Please, Jerry, don't ask me to say any more."

"You are so mysterious... I can't help thinking that this has something to do with baseball."

She poured the coffee. "Let's talk about something else. Are you going to leave me your address?"

"Of course. Please keep in touch." He realized that their talk had petered out. Soon after, he left.

Annie sat down at the breakfast table and picked up a portfolio of Johnny's sketches. He loved drawing and was taking lessons on Saturday afternoons at the Cleveland Museum of Art. Annie always drove him to University Circle and waited in some other part of the Museum while he took his instructions. She was especially taken with the Egyptian mummies. Johnny talked of nothing but art. But his grandfather, although himself deeply interested in literature, wanted the boy to go into banking, like his father.

The series of Johnny's sketches that Annie liked best showed ancient Greek athletes in action, their subjects taken from Greek vases in the Museum's collection. She started thinking of her last conversation with Johnny about those sketches. She was still startled with how revealing they were.

"Why are the athletes all shown as naked, Johnny? Was that just to show off their muscles?"

"No, Mom. My instructor, Mr. Leontius, says the drawings of the athletes are authentic, that in the ancient Olympics, the men all participated naked, probably for more freedom of action, or maybe for some reason related to their religion. He says that women had separate competitions. But running is all they were allowed to take part in. And their races were just for the young unmarried women. Here, look. I sketched one of the two women I saw on the vases. She wears a very short dress, see? And you can easily tell it's a woman or girl, because, uh, one strap of her dress is down."

Annie saw a graceful figure, her arms and legs seemingly in motion, her face happy. The short dress she wore was depicted in detail: It seemed made of pleated material. And Johnny was right: It exposed her right shoulder and breast.

Well, she thought, he's got to know sometime how we look naked. Better from ancient Greek statues than from girls he knows. This girl in the sketch is certainly lovely. Enjoying herself, too. Running. I haven't done any running in ages. Maybe that's something I could get back into. Not around here, though. The neighbors would think I'm crazy. Where could I run?

Euclid Beach Park. Right along the beach. As soon as spring comes.

14

CHICAGO TRIBUNE, January 1942

Commissioner Landis arrived in Florida rather early. He says he wants to "lie around in the sun." Probably, he's still recovering from the bout of bronchial pneumonia he suffered from last fall.

Annie's phone rang. "Anna! Something bad has happened."

"What, Mama? We talked yesterday, didn't we? A war has started, war with the Japanese. You know that."

"Not just the Japanese, Anna! With Italy! And now your Papa has a letter, a notice. It says he must go to the post office because he is an enemy! Anna, how can your Papa be an enemy?"

"What do you mean, go to the post office?"

"He must go there to ... register, that's the word. Register because he is an enemy! Oh, Anna, I am so afraid! Is this because of my boys? Is the government punishing us because of what my boys have done?"

Anna's heart sank. "I'll be right over, Mama."

It turned out that Giuseppe Cardello had never completed the process of naturalization for citizenship. Every Italian citizen in the United States must register as an enemy alien, and the easiest place for the government to collect the information was at local post offices. Giuseppe (and, it turned out, his brother Paolo) had neglected to become American citizens, although they had filled out initial applications, and so must report at the local post office to register as aliens.

"Mama, the word is *alien*. Not *enemy*. There's a difference." But not much.

Annie thought: Papa, where is your Lodge now?

When asked why he had never completed his application for citizenship, Giuseppe looked ashamed, but he expressed anger, too. "How long have I lived here as a good citizen?" he asked rhetorically. "Thirty-five years! Isn't that long enough to show I mean no harm?"

"Papa, you are not really a citizen until you fill out all the forms, learn

138

some American history, and swear in front of government people that you will follow all the laws of the United States."

"I am willing to do that. Why will they not let me?"

"It's too late, now that we are at war with Italy as well as Germany and Japan. I wish you had... Never mind. Call Uncle Paolo, and I'll take you both to the post office."

The room was crowded with frightened-looking people. Anna wondered why they weren't talking; after all, Italians were such volatile people. One woman was even hushing another. Then she saw the poster on the wall:

DON'T SPEAK THE ENEMY'S LANGUAGE!

SPEAK AMERICAN!

Anna's heart sank. This is really cruel, she thought. Now these people cannot even express themselves naturally. But she said nothing.

She helped her father and uncle to fill out their forms. One question was "Do you own a short-wave sending and receiving radio?" Giuseppe was about to answer "yes" when Anna stopped him. "Papa, that is not the kind of radio you own."

Another question was "How close do you live to a defense plant?" Nobody knew the answer. Anna had to inquire at the desk. The clerk replied, "Just say you don't know."

The form also warned that aliens might be subject to curfew; Anna had to explain what that was. They must also keep their alien registration cards with them at all times.

When they left, Annie was exhausted. And she was worried about her family's mental health.

How are they going to handle this?

She began to feel ashamed that she had been thinking so much about her own problem: How to punish Commissioner Landis.

"Hi everyone!" Annie called, and got off the bus at the entrance of Crile Hospital, where the wounded servicemen were standing or sitting in wheelchairs. "Time to go to the show! All aboard!" She saw a few smiles of anticipation as the nurses began wheeling some of the patients toward the busses.

"Hi, fellas! Welcome to the bus for the Hanna Theatre." Annie kept her voice cheery as she folded the wheelchairs and stored them in a corner of the bus behind a big strap. "Ready to see a Mae West movie? Let's go!"

One of the accompanying nurses started a song. "Twenty-nine bottles of beer on the wall…" and several voices joined in.

At the Hanna, the new manager Milton Kranz welcomed the busloads of wounded to the free showing and helped them find seats. After parking her bus, Annie joined the group, sitting in the back next to a tall soldier. She was thinking of the last time—which was also the first time—she had been inside the Hanna. With John, of course, viewing the garish gold carvings and the murals representing Greek and Roman history. She had avoided taking Johnny to see the new film *Fantasia* because it was shown at the Hanna. Now here she was again, fighting memories.

The question, "What's your name?" brought her back to the present.

The soldier next to her was asking. He had placed his crutches in the empty seat on the other side.

"Annie. Annie Smith."

"I'm Orlando DeMarco."

"You're Italian. So am I… I mean, Italian American."

"How can *Smith* be Italian?"

"That's my married name."

"Oh." He became silent.

The theatre director, Milton Kranz, spoke again, more formally, and invited the men for beer and sandwiches at Otto Moser's restaurant after the show.

The film, *Catherine Was Great*, proved to be a forgettable Mae West vehicle, redeemed only by Mae's forthright sexuality. After the soldiers were helped into Otto Moser's, Annie discovered that Orlando DeMarco had managed to get himself seated at her table. "This is a nice place," he said, looking around at the photos of vaudeville and film stars on the walls.

A blonde soldier next to Orlando thought he was being addressed and replied, "Haven't you ever been to a fancy place like this, Lanny?"

"Sure, in New York. Better places, like the Stork Club."

Annie was interested. "You're a New Yorker, Lanny?"

"Yes. Say, Annie, this guy who thinks this restaurant is fancy is from a small town: Boston. Charlie Jones. Annie Smith."

They all laughed at the conjunction of common names. Lanny continued, "It's actually Staff Sergeant Jones."

"Oh, and what's your rank?"

"Captain."

"I'm impressed. With both of you, of course. Most of the fellows I've met have been privates."

"The lower ranks get hurt more often."

She wanted to ask how it happened that Captain Orlando DeMarco got hurt, but she held back, thinking it best to keep the situation off the subject of injuries. "Tell me about New York." Sergeant Jones realized he had been dismissed and turned to the nurse next to him: "Nurse Anders: Do you want to hear about Boston?"

Lanny went on, "Haven't you been to New York? You seem ... well, sophisticated. I assumed you traveled a lot."

"I stopped there only briefly, on my way to and from Europe."

"What does your husband do?"

"He was a banker, but he passed away."

"Oh, sorry. In the war?"

"No, before." She felt that she ought to add, "You see, I'm much older than you are." But she thought that might give him second thoughts about talking to her, and she wanted to keep talking to Captain Lanny DeMarco. "Now, about New York. Tell me about the Stork Club."

"Well, it was hard to get past the golden rope at the entrance, especially if you were a little dark-skinned, like me. But if you had connections, or a big name, or a lot of money, you might get in, particularly if Walter Winchell had written about you in his column in the *Daily Mirror*."

"And you ... were important enough to get in?"

"Let's say I knew people," Lanny said. "Not that the food was any good. But being seen there with my beautiful girlfriend, and having our pictures appear in the tabloids, was good for business."

"What business is that?"

"Imported olive oil. I worked for an Italian family named Profaci in Brooklyn. They were devout Catholics, gave a lot of money to the church, and often invited priests into their home to celebrate mass."

Annie said nothing about having heard the name before. "How nice."

"They had about twenty other businesses, too, including some in the New York garment industry, and they owned a big farm in New Jersey. Hundreds of acres. It had a private chapel and a private airport. Originally, the house had been owned by Teddy Roosevelt."

"Really?"

He nodded. "Once when I went out to the farm in New Jersey I met a guy from this town. Cleveland. A guy named Ricardo. Never thought I'd end up in his city with a half-ruined leg."

"Ricardo?" Now she was listening more closely.

"Yeah. On Profaci's farm," Lanny repeated.

"Tell me about his business."

"One of Joe Profaci's businesses was selling protection to other businesses. It's not something that the law approves of, you understand. But it's the way things are done in Italy. Profaci collected a lot of money from companies in New York and Brooklyn who needed protection."

"Protection? Why should a business need protection? From what?"

He looked at her, then around, to see who might be listening. Then he added, "It's hard to explain. Profaci wasn't exactly an upstanding citizen. He owned a lot of illegal businesses as well as legal ones. He was a member of an Italian American group, known sometimes as the Black Hand."

Annie knew Profaci was part of the LCN, the Cosa Nostra. A gangster. So evidently one of his businesses was to sell protection from himself, or others like him. "And your friend Ricardo from Cleveland, at the farm: Did he work for Profaci, too?"

"Sort of. He was being hidden there with others, so that the draft wouldn't get them. Keeping them on the farm meant Profaci could claim they were essential workers, although they didn't do much work."

She thought for a moment, then decided. "Maybe I knew him. What was his last name?"

"Mmmm ... Costello? ... uh, Cardello, I think. Nice guy. Family was originally from Sicily; mine was from Como, on the mainland. This guy Ricardo and I played cards and drank wine together a couple of evenings. I liked it out at the farm. Maybe one day I'll buy a farm. I can still do a little work. My leg is healing, though the docs say I'll always have a limp. I don't mind that. My girlfriend in New York might, though. I've been writing to her, but lately I haven't had any answers. Her name is Honey. She's a model."

"Why didn't *you* get protected on the farm?"

"Didn't want to be. Figured it was my duty to serve." So even gangsters might want to be patriotic, she realized.

"The busses are here, guys. Time to go." Nurse Anders started helping the men toward the exit.

A call Annie received from Vincenzo revealed that he was still procrastinating in executing the project she had asked him to take care of so long ago. "I can't get the extra gas coupons. And it's hard to escape from my work."

"What work?" She let her voice become cynical.

"Well, I'm always being sent here and there to take care of somebody. Or something. My boss doesn't give me enough free time. He depends on me to get things done. It's not easy to get away."

Chicago Tribune, December 1942:

Surgeons have operated on Commissioner Landis at Chicago's Presbyterian Hospital. There are no reports as yet on the reason for the operation.

Annie got home tired from her volunteer work with wounded soldiers. She considered not even answering the phone when it rang. She put her head back on the sofa, but the ringing didn't stop. She finally picked it up. Her mother was crying. Giovanni had fallen and couldn't get up. He wouldn't or couldn't respond when spoken to.

"I'll call the ambulance and come right over."

But Giovanni never rose again. Within three days he was gone.

After that, Annie's mother began to demand more attention. She was lonely, unhappy, and couldn't understand why Annie didn't spend more time with her. Annie decided that there was one thing she could do: Ask her mother to teach her Sicilian cooking.

Chicago Tribune, March 1943:

As the result of an argument with the Ambassador East Hotel management over an increase in his rent, Commissioner Landis and his wife have moved out of the hotel and rented a house to be near his family. Commissioner Landis confided to a reporter that he was "feeling mortal." This year he will be seventy-seven.

Now it's too late to approach him in the hotel, Annie realized. I'll have to think of some other way to get at him.

Charles "Lucky" Luciano looked up at Gennaro, now known as Jerry Finch, who was standing over him in one of the three visitors' rooms at Clinton Correctional Institution, a place known widely as Dannemora, after the local town. The room was empty except for Luciano and his questioner.

Police had broken up Luciano's prostitution ring, and as a result of his conviction he was confined to prison.

"No, I don't support Mussolini. I thought I made that clear. Mussolini tried to destroy the Mafia in Sicily. Sicily is where I was born, in a small town with sulfur mines."

"Yes, we know."

"Besides, I'm a loyal American, been one since ten years old. Why would I support Mussolini? He never done nothing for me."

Luciano was seated comfortably at a table. He turned his thin, arrogant face away.

"And you agree to help the Allies against Italian fascists?"

"I said so, didn't I?" Luciano's lower lip stuck out belligerently, and his right eye, injured in 1929, seemed to droop even more than usual as he turned to look at Gennaro. "I've already told you I'd have my people working on the New York waterfront watch for enemy agents. Every day they load hundreds of tons of supplies bound for Europe. They service troop ships, too. My longshoremen will find any spies that try to get into the United States, I guarantee it."

Gennaro nodded. "We've set up conduits for them to report to, and we appreciate that help for America. Now about the coming invasion. You know that it can't be long before the Allies invade Europe. Some of our troops will come through Sicily. Can you use your contacts there to make it easier for an Allied invasion of Sicily?"

"What do I get in return? You going to let me out of prison?"

"Not yet," said Gennaro. "It would look bad, since you've just been convicted of running a big prostitution ring... And there's something else we need. We're concerned about Communist influence in the Italian resistance movement. We want to be sure that when it's all over, Italy won't have a Communist government. Can you get in touch with the resistance groups and tell them they must reject any Communists?"

"What does *not yet* mean?" The ugly scar on Luciano's cheek seemed redder than ever.

Gennaro sat down. "First tell me if you can help smooth the way for the invasion and tell the resistance to keep Communist members out of their organizations. We can't help to build a Communist Europe after the war."

"Of course I can," Luciano sneered. "Of course I can. There's still an LCN organization in Castellammare del Golfo and other big towns all over Sicily. The biggest boss is in the town of Villalba. He is Don Calogero Vizzini."

"Where's the town of Villalba? On the coast?"

"No, inland. Near the city of Caltanissetta, right in the middle of the island."

Gennaro thought a moment. "From that position, Vizzini could hardly help a coastal invasion force."

"You're wrong. Don Calo, as he is known, has power everywhere in Sicily. I can get in touch with him. For this, I need a free hand to contact my people. If I send for one of my soldiers, I expect to see him here pronto." He tapped the table for emphasis.

"The government has agreed to facilitate your efforts, Mr. Luciano."

"And my reward?"

"You'll get your wish to have your private Italian kitchen, right here in Dannemora. A prison cook who knows Italian cooking will prepare Sicilian specialties for you. And later on, you'll be paroled. To Italy. You're lucky, Mr. Luciano."

Luciano considered this, then nodded.

Gennaro rose and left the room, stopping in the hall outside to check the vending machine. But he found nothing he wanted, so he went out to his car.

The village of Dannemora, in the Adirondacks, was a plain hometown place, paradoxically burdened with the Clinton Correctional Institution built right on its edge. Gennaro stopped at a donut shop on Reservoir Road to write his report. On his way out of town he passed an athletic field named with a sign proclaiming it as LaFontain Park, where two teams of boys of about Pony League age were at play. The boys with red jerseys were positioning themselves in the field while a hopeful kid in a white jersey started shifting his feet at bat. Their play reminded him of Annie. I wonder what she's doing now.

Then he drove back to New York, where the city residents were suffering not only from the heat and humidity but also from a plague of bedbugs.

It was a successful trip, Gennaro thought, but I hate playing these negotiating games with such people.

Annie was breathing hard. Since Johnny had been at Roosevelt Country Day Camp she had been driving to Euclid Beach Park nearly every morning, after his bus pickup, to run on the hard-packed sand nearest the grassy bluff.

A few curious bathers watched her but never approached. She kept them at bay by avoiding eye contact.

Running seemed to bring her more peace than she'd had since Johnny's diagnosis of polio. While running she felt more free, more expressive, less burdened with guilt. She stopped wondering if Johnny's illness was the result of her participation in the death of her husband.

If my actions are the cause of Johnny's poor health, I regret that, but I accept it. Johnny is still a fine boy and is able to do a lot. He's overcome his self-consciousness, too. Getting involved with art lessons, where he can really become absorbed, has helped him.

At the camp, where Annie had spent a day observing, she saw that although her son could not take part in the sports and games, he could referee, and he could enjoy the swimming and even the horseback riding, though his favorite activities were the arts and crafts. He liked nature study, too.

On the last day of June at about eleven in the morning, while she was running she began to feel too warm. The weather felt more like August, so she pulled off the sweater she wore over her long-sleeved blouse. The blue cotton trousers she used for running felt heavy, too, but she believed them to be necessary. Wearing shorts among strangers would call too much attention to herself, she thought.

She slowed down to a walk, then moved up to the grassy bluff and sat down to rest and think. Without direction, her mind returned to what she thought of as her "problem."

It came to her again and again: I still need to punish Landis, the man who ruined my life.

Suddenly a man's voice intruded on her thoughts. "Hello, Mrs. Smith. I didn't expect to see you here."

Looking up, she saw a face that seemed familiar, but she couldn't place it. The man had a nice smile.

"You don't recognize me. I'm Carl Morris, Johnny's science teacher. I remember you from Parents' Night. I recall my surprise that a lanky blond boy like Johnny had a small, dark-haired mother. Then I realized I had already seen you when we were in high school. Do you come here often? Have you heard lately from our mutual friend Gennaro Finocchio? Or Jerry Finch, as he's called now. Mind if I sit down?"

She remembered then, recalling that she came home from that school visit thinking that Johnny had a handsome science teacher. Now she began wondering if he would ever stop talking. But he kept on. "Probably you don't realize that we attended Collinwood at the same time. I was two classes ahead of you and Gennaro. In the same one as his big brother Vito. Did you ever meet Vito? I think he left school before you got there. In those days I didn't use the name 'Carl Morris.' I was Carmine Morrissetti. I was crazy about Mary Finnochio, Gennaro's sister, but she ignored me. She's a nurse now, and working in Europe, on a hospital ship. I changed my name when I started studying to be a teacher."

"Now I know you. Why are you here?" She was studying him. Everything about him seemed definite and clear: His carefully etched eyebrows, his confident chin, his slightly wavy brown hair, even his strong shoulders in a white shirt with sleeves rolled to the elbows. She felt good in his presence.

"Because I'm 4F. Something to do with osteomylitis. Oh, you mean, why am I at Euclid Beach. I was over at the office arranging a family picnic for the Fourth of July. The Morrissettis will be gathering from all around the Midwest, so I reserved six picnic tables for the group. After going to the Humphreys' office here, I just thought I'd walk down to the water, and there you were."

"So you're still in touch with Gennaro? I mean, Jerry. I haven't heard from him for some time."

"That's probably because the Finocchios have all moved away. They're in New York now, where Jerry's brother Vito lives. Vito's in politics, you know, and family is good for his political image. He has a wife and five kids."

"What about Jerry?"

"He's somewhere in Europe, with the military. He has an apartment in New York. After the war he plans on going into the FBI."

Annie was startled. "FBI?"

"Federal Bureau of Investigation."

"I know, but... They go after the Mafia, don't they?"

"Among other criminals. Why? Are you in the Mafia?"

She responded to his attempted joke with a weak smile and changed the subject. "School is out now. What do you do all summer?" She found that she was really interested. She liked his looks and his manner.

"It's really only two and a half months. I study and get ready for next term. Right now I'm also teaching a chemistry course at Fenn College, in the Evening Division. It's for adults. Interested in chemistry?"

"I don't know anything about it."

"Several Cleveland companies send their employees to take Fenn's evening courses. Companies like Warner & Swasey, Thompson Products, G.E., Cleveland Graphite Bronze ... Learning more about chemistry and other science subjects helps employees get ahead in their work. They can contribute more because they know more. The companies in turn have shown their gratitude to the college by developing a fine new laboratory on the third floor of Fenn Tower. It's easy for me to demonstrate science principles with experiments there."

"What kind of experiments?"

"Well, last evening I gave a demonstration with sulfur, which is used industrially in several compounds. I showed how two separate elements, sulfur and iron, can form a different compound, iron sulfide. I demonstrated what happened when the two elements were mixed and heated together, and then some of the students tried the experiment themselves. Of course, you have to do this carefully, and in a well-ventilated lab, and avoid heating the test tubes too much, because if the sulfur becomes too hot it may form sulfur dioxide, a toxic compound that causes coughing and throat burning."

"Sulfur. Isn't that known as brimstone?" Carl Morris seemed to know a lot.

"Why, yes. Some people associate it with fear of the devil because of references to it in the Bible and the Koran."

"Do you fear the devil?"

"Not at all. I fear nothing, certainly not the element called sulfur or brimstone. It simply occurs in nature, especially in volcanic areas like Sicily."

"Sicily?"

"Yes, do you know Sicily?" When she didn't respond immediately, he went on—as was his habit. "Sulfur deposits occur all over the island, so there are workable sulfur mines in several places."

She smiled at him. "You're such a confident person."

"Why not be confident? Knowledge makes one confident and free. With knowledge comes the realization that there's nothing to fear. Anything can be controlled."

"I wish I had your confidence." He looked at her curiously, but said nothing. "Does Fenn College have an athletic field?"

"The Board is looking into it. Students need sports for exercise."

"Women students, too."

"Why, yes..." He looked at her in surprise. "The full-time Day Division students should all have a chance to enjoy sports. Now I remember: You were in sports. Baseball, right?"

"Yes, but Collinwood High didn't offer baseball to girls. Everyone just assumed girls didn't play or didn't like baseball. I played with independent teams. It was only after I graduated and started working that I found chances to play on sponsored teams." Why am I telling him this? He inspires trust.

"And I recall that you were known as The Card. From your last name, Cardello, and from being the team's drawing card. Do you still take part in sports?"

"Not in baseball. A little tennis or golf now and then. But I've just rediscovered running, and I'm enjoying it."

"Good for you. Do you know that Cleveland runner, Stella Walsh? The Sokol sponsors her. You know, the Polish sports organization. She's their drawing card."

She shook her head. "What sports do you like?"

"Boxing. I'm in the Cleveland Golden Gloves tournaments. Ever attend those?"

"No. Maybe boxing helps makes you so confident."

"Or maybe I can box because I'm confident."

They shared smiles. Annie decided she liked talking to Carl Morris because he gave her new ideas.

When she stopped talking entirely, Carl got up. "Well, I'm off. I'll be in touch, Mrs. Smith."

She smiled again, this time at his confidence. He didn't ask if he could phone her. "Call me Annie."

While he was driving home he was thinking: For the first time since the death of my wife, I'm interested in another woman. But perhaps it's pity I feel for her: She seems like such a lost soul. Imagine asking if I feared the devil! How primitive. She's haunted by something, perhaps guilt. She's a throwback to our superstitious island ancestors.

15

NEW YORK TIMES, July 10, 1943:

Today the Allies invaded southern Europe. Plans made since 1942 called for an invasion of Sardinia, nicknamed Operation Brimstone, and of Sicily, named Operation Husky. Sardinia seems to have been sidestepped, for today British, Canadian, and American forces made landings on several beaches in the south of Sicily at places between Licata, the location of ancient sulfur mines, and eastward toward Gela, one of the oldest Greek sites in Sicily but now an unattractive town full of rubbish and dirty alleys.

At Licata, an artillery observer launched a Piper Cub from a runway that has been improvised on a landing ship, and in order to call in support fire he circled his plane over the beach for hours.

On the ground, War Correspondent Ernie Pyle, who landed in Licata, said the Licata-Gela area was very different from the way it was described in the guidebooks. It was not lush and Mediterranean but dry and dusty. Water was scarce, and most fields were empty, since all the grain had been harvested, but the troops landing at Licata did find a field of tomatoes to enjoy. They encountered only light resistance from residents of the village. Refugees walked past dead bodies and did not try to bury them, fearing the "evil eye."

New York Times, July 10, 1943:

By late morning the last real danger to invading troops at Licata had been eliminated when naval salvos destroyed a four-cannon Italian railroad battery there. Resistance proved to be light, and the Americans at Licata advanced steadily, distracted somewhat by the strong smell of sulfur. Other soldiers kept comparing the sere landscape with the dry, hot region of North Africa where they had come from.

At one point a soldier came up to his commanding officer to say, "Sir, there's a cave full of bint up here."

"Bint?" The officer had not served in North Africa, where the Arabic word *bint*, for women, had come into common usage.

"Women, sir. Young women."

The officer and the rest of the men moved forward just as the young women of the village were emerging nervously from their smelly hideaway, some of them praying loudly, others crying, a few summoning up angry looks. "Sir, they're afraid of us."

But the men were already bringing out candy and cigarettes to give away, and soon the women seemed reassured. One who was hugely pregnant seemed attracted to the officer and moved up close to him. A tiny child also toddled forward, hanging onto the hem of her skirt. "I speak English," said the pregnant woman. "My name is Stella."

"Good for you, Stella. Better keep your group in the cave until headquarters can be established." And he left, his detachment following. Surly looks from Stella failed to delay him and his men.

A group of infantrymen found an abandoned command post, and when the phone rang, an Italian-speaking American picked it up, saying "Chi c'è?" (Who's there?"). He found that he was talking to an Italian general who wanted to know if the Americans were landing. The American infantryman assured him that they were not! This reply satisfied the Italian general. The Americans collected all official-looking documents at the command post and eventually delivered them to headquarters.

By evening the troops invading Sicily's southern coast were well established ashore. Preparatory bombings had softened resistance, and Italian defenders surrendered in droves. Some were in tears. "We have been invaded again," said one sad old man.

Prisoners who spoke English asked soldiers for news of Chicago or New York. Intelligence officers who had landed with the troops drew some prisoners aside to ask them about certain Mafia members in Sicily. The intelligence officers carried papers with long lists of names.

At Licata the Americans under General Truscott set up headquarters in a narrow street of the town at a yellowish building called Palazzo La Lumia ("the Light Palace" or "the Palace of Light"), but it proved primitive rather than palatial, and the soldiers complained of the layers of dirt as well as the smell of sulfur, which they said could not be scrubbed away.

New York Times, July 11, 1943:

General George Patton, who knows a lot about war history, went ashore on the southern coast of Sicily today, recalling for his staff the ancient empires that had once ruled the island, one after the other. But Patton appeared to scorn the local residents, calling them "dirty" and "destitute."

New York Times, July 12, 1943:

Last night the hospital ship S.S. *Talambo*, carrying at least two hundred wounded soldiers collected from Sicilian beaches, was sunk by aircraft attacks, despite the ship's brilliantly-lit red cross painted on her white deck, displayed for all to see. When her lights disappeared and she began to sink, the destroyer *Tartar* sped to pick up survivors, but few wounded could escape from the small portholes before the ship went down. More than thirty nurses had been working on the hospital ship. Only six of them were rescued from the dark, cold water.

New York Times, July 16, 1943:

Today General Patton's forces took Agrigento, the ancient city once called Akragas, founded by Greeks in 582 BC and still full of many Greek monuments from the days of Greater Greece. It was once the most beautiful of Sicilian cities, described as such by Pindar, an ancient Greek poet.

Long ago Agrigento was notorious for its pleasure-loving citizens, who had become extremely rich, particularly through its exportation of olives. Now it is merely a strategic point in the capture of Palermo, Sicily's capital. General Alexander's forces are working on taking this key city and on ways to split the entrenched German forces on either side of Mount Etna.

New York Times, July 23, 1943:

The Germans have begun evacuating their troops from Sicily. Meanwhile, Patton is ensconced in Palermo, the capital of Sicily and its largest city, where he has made the Royal Palace his headquarters and where he dines in the huge state drawing room.

As part of the drive for Palermo, the Allies entered the tiny town of Villalba, northwest of the central Sicily city of Caltanissetta. In Villalba lives Don Calo Vizzini, Sicily's most important Mafia chief. In the past, Don Calo has aided the Fascists, but now he finds it convenient to cooperate with the Allies, who have made him mayor of the town.

New York Times, August 17, 1943:

Italian soldiers have been evacuating the island, using mostly eastern ports like the lovely resort town of Taormina.

Major Harry Llewellyn of the British Eighth Army, hearing that Taormina was free of the enemy, took a squad into the town center, where he unexpectedly found an Italian officer and his troops. Llewellyn told the officer that Taormina was surrounded, so the Italians surrendered.

Then Major Llewellyn and his squad proceeded to Taormina's finest hotel, the Albergo San Domenico Palace. Meanwhile, his senior officer, Colonel David Belchem, arrived in town, and the two walked in on local Sicilians who stood stone-faced around the hotel lobby. Llewellyn and Belchem, ignoring them, reserved two rooms for themselves at the palatial hotel, then proceeded to its beautiful restaurant, where many well-off Sicilians were dining, and ordered a gourmet meal.

The Sicilians, beginning to warm up to the Americans, revealed that only a day earlier they had dined at the Albergo San Domenico Palace with German and Italian officers instead. So Taormina's finest hotel had a changed clientele.

The players were fanning out onto the field. They moved athletically, with strong, sure steps. A few even trotted. But instead of wearing baseball pants, they wore short, flared skirts, like tennis or skating skirts.

Skirts? On baseball players? How could they slide safely?

Annie shook her head, then turned to her neighbor in the stands. "Who's that short, skinny girl at bat?"

"That's Betty Trezza."

"Trezza. Italian?"

"I suppose so."

"Where's she from?"

"New York. Used to be a garment worker."

"What position?"

"Infielder. She plays short for Minneapolis."

"She's not even five feet tall."

"So? She has a great arm and gets the ball away fast. She's not the team's best batter, but she hits in the pinch, when it counts. I've seen her bunt, too. And she can steal a base—one of the fastest runners I ever saw. You're not from around here, are you?"

"No, I'm driving to Chicago and just stopped in to see some of the game."

The woman looked at her curiously. "Well, it's a good league. You'll be surprised at what these women players can do."

Annie looked at her, thinking "I doubt that I'd be surprised," but said nothing, so the woman turned back to her family and her peanuts.

Annie watched, hearing shouts of encouragement. Trezza stood at home plate, slightly bent over, her short, fuzzy black hair sticking out from under her baseball cap. Then, ready to hit, Trezza waved her bat.

Annie couldn't stand it any longer. She knew she should have been in this game. She got up and left. She was thinking: That could be me. That Trezza girl even looks like me. Small, thin, dark. If the league had started ten or twelve years ago, I could have been this girl, playing professional baseball in a well-backed women's league. I was good enough to be in it. What am I now? Nothing. A widow with a twelve-year-old child. A child with infantile paralysis. At least now the child is well enough to attend school.

And my new housekeeper takes care of him after school. But that won't bring my baseball career back to me. It's over. I'm too late.

Watching the game would have been too painful. She left the South Bend ball park and started driving out of Indiana toward her destination in Chicago. On her way through the town of Warsaw, she passed a playground full of joyous children. Some pushed themselves back and forth on swings. Others see-sawed up and down. A few just chased each other.

I wish my child could run and play like that.

As she drove, her anger faded. She began to think of the reason she was driving to Chicago. She wondered if she really wanted to fulfill her goal of punishing the man who had ruined her career.

What if I'm caught? I'd go to prison. Then who would care for my child? His grandparents? I can't see Father Smith as someone who would give Johnny the daily attention he needs. And my mother is unprepared for such a task. Nor does she have the resources.

But if I don't do it, I will regret that Landis got away with what he did to me. Especially grating is his allowing some baseball men to develop a women's professional league, a league that I could have played in when I was younger. Why couldn't he have let that women's league start earlier?

She thought again of the cocktail shaker in her luggage, the bird with the pointed feet, the dangerous weapon.

Maybe it would be worth it, for the satisfaction. Maybe after I get there I'll decide what to do.

When she reached her hotel, Annie phoned home and asked for Johnny. She could hear him crying while the housekeeper reported that he had fallen and broken his arm. Annie stood at the phone, breathing hard. She made a sound like a groan. Then she picked up her suitcase and drove back home.

The Chicago Tribune, November 1944:

Commissioner Landis has been admitted to Chicago's St. Luke's Hospital with a reported respiratory condition and heart attack. His wife Winifred was admitted the same day with a broken wrist. But the major leagues, in the confidence that Landis would recover shortly, extended his contract as Commissioner for seven more years.

The Chicago Tribune, November 23, 1944:

A hospital spokesman reported that Landis had a better day.

The Chicago Tribune, November 24, 1944

The Commissioner's condition is listed as satisfactory.

Annie was on a plane to Chicago on Thursday morning, even though her widowed mother had finally agreed to join her for a Thanksgiving dinner.

It's now or never, she said to herself. My mother and Johnny will have to dine alone.

Annie unpacked her cocktail shaker at the Ambassador East Hotel and began reviewing her plan.

This is the way it will happen: At the hospital this evening, when visiting hours are over, I'll get someone to find out his room number. When the nurses aren't looking, I'll go to his room. I'll find him in bed and all hooked up to machines. He'll probably be asleep. I know what he looks like: A slight figure with an unruly mop of white hair. I'll stand over him for a while.

Then I'll awaken him. I want him to know what's happening and why. I'll tell him, "Do you know who I am? A person whose life you ruined. You kept me from doing what I wanted to do, and what I was qualified to do: Play baseball under my contract with the International League. What right did you have to cancel my contract just because I was born a girl? What right did you have to prevent me from doing what men do every day?"

As she thought about it, her breath came faster, her face reddened, and she became more resolved to carry out her plan.

The Chicago Tribune, November 25, 1944:

The Hospital announced unexpectedly that Commissioner Kenesaw Mountain Landis had passed away early in the morning, just a few days after his seventy-eighth birthday.

Later that morning Annie repacked her cocktail shaker and left the Ambassador East Hotel.

At home the next day, Annie's mother phoned. "Why did you go to Chicago? I suppose to see that boyfriend of yours there, Vincenzo del Vecchio. Am I right?"

"Yes, Mom. You're right."

16

MARTINO LEANED BACK IN HIS CHAIR and announced, "I don't want nothing to do with Capone, Luciano, or Anastasia. They're different. They're not Sicilians. They're more like Americans, who don't understand us. They even bring in *Napolitani* and Jews." The dining room of the small house in Long Island held the group of seven.

One of his men, Enrico Tameleo, waited, then said, "Sure, Joe. I've got to say, though, that Luciano guy is as lucky as his name. Look how he survived that beating by Maranzano's men back in 1929. Then how Lucky just happened to be in the men's room when Bugsy Siegel walked into the restaurant and got rid of Masseria. Maybe Lucky's right; maybe we should cooperate with the successful younger guys, whether they're Sicilians or not."

Martino took off his dark-rimmed glasses. "No. They can call us old-school if they want. It's important to keep the old Sicilian values. Honor. Tradition. We live as we have lived in Sicily. We recruit only from the old country. And mostly from my home town, Castellammare del Golfo."

"Is Cardello from the old country?"

Martino looked up in annoyance. He patted Rick Cardello on the cheek. "Born here, but his parents are from Sicily. Ricardu lived there recently. In Licata. He mined the sulfur ore. He knows the old ways." He turned and dictated: "We are simple people. We don't dress up fancy or go to those Manhattan restaurants like the others. We operate the way we always did."

"Sure, boss. Now will you tell us about your new idea?"

Martino leaned back. "It involves my funeral parlor." He looked around proudly. "I'm having double-decker coffins built. We can get rid of dead bodies quietly by putting them in the second deck of the coffins. No need to leave them around at places where they'll be found. " He looked around and grinned. Others caught on and did the same. Rick Cardello, too, looked amused.

Then Martino called for the dinner. He poured glasses of a Bartoli red wine. His wife set the new baby in his crib, reminded the other two children to be quiet, and began serving a complete Sicilian meal, starting with steamed mussels, grilled octopus, fried squid, and chicken scallopini, then going on to big bowls of chickpeas in lemon sauce and tube pasta with green pesto. They ate for a long time, disposing of many bottles of wine and toasting often—to the Old Ways of Sicily.

Cleveland *Plain Dealer*, October 23, 1945:

> Today Branch Rickey announced that he had signed Jackie Robinson, a black player, to a contract. Robinson will play with the Montreal International League team, the Royals. Obviously, Rickey plans to bring this player up into the majors.

And in my league, too; the league I could have played in. *Should* have played in: The International League.

A black man has made it into Organized Baseball before a woman. Same as with voting: Women always get considered last.

Annie took a deep breath and, to calm herself, went to her shelf of records and selected one with the opera singer Giacomo Lauri-Volpi singing "O Tu Palermo," from the opera *I Vespri Siciliani*, Sicilian Vespers, about the revolt against the French in 1282. Then she picked up a copy of *Vogue* and started to open it when she stopped: The woman pictured on the cover looked familiar. It looked like—yes, it was Katy Reiner, the pretty blonde ball player who kept changing boyfriends. But she looked different, her hip jutting out in a sexy pose, her heavily painted mouth hanging open. The strapless red dress flopped sideways, and on her head perched a cone-shaped hat something like what a Chinese peasant would wear.

Annie looked inside for the identifying information, which called the model not Katy Reiner but "Honey Myne." She knew that both the Powers and the Conover agencies renamed their models. Then she remembered a phone call from Katy asking to borrow five hundred dollars; her old friend wanted to go to New York and try out for a modeling job. Evidently, Katy made it. Annie never got her five hundred back, though.

Annie got up and moved restlessly to the kitchen.

I've got to get my mother to show me how to cook Sicilian food. The last time I asked her, she complained of the impossibility of buying freshly-caught sardines. And how was she going to find green and black olives right from the tree? Well (I told her), there's got to be something you can show me how to cook with ingredients available here.

Celery soup, she replied. It's made by frying chopped celery in oil with onion, then adding barley, stirring for a minute, and finally adding chopped tomatoes with bay leaves and water. Cook it for a long time. Then mash it all up and cool it for a long time. Serve it cold. After the soup, serve roasted prawns with artichokes.

Oh, mother, I asked, isn't there something simple? Sure, she said. Fresh tuna. Salt your tuna steaks, then rinse them. Sprinkle with pepper, fry quickly in hot oil. Remove the tuna from the pan and pour in some Marsala and honey. Cook this sauce, then cover the fish with it. Let it rest until dinner.

I remember eating your tuna. So what do I serve with it, mother?

Roasted onion halves stuck together with pesto.

Honestly, mother, I don't know any American who would eat roasted onion halves. Isn't there some simple pasta dish I could try?

Of course, she said. Greek pasta. Don't you remember eating it? The sauce is made of ground pork and onions with pecorino cheese and freshly grated pepper. You pour it over the pasta and coat every strand with the sauce.

Now I remember. It tasted so good!

Do you remember the pasta sauce with green tomatoes and purple onions?

No.

Her mother sighed: You were always rushing through dinner so you could leave the table to run outside and play ball. I wish I could get fresh figs. I wish I had my boys back.

The following summer Annie's mother was ready to move out of her lifetime home on Pythias Avenue, near Euclid Beach. "A riot!" she told Annie on the phone. "A riot in Euclid Beach Park! Just two streets away from me!"

"Well, mother, the Negroes want to enjoy Euclid Beach Park, too."

"Why don't they have a park of their own?"

"I don't know. They have baseball teams of their own, and even leagues of their own. But of course, it isn't the same as being accepted in places where white people can go, or being accepted in the white leagues."

"You sound as though you think we should mix with them."

"I used to think they should to stay separate. But now I'm beginning to realize how they feel. It's like the way I feel about keeping women out of the baseball leagues."

"Well, your Uncle Paolo and his family have suggested I move out to

Painesville, where they bought last year. I'm thinking about it. This neighborhood is changing anyway. People whose languages I've never heard before are moving in."

Annie thought: My father used to think that nothing would ever change. But everything is always changing. Even us.

"Yeah, Ma, yeah. It's me, Dominic. Merry Christmas! How are things in Cleveland?"

"Well, there was a celebration for the city's hundred and fiftieth anniversary. You know, parades and pageants. But there were also riots this summer in Euclid Beach Park. The Negroes want to come to the park. But the park owners think if the races mix, there will be trouble between them. Well, there's trouble anyway."

But Dominic Cardello hardly heard. His own activities mattered most to him. Lounging in Bugsy Siegel's wing on the fourth floor of the new gambling hotel that the mobster was building in Vegas, Dominic thought only of Bugsy's plan. Bugsy believed that Vegas was ready, in the winter of 1946, for postwar expansion.

Dominic soon began to get annoyed over his mother's entreaties to "Come home! Don't you want to see your own mother?" It's always this way, he thought; she never thinks that maybe I don't want to come to Cleveland, that maybe I'm involved in important things here.

"Ma, I work here. ... Yeah, all the time. Even on Christmas. ... Ma, we open this hotel tomorrow, with a lot of Hollywood people due to arrive, and it's not even finished, but we gotta open so we can make some money. ... What? ... Oh, yeah, it's true, the contractor building the hotel owns the New York Yankees baseball team. ... Why is he building a hotel? Because he's a builder, Ma. Some guys have more than one business. ... Yeah, you can own a ball team even if you're a builder. ... Listen, Ma, I got to go now. There's lots of work to be done, and Mr. Siegel needs me. ... Yeah, sure I'll write. Bye."

Dominic was thinking: I'm going to be the one to do something big. Ma is always expecting Rick to suddenly make a good career for himself. I haven't seen any sign of it. He even worked on a farm! What kind of work is that?

Now I got to be sure to go down the right stairway because Bugsy had some false ones built; they lead nowhere. He sure has some good security—

even a secret trap door in the floor that leads down to the basement. Imagine Del Webb building all these escape hatches for Bugsy ...

"Hey, Babe," he called, reaching the ground floor, where his girlfriend sat in a deep chair holding a gin fizz and swinging her long legs. "Let's go get something to eat."

Over burgers he continued his reflections out loud, now that he had a listener. "When this place is ready, it's really going to make dough. I'll be Mr. Siegel's right hand man, really show up my brother, who is nothing. As for my sister Annie, she's rich only because of who she married. I stopped asking her to invest in projects I'm involved in. She wants to spend her time pretending to be important with those socialites, and moping because she never got a chance to play big-time baseball. Silly. Here, I'm mixing with real big shots..."

"Sure, Hon." Babe flicked her false eyelashes in a way she thought was sexy. She knew the hotel would be a big deal, with all those Hollywood stars coming. But she wasn't much interested in Dominic's future. Her mind was on Hollywood.

"Yeah, Bugsy and Meyer Lansky have great plans, and I'll be part of them," Dominic went on. "This Costello guy has a million bucks invested in the place, so he's gotta be a good one to know, too. Wilkerson, the one who started the project, seems to be the weak link now."

"He's probably losing interest in it because it's costing so much more than he expected."

"The one who's really worried is Del Webb, the contractor. He can't meet his deadline. So..." Dom leaned forward. "He's afraid somebody's gonna bump him off!" He gave a short, sarcastic laugh. "I told him, don't worry, Mr. Webb. We only bump each other off!"

Babe leaned into Dom and grinned, starting to rub up against him.

"Dominic! Stop mooning around and help Umberto! We got to have some rooms ready." Siegel, move-star handsome in a striped suit and loud tie, turned briskly and walked away. Babe's eyes followed him.

When Rick's phone rang in June of 1947, he raised his eyebrows in surprise at the voice on the phone. "Dominic? It's really you? How are things in Vegas?"

"Not good. I left. My boss, Bugsy Siegel, got killed today."

"Are you involved?"

"No. Lucky Luciano did the job. Him and Meyer Lansky. For months they suspected Bugsy was skimming. You know, because the hotel he was building had such big cost overruns. They thought Bugsy was cheating them."

"Well, was he?"

"I don't know. But anyway, I thought I'd better leave. I think I've been here long enough."

"Where are you?"

"In Beverly Hills. I have an apartment here. Bugsy lived part of the time in Beverly Hills, too, with his girlfriend Virginia. I went there early this morning. He was lying on a living room couch—blood all over it. I got out of there fast."

"What made Luciano and Lansky think Bugsy was skimming?"

"Virginia—you know, Bugsy's girl—kept making trips to Switzerland to deposit a lot of cash."

A pause.

"What'll you do now?"

"Geez, I don't know. I wondered ... could you help me?"

Rick was silent, thinking. "Profaci doesn't care much for the California guys. I'll see what I can do. Meanwhile, I myself got into trouble with Joe Martino."

"What happened?"

"I was dating a showgirl from the Copacabana Club in New York, and one night between shows she was sitting at my table having a drink with me when Martino showed up and grabbed her arm. He asked, 'Why are you drinking with him?' I didn't realize it, but she was dating him, too. He started giving me hell. I thought sure he was going to get one of his guys to beat me up. Just then a fight broke out in the club: A bunch of drunken ball players from the New York Yankees got into a fight with some drunken bowlers at a next table, and the club manager called the cops. I took advantage of that distraction to get out of there fast."

"Gosh, I guess you can't help right now."

"I'm still on good terms with Profaci, and also with Costello, who owns the Copa. Let me see if I can do something for you. But I'm going to see if I can hook on with Tommy Lucchese. Martino hates the Lucchese Family, but they're one of the most successful of the Five Families in New York."

On Friday morning a messenger brought Dominic two tickets to a Saturday night professional basketball game. He was sure they came from a guy in the food service business who owed him money and promised him a gift

162

for waiting a little longer to be paid. Babe agreed to go with him to the game, so on Saturday evening he took the elevator down to the parking garage and got in his car. He suspected nothing until he felt the cool steel on the back of his neck.

"Oh, no, guys, please..."

"Sorry, Dom. Bugsy had to go, and you're one of Bugsy's guys, so it's your turn."

Dom's mother learned of his death when her friend and neighbor, Yolanda, spotted the news in the *Plain Dealer* and brought the story over to the Cardello home on Pythias Avenue. Bianca, his mother, was inconsolable. She kept mourning, "In a parking garage! Died in a parking garage!"

Yolanda kept saying, "I knew it would happen. I knew it. I wonder how long your other son will survive."

Bianca got up, went into the bedroom, and closed the door. Yolanda, insulted, left.

Cleveland Plain Dealer, October 10, 1948:

A huge crowd of enthusiastic fans in the Cleveland Stadium cheered the band as it marched around the field before the game, led by a couple of small girls in short satin skirts twirling sticks decorated with pompoms.

Many fans wore long coats, the men doffing their fedoras only for the flag-raising ceremony. A tie could be seen beneath the coat of Hank Greenberg, the Cleveland general manager, but Cleveland club owner Bill Veeck, seemingly impervious to the cold, wore his usual casual jacket over an open-necked shirt.

A pink scarf filled the neckline of Annie's warm blue woolen suit, but she still felt chilly. Her friend Jerry, home on leave and visiting Cleveland, liked the traditional baseball foods and summoned the ice-cream seller, a uniformed boy with a box carried on a sling around his neck. Sixteen-year-old Johnny, in his Indians' cap bearing the likeness of the mythical Chief Wahoo, exulted in his seat behind first base and bit delightedly into his chocolate-covered ice cream bar. The chocolate tasted like wax, but he ate it anyway.

So many people wanted to see this fifth game of the series in Cleveland that the overflow fans were allowed on center field behind a hastily-erected fence, where they had to stand for the entire game, all but obscuring an advertisement for tires bearing the word ATLAS.

Glancing at the swarm of standees, Annie remembered, from a class about ancient Greece that she took at Cleveland College, that the name

Atlas came from a Greek myth about the Titans. They lost a war with the Olympians, so the great god Zeus condemned one of their number, Atlas, to stand at the western edge of the Earth, Gaia, and hold up the sky on his shoulders. The name Atlas had come to symbolize strength and stoic endurance.

How is it that these mythological gods still have meaning for today? she was thinking. At least, the male gods do. Men like to believe that their strength and endurance help hold up the world. What about women's strength and endurance? Aren't there any strong goddesses?

Feller's fastball wasn't working. He was hit hard, and by the fourth inning the score was Boston four, Cleveland one.

Then the Indians rallied. Even the catcher, Jim Hegan, hit a homer. But the Braves caught up and surged ahead, and soon the score was Boston eight, Cleveland five.

When Boston scored again, Feller left the game, and in walked Satchel Paige, the first black man ever to take the pitcher's mound in a World's Series game. He moved slowly and deliberately, approaching the mound to the accompaniment of cheers. Picking up the resin bag and dropping it in his usual relaxed manner, he prepared to pitch.

Annie felt herself tensing. That black pitcher is a lot older than I am. He's been in the Negro leagues just about forever. I should be out there trying to save this game. I have strength and endurance, too. Why does Paige have the right to play and I don't!

The Braves continued hitting, despite Paige's efforts, and won the fifth game of the World Series against the hometown Indians eleven to five.

Annie tried not to smile, but her face wore a gratified look. Jerry asked her, "Did you enjoy the game?"

"Yes, it was better than I thought it would be."

Jerry looked at her strangely, wondering what she meant. Then he forgot about it.

The immense crowd left the park without enthusiasm. Disappointed local fans walked slowly through the huge parking lot to their cars, so Johnny's languorous walk, necessary for dragging his leg brace along, wasn't readily apparent.

"Annie, would you like to go to Boston with me to see the sixth game?" Jerry asked just before they reached his blue Ford.

Annie deliberated. Jerry was nice, and she felt comfortable with him. But seeing black players participate in big-league games kept reminding her that they had made it to Organized Baseball before white women, who had to play in a separate and unequal league. She knew she didn't want to see any more of that.

She gave Johnny as an excuse. Jerry didn't call again.

"Rick, I'm so glad to see you! How long are you staying? Are you back for good? I have so much to talk to you about." She released him from her hug and led him from the foyer into the living room.

"I'm not sure it's safe for me to be in town, but I wanted to talk to you. Where is your son? I'd like to see him."

She noticed how nervous he seemed. "He's long since gone to bed. Stay in one of the guest rooms tonight, and you can see him tomorrow. Why did you come so late? Does Mom know you're here?"

"Hold on, little sister. I'll stay here tonight and go to Pythias Avenue tomorrow. Then—"

"Don't tell me you're leaving again!"

"We'll talk about that later. Do you have a glass of wine for me?"

"Of course!"

"What is that odd-looking thing on the bar? A bird?"

She spilled the wine she was pouring, and he retrieved the glass from her shaking hand. "What's the matter, Annie?"

"Oh, Rick, I have to tell you something. It's something terrible that I've done."

"Still making confessions? What good does that do?"

"I'll feel better if I can tell what I did. And I can tell it only to you. Nobody else would understand."

"Do you mean about what happened to your husband?" He put down his glass. "Vincenzo told me. He did it for the both of us. I know it wasn't a good thing to do. But I think you were relieved to be free of him." He sipped the strong red Chianti. "His usefulness to us was over."

Annie remained quiet, looking down at the carpet. "I suppose you're right. But I can't forget how easy it was for me to agree to it."

"Vincenzo is persuasive. He can be controlling. He uses people, too. You know that."

She nodded, remembering. "But there is more. Something else I've done. Something even worse."

He looked up, surprised.

Just then the lights of an approaching vehicle lit up the entire room. Rick dropped to the floor and whispered harshly, "Get down!"

Instead, Annie moved into the foyer, where she took up a position behind the door. From there she could peek through the corner of a curtained window to identify the visitor.

"Annie! Get down!"

"It's just Carl. You remember him from Collinwood. His name then was Carmine Morrissetti."

"A visit from a man? At this hour?" Rick got up. They heard the car door slam, then steps on the walkway.

"He teaches a night class and comes over afterwards." She opened the door as he approached it.

"Carl, come in. You remember my brother Rick?"

"Oh. I'm disturbing a family visit."

"Hello, Carl. Nice to see you. Annie and I do have a lot to talk about."

"Sure, I understand. I'll call again. Good evening."

"Sorry, Carl. Listen, don't tell anyone you saw me here. Okay?"

He raised his eyebrows slightly but agreed quickly. "Sure, Rick. I'll see you again, Annie."

After the door closed, she turned to Rick. "You're still working for those crooks."

"Annie, let's talk another time. I'm tired and need some sleep."

The next morning Rick told Annie he was in trouble with a racketeer named Joe Martino and was "laying low" for a while.

The Indians thrilled the city's fans when they took the World Series by beating the Boston Braves four games to two. One of the stars of the Series was Larry Doby, the team's top hitter. Cleveland's celebration continued as crowds gathered to greet the team arriving in town at Terminal Tower and filled the sidewalks of the downtown streets. Smiling fans standing patiently on Euclid Avenue watched a parade in which Manager Hank Greenberg and Owner Bill Veeck waved from the back seat of a beautiful white 1947 Cadillac convertible. Veeck's wife sat between the two men, her suit decorated with a fur piece, in the fashion of the day.

"Are you sure you won't be marked absent today?"

"I won't, Mom. The teacher said we could welcome the Indians home if we wanted to. Honest."

Annie stood on the sidewalk in front of the Lindner-Davis store, watching with Johnny, who cheered excitedly. Despite the excitement, Annie remained stone-faced. She was there only to gratify Johnny, who loved the thrill of feeling part of a winning team. Besides, he'd come to admire Bill Veeck since learning, from the *Cleveland Press*, that Veeck reached his success despite a severe limp from a war wound.

I wish my son weren't handicapped, Annie thought for the hundredth time. I've got to see that he enjoys life anyway.

Vincenzo was in trouble. He phoned Annie from Chicago to explain. "I'm in dutch with Maranzano, my Boss. I want to come to Cleveland and stay with you for a while. Maybe this will blow over."

"Vincenzo. That isn't convenient. I ... well, I'm seeing a man, an old beau of mine. I can't have a guest now. I just can't."

"You mean you're refusing to help me?" There was a pause. "Remember, I know a lot about you, things you don't want those society relatives of yours to ever know. Or that precious son of yours."

Annie was shocked. Vincenzo was threatening to reveal their conspiracy to kill her husband.

"Vincenzo, how could I let you stay here?"

"Remember, I'm a cousin. A cousin from Sicily."

She finally relented. "You'll have to stay out of sight. I'll prepare the room over the garage."

But when he arrived the next morning after an overnight train ride and a taxi from the downtown terminal, he was talkative. Annie didn't appreciate his boldly walking in during breakfast with her son, but she had to accept it. "Johnny, this is my cousin Vincent from Sicily. He's going to stay in the room over the garage for a while."

"Oh. Why? Can't you stay with me, Cousin Vincent? I have a spare bed in my room, and we could talk. What's your last name?"

"I need a long rest, Johnny. I'm very tired. We can talk another time."

"Will you have some eggs, Vincent?" She noticed that he looked as handsome as ever, in a slick, hard, aggressive way.

"No, I ate in the terminal. I've been traveling all night, so I want to get to bed. See you later." He left by the back door.

"Golly, I didn't know you had a cousin in Sicily, Mom."

"I seldom see him. Now, finish your toast. Here's your lunch money."

Then she thought: My son has just met his father's murderer.

About eleven the next morning, when Annie was returning from a trip to the drugstore, Vincenzo came into the house with his usual lounging pace. She was still thinking of his threat to reveal the way John had died. But with his tousled hair and flashing black eyes, he remained attractive to her.

"I've got more to tell you, Annie. Want to hear it?" He seemed to be flaunting his knowledge, proud of his hold over her.

"I don't know." And she sat down in a living room chair, discouragement and fear on her face.

"It's about your husband. You didn't know everything about him. But Joe Martino did."

"Your boss?"

"No, a friend of my boss. Martino is the head of one of the Five Families in New York."

"What was there for him to know about John?"

Vincenzo sat down and looked at the nails on his left hand. "Banking, that's what. Crooked banking." He paused, letting his eyelids lower a bit, while Annie gathered her mental defenses.

"Martino's organization was using several banks to ... process money. Through your husband's bank, he somehow found out about it. By blackmailing Martino, John Smith diverted a lot of it to an account he set up in Europe at a tax haven country. A place called Andorra. That money belonged to the Martino organization. But Joe Martino could not think of a way to claim it. So he had to stop the money from draining away."

"Stop it?" She began squeezing the arms of the chair.

He sat up straighter. "Did you think I killed your husband just for you?"

He let that question resound within her for a moment. "It was convenient that you brought him to Sicily, where we could easily stage his accident."

She put her head back and looked at the ceiling, then at Vin. The room seemed to suddenly tilt.

"That stopped the draining away of the money. The only problem was that Martino still couldn't get at the account. He figures either you or your brother Rick has that account number."

She was breathing hard now. "You let me believe that I was entirely the cause of John's death."

"Why not? You wanted it done, and you liked my attentions." He got up and approached her. "I think you still do."

She hung her head. "Oh, God. What have I done?"

He took her hands and helped her stand. With his arm around her, they ascended the stairs together.

Before he left, Vincent told her one more thing. "When Martino does something for you, he expects something in return."

"Does something for you?"

"He arranged to take care of your brother in Sicily for a while, when Ricardu needed to let his enemies and the law cool down, and he arranged to get rid of your husband because he knew you wanted to escape from your marriage. He knew because Rick told me, and I told Martino."

She let these facts begin hurting her before replying, with trembling lips: "What can I do?"

"Give him the number of your husband's bank account in Andorra. It must still be full of Martino money. Your husband didn't have time to use it all up, so it's just sitting there earning interest. Think about that. Martino's money."

"But I don't have it!"

Vin shrugged, in the timeless Sicilian way. "Find it."

17

ALTHOUGH ANNIE SLEPT ONLY FITFULLY after hearing of John's blackmailing of Joe Martino, everything looked better the next day. How serious could that be? Surely Martino wouldn't expect her to find the money.

When the phone rang, she felt relaxed. "Yes, I can lunch with you tomorrow, Isabel. Union Club? Oh, Women's City Club. All right, noon."

Annie sat back in her chair and mused. I'm glad Vincenzo left yesterday. My sister-in-law: If it weren't for Isabel, I'd be a recluse. She insists that I get out and do things. I can't be as active as she is, though: Horseback riding, getting her pilot's license. She's a real sportswoman. The kind I read about in magazines.

The phone rang again. "Yes, I'm Anna Smith. Your name, again ... is what?"

"Joe Martino."

Her head moved back on her shoulders, as though someone had hit her in the face.

He went on, "I wonder if you can tell me where Rick Cardello is."

A pause. "Why do you want to know?"

"I have a reason. Aren't you his sister?"

"Yes..."

"Then you should know where he is."

"I don't know why I should tell you."

Another pause.

"I need to know. He owes me something. Or perhaps it's you who owes it to me."

Annie sat back. "I don't think I want to speak to you." She hung up. Sitting there, leaning back on a bright blue pillow, she worried: So it's started already. How does he know who I am, where I live? I can't talk this over with anyone. Not even my mother. *Especially* not my mother.

This can't be real. Is it actually happening to me?

She walked into the bedroom and started packing.

When the phone rang a third time, Annie hesitated for a long time, then finally picked up the receiver. It was her mother, with a surprising proposal.

"You want to move in with me? Here? I thought you didn't like this house. ... Well, I know you don't approve of ... my men friends who visit. ... Yes, some stay overnight. ... No, I'm not going to stop having visitors. ... No, I'm not going to consider marrying again. You know I depend on the Smiths to support Johnny and me. They would cut us off if I remarried. ... Mom, I have to go and pack now. Johnny and I are getting ready to spend two weeks at that cottage in Canada that I told you about... We leave Saturday. ... Yes, of course I'll call. Goodbye."

Women sat four to a table, chatting over lunch at The Women's City Club on Euclid Avenue. Isabel and Annie, unable to find a private table, asked permission to sit down with another club member who was just finishing her lunch. "My friends left already," she said. "My name is Dorothy. Glad to meet you."

With her blonde hair in a bun and wearing a conservative suit, their new acquaintance looked like the schoolteacher she was. "I teach first graders how to read," she explained. "It's challenging but very gratifying to see them change from non-readers to children who can enjoy books. I'm sure I heard of you, Isabel, as a sportswoman. Do you enjoy sports, Annie?"

"I used to. As a girl I was a member of an industrial girls' baseball team." I haven't admitted that in a long time, Annie thought; this woman seems so relaxed and receptive.

"Interesting. Did you know women have been playing baseball since at least the 1870s?"

Amazing, thought Annie. Not that women have been playing baseball that long, but that she didn't respond by saying *You mean softball.* "How do you know that, Dorothy?"

"I'm working with my husband on a scholarly book about the history of baseball. It includes women's baseball, of course."

"I'm surprised to hear about that. I'll be looking forward to reading the book."

"Now I must go. I'm spending the afternoon doing research in the Cleveland Public Library. It was nice to have met you both."

The cottage her sister-in-law had found for Annie in the Gravenhurst area north of Toronto was suitably private. It stood on an island, so it was accessible only by boat.

Finding a snake on the cottage porch annoyed Annie. The boatman was about to leave, but she called him back again, and he killed the snake for her. Johnny's eyes were wide. "Wow! A real snake! Is it a dangerous one?" The boatman replied, "Aye, he's a killer, that one. " Then, winking an eye, "Nah, just an old black snake, taking a rest, he was. Well, McKaye says good-bye once more. Be back for ye in a fortnight."

Johnny watched McKaye paddle away. "Why does he talk funny, Mom? And can I go swimming right away?" He couldn't wait to unpack his swim suit, but he first checked his room for snakes.

He thumped off toward the dock before Annie was ready. "Wait till I get there!"

Johnny wants so much to do everything... Maybe this wasn't such a good idea, coming here alone, just the two of us. I'm glad I insisted on a phone. I hope ... that man doesn't decide to hunt for us. And where have I heard of that country called Andorra?

She left the bags of groceries on the porch, rushed to change, and got to the lake in time to see him pull off his brace and limp from the small beach into the water. "Don't go far! Wait for me! This is a big lake..."

When he finally tired and returned to shore, she realized she'd forgotten to unpack the towels, so they walked back to the cabin dripping.

"I'm hungry, Mom."

"Good. Dinner will be ready in no time."

Johnny turned brown in just a few days. His skin, like Annie's, took a tan well. His blond hair bleached lighter.

The two of them explored the island or played catch on the beach. It felt strange for her to throw a ball again. Annie had to be careful not to pitch hard or away from the target. Soon she got the range just right, and he was catching the ball easily. One day they took a long walk up the beach and picnicked, sitting on a log next to an extinguished bonfire. They built a small fire on top of it and roasted marshmallows.

As she watched her boy turning into a teenager, Annie thought, he must never know the things I've done. I must keep him innocent.

The time went quickly. They were outdoors most of the day. Evenings they sat on the porch, talking. Some mildewed books, a set of Chinese checkers, and a Monopoly game Johnny found on a shelf kept them entertained when it rained. Then it was time to pack.

The lights of the Bratenahl house seemed to be off when Annie pulled up to the driveway at about 12:30 in the morning. Johnny was asleep after the long ride from Ontario. She stopped the car and sat there quietly, thinking: I talked to Mrs. Armbruster day before yesterday and told her to leave one living room light on. What if something's wrong?

And she thought of the worrisome phone call from Joe Martino. Then she saw a flash somewhere at the back of the house; a light had been on, and someone inside had just turned it off.

Then Johnny awoke. "Mom. Mom, we're here. Let's go in, Mom." And he started to open the car door.

"Wait, Johnny. We're leaving. Close that door. I'm going to drive to your grandma's house."

"Leaving? What for?"

"I think something's wrong." And she had started to back the car into the street when she saw a figure rushing out the side door. As she paused to make her turn, the explosion happened.

The loud sound frightened Johnny more than the spectacular flames and the smoke from his burning home. He jerked into hyperconsciousness. "Mom, Mom! Our house! My room! My drawings!" Then he sank down and began to whimper.

A dark sedan that had been parked behind her pulled past.

Annie straightened up. Fear for her son and anger at this terrible occurrence made her react. Instinctively, she started to follow the sedan, paying no attention to lights in the nearby homes that were starting to snap on. The sedan began to speed. Emerging from the private streets of Bratenahl, the driver, followed by Annie in her roadster, raced along Lake Shore Boulevard.

She forgot everything but the chase. On she pressed, feeling as though she were running, trying to catch the leader in a race and pass him. Vaguely, she heard Johnny's protestations, the roar of the motor, the hum of tires on the road. She became aware that Johnny was questioning her, but she shook her head. "Not now."

The sedan pulled ahead of the 50 mile-per-hour limit, and Annie's wrath rose.

First it was the destruction of my plans for my future. Then it was Johnny's illness. Now it's destruction of my home, my comfortable retreat, my nest for my child and me. Why does life treat me like this?

Then the sedan passed East 156th Street, where Annie had planned to turn off the Boulevard so that she could take Johnny to his grandmother, who hadn't moved away from Pythias Avenue. There Annie began to lose her desire to follow. She felt very tired, and Johnny was whimpering again, so she let the sedan escape and turned back to the street leading to her mother's home. Her own tears, of frustration and anger, were beginning to flow.

The house on Pythias was dark, so Annie tried to think whether to go to a hotel. Realizing she knew of no place nearby where they could stay, she decided: I'll just have to wake my mother. Besides, I need to use her phone to call the police—why didn't I try to get the car's license number?

Mrs. Cardello's old brown robe flapped around her thin figure in a long pink flannel nightgown. Her frightened eyes revealed her concern, but she bustled Johnny into bed in the small "spare room" before finding out what the emergency was. Annie soothed him until he relaxed, then left his room to explain.

"I'll use your phone, Mom, to call the police."

"The police! Is it your brother?"

Annie thought for a moment before replying, "I don't really know why this happened." She realized that if she told about the figure she saw leaving her house, the one she was pursuing, she would be asked who it might be and why her home was targeted. She resolved not to mention that figure.

Her mother listened to Annie's call with a disturbed expression. "Have you been carrying the little stones I gave you?"

"I ... They're in my purse." She picked it up and looked inside, taking out a handful to put in the pocket of her jacket.

My good luck charms. Maybe my mother is right. I really feel better when I'm fondling them. "I'll keep them in my pocket."

Bianca shook her head, then left to make coffee. When the police arrived, they reported that the house had been consumed in the fire. A detective asked if she had any idea why the explosion had happened, so she told him that she thought she had smelled gas. And when Rick phoned after learning of the event, she let him think the same thing.

At noon came a call came from Isabel, announcing, "Annie, you've been summoned into The Presence. Your father-in-law wants to see you here. He's sending a car for you. Bring Johnny, and I'll entertain him."

Instead of receiving Annie in the living room of his Shaker Heights home, Emmet Smith welcomed her in his home office, where he managed his investments. He had sold his Euclid Avenue establishment when commercial interests began buying up the old mansions formerly occupied by the early founders and developers of the city as the population began shifting to the suburbs. In Shaker Heights he was again surrounded by the rich and important, many of whom had moved to this attractive suburb with even larger home lots than the old-fashioned places on Euclid. His daughter Isabel, unmarried still, kept her suite in his home but also lived in an apartment in the Hollenden House, a fashionable Cleveland hotel.

"It's time for me to intervene," he declared after offering her a sherry, which she declined. "I want young Johnny away from ... questionable influences. He must go to a well-recognized boys' school. The education available in Cleveland for children of important families is too limited. I've chosen Braithwaite, in Connecticut. It has a fine reputation, and there he will meet boys with the right background. Besides, he needs to get acquainted with New England, where his forebears came from. After Braithwaite, he will matriculate at Harvard."

Annie began breathing hard. His forebears in New England? How about his forebears in Sicily? But she held her remarks to herself, instead asserting, "You can't take my son away from me."

"I'm not proposing to take him away from you. I suggest you go along."

"Where?"

"To New England, of course. I have inquired about places in Boston, and I have found a good house in a suburb called Newton. Young Johnny can visit you there on some weekends. New England offers old cultural and historical background that will be suitable for both of you to be exposed to. After all, Cleveland is only the Western Reserve of Connecticut. New England is where the nation formed."

How pompous and overbearing, Annie thought. And I learned in school that the South had a lot to do with forming the nation, too. "But my family ... my mother, my relatives ... they will feel deserted. And Cleveland is my home."

"I won't hear a word of it. Johnny's best interests must come first, so you must adjust. All the arrangements are made. You both leave on the train next week, Wednesday. We mustn't delay; the school year in Connecticut has already begun. Mrs. Allen will furnish you with details and funds for new clothing, furniture, whatever you need. After you are both settled, I will telephone to check on you. I'm sure you will both thrive in these new surroundings. Good afternoon."

She bowed to the inevitable, her stomach churning with fear and anger, then rose to face the housekeeper, Mrs. Allen, in her lair, a small office next to the library. Mrs. Allen served as secretary and assistant to the elder Smith. The steep and regular waves in her hair almost induced seasickness, and her pursed lips discouraged chit-chat. With a few words of instruction and no sympathy, she handed Annie some papers in a fat envelope, wishing her well politely but firmly.

The people who have the money have the power, Annie thought ruefully. Will I ever be able to control my own destiny?

At hearing the news, Johnny seemed surprised but undisturbed. He appeared to think of the change as an adventure. "Wow," he responded, beginning with his favorite expression, "I get to go to a school where I sleep overnight. I'm getting to be a really big boy."

"I'll get someone to drive us to the new school so we can look around together. While you're getting settled there, we can talk on the phone every night, and you'll come home weekends." She was starting to miss him already. And Carl. She would miss Carl, too. Summoning up his face, she closed her eyes and thought, I wish Carl and I weren't being separated.

Annie had never been in Isabel's Hollenden Hotel suite, so when she received an invitation to come there for a farewell luncheon, she was surprised. When she arrived, she learned why: Isabel lived there with someone, a young woman Isabel called "my girlfriend," a delicate-looking blonde in wispy violet chiffon named Tina. Isabel answered the door in her usual jodhpurs and classic silk shirt and was soon striding around the room looking the picture of the modern healthy sportswoman, pointing out her latest equestrian award for excellence in dressage. Who Isabel really was began to sink into Annie's consciousness.

"Tina doesn't go out much. She's a delicate girl, subject to many illnesses." Isabel was giving a reason for her girlfriend's remaining invisible for so long.

"I love reading and cooking," the delicate girl volunteered, "and making a nice home for Isabel. So I'm happy here."

Gradually, Annie became comfortable with this newly revealed situation and began to talk about reading.

"Tina reads cookbooks," Isabel boasted.

"I like the Betty Crocker and Good Housekeeping books," explained Tina.

Isabel added. "Tell Annie about the Vienna cookbook."

"Yes, do." Annie had never thought of ethnic cooking as especially elegant, but she found that viewing and tasting Tina's Austrian lobster salad in sherried aspic, with asparagus and pimiento, was a true dining experience—and said so.

Then came dessert. "I found the recipe for this blueberry pudding in the Good Housekeeping book."

"It's become a favorite," Isabel added.

Annie was impressed. "What a talented person you are, Tina!"

"Isn't she?" Isabel's smile for Tina was warm and loving.

Over the demitasse, Isabel gave Annie some advice. "Phone me here whenever you like, and let's talk about how you're getting on. My father has a great friend in Boston and goes there often; sometimes I go along. I'll visit you around Christmas."

Before leaving Cleveland, Annie and Johnny paid a different kind of visit: To the site of their home in Bratenahl. Annie parked the car in front of the rubble that was left of their comfortable house. Although it was drizzling, they took the time to look through the detritus for anything recognizable. Johnny found a sketch tablet that hadn't entirely burned because it was covered, front and back, with heavy shellacked boards. Inside were some of his sketches, so he picked it up to save. In among some blackened bottles, melted vinyl records, and burned furniture, Annie spotted something curved: It was The Bird—she thought of it with capital letters.

No, I will not save it, she thought. I don't ever want to look at it again.

Before I leave for Boston (she realized), I must collect the contents of my safe deposit bank. I don't recall anything hinting at a bank account in Andorra, but I might have missed it.

At the bank she slipped the papers into a briefcase and brought them back to her mother's house, intending to look them over. But she soon got caught up with plans for their move, finding out details of Johnny's school, buying him his uniforms, arranging their train trip to Boston, speaking on the phone to her new housekeeper, and hiring a driver to take the two of them directly to Braithwaite.

When she talked to Carl, she was surprised when he asked for her brother Rick's phone number in New York as well as her own in Boston.

"The house is drafty, Father Smith," she reported on receiving her first phone call at 22 Moreland Street in Newton. "It needs weatherproofing. I'm colder here than I've ever been."

"Have it done and send me the bill. Now tell me about Johnny."

"He seems comfortable. He's rooming with a boy named Rodney Williams, who is related to the Williamses of the Sherwin-Williams Paint Company in Cleveland. Johnny says the other boys talk funny, like having a 'bahth' and wearing something called 'sneakas' and going across the 'quad.' He seems to have an ear for language. His favorites are the art and music classes, and he is beginning to find poetry interesting. Of course, he misses his old home and me. And because he was late in starting the school year, he has some catching up to do."

"How about his disability?"

"He's been accepted on the swimming team. That's a sport where he can easily reach the minimum standard. He has volunteered to schedule games for the baseball team, which does some traveling to meet other boys' schools. He also says he plans to draw cartoons for the school paper."

"It sounds as though he is settling in. I will come up for Thanksgiving. We will all have our holiday dinner at the Parker House, where I will be staying."

"Oh." She was surprised, but she found the prospect of spending Thanksgiving with him and Johnny not unpleasant.

When she discovered the subway, Annie found it easier to get around the city. The housekeeper who had been engaged for her was her best informant about Boston. Driving in the city was difficult, Mrs. Kane told her, and "the subway takes you everywhere." And "everywhere," Annie found, included two wonderful art museums within walking distance of each other, one of them created by a Boston society woman inside a beautiful old mansion.

Mrs. Kane, a tall, bony Irishwoman with black hair and a frilly pinafore worn over a dark cotton dress, even furnished Annie with a subway map. Mrs. Kane was not really married, Annie learned, but used the title as an honorary one. As the eldest of seven daughters, she had always been the motherly type, she explained, and went out "into service" early. Her talents included hiring window washers, having the basement cleaned, and taking care of Annie when she came down with one of her upper respiratory infections, which seemed to attack her more often than in Cleveland. Annie saw to it that Mrs. Kane had an apartment in the house so that she could spend some nights there.

Annie's phone calls to Isabel were more detailed than those to her mother. She told her sister-in-law that she didn't miss Johnny so much when she kept busy finding places to visit, like the Old Oyster House, where she found the fish chowder too bland and creamy, and historic Faneil Hall, where she took the standard tour and learned about the early history of Boston. When Johnny came home on the train and spent the weekend with her, she showed him around. As she expected, he found subway trips to the Fine Arts Museum and the Isabel Stewart Gardner Museum inspirational. "Some day, Mom, maybe I can be a good artist. Now let's get on the subway again."

"Why do they call it the subway?" She asked Mrs. Kane. "Most of the time it runs above ground."

"Beats me," replied the housekeeper. "When are you going to have a party, Ma'am? All this fine Rosenthal china you bought needs to be put to use." Her ruffles quivered as she polished the silver bread tray for the second time, even though it needed no polishing. "I don't know why you didn't buy good Belleek china from Ireland, especially since there's a sale on it at Filene's." Mrs. Kane always offered her opinions even when they weren't required.

At the subway stop in the center of town, right near the State House, a gold-domed government building, Annie found the Commons and the Public Garden, both good places for brisk fall walks and for viewing the changing colors of the season.

If I haven't found a place to run, at least I can take some pleasant walks here.

Boston was very much a baseball town, she found. Many citizens identified with the Red Sox. She saw evidence in the store merchandise, she heard people talking about baseball, and she found the Boston Globe always full of baseball news even in the off-season. Then she realized that Fenway Park was on the subway line, only two stops from hers.

"No," she said to herself. "I'm not going to a professional baseball game." But she found she could hardly avoid hearing about the Red Sox, a team that usually came second, third, or fourth in its league and a perennial rival of the New York Yankees, long considered the best and most important club in its league. For the first time she began to read about men's professional baseball.

All the while she was becoming interested in the old city, she knew that eventually Joe Martino would find her. Would the retaliation he had already done enough? Or would he still expect something else? She knew the answer: Destroying her home was just an expression of anger, a way of getting her attention. She could expect to hear more from him.

Bianca Cardello remained bitter about being separated from her daughter. When she phoned, she subjected Annie to quizzes about her personal life. Had she met any nice men? "Well, I've met the yard man," Annie teased. "And two other men who filled the attic full of weatherproofing. I don't care for the smell of it, but the house is warmer now." She invited her mother to visit, but Bianca, who had never left Cleveland, said she would feel uncomfortable traveling, especially alone. Uncle Paolo had invited her to his family's Thanksgiving dinner.

"By the way, Anna," Bianca added, "your Uncle Paolo told me that when young Tony lost his job right after his baby was born, you sent him money all summer, until he got his new job. That was nice of you. And I don't think I ever thanked you right for all the money you've been giving me. I wish my sons were as thoughtful as you are."

"Mom, I have extra money, and I'm glad to see it go where it will do some good. I'm sure the boys would both have done it if they could."

Bianca started to cry, so Annie urged her again to visit Boston, but again she refused.

On Thanksgiving Day, Father Smith picked up the *Boston Globe* at breakfast in the Parker House and learned that Cleveland was in the midst of its worst snowstorm in years. Everything had closed down, and the governor had called in the Ohio National Guard. Father Smith decided to extend his stay at the Parker House.

Johnny lifted the napkin away from the breadbasket and stared at its contents. "Now I know why they're called Parker House rolls!" he exulted. "They must have been invented here!"

Father Smith smiled as he watched his grandson discovering new things. Looking at them, Annie realized that Emmet Smith's connection with the boy could be a source of pleasure for them all.

"This hotel is noted for more than its food," he remarked. "Important writers like Charles Dickens lived here for a while. Ever hear of him?"

Startled, Johnny replied, "You mean, the man who wrote A *Christmas Carol?*"

"And many other fine works. The Parker House was long the gathering spot for Emerson, Thoreau, Hawthorne, Longfellow ... Do you know those names?"

"Poets!" Johnny exclaimed. "They were real people? Who came to this same hotel?"

"They met here on Saturday evenings to talk and dine together. They wrote a lot besides poetry. They set the literary tradition for this country."

"Wow. And I'm right in the same building."

"Tremont Street: Is that a French name?" Annie asked, realizing that Father Smith would know why the main street bore that name.

"No, the word 'Tremont' is just a shortened form of 'Trimountain,' the original name. The original settlers built their city on three small hills they thought of as mountains. Anna, you must walk with Johnny up Beacon Hill, one of the oldest areas of town. It looks quite European."

European, she thought. Probably like Italy. Not sure I want to go.

After Johnny had left to return to school, Emmet, still ensconced at the Parker House, phoned Annie with an invitation to lunch at the Copley Square Hotel. She knew where Copley Square was: On the subway line and very near the great library. "I'm bringing someone whom I want you to meet," he said mysteriously.

Annie took a cab so that she would not have to wade through snow in getting to and from the subway. She found the hotel entrance so classically lovely that her mind returned to the day so long ago when she entered the Society for Savings Hotel in Cleveland, admiring the ironwork at the doorway.

Emmet Smith rose politely as she entered the lobby. Seated in a chair next to his was an elegant-looking woman, her grey hair carefully set and twisted high on her head, which she held in a regal manner. Her luxurious sable coat lay open to reveal a richly-textured woolen suit that matched her hair. The pearls at her neckline were multi-stranded.

"Anna, I want you to meet an old friend, Regina Jones."

"Not old friend, Emmet. *Long-time* friend." She allowed herself a slight smile. "How do you do, my deah?"

Annie felt unsure how to reply. Finally, she said, "I'm happy to meet you, Mrs. Jones."

"Welcome to Boston. Here comes Charlie now." And a young blond fellow using a cane limped toward them.

"Hello, Mrs. Smith," he said, as if he knew her. And he did. "I met you at Crile in Cleveland, when you were one of the volunteers taking us patients by bus to lunch and a show downtown... Mr. Smith, sir, how are you?" And he hugged Regina Jones, murmuring "Mum, dear."

Annie could hardly speak. She was receiving more information than she could easily deal with, especially when Father Smith (as she still thought of him) took Regina's arm on the way to the dining room and started calling her "Darling."

"I hardly thought I'd have the opportunity to meet you again, Mrs. Smith," continued Charlie Jones as they approached their table. "What luck that you are related to Mummy's ... well, you know ... and that you have, I hear, moved to our neck of the woods." After the waiter took her coat and Charlie adjusted her chair before giving up his cane, Annie's eyes lingered on the bludgeon-shaped object, and Charlie explained that since graduating from crutches he was carrying an Irish stick made of heavy bog oak. "Mum sprang for a trip to Ireland and Scotland last summer, and I picked up this cudgel in Dublin. A bit heavy, perhaps, but I can always use it to beat off attackers," he grinned.

For the entrée, Father Smith recommended the schrod, so Annie had to find out what it was. Then he began suggesting tours she might take once the weather cleared, tours within fifty miles of town that would give her an idea of what New England was like, such as to the town of Rockport, and then to the historical points of Lexington and Concord. Thinking of driving around the Boston area made Annie realize how alone she was and how enjoyable such trips might be in the company of a man. Carl came to mind; she pushed the thought away.

The luncheon proceeded pleasantly, and Annie realized that she was finally seeing a different side of Emmet Smith, his human side.

He must have been as frightened as we were when our house was burned. That's why he so precipitately moved us out of Cleveland.

"My deah," Regina Jones was saying to Annie, "You must go to Symphony with us. Now that we have Charles Munch as conductor, we are hearing ravishing French music like Debussy and Ravel. Munch is Alsatian, you know. But we still get the fine old standards like Mozart, Brahms, and Haydn. Even some Wagner. What is your taste in music, Anna?"

"I really prefer opera. Verdi and Puccini are my favorites. Although I lost many records in my house fire, I have found some other recordings I enjoy, like a 1922 record of Rosa Ponselle singing an aria from the Verdi opera 'Sicilian Vespers.' Do you know the opera? It's about the revolt of Sicilian peasants against the French occupation. I've never attended a performance of the opera, but I've read about it. Anyway, Ponselle had a wonderful coloratura voice, not as thin as Galli-Curci's."

Regina Jones was nodding, but it was Emmet who responded. "Why, yes. I've heard recordings of Ponselle's voice," Emmet contributed. "And Galli-Curci's. I didn't realize you were such a connoisseur of opera, Anna."

"Music keeps me from getting lonely, and I collect recordings of well-known arias, especially from Verdi and Puccini operas. I think Johnny enjoys music, too, although art is what he loves best."

Charlie Jones listened intently. He realized that Anna Smith must be about eight or ten years his senior; yet he found her increasingly interesting. She has some depth, he thought; not only is she attractive, she might be enjoyable to date. He asked for her phone number.

Regina Jones had sized up her new acquaintance, too. "Emmet, I think Anna is the kind of person who would enjoy the Ath. I'll give her a membership."

"Good idea. The Ath is old New England at its best."

As Annie wondered what they were talking about, Regina explained, "We're talking about the Athenaeum, a private library in a charming old building on Beacon Street. In the nineteenth century it was the center for all Boston intellectuals. You'll want to browse there."

After Johnny's return to Braithwaite and Emmet's departure for Cleveland, Annie took the subway downtown and began wandering up Beacon until she came to "the Ath." Inside, the quarters seemed smaller than she expected, but the atmosphere was one of culture and scholarship. Beginning with the second floor, each one of its five floors had its own gallery looking down at the others. Paintings and sculpture accented the museum-like quality of the institution. When she visited the women's washroom, she saw that the marble sink featured gold fixtures, thus hinting that members assumed the importance of wealth as well as culture.

While browsing, Annie picked up a book of essays by Matthew Arnold. Leafing through it, she realized that Arnold was an accomplished poet as well as a critic of art and beauty. Chancing upon a poem with the word "Etna" in the title, she read it with growing horror, realizing that in it the main character, an intellectual named Empedocles, felt so depressed that he had decided to throw himself into the Sicilian volcano.

She closed the book and looked around. Am I becoming as withdrawn as Empedocles? Why can't I become involved in life? Am I so influenced by the negative things that have happened to me, the bad things I have done, that I will never feel normal again, joyful again? Am I, like Empedocles, heading for suicide?

She left the book on a table and walked out into Beacon Street, suddenly needing the cool, fresh air.

That evening Annie stood at the front windows of her house in Newton, watching the snow fall. The lawn was nearly covered. The scent of roasting beef filled the air while strains of Brahms's Third Symphony came from the living room record player. The first movement was reaching its crescendo when she remembered her dream:

She was in the Boston Public Library at Copley Square. Walking through the entrance of the original building, with its carved head of Minerva, goddess of wisdom, to check on the country of Andorra in the card catalog, she realized she that she was standing in the newspaper reading room. Someone hiding behind a newspaper was stalking her. She had to get out of there. She knew that a corridor connected the two buildings of the library; where was it? Looking around, she spotted a narrow staircase. The steps loomed ahead of her; she began to climb. Faster, I must go faster! Danger lay just behind her. Her legs began to ache. Finally the staircase ended, and she found herself in a narrow hallway—a perfect place for an ambush. She ran until she came to a door. Pushing through it, she saw that she had entered the other building. The room was full of people studying at tables. She knew she was safe with them around her. Slowing down, she walked determinedly through the reading room to the exit. A blast of hot air met her as she left the building. Is it summer? Or is it hell?

The dream ended.

In Chicago, Jean Stewart sat in the nurses' break room at St. Luke's Hospital talking about her favorite mystery, the sudden appearance at her desk in 1944 of a volunteer named Betty who, after asking a few questions, disappeared just as suddenly.

"I think she was a Negro woman," Jean said to her friend Dora. "Her hair was black and kind of frizzy, even though she wore it pulled back flat."

Dora pulled on her Chesterfield. "I remember seeing her, but I didn't talk to her. I thought she was white."

Jean put down her coffee cup and picked up her cigarette. "She was dressed up like a white woman, but her skin wasn't real white. I remember she was a small person, and she wore a dark suit and glasses. Imagine claiming a couple of the doctors asked her to check on whether some patients were still registered! Later, when I asked both doctors about it, they'd never heard of it. I still wonder why she did that."

"Well, the only important patient we had at that time was the baseball commissioner, and he died. So there's no use wondering."

"Yeah, I think she was a Negro."

"Oh, Jean, you're obsessed with fear of the Negroes." Dora stood up and brushed cigarette ashes off her white uniform.

"Well, they're filling up this city." Jean had her "frown face" on. "They're everywhere you look—in the stores, in banks, everywhere. Those black baseball clubs—they call themselves league clubs—they even get to play in Comiskey Park sometimes. And White Sox Park, my husband says. We're thinking of leaving."

"What? Leaving Chicago?"

One more drag on her cigarette, and Jean replied, "He's had a job offer. In Boston. They're plenty of hospitals there where I could work, like Brigham and Women's Hospital. It has a good rep."

"Why would you want to go there? Do you know anyone in Boston?" Dora stood up and took her coffee cup to the sink.

"Just a cousin and her husband. They live in a suburb. They can help us find a place to live."

Dora checked her watch, and they left to resume work at their posts.

Part Six:
John's Legacy, 1870,
1879, and 1888

18

COME IN, COME IN, STRANGER! Come and look at our wares! Do you need needles from Birmingham? Cotton cloth from Leeds? Ships' bells and binnacles? We have them, and a lot more. Look us over! You'll surely see something you like. Here be calico. ...

Oh, you just came in for directions? Of course. Yes, our town is crowded; we're having a special occasion today. A race. It's called a smock race. Do you know about smock races? They're common in this area. I understand they're held in Europe, too.

No, not for men. It's a women's race. They run for a prize: A smock. It's a she-shirt, made of soft, unbleached linen cloth, and it has been smocked—that is, sewn with tiny tucks, and embroidered. Very pretty. Furthermore, it's been decorated with ribands. ... Yes, ribbons, they're the same thing. The prize smock was procured right in this shop, of course, from our wide selection, purchased by the town fathers, who like the races, which bring in strangers like yourself, who then patronize the various businesses in town, especially the taverns, heh heh!

And your name is? ... Ah, Mr. Trevor E. Smith. Good, solid American name. Glad to make your acquaintance, sir. Feel free to look around at the merchandise. And are you planning to stay here in New London? ... No? ... Ah, from upstate. ... Oh, all the way to Ohio? So you plan to travel to our Western Reserve. Are you sure you want to be so far from New England, the center of American civilization? ... Well, I wish you well, Mr. Smith. Now that we have the railroad, you no doubt plan to take advantage of that modern mode of transportation. We pride ourselves on being up to date here, in this year of 1870.

I hope you enjoy your stay in our town, Mr. Smith. I'm Joshua Bright, proprietor of this establishment, formerly of the U.S. Fourteenth Infantry. Trained here at Fort Trumbull under Commander John Reynolds, who was killed right in front of me at the Battle of Gettysburg. ... Yes, difficult times indeed. We're all glad it's over, and slavery is outlawed. In the war we had a couple of colored regiments. ...

Yes, of course we have baseball here, as we do all over Connecticut. A few years ago we had a state convention of thirty organized clubs. ... You played while working in your father's shop? ... I'm impressed that your excellent play was mentioned in the local newspaper. No doubt if you settled here you would— ... Ah, you prefer to remove to a more distant place; perhaps your talents were unappreciated in— ... I wish you luck, sir, in your plan to make your fortune in one of the populous new industrial cities out there in the Western Reserve.

Yes, the sounds outside are getting louder. Shall we repair to the porch, where we can view the goings-on?

... That group to your left? Yes, that consists of the wenches who will be running this race. ... The man on a horse? That is our sheriff. He will settle all fights, for the action is likely to be punctuated with disputes among the runners. And yonder tree, along to our right, with the white sign, that is the goal. Some of the town fathers stand there, to observe and adjudicate.

We do see a bit of jostling among the contestants. But there is quite a crowd of them, is there not? Not much room. Yes, they wear what looks like under-dress, what the British call "smalls." Or "smallclothes." But the theory behind their choice of costume, you see, is that, the fewer the items of clothing, the faster the runner. The skirts are short, the bodices are scanty. But, you see, Mr. Smith, the young women race not only to win the smock, they enter to display their charms—if any—so that they can attract young men as husbands, or what they choose to call husbands, since trips to my office to register marriages, in my capacity as city clerk, remain few...

... That gun was fired to start the race! Yes, the wench in blue has tripped another. ... That one? No, she fell over that cur, over-excited as it was by the noise. ... Oh, the tall, black-haired one? She used her sharpened elbows, I believe, on both her neighbors in line. An Irishwoman. You know the Irish have been coming here since the potato famine of 1846. A great bony-looking frame she has, but see how fast she runs! No, from our perch here we won't be able to see the winner, but the town fathers...

Well, well, he's gone, is Mr. Smith, probably to find himself one of these wenches. I warrant I won't see any application for a marriage license from Mr. Trevor E. Smith and one of these chippies. I never saw such bold looks and carnal movements in my life. Hmph. They're already finding themselves some young swains who were much excited by the revealing clothing, what there was of it. Such displays of loosened hair, of heaving bosoms... I myself, in fact—

Mattie! Mattie, go and find out who the winner is. Not that it matters. And come back quickly.

"Oh, Maud, don't be such a stick-in-the-mud. There's no harm in it. A lot of the men I know are going. You could come along, too." Trevor Smith could be persuasive, but this time his wife would have none of it.

"Don't insult me, Trevor," she said, making what he called her "uppity" face. "I wouldn't make an appearance at such an occasion. What would my mother think? Nora, remove the casserole and bring the coffee."

"Your mother need not know of it, my dear."

"Trevor! Now you recommend attending clandestinely?"

He smoothed his moustache a bit nervously; he prided himself on its luxuriance. "I wouldn't put it like that."

"I thought that you might want to pattern your behavior after the actions of pillars of the Cleveland community—men like Mr. Hanna and Mr. Case." As she rose, her bustle rustled.

"Now Maud." He put down his cup. "Try not to be too old-fashioned. Leonard Case wouldn't go; he isn't even a well man..."

"It's Saturday. Alice and I will be attending the weekly meeting of the Women's Christian Temperance League this afternoon. We're taking her carriage. I shall see you at dinner."

"Wait, Maud! Please don't go away angry... Stop fussing at the table, Nora! Maud, listen."

She paused at the dining room door, but not for long. "I shall not hear another word about this vulgar exhibition you want to attend. If that's what you desire to do, I ... I have nothing more to say. Good day."

Trevor sat there pouting for a few minutes. Then he got up and went about his business. Opening the door to the hall, he directed, "Get the trap, Dewey. I'm going to see a baseball game."

August of 1879 proved to be a hot month in Cleveland, but Trevor wore his stylish three-piece lounge suit; the points of his shirt collar were pressed into wings, and he fastened his ascot tie with a silver stickpin. As an up-and-coming Cleveland banker, he had to keep up appearances. And now that he had a wife who claimed descent from a prominent local family, he wanted to reflect her importance, too.

"Mr. Smith, sir. To the Kennard Street baseball grounds?"

"No, Dewey, to grounds on the east bank of the Rocky River, at Detroit Avenue."

Dewey halted. "The league team has changed its grounds, sir?"

"Not at all. The league team has a game at Kennard Street today. But the teams I shall watch are touring teams." No need for Dewey to learn any more than this, thought Trevor.

The up-and-coming banker had plenty of time to think about what he was doing, for the trip to Rocky River took nearly an hour. And think he did.

After all, I'm the man of the family, and I have the right to select my entertainment. Maud is excessively prudish. She has been my wife for three years and has hardly even mellowed. Stiff-waisted, stiff-necked. Wound up as tightly as a clock. No wonder she has still not presented me with a son. Perhaps I shall have to be a bit rough with her. Loosen her up a bit. Insist on more frequent sessions. Meanwhile, I look forward to spending the afternoon with my male friends, just as she enjoys being with her radical Temperance ladies. Pretty soon they're going to want to do everything men do. Even vote.

As the horses trotted up to the grounds, which were surrounded only by a low fence, Trevor and Dewey read the sign next to the entrance:

Red Stockings vs. Blue Stockings
August 15, 1879
2 o'clock

Dewey could not suppress his exclamation: "Sir, are the famous Cincinnati Red Stockings here? The team that became the Boston Red Stockings?"

"No, Dewey. This Red Stocking team is a different one, from Utica, New York. Let me off here, and pick me up at five."

Trevor paid the ten-cent admission charge and began looking for his friends. They were easy to find in the small baseball grounds: Franklin Backus, the attorney; Gregory Gardner, the ex-mayor; Edward Higbee, the department store owner; and Charles Brush, the inventor, who had just this spring installed electric street lights on Public Square. Sitting down near them, Trevor was recognized and made a part of the conversation.

"Have you seen these players before?" asked Attorney Backus.

"Never," Trevor replied, "but I'm looking forward to the experience." He grinned, and Gregory contributed a nervous laugh.

"There must be about a thousand people here," Trevor said, looking around with surprise. "Mostly men, of course."

Charles called their attention to someone they knew, George Stephens, an accountant, who had walked out onto the field toward the entrance. "Why, George looks a bit embarrassed," said Charles. "I believe he's going to act as umpire for this game."

"Well, he has plenty of baseball experience. When was it he played with the Forest Citys?"

Charles replied, "Back in the sixties, during the War, I should think. Before you came to Cleveland, Trevor."

Just then a large van pulled by four horses stopped at the entrance and began discharging the players. At that moment, George was joined on the field by an announcer, who declaimed, "Ladies and gentlemen, I present to you, fresh from their successful appearance in Buffalo, New York, the Red Stockings and the Blue Stockings of Utica, New York, in their first appearance in the City of Cleveland."

The two teams filed onto the field, and the onlookers began to chatter loudly, commenting on the women's appearance. Ed Higbee said, "Why, they really are wearing red or blue stockings, long ones that must extend above their knees." Ever the businessman, Ed added jealously, "I wonder where they found such items. My department store doesn't carry them."

"Those skirts," remarked Attorney Backus, "are uncommonly short."

"That's so that they will flap around the knees seductively," added Charles Brush. "Otherwise, the costumes look quite modest and demure," he intoned through his great nose.

"They look very much like women's bathing attire," said Ed Higbee, the merchandiser. "My store carries such costumes."

"I've never seen so many women's legs before," said Charles.

"Some of these girls are quite pretty," Trevor ventured. "Look at the small blonde girl. And that redhead... Nice figure."

"Now, Trevor," smiled Ed, "keep your mind on baseball."

They all laughed. Trevor did feel a bit uncomfortable. But why should I? He thought. All of us are here for the same spectacle. And we're all staunch members of the Old Stone Church. So what could be wrong about it? he told himself firmly.

By then the young women were tossing the ball about. Gregory adjudged a few of them as "pretty good at throwing. However, most of them aren't."

"That black-haired one catches the throws pretty well," was Trevor's assessment. "The rest are woefully deficient at the skill. Three of them have already dropped a ball thrown to them."

"And a couple of them let it go over their shoulders," added Gregory.

"Gentlemen, shall we indulge in a little wager as to which team will win the game? I propose to bet five dollars upon the Red Stockings. Who will take me up on this?" Before long their bets were laid.

Then George Stevens, the umpire, announced "Play ball!" The chatter in the stands died down a bit as the players took their places, the small blonde batter at a twelve-inch-square slab and the tall black-haired pitcher in a box four feet by six feet. The batter called for a low pitch, so the pitcher obliged with one at the height of her skirt hem. In an attempt to hit the pitch, the blonde nearly turned herself inside out. Laughter arose. But the batswoman persevered.

The pitcher's right to take a running start from the box made it almost impossible for the small hitter to time her strike at the ball or even reach it. She struck out on three pitches. Someone clapped, and a few others joined in, on the assumption that the applause was directed at the performance of the pitcher—who made the same assumption, turning and smiling before addressing the next batter.

"Now that Cleveland has entered a team in the new professional league, I don't know why we're watching this poor level of baseball," declared Attorney Backus.

"You know why," Trevor remarked.

"Of course he knows," agreed ex–Mayor Gardner. "Uncommonly humid," he muttered. "Beastly weather." No longer feeling the necessity for a careful appearance before the public, the ex-mayor unbuttoned his shirt collar and pulled off his straw boater, fanning his bald head for a moment before replacing it.

"It's those flapping skirts," said Brush. "We all pay attention when the pitcher goes into her motion, because there's a lot to be seen."

Ed Higbee hooted.

"What's her name? The pitcher, I mean."

"A small sign I saw outside said the pitcher for the Red Stockings is named Tillie Sheldon," said Gregory Gardner.

"Well, Miss Sheldon is worth watching," asserted Trevor. By then the Blue Stockings had actually scored a run, and soon the Red Stockings responded with four of their own. Most of this scoring was awkwardly achieved or occurred because of errors, Trevor and his friends agreed.

The only real excitement occurred when a tall, athletic-looking Red Stocking batter struck the ball fairly and ran so fast to first base that she slammed into the smaller Blue Stocking first basewoman stationed there and her momentum carried her onward so that she somersaulted into the field beyond the base defender.

"Good heavens!" exclaimed Trevor.

"Well, I never!" agreed Ed Higbee.

"I enjoyed that!" admitted the ex-mayor.

The attorney and the inventor merely smiled hugely, while the level of sound from the audience rose considerably, with snickers and cackles prevailing.

Scoring continued, but as the humidity increased, the weather deteriorated. By the end of the fifth inning, when the Reds had made 28 runs while the Blues had only 16, the game was stopped in the fifth inning on account of rain.

"I think that was a rewarding afternoon," Trevor remarked, "and not only because I won my bet." His friends agreed.

"I'm glad I didn't miss this game," remarked Charles Brush. His large nose had turned pink in the sun.

"Yes, it was a better choice than the league game being played at the same time," said the ex-mayor as they stood under an overhang waiting for their rides.

"Who were Cleveland's opponents in today's league game?" asked Frank.

"The Chicago White Stockings." Gardner replied.

Charles Brush said thoughtfully, "I wonder... Surely, these girls know they are merely objects of curiosity, if not ridicule. I wonder why they continue to play baseball."

After considering this thought, Trevor responded. "I think I know. The reason is the same one you and I played baseball as younger men. We enjoyed it."

Gregory nodded. "I think you're right, Trevor. They seem completely unconscious of the attractive picture they present. Instead, they appear to be concentrating on playing the game."

Nobody commented further on this novel thought, and it was soon forgotten.

Dewey drove up smiling. His greeting to Trevor revealed that he was better informed now than before: "How were the ladies, sir?"

"Only fair, Dewey. Only fair."

"Well, sir, I think my own team might be better."

"Your team? You play on a local nine, Dewey?"

"Oh yes, sir, oh yes. I play on a crack colored team. Last Saturday we beat a local white team 24 to 17."

"Twenty-four to seventeen?"

"Yessir. Oh yes. Twenty-four to seventeen."

"Well. Good for you, Dewey. Good for you."

"Yessir. Thank you, sir."

Dinner was very good. Nora had prepared a roasted hen stuffed with onion-flavored bread, and Maud, seemingly forgetful of her earlier pique, talked animatedly about the plans of the Temperance women. Afterward, the evening was spent in reading, Trevor enjoying *Travels with a Donkey in the Cevennes*, by Robert Louis Stevenson, where he learned how one used something called a "sleeping bag" and thought what a cozy little bed it might be for a couple on an outdoor sleeping adventure, and Maud discovering, in George Meredith's *The Egoist*, that women were sometimes used by fathers and husbands to cement the male bond between them. I wonder, she thought: Did I marry Trevor because he and my father were friends?

At breakfast, Trevor eagerly picked up the *Cleveland Herald* to read the reporter's story about the baseball game he had watched the day before. The writer, Trevor recognized, supported his own opinion about the uneven quality of play, calling it "little more than a variety show." Admitting that the display was "not quite indecent," the reporter thought it "sadly out of taste."

Feeling generous, Trevor read this statement aloud to Maud. She seemed subdued and avoided comment. Finally, she began talking about baseball. "It seems," she revealed, "that Alice's daughter plays baseball at that women's college she attends, Vassar." She raised her eyebrows at Trevor but let them return to their usual position. Although her lips remained a bit pursed, she seemed to be in a forgiving mood.

"Alice's daughter!" He was genuinely surprised. "I had no idea that the fad of women playing baseball had affected girls in college."

"Yes, Sophia told her mother that the girls had been playing baseball ever since she was a freshman. At times, as many as five teams played games in the fall and again in the spring."

"How did that happen?"

"It was their college physician who suggested it, thinking it would contribute to their health."

"And did it?" Trevor, feeling vindicated, took some of the raspberry jam and applied it to his scone.

"Apparently, until the accident."

"What happened?"

"One girl fell while running the bases and hurt her leg. For a while, the teams stopped playing, then started again. Sophia is about to enter her senior year, and they're still playing."

"Hmmm. I hope they ... dress conservatively."

"They wear their regular clothes—gowns that reach the ankles—but they have adopted small, fashionable-looking caps that show the team colors. And they've given their clubs clever names like the Resolutes and the Daisy-Clippers."

"You sound almost approving."

"Sophia seems none the worse for having indulged in this athletic exercise, Alice told me. I suppose it will not hurt. After all, the girls play without an audience, in a remote corner of the campus. No public displays, of course," she emphasized.

Trevor took his implied scolding with good nature. "Of course." Perhaps she is mellowing a bit after all, he thought. Maybe tonight she will be more amenable to my advances. She seems to have loosened up. I want a son; I need a son. All my friends have sons. I will give him my middle name, Emmet, and he will join me in the bank.

Flappers made Emmet Smith a bit nervous. They flaunted their sexuality, letting their soft galoshes flap around their ankles as they walked. This rhythmic movement called attention to their legs. Those short skirts! They revealed just enough to make him want to see more. Whenever a flapper came into the bank, Emmet withdrew deeper into his office. Then he discreetly looked out the side windows at her, glancing around to be sure his father, Trevor, wasn't watching him.

Emmet thought of himself as up-to-date, spiffy, and quite "the berries." He wore his hair parted in the middle, in the popular manner of the day. His favorite suit, made of muted glen plaid, was double-breasted. He considered that name for the style of suit to be a particularly good one, since it called attention to his wide chest.

Emmet reveled in the important events occurring in Cleveland. He spent little time at the bank, attending the National Air Races and as many games as possible of the Cleveland Indians at League Park, joining the Cleveland Yacht Club, haunting the new downtown theatrical district at Playhouse Square, and celebrating with pals at speakeasies when the Indians won the American League pennant and then took the World Series. He learned to smoke because it made him look sophisticated.

Emmet's father, Trevor, considered his son a callow youth, a boy without much success in the bank and more interest in his good looks than in anything else, but Emmet, a recent graduate of Western Reserve University, thought he was a Big Cheese. Trevor went after the business of Spang's Bakery and Race's Dairy, but his son Emmet favored the "joints" of Short Vincent Street, where bookies showed little interest in savings accounts. Emmet thought of his father as a funny old bird, a flat tire instead of a live wire. He reveled in the slang of the day because he thought it was part of being modern. When he was out with his friends, Emmet felt himself to be on top of his little world.

That is, until he met Frenchy, a girl who had entered Mather College of Western Reserve University to major in what she already knew: The French language. Knowledge of French had high value in the circles where Emmet traveled. If you memorized a few French nouns and tossed them into the conversation, even where they failed to fit (as did some of the characters in the opera *Die Fledermaus*), you were considered worldly-wise, blasé, not born yesterday, a cosmopolitan, and dry behind the ears. So when Frenchy, whom he met at an alumni tea, unloosed a barrage of French phrases complimenting Emmet on his appearance, his education, and his athletic ability (he had played football at Western Reserve whereas she had merely taken a class in archery), Emmet was hooked.

Frenchy's real name was Suzette. Emmet thought that a particularly cunning name—sweet, darling, and, above all, French. She claimed descent from an officer in the army of Charles of Anjou, who, she asserted, ruled France in the thirteenth century. Her popularity arose from her vivacious and charming nature as much as from her pretty face and auburn hair, worn in a short and bouncy "finger wave" style.

Ambitious beyond her years, Suzette persuaded her father Claude Moreau, a Cleveland pharmacist, to pay for her matriculation at Mather College, the women's education unit of Western Reserve University that had opened for "females" in 1888. She knew that there, during the parties that combined students of Mather with those of WRU, she could meet men on a social level superior to hers. Encountering Emmet Smith at a university mixer to which recent graduates were invited proved that she was right. She brought him tea and cookies, sat close to him on a soft sofa, and showed him in her attentions that he had greatly impressed her.

The courtship that followed proceeded much faster than Emmet's father Trevor desired. "She's just a baby, Emmet. Barely sixteen. And I didn't like the way she studied everything when she was here. It's as if she's planning to copy our décor, the food we serve, even the way we speak to servants." Trevor had correctly pegged her as a social climber.

"Father, she just wants to please us by emulating our style. Believe, me she's very much like us."

"She lacks our taste in clothes."

"She's modern, Father. Try not to be a wet blanket. She dresses the way the other girls dress."

"We haven't even met her parents."

"They're abroad. Besides, I'm not marrying them. I've never felt for any other girl the way I feel for her. I'm taking her to a party tonight, and afterwards I'm going to propose. I've already bought a ring from Sam Deutsch, the jeweler."

Trevor looked at Emmet with disapproval. "Isn't Deutsch also a boxing promoter?" Trevor thought Emmet not only acted without thinking, he mixed in unsavory circles.

"Yes, and he's just bought a football team and entered it in the National Football League. He's an up-and-coming kind of fellow, and I'm glad to have him as a friend."

Trevor, hearing the defiance in Emmet's voice, pursed his lips. "I see that you've made up your mind. Have you spoken to your mother?"

Emmet paused. "Not really. I just told Mother that I was falling for Fren—Suzette. But if you like..."

"Never mind. I'll talk to her." No use trying to change his mind now, Trevor realized.

"Thanks, Father. I have to go. I must pick up the corsage." Emmet had arranged to leave his roadster at Sam's house so that before and after the party he could ride with Frenchy in the rumble seat of Sam's small car. The seat was so small that ... well, it was cozy. Not for nothing was that seat called a Struggle Buggy.

Two weeks later the Moreaus, just returned from Europe, were invited to dinner at the Smiths' imposing Euclid Avenue chateau. Annette Moreau, a chubby woman, sweated in her satin gown, while Claude Moreau squirmed in his unaccustomed formal wear, which he obviously detested. Suzette, having made her conquest, didn't bother with a long dress but wore a cute little number so tight that, when she was seated, climbed halfway up her thighs. Emmet had the grace to feel a bit embarrassed.

Halfway through the meal, the Smiths began to learn more about the Moreaus than they really wanted to know.

"Where in Europe were you traveling, Mr. Moreau?" led Trevor, trying to act gracious.

"We went to Messina, in Sicily, where my ancestors come from. My family traces its lineage from a Lieutenant Moreau, originally from Provence but for many years stationed in the town of Messina, in the eastern part of the island. Count Charles of Anjou, the ruler of Sicily at the time, brought a considerable army with him when he occupied Sicily. My ancestor was among the soldiers. That was in the thirteenth century."

"You are saying that … your family comes from Sicily?" Trevor Smith, startled, stopped eating.

"Yes, with French lineage through the occupying soldiers, who were mostly slaughtered in the battle of the Sicilian Vespers of 1282 when the local peasants revolted. But not all of the French occupiers were killed. Those who had ruled benevolently, such as the French administrators in Messina, were allowed to escape. They took with them their Sicilian wives, of course."

Trevor's wife Maud seemed to be struck dumb. Like Emmet, she had expected the revelation of French nobility, at the very least. Now she learned instead about a French soldier and his Sicilian wife running away from revolting Sicilians.

"And the lieutenant escaped to France?" Trevor inquired.

"No, he and his wife settled in Tunis, which was also governed by Count Charles of Anjou. Lieutenant Moreau's descendants lived there for generations. We visited Tunis on this trip, after a stop at a resort town in Sicily called Taormina. "

Emmet, taken aback, was following the conversation avidly, turning his head from one father to the other as Claude Moreau responded with information to Trevor, the only one asking questions.

"Ah. Tunis. That is in … North Africa, I believe?"

"Yes, my forebears lived there for three generations, before removing to the south of France, where my wife and I were born and grew up. There my parents continued many Tunisian customs. We came to the United States as young newlyweds, so our daughter was born here."

"I see. And what language does the family speak at home?"

"Tunisian Arabic first, French second, English third. And what languages do *you* speak?" Moreau began to show a bit of annoyance at being so closely questioned.

"I'm afraid we can't compete with such a cosmopolitan household as yours, Mr. Moreau." Trevor tried being more circumspect.

"It's *Doctor* Moreau. I hold a doctorate in science from the Ecole Technologique of Provence." Score one for the soldier's descendent. "And do your forebears come from Europe, too, Mr. Smith, or are you descended from the aborigines?"

At first taken aback, Trevor finally laughed with everyone. But the Smiths never found it easy to welcome Frenchy into the family, especially after learning that the name "Moreau" means "son of the Moor."

After this difficult evening, Emmet acted more subdued. He had flubbed, and he knew it. Thinking he was bringing a pearl into the family, he had instead brought in what his parents considered a bracelet of brass.

Trevor and Maud hastened the wedding along after learning that Frenchy was already, as Annette Moreau put it, *enceinte*. Suzette's daughter Isabel was born seven months after the wedding ("a premature birth," Maud told everyone), in the Euclid Avenue mansion that Trevor found for them. Baby John came along ten months later.

Emmet, now a more sober and serious person, started paying attention to his job and spending less time with people his father called "loafers." He had learned his lesson, and he never forgot it. He stopped making assumptions, trusted nobody, eschewed bookies, and became a staunch Republican and solid businessman—in other words, the ideal banker. Although disillusioned with Frenchy, he supported her as his wife and kept his dalliances with other women discreet, confining them to contacts made during visits to Boston and New York for checking on his growing investment portfolio. In New York he was not above a trip to a peep show at Times Square.

Much later, the Smiths learned that Annette Gambetta Moreau was the daughter of a Marseille grocer. Clevelanders, however, knew her as a prominent member of the Horticultural Society who grew prize-winning roses. Besides, remarked Emmet's father Trevor when *en famille*, I'm the son of a Connecticut grocer myself; and everyone knows, from the name Smith, what my early ancestor did for a living.

Suzette Moreau Smith developed into a collector of fine carpets from the Arab world, furnishing her stylish mansion with some of the best in the Midwest. Their rich, glowing colors set off the mahogany and chestnut furnishings popular in home décor at the time.

Rug salesmen often visited Suzette's private suite on the top floor of the Smith home to unroll their wares before her, and after dealing with the salesmen she fed them couscous. They politely called her "Sayyida" (Lady), and some even regaled her with stories from the Koran, to which she replied that Islam discriminates against women and prevents them from acting in the world as men do; Muslim women could never, for example engage in sports. One dealer then claimed that Aisha, the young wife of the prophet Muhammad, enjoyed running footraces against her husband. Suzette replied, "Ibrahim, games played with your husband don't count as equality in the world. How much for this small Berber carpet?"

It soon became whispered that many of these darker-skinned dealers, some of them Coptic Christians and some practitioners of Islam, were distant relatives, or claimed they were. In any case, they were people with whom Frenchy could speak her favorite language: Tunisian Arabic.

PART SEVEN:
HOW IT ALL PLAYS OUT

19

BY NOVEMBER, ANNIE FELT SETTLED in her Newton house. One evening, just as Mrs. Kane was about to leave, someone knocked at the door. "Rick! It's great to see you. What a good surprise. Mrs. Kane, meet my brother Richard Cardello."

"Why, the two of you look a lot alike, except you're a big man, Mr. Cardello. Glad to meet you. Can you stay? I'll get a guest room ready."

"I'll take care of it myself, Mrs. Kane. You go ahead home. See you in the morning."

While Annie prepared a sandwich and coffee for Rick, she encouraged him to talk. "Things are going better with my work," he told her. "I was lying low for a while. Joe Martino seemed to have some grudge against me, but I think he's forgotten about it. If I keep buttering him up, I may get invited to take part in a big convention of the Five Families of New York that's scheduled for a few weeks from now. I ought to learn a lot from sitting in. As long as nobody there makes trouble. So many of them hate each other!"

While he was eating, Annie thought about telling him of her phone call from Joe Martino as well as Vincenzo's story about a bank account in Andorra. Then she decided against it; what good would it do? I can't involve Rick; and it might make more trouble for him.

Instead, she told him she wanted to confess something.

"Confess? Are you still doing that?"

"Yes, I have a terrible story to tell. You know how much I wanted to play professional baseball, how important my contract was to me, how devastated I was when Commissioner Landis cancelled it. I never got over that, never forgot what he did to me. It was cruel." She looked at him fiercely. "I needed to get back at him for that."

"Get back at him?"

"I kept my anger in my heart and let it build. I thought of it often, imagining ways I could hurt him. I asked Vincenzo to do it for me, but he never got around to it."

"He mentioned that. But he thought you gradually forgot about it."

"Never. I *never* forgot about it." She was getting riled up. "And one day ... one day ... I did it."

He waited for a few moments. "This is what you were trying to tell me the last time I saw you." He settled himself. "All right. Tell me what you did."

She got up and started to pace the living room, wringing her hands. "I planned it all out carefully. He was still in the hospital. In the Cleveland Public Library I looked up the management of St. Luke's Hospital, getting the names of the director, the board members, all the doctors, finding out the times of visiting hours, the layout of the hospital, everything I could think of that I might need to know."

She stopped pacing and put one hand on the back of a chair for support. "Then I prepared my appearance. I wore a dark business suit with a white blouse. Low-heeled shoes. I put my hair in a tight knot at the back of my head. I wore a pair of glasses with dark rims. And around my neck I had a chain with a plastic identification card; one side had the name of the hospital printed on it and the other had the word 'Volunteer.' I bought the most official-looking clipboard and heavy pen I could find. And I bought a small leather bag, something like a doctor's bag, for my ... bird. The penguin cocktail shaker.

"I took the noon plane to Chicago and picked up a car at the airport. My reservation at the hotel was under the name Mrs. A. Smith. That evening after dark, I checked my appearance, then drove to the hospital, arriving at 9:30, parking as close to the door as possible, for I wanted to leave my coat and heavy boots in the car. I left my purse, too, taking only the clipboard and the bag. I wanted to look as though I had been working there all day.

"When I entered the hospital, I stopped, pretending to check my clipboard, just in order to get used to the surroundings. I walked around the waiting room as if I knew it well, flipping the pages attached to my clipboard. I smiled and said 'Hi' to the two women who ran the coffee bar. And I greeted the girl at the small gift shop. Twice I sat down and pretended to work on my clipboard. That gave the staff time to get used to my being there.

"Then I approached the nurses' station at the end of the hall. I stopped again, looking at my clipboard and flipping through the sheets of paper on it. I listened to the conversation in order to hear what name the nurses were using for the receptionist. Then I stepped up to her.

"'Jean, I need to check some names with you. How about Martin, T.? Is that a patient on today's list?'

"'Why, no. Who wants to know?'

"'I think it was Dr. Abbot. Or maybe it was Dr. Perry. Anyway, one of them asked for a double check of these names. How about a Landis, K.? Is that a patient today?'

"'Yes, Landis is still here. I don't believe I know you.'

"'Oh, sorry, I'm Betty Payne. I thought everyone knew me! Anyway, I've got to get this list checked tonight. Is there a room number for Landis, K.?

"'Yes, 303.'

"'Thanks, Jean.'

"I stood around pretending to put marks on my papers while others came up to the receptionist. When she seemed busy enough, I disappeared in the direction of the elevators. I knew that a visitor to 303 that late was unlikely. Landis's wife was sick in the hospital herself, so she wouldn't be with him. And on big holidays the hospital always had little more than a skeleton staff. If a nurse was around, she probably wouldn't stay long.

"It took me only a few minutes to find room 303. I tapped softly at the door. No answer. Slowly, I opened the door. The lights had been dimmed. It was a big room with two beds. It even had two doors. The bed nearest the door I had opened was empty. I walked slowly and quietly toward the bed with Landis in it.

"As I'd expected, he was hooked up to a machine by tubes that ran into his nose and arms. His eyes were closed. What a small figure he was! And his white hair looked even messier than it did in pictures. His mouth was like a small, straight slit. He breathed noisily.

"I hated him. Hated him! The Commissioner of Baseball, indeed. He was not *my* Commissioner! I was glad to see him helpless, glad to see that he could do nothing to stop me.

"I came close to his bed and started to unpack the bird. Somehow, I dropped my clipboard on the floor! It made a clattery noise. And he woke up.

"His eyes were dark, and at first he showed no reaction to me. But when he saw the look on my face—a look of anger and determination—he began to show fear. I was glad. Glad! His mouth started to move, but he seemed unable to produce a word. A few sounds came out as I took my bird out of the bag. He seemed to be gurgling. I picked up the bird and held it in front of me. His mouth twisted, and awful sounds began to come out of his mouth. I began to lift the bird and turning it so that it would land on his head with the bird's feet first. He started to lift his head from the pillow.

"Then I heard the ringing of a bell. It was connected with his bed. It must have been set to ring when his body was stressed. Then his head fell back, and he was still. His eyes stared. By then I was repacking the bird and picking up the clipboard. I left quickly by the second door as a nurse entered by the first. There was a commotion. A doctor arrived as I reached the stairway. I got out of the building as soon as I could. The next morning's newspaper said that Landis had died during the night.

"So I am the one who killed him."

Rick was silent. His nervousness was gone; he was thinking. Then he got up and poured himself another glass of wine. "This," he said, "will go away. After a time, you will feel better."

She sat down. "I doubt it. The whole thing rankles in me. My act settled nothing. It reminds me of a music course I took at Cleveland College."

"Music course? What do you mean?"

"Bruckner's Seventh. Do you know it? It's full of unresolved themes. They remind me of life. Like the motifs in Bruckner, the themes in life don't always resolve themselves. They keep rolling along, or they halt in a minor key instead of returning to base. Meanwhile, a new motif appears, bowing to introduce itself to us, and we become taken up by it. The way my attention was taken by my son."

He raised his eyebrows. "You mean, before we can really settle a problem, something else takes our attention, so the problem is always there. Do you think life is really like that?"

"I think so. Nothing from my earlier life seems resolved. Yet other things have come into it. Just as in Bruckner. As soon as you think you've caught the ball, it dances away from you."

He began to frown. What was she talking about?

"Why can't it be like Mozart?" Her voice became shrill. "In his music, everything has an ending. Every play gets completed before the next one starts. With Mozart, you always know where you stand. By the time you get into the ninth, you know exactly how the game's going to end. Everything gets sorted out. Not with Bruckner.

"And he keeps changing keys. Why does he do that? Why can't he finish each inning, like Mozart, so we know where we stand?" Her voice trembled.

"Annie, what are you talking about? Get hold of yourself!"

"I'm talking about not knowing where I'm going in this life." Her voice sounded harsh and shaky. "Nothing seems to move along smoothly, with each inning tying up loose ends before the next one starts. The base paths are too full of bumps."

"For heaven's sake, Annie. Life isn't baseball, and it isn't music. You have to make life for yourself. Decide how you want it to turn out, what your goals are. Then take charge of your life."

"But is that possible? I feel pulled in different ways. It's as if my distant past is controlling me."

"Distant past? What distant past?"

"I felt it in Sicily. Ancient ancestors, ones who were like me, did things..." Her voice trailed off.

"Nonsense. Your ancestors are mine, too, and they don't control me. Why should they control you? You're imagining things."

"Have you read about the ancient Greek idea of Fate—how we're forced to some ending we don't even want, by what our ancient ancestors decided?"

"That's crazy. Our ancient ancestors don't set us on our paths of life. We do."

"Maybe you set yourself on your life path. I seem unable to do it."

He became impatient. "Don't be ridiculous. If I can choose my path, you can. And I've chosen." He paused, then looked at her closely. "I'm going to tell you what it is, if you promise not to reveal it to anyone."

Now she became attentive, even calm. "All right."

"I'm doing dangerous work. I'm a secret informant for the FBI. I keep the FBI aware of what's going on in the five New York families, as they call the five Mafia organizations in New York."

"But Rick. That's really frightening. How did you get into this kind of work?"

"I think I'll keep that to myself. Don't forget, you've promised not to tell anyone. Even our mother."

"Yes. I promise." She sat back in her chair, thinking. Her mind had finally moved off her own situation. "I can't imagine doing anything that dangerous."

"We do what we think we must."

"Now you're the one who sounds as though you're being controlled by Fate."

"Baloney. I just ... realized one day that I had some special knowledge, and I didn't like having it. I decided that I wasn't going to end up like Dom."

Annie thought about that. "How am I going to end up, after what I've done?"

Then another thought: I wonder if anyone suspects me of either of my crimes. She felt tired and began coughing. Rick thinks I will forget. But what I did in Chicago I will never forget.

In Chicago, another person did not forget a volunteer named Betty Payne, a stranger who asked questions on the day of the baseball commissioner's death and never came back. Jean Stewart, the woman at the main nursing station at St. Luke's Hospital, thought about the stranger now and then, wondering why she showed up suddenly and then disappeared.

Annie invited Isabel to stay for a few days during the Christmas holidays. While Mrs. Kane made plans to treat Annie's guest, Annie decided to examine the papers she had brought back from the Cleveland bank deposit box.

Walking into the small room she had furnished as an office, she sat down at her French Provincial desk and began methodically going through the papers. Immediately, her mind went back to the day in Taormina, in the elegant San Domenico Palace Hotel, after her husband John had lost his life and she was looking through his wallet and his envelopes of money, tickets, and information about their tour. She realized that she had been postponing this work because it would bring back too many memories.

Then Charlie Jones phoned. Do I really want to go out with him? she wondered. He seems like a dilettante, just moving through life at a leisurely pace. But then, perhaps I'm a dilettante, too. I think I'll put him off for a while; I have too much to think about. She told him she was suffering from a cough, which was true.

Bringing herself back to the present, she thought: If there was a number—or perhaps a key with a number, or a paper describing the account in Andorra—I don't recall seeing it the day I looked through papers in Taormina.

Now she was coming across other papers: Life insurance policies on her and on Johnny, certificates of vaccination, diplomas, the deed to her new home, the certificate declaring Anna Cardello married to John Smith, and a multi-page trust agreement in which Emmet Smith bestowed a lump sum and a monthly stipend on Anna Cardello Smith.

As she opened the trust agreement, a letter fell out of the back, a letter from a bank in Andorra. The bank manager was writing to Mr. John Smith, Esq., assuring him that the "sums on deposit" in the bank would be "safe from discovery" by anyone, according to the laws of the country. It advised him that he would receive "an annual accounting" of this deposit and invited him to visit Andorra at any time to receive additional assurance from the bank's staff and enjoy touring their "delightful little country." The letter failed to state the number of the account.

Annual accounting. Where were the notices of annual accounting? She had seen none. Where had they been sent?

Then she began thinking of the safe deposit box. She was not the only holder of a key to the box in which these papers were kept; Emmet Smith, John's father, held the other, and it was he who had obtained the box for her in the first place, on her return from Sicily to Bratenahl. Probably, he had gone through the papers before handing them to her to place in the box.

Why, yes! It was Father Smith. He's the one who must have the number of the Andorran account. Had he any idea what that account contained and where the money came from?

When the phone rang again, she didn't expect to hear the voice of Carl Morris. "I'm in town for a science teachers' convention. May I see you?" She welcomed his presence, inviting him for a meal, which Mrs. Kane gladly provided. Visitors gave the housekeeper a chance to shine, and shine she did, whipping up a four-course meal out of the contents of the refrigerator. Being a discreet as well as a clever woman, she left after cleaning up.

Annie was so glad to see Carl that she gave him a hug at the door. Over the salad at dinner he shared his news: "I've left high school teaching for a full-time instructorship at Fenn College. I prefer working with older students. They're usually more serious about learning. And this is a step upward for me."

"I admire your pursuit of a fine career, Carl. I wish I had your determination." She looked at him carefully; she liked the way he looked.

"You could do just about anything you wanted, if you turned your mind to it, Annie."

She shook her head sadly. "I'm too distracted by events in my life over which I seem to have no control." She turned her head and picked up a tissue for her nose.

"Anne, that's a terrible cough you have. What does your doctor say about it?"

"He says it's not a germ; I must have some kind of allergic response to something in my house. I don't cough when I'm not home."

He stood up and looked around. "When I came in I thought I there was a recognizable odor in the air." He turned to her. "Have you had your house weatherproofed recently?"

"Yes. Why?"

"That smell is from the solid foam sometimes used in weatherproofing houses. It's installed in the attic. May I have a look at it? How do I access the attic?"

He refused to take no for an answer and followed her upstairs, where he pulled down the steps that led up under the roof. For a few minutes she heard his footsteps marching around above her, along with some tearing sounds. Then he descended.

"Annie, you are breathing toxic fumes of sulfur dioxide, the gas that forms when the sulfurous compound in the weatherproofing gets wet. Water is seeping into it through the roof. That's why gas is escaping. Behind it is some drywall that is releasing hydrogen sulfide, another toxic gas. Get this drywall and weatherproofing replaced as soon as possible with something more up-to-date. And have the roof redone in the spring."

"Sulfur gas?"

"The weatherproofing and drywall are exuding the same toxic fumes released by a volcano when it erupts. They smell a little like rotten eggs. Eventually, you could be poisoned to death."

Frightened, Annie stumbled to her small office to check the phone book. "I'll call the company right now."

"Have them tear it all out and replace it with something without sulfur that will not react to dampness."

When Carl left, he held her close. "Annie, you're important to me. I want you to take care of yourself. Perhaps I will some day persuade you to return to Cleveland."

She thought, I feel warmly toward Carl. I love being close to him. But I don't deserve happiness.

She remained sitting in her living room, feeling numb. Poisoned by sulfur. It seems to be following me. Sulfur, that devil's gas from hell, could have been my punishment for the terrible things I've done. If I hadn't met Carl, that is. He saved me.

When Annie talked to Mrs. Kane about the odor, the housekeeper declared, "I thought it was the drain cleaner I've been using on these old toilets because it contains sulfur. How awful that you have been breathing poisonous fumes all day and all night! In fact, you would be closer to the attic at night, when you're asleep upstairs. It's lucky your friend Mr. Morris is a scientist."

The workers came to tear the attic apart, and the house was a mess for a full day, but the job got done before Annie's company arrived. For Isabel made good on her promise to come to Boston and visit Annie during the Christmas holidays, while Johnny would be at home. Mrs. Kane, informed of the impending visit, bustled about importantly, calling in the window cleaner, furnishing the blue guest suite with crisp new sheets and scented soap, consulting with Annie about Christmas decorations, and planning meals to include New England specialties. "Corn cakes for breakfast, with the best maple syrup. Baked beans for lunch, served with steamed brown bread. Some good Vermont cheddar for hors d'oeuvre..."

Annie asked for crab cakes and wondered aloud whether lobster was available. The day before Johnny was to get home, Mrs. Kane busied herself with baking a Boston Cream Pie as well as shopping for what she already knew Johnny loved: Cider and freshly-made doughnuts.

Isabel, delayed in Cleveland for several days, arrived when Johnny's school vacation was nearly over. She came in wearing long leather boots, tight woolen ski pants, and a short fur jacket with matching hat. Shaking off the snow, she handed Mrs. Kane two shopping bags full of gifts and cried "Merry Christmas to all!"

Removing Isabel's hip-length boots and applying cozy pink slippers took Mrs. Kane ten minutes, Isabel all the while exclaiming about the charm of Annie's living room and its holiday décor. "You could charge for admission; it's like a Christmas museum. You know, speaking of museums, when I was young I thought I was named after Isabel Stewart Gardner, who created that Boston museum in her home, until I found out otherwise."

"Mrs. Kane is the decorator, with Johnny's help." The boy hugged his aunt and stood there grinning with pleasure.

When they were settled around the fireplace, Isabel began talking about her family. "It's so pleasant to be with family during the holidays. John and

I used to love to hear the stories my grandfather Trevor Smith told about his youth when we had family gatherings.

"My favorite is the one about his working for his father, a shopkeeper. In the shop he met a woman whose family members, the Beechers, were abolitionists. They wrote and spoke against slavery. Isabella Beecher used to come into the shop owned by Grandfather Trevor's family, and she would rant against the laws, including one that said a woman has no legal existence separate from her husband's. Grandfather was so impressed with her he fell in love.

"Of course, Isabella Beecher was already married to a law student named John Hooker, but that didn't stop Grandfather Trevor. He followed her around and sent her mash notes. When the abolitionists in Hartford formed committees calling themselves Wide Awakes, Grandfather Trevor parodied their efforts by establishing a baseball club also called the Wide Awakes, claiming that he gave the team that name because the players met to play their games early in the morning, before going to their jobs.

"But the townspeople serious about abolition were not amused, and they sent a delegation to Trevor's home to request his departure from Hartford. His parents were so embarrassed that they sent him away. He told us he was drummed out of town. That's how he came to Cleveland to start a new life. And that's why I was named Isabel, after Isabella Beecher."

Johnny found his aunt's tale mesmerizing. "Gosh, Aunt Isabel, I've heard of the Beechers in history class at school. What a story!"

"And maybe it's even true!" Isabel replied with a grin.

It was seven in the evening of Isabel's second day, after Johnny had discovered that Boston Cream Pie was really a cake, and Isabel was suggesting a luncheon at the old Boston bar and restaurant called Locke-Ober, when the phone rang. It was Mrs. Allen, Father Smith's housekeeper, asking to speak to Isabel, whose face dropped as she listened. The holiday cheeriness disappeared. "I'll be there as soon as I can. Probably by tomorrow afternoon."

To Annie's questioning look, she responded, "Father has had a massive heart attack. He's in a coma and isn't expected to recover. I must go back to Cleveland."

20

AFTER JOHNNY RETURNED TO SCHOOL, Annie left on the train to join Isabel in Cleveland. At Isabel's request, she stayed in the Smith home in an old-fashioned room with wicker furniture, a pottery bowl of fake nasturtiums, and somebody's unfinished knitting in a basket. By then Emmet Smith was gone from this life. Annie arrived in time for a funeral attended by people with important names in Cleveland, like Sherwin, Williams, Mather, Case, and Severance. Half the parish of Old Stone Church paid their respects at the Ridgewood Funeral Home and signed its guest book.

The formal reading of the will took place in Emmet Smith's comfortable home office. As expected, aside from bequests to people like Mrs. Allen and donations to his pet charities, Emmet had left half his estate to his daughter and the other half divided among Annie and her son. Trust funds guaranteed their lifelong support.

Afterwards, Attorney Ellison handed Annie an envelope labeled, "Personal to Anna Cardello Smith." Surprised and curious, she waited until she could be alone in the guest room assigned to her before opening it.

Dear Anna,

A matter relating to my son's effects is not covered in my will because it has to do with something delicate. When I found, among the papers in John's safe deposit box, correspondence about an account in the country of Andorra, I knew it must be something less than above board, since he had kept it from me, and probably from you as well. Andorra is a country where Americans and Europeans hide money from the government.

Shortly before his marriage to you, I realized that John had suddenly come into a great deal of money for which I did not know the source. Although he declared he had become very rich and would not work another day, he never explained how it had happened, acting rather furtive about it. Perhaps the money came from gambling, which he engaged in frequently, despite my disapproval. He must have placed those questionable funds in the Andorran account. He doubtless expected to live on this money for the rest of his life, doing nothing at all.

Before you returned from Sicily, I gathered the correspondence about this account, but I could not access the money, since you are his heir and I am not.

So I had a document drawn up in which you assigned this account to me. You signed this document unknowingly, among many others that I presented to you on your return, telling you only that they were formalities. I regret this deception, but I felt responsible for all your legal matters, so you signed over this money to me without realizing it.

Upon inquiry to the Andorran bank, I discovered that the money in the account amounted to a great fortune. I withdrew about half, placing it in various banks here and abroad, in accounts bearing your name. I believe you deserve this money, to help make up for your aborted marriage. I left the rest of the money in the account.

Enclosed is the number of the Andorran account and the bank books for all your new accounts, along with a document legally returning the Andorran account to you. If you have any idea where the money left in the Andorran account really belongs, please see that it gets to that person. All you need to do is send it to the person with a document, prepared by an attorney, stipulating that you, the legal owner of the account, give its contents to that person.

"I was really just getting to know him," she told Isabel when they were finally alone in Emmet's study, having a glass of sherry. She was not about to share what she had just learned; it opened too many difficult subjects.

"He was a solid person, a fine man. I'm glad he left you a personal letter." Isabel was too polite to ask what the letter contained.

Annie was thinking: All of us have character flaws. He took something he believed belonged to me; then he gave it back.

"The death of a parent is traumatic. It was hard losing my mother so soon after John's death. She was a rather exotic person, with Eastern European tastes. And she told everyone I was a premature baby, whereas my grandmother Maudie said Nonsense, Isabel was a fully-formed, hearty and healthy child, whereas John was puny! Now I'll miss my father greatly," Isabel went on "I'm almost sorry I arrived before he passed on; I prefer to remember him in life. Death is not a pleasant thing to witness."

Immediately a scene flashed before Annie's eyes: A figure rushed forward from behind her, grasped John, and hurtled him to his death like a twig in a storm. She heard a scream, her own. Death is not a pleasant thing to witness.

"Annie, are you all right? Oh, again I am speaking of death. This must be as hard on you as it is on me. It brings back difficult memories." She put an arm around her sister-in-law's shoulder. "Let's speak of something else. In fact, let's do something else. We should get away for a few days. How about New York? We could see some shows, visit those museums we both love, try some new restaurants. We can stay at Father's club."

"But what about Tina? Wouldn't she like to come?"

"Tina is a complete homebody." Isabel rose. In a nod to custom, she wore stockings and a black silk dress that floated gently as she walked across the room, then came back again. "She would like nothing better than to think of some new treats she can prepare for my return, practice them till they are perfect, and put on a big homecoming welcome."

"Maybe you're right. A change like a visit to New York sounds like fun. The city won't be so crowded with tourists in January. First, I'll visit my mother. Meanwhile, would you go ahead and plan the trip?" Isabel left to get started on plans.

Now, Annie thought, sitting in a padded wicker chair in the old-fashioned bedroom: This Andorran account. Emmet Smith did what he thought was right. I must carry through with his request... I think I know now why he said he wanted to get Johnny away from "questionable influences": He suspected that whatever questionable person owned the money in the Andorra account caused the house disaster! No doubt he was right. I have to get rid of this money by seeing that Joe Martino receives it; then he will stop bothering me. But how? I certainly don't want to meet him or have anything to do with him. My only way of contacting such people is—of course—my brother Rick. When I get to my mother's house, I'll phone him in New York. Meanwhile, I'll find an attorney, a discreet one.

That afternoon Annie took a cab to her mother's home in the old Collinwood district. The house seemed smaller and more drab and dreary than ever. She asked to stay there for a couple of days. Her first job was to look for and find the business section of the phone book and study the list of attorneys. Selecting one took only a few minutes. Then she began phoning.

I'll be glad when this is all over with and I'm rid of this Andorran money, or what is left of it. I don't even want to know how much it is.

That evening Isabel called. The New York trip was all arranged.

Jerry Finch woke up early in the apartment on West 73rd Street. He was getting used to the speed and intensity of New York life; it was not unlike his work for the FBI, he thought. Something new was always happening.

"Some streaky rashers, Love?" Molly called. "With a pile of scrambles?"

He smiled at her use of Irish terms, an affectation that had become a joke between them because she had been born in New York. "If there's lots of coffee, yes. And some of those scones you made Saturday."

As he shaved, he savored the tip from an informer revealing that the Five Families in New York planned a convention with members of the mob from all over the country, to meet in an upstate New York town not far from Binghamton called Apalachin. It would be held at a gangster's private estate, its access road always carefully roped off from the public.

This is finally our chance to net some of those elusive characters such as Joe Martino, he thought. We'll start getting our strategy mapped out today.

As he walked into the kitchen, he paused to watch his wife serve the breakfast and congratulated himself all over again at finding her. Her orange-red hair tumbled about as she bent to put plates on the table. Looking up at him, she gave him that joyous smile that had first attracted him to her.

Her bright blue eyes softened, and he just had to give her a hug.

"Careful, now. Soon we're to have a wee bairn."

"Molly, 'wee bairn' is Scottish."

"Oh, that's right, I'm Irish!"

"Besides, it had better not be soon, if you're only three months along. Did your boss seem happy about your leaving at six months?" Jerry sat down and picked up one of the "streaky rashers" of bacon.

"Not happy, mind you, but accepting. He's talked to a couple of candidates who could probably run the office as well as I do." She poured the coffee.

"Nobody could treat the radio stars who come to the studio as well as you do."

"I just butter them up; that's all they need. Also tell them where to sit and how to use the microphone."

"Speaking of butter—"

"Here, me lad; right here."

How could I ever have thought that Annie was the one for me? Molly is a revelation: Always cheerful, never moons around regretting her past or wondering why her life isn't perfect. Molly is so warm and loving. I'm glad

I finally grew up. Then, aloud, "I'm glad I walked into that radio station last summer and found you there."

She put her hand over his. "So am I. Never thought I'd fall for a detective... Well, an agent, with a pol for a brother and five loud kids for nephews." She buttered a scone. "Your brother Vito is very effective on the radio."

"More important, he loves the way you treat his noisy kids."

"I'm crazy about them. And I can hardly wait to have our own. I'll teach them to eat boiled praties with the skins on."

He smiled as he thought how wonderful it was to have a woman to be close to. He thought of his friendship with his sister Mary, who had perished on a hospital ship during the war. This more than makes up for the loss of Mary, he thought.

Joe Martino was miffed. He muttered to some of his men, "I don't know why we have to meet in another national convention. We just had one of those last year; I ran it myself, and it went smoothly. As for the recent Albert Anastasia killing, we could have straightened that out among ourselves here in New York; I'm pretty sure some of his own men did it. This new convention is Tommy Lucchese's doing. He's always trying to undermine me in some way."

They sat there looking at him, some of them nodding.

I wonder why I even bother talking to them, he thought.

Martino decided instead to undermine Lucchese by going upstate a day in advance of the convention and having a private talk with his influential cousin Stefano Magaddino, who held property in nearby Endicott. Let the others meet the next day in Apalachin; I might just stay away from there entirely. I can sit back and see what happens without me.

Rick Cardello lay there thinking: I need to be persistent but still act supportive. So far, I'm not getting much information except that the Five Families plan to meet others in convention soon.

Then Rick got a break. Martino phoned and asked for his company in Smithtown, on Long Island, to help plan the Martino Family's strategy concerning the convention.

After a few minutes, Rick got up and made a phone call to his FBI boss: "I hope Martino doesn't have in mind punishing me for something. I don't know what I did to annoy him. At least now he seems friendly." Rick got dressed, ate some cereal, and packed an overnight bag.

Then, leaving his third-floor walkup on Murray Hill, Rick strolled west toward Fifth Avenue, avoiding the slush, and walked north to catch a train at Grand Central.

He missed the phone call from his sister, which was recorded on his Tel-Magnet, an experimental answering machine the FBI had given him.

Rick spent several days in Martino's home discussing tactics to be used with the other mobsters like Lucchese, beginning with how to open the subject with his cousin Stefano Magaddino, who had a country place in Endicott, a town near Apalachin. In the end, Martino finally confirmed his decision not to attend the convention at all but simply to spend time continuing to talk things over with his cousin Stefano and letting the Apalachin convention go on without him. He decided that Rick would be one of the men he would take with him to Stefano's house in Endicott.

Sam Giancana of the Chicago Family welcomed the invitation to a convention in Apalachin. The previous gathering, held at the same Apalachin estate and run by Joe Martino, had been conciliatory. This time Giancana decided to take along his right-hand man Frank Nitti, along with Tony Acardo, Paul Riccia, and Vincent del Vecchio.

21

MARTINO TOLD HIS MEN THAT THEY would start out for Endicott in two cars the following day. That was two days before the big meeting in Apalachin. Rick rode in the same car as Martino.

They had hardly left Martino's driveway in Smithtown when Rick asked to stop in Manhattan at his apartment. "I need some clean clothes and to check my phone messages."

Martino thought for a moment before replying, "Okay. I'm coming into your apartment with you."

Startled, Rick warned, "I live in a third-floor walkup, Boss, and you're just getting over the flu."

"It's okay. I want to see where you live."

"Sure, Boss." But Rick worried: What if there's a message from my FBI leader? And what if I've left something lying around that connects me with the FBI? Martino's move also revealed (Rick thought) that The Boss suspected his newest Family member of being a traitor. He felt nervous. "By the way, where did you get that phone-answering gadget you use, anyway?"

"A Jewish guy I know had one for answering the phone on the Sabbath, when he's not supposed to work. He got me one like his."

As soon as they walked in—Martino showing a few signs of his age after walking up three flights—the flashing light on Rick's answering machine became obvious to them both. "Go ahead, get your message," challenged Joe Martino, looking Rick full in the eyes.

"It could wait," Rick muttered, on his way to the bedroom.

"No! It can't wait. Get it now!"

Rick turned, hardening his face in a frown. Then he moved toward the machine, hoping. They both listened to the following message:

"Rick, this is Annie. I need your help. I just found out that my late husband John used a bank account in a country called Andorra in order to hide money that he extorted from someone else. My father-in-law, who died last week, discovered it in some papers John left. It seems that John was blackmailing Joe Martino, someone you know. Vincenzo knew about it. A few months ago, Vincenzo told me there was such an account, and that the money in it belonged to Martino. I couldn't believe it. But it must be true, because when my father-in-law's will was read, he left me a private message about it. Since the money was left to me, I've had an attorney prepare a document transferring ownership to Joe Martino, and I'd like to get this document and information to him. I'm on my way to New York with Isabel, staying at the University Club, and I'll have the papers with me. If I bring the papers to your apartment, can you get them to Martino? Vincenzo hinted that Martino was the one who had my home destroyed, in the mistaken notion that I had his money. Well, now that I do have it, I want to get rid of it. Please, Rick, call me at the club."

Martino sat down. "Well. That clears something up. So your sister has the account number. And now she knows that money is mine. She's even willing to give it back. So you didn't know about it. Well... Listen, Cardello, call and tell her she has to bring it to me." He was thinking, I was suspicious of him for nothing.

"Bring it to you? Where?"

"In Endicott, where I'm going. I want to get my hands on it immediately."

"You mean, you want her to drive to Magaddino's place?"

"That's just what I mean. Call and tell her. Now."

Rick hesitated. "I don't like to have my sister mixed up with these guys. Are you sure she won't be in the way?"

"She can have a room for staying overnight. I want that account brought to me. Today."

"Okay, Boss. I'll call her. But you said Magaddino's place is way out in the country... You'll have to give driving directions."

"Pick up the phone. Right now. Tell her. Then I'll get on the phone with directions."

Annie lay back on the bed, reeling from the words she'd just heard on her answering machine.

I don't want to do this. But I suppose I must. Rick seems to think it's absolutely necessary. Now what am I going to tell Isabel?

Annie and Isabel had just returned from a visit to The Cloisters, where they were surrounded by medieval art and enjoyed walking through the building's arcades, with their views of the Hudson. Isabel wanted to go to her room to rest and call Tina, then check on their show tickets for the evening.

Annie decided: I'll have to avoid explaining it all. But I'll need Isabel's help.

Calling Isabel's room, Annie just said that "something has come up. I need to go upstate for a day and night to help my brother Rick. Could José at the Club desk find me a driver?"

Surprised but supportive as always, Isabel said, "I'm sorry you'll miss *Damn Yankees* tonight. But I know my father had a regular driver he always called in New York. José will get him. Let me know if there's anything else I can do." Afterwards, Isabel thought: Rick is the brother who left the country with her and John. I'm sure he was in trouble; that's why Annie took him to Sicily. He must need help again. Annie always responds to his appeals; she's too nice to this black sheep.

José told Annie that Mr. Smith's regular driver, Anthony, although he lived in Astoria, Queens, worked in Manhattan. "I'll contact him right away." She waited at José's desk while the dispatcher got through to the driver. Anthony responded that he was just dropping off a fare at Grand Central. "I'll be right over. Sure, I can do an overnight. Just let me phone my wife. Yes, I know where Endicott is. Big shoe company there." Anthony, although he didn't know Annie, was confident that he'd be well compensated for his time by any member of the Smith family.

When Joe Martino returned to the car after visiting Rick's apartment, other members of the party had become restless. "Dice" Aiello, who was driving, started grouching: "What were you doing all this time, Cardello, having a bubble bath?"

Martino put a stop to complaints. "None of your remarks, Dice. Something got settled. We're going to have an extra visitor at Magaddino's place. You'll find out more later."

Anthony the driver muttered aloud as he left the University Club with Annie. He was planning his route to their destination. "Lucky we got such clear weather. I think I'll take Route 17 north, and we can make a stop at Red Apple Rest. We won't have to stop again till about Tarrytown—ever been there? Very nice. Or maybe Monroe. That's sort of a resort area. Then we'll go up into the Catskills, maybe stop in Liberty. This is scenic country. Binghamton is the nearest big town..."

Annie was barely listening, until he mentioned baseball.

"Johnny Logan, the baseball player on the Braves, comes from Endicott. He was a pretty good player. Know anything about baseball?"

"Yes, but not the male professionals. I played women's ball."

"Oh, softball?"

"No. Women's baseball." Anthony heard a touch of irritation in her voice, so he paused, but only for a moment.

"I once saw a couple of women's teams from the All American Women's League play a game when I went out to the Midwest to visit my sister in Wisconsin. An outfielder named Kurys. Sophie Kurys: Could she ever hit! Stole bases, too. I was surprised."

Annie, looking at New Yorkers negotiating the slush in the streets, failed to respond. Her sour looks, caused by her jealousy of players like Kurys, who'd had a chance to play real pro ball, made Anthony decide not to continue that line of talk.

She was thinking: From the sublime world of antique art in the serene setting of The Cloisters, I've been jolted back to reality. Fearful reality. I don't really want to meet Joe Martino. Or any of his cohorts. But it seems that I must. What will his attitude be? Will he be full of anger? Will he demand to know what's in the account? Am I going to convince him that I knew nothing of John's effort to cheat a gangster by blackmailing him? Above all, are Rick and I going to come out of this safely? But why do I think of myself as better than those mobsters? I've killed two people myself.

At Red Apple Rest, which proved to be a touristy restaurant with busy toilets, she and Anthony stayed fifteen minutes. Anthony drove through the Tarrytown area without stopping. After passing through a state park, Anthony found a drugstore in Monroe that served ice cream sodas; Annie treated him, watching the sky darken. At Liberty, Anthony gassed up the car. Soon after, they were driving due north through another park-like area. At Deposit they turned west to Binghamton, with another stop at a luncheonette, for coffee and to use the toilet.

By then she had found out that Anthony liked music; that his mother had sung him and his four brothers to sleep with an Italian lullaby called "Dormi Dormi," which he sang for her; that his family came from a Sicilian town called Marsala (same name as the wine, an Arabic word that meant "the port of Allah"); and that his own last name was DeLuca.

"That Italian lullaby you sang is addressed to a daughter, not a son."

"What, you know it? You are Italian?"

"My parents are Sicilian Americans. The song is sung to the mother's *bella figlia*, pretty daughter."

"True, true. How strange that you know this."

"I think I should tell you, Anthony, that the place you are taking me to in Endicott is owned by a member of a crime family, a man named Stefano Magaddino. I must see another man there in order to give him something that belongs to him, something I didn't realize I had until last week. I'm not comfortable being at this place, but at least my brother will be there, and he will protect me."

"Oh. I never thought I'd ever meet any of those guys," Anthony remarked thoughtfully. "Not that I want to. Is it all right if I drop you off at the house and go to a motel? There's one just south of Endicott; we'll come to it soon. It's called the Parkway Motel, in the town of Vestal. I'll stop and pick up their card so I can leave you the phone number; you can call me there when you're ready to leave."

Darkness fell just as Anthony entered Vestal. The Parkway Motel, well lit, stood on their left. Picking up the card took Anthony only a few moments, although he thought the owner looked at him curiously when he reserved a room for one night, saying he'd be back again soon.

The Susquehanna River arises out of Lake Otsego in Cooperstown, New York, where the Baseball Hall of Fame was built in 1939. In the so-called Southern Tier of the mountains, the river meandered on either side of Route 17; sometimes it lay to the north of the road, sometimes to the south. A bridge over the river connected Vestal, on its south side, to Endicott, on its north. Anthony negotiated the bridge and turned onto Endicott's Main Street, after which he followed the directions to Magaddino's farm that Annie had copied from the phone message Rick initiated and Joe Martino completed.

Driving slowly on the narrow roads, they finally came to the house, a large wooden structure set between snowy meadows. It seemed to be a renovated farmhouse. The long driveway had been cleared, so Anthony drove to the front door and stopped. A light over the doorway went on. Anthony opened the car door for Annie and handed her an overnight bag. Turning, he saw a big, square man standing there. Anthony waited nervously as Annie walked up the front steps and said, "My name is Anna Smith."

The man nodded, took her bag, and said "Come in." Anthony waved and left.

Inside, Annie looked at the square man. His face looked square, too.

Although his upper lip curved, it was pressed against the lower one so that his mouth looked thin. Heavy brows bent protectively over intense brown eyes. His hair was starting to recede, but his hard face and demeanor spoke power, the kind exuded by the kind of person who expects to be in charge.

"Joe Martino. Meet my cousin, Stefano; my Uncle John; and my friend Gaspar." The men nodded at her but did not rise. "We will go into the next room to talk."

Still carrying her bag, he led the way to a dining room. As in so many old homes, a door had to be opened each time a different room was entered. The dining table had been cleared, but obviously a meal had just been eaten there. "May I give you a glass of wine?"

"No, thank you. I just want to get this over with."

"Well, I think we need to talk first." He put the bag down and indicated the chair she should take, while he took the one at the head of the table. "Now, I want to make some things clear." He spoke deliberately and assertively. "Among the people of my tradition, I am highly respected. As a man of honor, I enjoy a reputation for fairness and tact. Others turn to me for counsel. Not everyone has always agreed with me, but they always know just where I stand."

He paused. Annie sat there silently, wondering where in the world this extraordinary speech would lead.

"Now, although I have been harmed, I am not angry, for I realize that you may not be the one who harmed me. And you say you are willing to make things right by returning what is not yours. I have a right to be angry against those who took something from me, but if they are no longer alive, then I cannot pursue my grievance against them. At least you are willing to make the restitution that they should have made."

Annie began to realize that this pompous speech came from a man who had to explain everything to himself, and do it before an audience.

She decided to fall in with the course of the conversation and do some of her own explaining. "Mr. Martino," she began, "I knew nothing about the existence of this account until my father-in-law, Emmet Smith, died, although Vincent del Vecchio hinted at its existence some time ago. When my father-in-law passed on, he left the account to me, explaining that it came from his son, my late husband John. As far as I am concerned, it is tainted money, and it is not mine. All I want to do is get rid of it."

"All right. That sounds like the right approach. Do you guarantee that the account is intact?"

She sat up straighter. "I guarantee nothing, except that the account is just as it was given to me. What happened to it, if anything, between the time my husband ... established it and the day my father-in-law died ... that's not my responsibility. So I am unable to tell you anything about it. Just take it, please, and have done with it. I have it right here, with the statement prepared by an attorney assigning ownership to you." And she started fishing around in her purse.

"You seem very anxious to divest yourself of this money."

"It is not money that I earned or anyone in my family has earned. I don't want it."

"And you were bold to agree to come here."

"I seemed to have no choice, since you did not propose coming to me for it. So I must come to you." Then she took a chance and reminded him of something he had already done to her. "Surely you realize now that what happened to my home in Bratenahl was a mistake and that I did not deserve it." She handed him the envelope.

That gave him pause. "The accident that befell your house was the result of over-enthusiasm on the part of some friends who mistakenly believed they could force the return of my property by damaging yours."

"It was a useless gesture, since I did not have your property."

After a few seconds, he nodded, accepting the implied criticism. But he avoided apology. Annie realized that he was not the type of person to offer one.

"So you have plenty of money of your own?" He took the envelope.

"I have money given to me by my father-in-law. Over the years, he made lucrative investments, and he left his money to me and my son as well as to his daughter."

"And what if I found the account short?"

That gave her pause, since she knew that Emmet Smith had dipped into it, if only for her own benefit. She decided she must stick to her claim of innocence about the contents. "I have no control over what happened before it came to me. If you are a man of honor, I am a woman of honor, and you must accept that I am not responsible for the content of the account. I instructed the attorney to state that whatever is in the account is yours. That's all I can do for you."

He was silent. He seemed nonplussed by her claim of being an honorable woman; that was probably a new idea for him. Could a woman have honor? And he still had not opened the envelope.

"Now, if you will show me to my room, I will be glad to retire, since it's very late."

He sat there, staring into the distance, thinking. She sat very still and tried not to show her nervousness. She made sure that her eyes and mouth showed determination: I can't let this man bully me.

Then he rose. "All right. I suppose I must accept your statements. They sound logical. For your sake, I hope they are correct. The housekeeper has left a tray in your room. I might not see you tomorrow, but you are welcome to stay for breakfast."

She didn't move. "Where is my brother? He said he would see me here."

"He's gone to Apalachin to make some arrangements. He will come to your room later."

She rose and took her bag. He opened another door, this one to a hallway full of doors, leading her to the fourth one on the right. "Good night."

Inside, she locked the door before even turning on the light. The room looked old-fashioned but comfortable. There was a musty odor. At least the bathroom seemed clean. On a desk lay a tray covered with a white napkin.

Suddenly Annie had to sit down. She felt exhausted from the tension. And some of Martino's words clanked in her mind ominously: Do you guarantee that the account is intact? What if I find the account shorted?

Since Annie already knew that Emmet Smith had removed about half the money in the account, she was afraid that Joe Martino would hold her accountable, whether she bore the responsibility or not.

What am I going to do? He will doubtless examine the account papers tonight. None of them mentions the amount of money that's still in the bank, but what if he makes an overseas call to Andorra and finds out? I think I must get out of here. But if I run away, he'll know I haven't told him the whole truth.

In the Parkway Motel in Endicott, Anthony the driver was undressing when someone knocked on his door. Who I the world could that be? he wondered. I don't know anybody around here. He waited a moment: Could it be one of those gangsters? Another knock. He pulled on his pants. In the doorway stood two men he thought were police.

"What's happened?"

"Nothing yet, Mr. DeLuca. We're New York State troopers, and we need to ask a couple of questions, that's all. We're looking for information. May we come in for a minute?"

Inside the small room, the two men sat on straight chairs. "I'm Sergeant Croswell," said the older man, "and this is Investigator Vasisko. We received a tip about a convention of soft drink distributors in Apalachin, to be held on the property of a crime figure named Joseph Barbara, who also owns a legitimate business distributing soft drinks. We've been keeping an eye on Barbara, and we've learned that the convention is supposed to take place at his home on McFall Road in Apalachin tomorrow. It's a big property, about fifty acres, with several buildings. We understand that you took a fare somewhere near there this evening. Was it to the Barbara home in Apalachin?"

"No, it was to Endicott."

Now, he wondered, what am I supposed to do? Tell these Troopers everything she told me? I don't think so.

"Who was your fare, and what was the name of the property owner in Endicott where you dropped your fare?"

"My fare was Mrs. Smith, and the property owner was a Mr. Magaddino."

"Mrs. Smith, eh?" smiled Sergeant Croswell. "Sounds like a fake name to me." He took off his hat and put it on his knee.

"Oh, I don't think so, Sergeant. I knew her late father-in-law, Mr. Emmet Smith. And I drove him often, when he was in New York. An important person, a banker and investor."

Croswell's face fell. "Oh. Well, how about this Magaddino fellow?"

Vasisko, the younger man, broke in. "That's a familiar name. He could be going to the so-called soft drink convention in Apalachin tomorrow."

The two troopers looked inquiringly at Anthony.

"I wouldn't know about that," Anthony stated circumspectly, thinking, I'm not going to say anything unless it's necessary. "What's the soft drink convention?"

Vasisko continued, "We suspect that instead of bringing in soft drink sellers, the convention will bring in criminals from all over the country. Yesterday we were here investigating a rubber check when Joseph Barbara's son came in to make reservations for six people attending tomorrow's convention in Apalachin. When we reported this to our head office, we were directed to investigate further." He sat back, more relaxed. "We just thought you might be able to give us more information, Mr. DeLuca. Do you come here often?"

"No, I haven't been to Endicott for a couple of years, when I took some sales people to the shoe factory there."

Croswell thought Anthony might know a little more. "So do you have any idea what Mrs. Smith's business was at the Magaddino residence in Apalachin?"

Anthony paused in order to get his words just right. "She said she was returning something that didn't belong to her, not to the man who owned the house but to someone else at that residence. I don't know who."

"Is she planning to stay overnight?"

"She indicated that, yes."

"Anything else you know?"

"I can't think of anything. I gave her the motel's card so she can phone me when she's ready to return to the City."

"She lives in New York?"

"I don't think so. She's staying at a private club, the University Club. I get business from the Club now and then."

"So where does she live?"

"I don't know. I never asked." Let them find out these details for themselves, Anthony thought; I'll do what I can to avoid getting her into trouble. Mr. Smith was always generous to me. She probably has no connection with those crime bosses. I won't mention her brother.

Croswell put on his hat. "It sounds as though her business is unconnected with the convention. Well, if you think of anything else that might help us, give us a call. The motel owner has our number."

"Sure, Sergeant."

Annie decided to answer the knock on her door. "Who's there?"

"Rick."

She hastened to let him in. "Oh, Rick, I'm scared. Are you okay?"

"Yes, yes. What happened?"

"Martino seems suspicious that I might have stolen some of his money. And I need to tell you that my father-in-law, Emmet Smith, did take out some of it, when the account was in his possession, and put it into several banks around the country under my name. So what I'm giving Martino is the right to an account with about half of what was originally in it. What if he finds that out tonight?"

"How could he? Do any of the papers you gave him mention the amount of money still in the account?"

"No, but what if he checks? He could call Andorra; it's morning there ... I think I'd better leave now."

Rick shook his head. "The bankers wouldn't give him information on the phone. And as far as the bank knows, you're still the owner. No, he can't do anything right now, not until he establishes ownership with the bank. You're better off staying here tonight, so that Martino won't become suspicious. Get some sleep. If you need me, I'm in the room at the end of the hall on this side."

As she tried to relax, she kept wondering: Am I going to get out of here alive?

22

WHEN ANNIE AWOKE to the unaccustomed sound of a cardinal calling, she realized that she had finally slept for a few hours. Peeking outside her window, she saw a large red spot on a patch of melting snow. No, not blood; she assured herself: The red feathers of the male cardinal, who had just found some seeds scattered by the branch of a nearby maple.

I must stop thinking of blood, she told herself, and get out of here. After getting herself ready—I'm as ready as I'll ever be—she opened her door, looked around, and went back to the dining room. No phone here. I'll try the living room.

She lifted the latch of the old farmhouse door. In the living room she saw the backs of some men who were talking quietly. Martino turned and beckoned. She came forward and said, "May I use the phone? I'll call my driver."

"It's in the kitchen. Use the side door from the dining room."

In the kitchen were two men drinking coffee and talking. They nodded to her and went back to their breakfast. The old-fashioned phone was mounted on the wall.

Anthony answered right away and promised to be there in fifteen minutes. "Listen, Mrs. Smith. Last night two state troopers came here and asked where I dropped you off and a lot of other questions. I told them only who you were and where you were going last night, nothing else. They're watching some gangsters in the nearby town of Apalachin. I think there's going to be a raid. Are you okay?"

"Yes. Yes, thank you, Anthony." She could not keep her voice from trembling. "I'll come to the front door in fifteen minutes."

Back in her room, she nervously wondered where Rick was and whether to check his room. Better not; he said to contact him only if I need help. I'll have to leave him to handle this.

In fifteen minutes she re-entered the living room. Martino and a few others were standing in a corner, smoking and talking. He turned and came over to her. She steeled herself for whatever he was going to do or say.

"I'm glad you came with this envelope. Before this, our relationship was in peril. I even thought your brother might be holding out on me. Now I think we have straightened it out. I want no trouble. Peace is the desirable state. I do not like to violate the peace established through my leadership."

Her jaw dropped during this flowery speech. She calmed down. "All right. Peace between us." Thank god Anthony's cab is approaching. I can't take much more of this strain.

Neither of them said thank you or goodbye. She opened the door to a different world, thinking what a good sign it was that a thaw had begun; the air was noticeably warmer, and the snow was melting.

"I'll feel better when we're out of this area," Anthony said. "I'm sure something bad is going to happen."

"Maybe not," Annie replied. "Maybe this meeting you mentioned will benefit the law. After all, if the troopers know about it, they can handle it and perhaps arrest the mobsters."

"You may be right, but..."

"I'm curious about it. I think I'd like to go to the town of Apalachin."

Anthony was startled. "You don't mean that, Mrs. Smith. It might be dangerous."

"I doubt it." She was thinking of her brother Rick and his revelation that he worked undercover for the FBI. "Maybe we can be of some help."

"Help? I'd rather not. Besides, what could we do? " By then he had reached East Main Street in Endicott.

"Drive back to Vestal so we can have breakfast in the motel coffee shop. We can talk about what to do."

"If you say so, Mrs. Smith. If you say so. Just remember: These men are seriously bad guys."

In Binghamton, about thirty minutes away, men moved around inside the local office of the FBI, collecting their gear in preparation for the raid. Jerry Finch was on the phone with the Vestal office of the New York State Troopers, arranging to meet the local Troopers in Vestal and laying out joint plans.

At their office in Vestal, Sergeant Croswell of the State Troopers was awaiting backup from police officers from nearby Horseheads, Waverly, and Whitney Point, all of them expected momentarily. Croswell realized this event could be a big one and hoped it would not turn out badly for the law.

In Apalachin, the warmer weather had inspired the preparation of an outdoor barbecue on the Barbara property. Around noon, men in city overcoats and fedora hats were already standing around a barbecue pit, enjoying the smell of cooking meat as the caretaker continued to bring wheelbarrows full of steaks, veal, and ham from the kitchen to the cook working at the pit. A fish delivery was expected shortly.

At the Parkway Motel in Vestal, over an ample country-style breakfast of ham and eggs with buttermilk pancakes served by Mrs. Schroeder, wife of the motel owner, Annie persuaded Anthony to drive to the edge of the Barbara property in Apalachin. Jacob Schroeder gave directions: "When you reach the town of Apalachin, drive down Main Street and take a left on McFall Road, heading south for about half a mile. You'll see the Barbara property spread out on a hilltop. The main building is a fine stone house."

Anthony still had misgivings. "This seems like a crazy thing to do, if you don't mind my saying so, Mrs. Smith. If there's going to be a raid, we'll just be in the way. There might even be shooting." He shivered.

"I doubt it," Annie replied, who was feeling strangely calm. "These people wouldn't take a chance on shooting policemen. That's one thing they avoid."

Anthony looked at her with impatience, but he could tell he would never be able to persuade her out of her decision.

By noon, Annie had decided not to wait any longer. She needed to feed her curiosity. And she was beginning to feel infallible: Since nothing bad happened to her at the Magaddino house in Endicott, what could possibly happen afterwards?

About a quarter after twelve, Anthony pulled the cab away from the Parkway Motel and onto Route 17 going west toward Apalachin. Immediately he realized that he was joining the end of a long line of cars, many of them police cars, all proceeding in his direction.

"I think we've just entered the raiding party," he said shakily. "What should I do?"

"Nothing. Just continue, and go where they go."

The cars parked on the road in front of the Barbara property.

Just then a vehicle that had been trailing Anthony's cab pulled into the driveway; the name painted on its side said "Fish." The occupants of the lawmen's cars permitted that car to enter the driveway.

Then the men in large troopers' hats or civilian clothes spilled out of the parked cars, walking up the drive and onto the meadows on melting snow, stopping at the cluster of parked cars, where they started checking license numbers.

Anthony and Annie watched as a man from the delivery truck left a large box at the barbecue pit. When the truck came back down the drive, however, two troopers detained it.

By then the mobsters in their dark overcoats and felt hats had begun to notice that invaders were checking their cars. Alarm spread among them, and some mobsters began rushing into the surrounding woods, dropping objects as they went. A few ran into the house, but most scattered, although they were soon halted by the lawmen, who began leading them back to the road.

"Don't you think we'd better go?" asked Anthony nervously.

"Not yet." She had just spotted two men who looked familiar as they walked toward the road. Yes, the tall, relaxed mobster lounging along with a familiar gait was none other than Vincent del Vecchio. His handsome face bore a look of complete disdain. His captor, whose demeanor showed only pleasure, revealed himself as Gennaro Finocchio, known as Jerry Finch. Jerry grasped Vin firmly by the arm.

"Let's go now," Annie said.

"Did you see your brother?" asked Anthony as he started the car and began backing and turning.

"No, but I'm convinced he isn't here. He's back at the farmhouse in Endicott. The man who owns that place planned not to attend this event, so my brother didn't show up, either."

Suddenly Anthony stopped the car. A trooper was waving him down.

"Oh, hello, Sergeant Croswell. I hope you've caught a lot of criminals."

"What are you doing here, DeLuca? Are you Mrs. Smith?"

Annie nodded. "We were just curious, Sergeant. We'll leave now; we won't get in your way."

"Have you some personal interest in these people?"

"Hardly. But it looks very exciting! What is it that those men are dropping in the snow?"

"Weapons. Guns and money. Better get out of here."

"Yes, Sergeant."

The Apalachin raid made all the papers because it netted so many mobsters. Tommy Lucchese had escaped through the woods and picked up a ride with a local delivery truck, but about sixty others were detained and questioned closely, although nothing specific could be pinned on them. Mainly, they suffered the embarrassment of nationwide publicity. Joseph Barbara's legitimate business license was revoked; he had to sell his fine estate in Apalachin. And the world realized that there really was a nationwide crime syndicate, which newspapermen dubbed the Mafia.

Martino and his cousin Stefano Magaddino escaped detection by staying away from the Apalachin convention. Martino and his men, hearing of the disaster, quickly drove away from the area.

Anthony got Annie back to the University Club in time to permit her to have cocktails with her sister-in-law. He gladly accepted a fee of $300 for his services. By that time, after only one sip of her martini, Annie decided she owed Isabel an explanation for breaking into their trip so abruptly.

First asking Isabel to keep the matter to herself, Annie gave her curious relative a sanitized version of her adventure. She began by saying that the letter she had received posthumously from Emmet Smith revealed that Emmet had discovered John's blackmailing of the gangster Joe Martino and, after obtaining control of it, had assigned the contents of the fund to her, Annie.

Isabel sat back in surprise. "My brother John hoodwinking a gangster? Well, I wouldn't put it past him. Just before he proposed to you, he became very secretive and stayed away from home almost every night. He refused to explain even to our father about what was keeping him so occupied. I thought he was just gambling and dissipating, and I was sure that marriage to you would cure both vices. It might have, if he had lived. So now the money he obtained by blackmailing that Martino fellow is back where it came from?"

"I believe it is. Martino as much as admitted that he had my house in Bratenahl destroyed because he thought I had his money. I didn't, but as soon as your father assigned it to me legally, I wanted to get rid of it, and I used my brother Rick, who has some acquaintance with Martino, in order to return it. Rick knew where Martino was staying upstate, and it happened to be near the town where the mob convention took place. I persuaded Anthony to drive there over there this morning so we could see the action. Quite exciting to see so many Mafia men apprehended!"

"Well, you had an unusual adventure. I'm glad it turned out right."

"I just hope it's all over with Martino and he won't bother me again."

Annie relaxed in the dusky atmosphere of the Club's bar—until the waiter came to their table with a message. "You're wanted on the phone,

Mrs. Smith." He placed the phone on the table and connected it to a wire, then handed her the receiver.

Nervously, she said, "Yes?"

"Annie, it's Rick. Are you okay?"

"Oh, Rick, I'm so glad to hear your voice. I'm fine, and I think it's all over. How did you manage?"

"I had no problem. And I think Martino will stay out of your life now, no matter what, since he came so close to being exposed at the Apalachin convention, which embarrassed so many of his colleagues."

"I hope so, Rick. I hope so. Thank you for your help in this matter."

"You're welcome. I think it helped my position, too. I'll phone you again in Boston in a couple of weeks. Goodbye."

"Bye, Rick."

Annie smiled at Isabel, who squeezed her hand. Then they drank a toast to Rick.

On Annie's desk when she arrived home in Newton was an elegant note from Regina Jones inviting her to a dinner party, along with a letter from Johnny about his latest adventure. She started with Johnny's message.

"I'm writing instead of calling," he wrote, "because you were away in Cleveland and New York. I wanted to tell you about the visit of the girls' school. First, sorry to learn about Grandpa Smith. He seemed like a nice man. Now about the visit. We've been working on our dancing (ugh!) for two weeks because we were told that if we didn't dance when the girls visited we'd get a demerit. Even boys with a limp, like me, had to learn to dance. (More ugh!) We also had to practice being nice to them, like offering to get them a glass of soda. Well, it all turned out pretty good. The girls watched a basketball game with us, then came to dinner with us, and then we all danced. It wasn't too bad. But I was glad to get back to normal. The editor of the school paper likes my sketches, so I made some called 'Visit of the Willowood School' and showed some of the girls cheering at the game, cutting their roast beef, and even dancing with the fellows. I'll send you a copy of the paper. Say Hello to Aunt Isabel."

She smiled delightedly. Then she turned to Regina's invitation. "Please come to a small dinner party at my home on Saturday at seven. I'll send a car for you at six-thirty." She added, "I hate to ask for formal dress, with all this snow, but the path will be clean for you."

I don't see how I can get out of this, Annie thought. To get a formal dress, she had to ask for shopping help; Mrs. Kane directed Annie to boutiques in Boston's Back Bay area where she would find gowns suitable for Boston dinner parties.

Promptly at 6:30 on Saturday, Regina's uniformed driver stood at the door saluting. On starting to enter the Rolls, Annie realized she was not alone. Taking in her breath, she almost backed away, then saw quickly that she knew the other passenger. "Mummy asked me to keep you company," said Charlie Jones, handsome and very blond in his black evening clothes, the white collar of his shirt standing out starkly against his winter tan. "We just returned from Nassau," he explained. "Do you ever visit the islands? We like to escape for a while from the cold."

"I haven't been any place more southerly than the towns just south of Cleveland. Well, perhaps I have, if you count Sicily."

"Ah, yes. Tuscany is my favorite part of Italy. What is Sicily like? I always assumed it was quite primitive."

She looked at him with irritation. "No more primitive than some other parts of Europe, I've heard."

He changed the subject. "I'm so glad it stopped snowing. What things have you been doing?"

She spoke of her trip to New York City, but only in the most touristy terms.

"Mummy wanted me to mention the passing of your father-in-law, Emmet Smith, her very close friend. She said I should make sure to tell you how sorry she was, and that she did not attend the funeral for the sake of appearances... Here we are. Chestnut Hill isn't far from Newton."

The driver turned in at a private road and stopped in front of a mansion with Doric pillars standing like brackets around the entrance. A butler welcomed them and took Annie's pale blue cape. "This way, Mrs. Smith," indicated Charlie, leading her to a sitting room where several people had already gathered and Regina Jones was starting toward her, hands out in welcome.

"My dear Anna, I want you to meet some of my friends. They're looking forward to your acquaintance. First meet my spiritual advisor, Canon Joseph McGuire... Now my friend Dr. Jacob Epstein, director of my favorite hospital, and Mrs. Rachel Epstein. Rachel and I are on several boards together."

"We also meet at the Intergroup Relations Council and the Mayor's Civic Committee," said Rachel Epstein.

Annie was curious. "What do those groups do?" She accepted a proffered seat next to Mrs. Epstein.

"We work on ways to promote cordial relations between Catholics and Jews," replied Rachel Epstein. "Vandalism and physical attacks on each other, especially among teenagers, have declined since we have been sending out informational speakers to schools and colleges, distributing literature, and campaigning through the media."

Canon McGuire added, "Information is the key, we find. When one group believes lies about the other, anger can lead to physical attacks. Those decline when the attackers discover that they are wrong about their assumptions."

Annie felt enlightened. So much is going on, she thought, especially with problems that I never think about. She accepted a glass of sherry.

Before she could properly absorb what for Annie was entirely new information (Catholics and Jews could be friends?), more guests arrived, and Annie began to understand that Regina Jones ran what in earlier times was called a salon. She collected people she found interesting, gathered them together for cocktails and dinner, and stirred them up by sprinkling among them the ideas going the rounds.

Looking around, Annie realized that she and Charlie were the youngest people in the room. She felt flattered to be included.

Now Dr. Epstein was addressing her: "Mrs. Smith, I understand that you have formerly volunteered in a Cleveland hospital, one that focuses on veterans. Would you consider doing the same at my hospital? Brigham and Women's is one of the top institutions here, and we always have openings."

She smiled, realizing that she had done nothing in Boston so far except to explore the city. "You make me feel guilty, Dr. Epstein. I'll certainly look into it."

Then Annie was addressed by a fortyish woman in a slinky silver satin gown, the diamonds in her earlobes flashing against her black hair as she turned her head: "I'm afraid I didn't catch your name, my dear."

"Annie Smith."

"Ah. I have the impression that despite your name, you are of Italian descent rather than English. I believe Regina mentioned that. I am Sonia Fancetta, and I operate a chain of pastry shops, mostly in the section of Boston called Little Italy. I am also active in several Italian American organizations, and I invite you to join."

Talking to Sonia revealed for Annie another facet of life she had left unexplored. Why didn't I think of doing that?

It was at the dinner table that Annie began to contribute to the conversation. She was seated between Dr. Epstein and a man of about fifty named Tito DeBono, who was addressed as "Professor DeBono"; she discovered that he taught languages at Boston University.

At first DeBono talked past her: "Dr. Epstein, now that we have had a Jewish woman selected to be Miss America, Bess Myerson, and a Jewish ballplayer elected to the Baseball Hall of Fame at Cooperstown, Hank Greenberg, do you consider that Jews are clearly accepted in the world of popular culture as never before?"

"I do," Epstein said over his shrimp cocktail. He opened his mouth to say something else, but Annie jumped into the conversation.

"Greenberg is certainly a star in the world of men's baseball. I wonder when women will have a star player elected to the Hall of Fame."

DeBono looked at her, nonplussed. "Do women play baseball?"

"Certainly."

Epstein contributed, "I remember a league of women baseball players who fielded teams during the war. Why didn't it continue afterwards, Mrs. Smith?"

"The men who started it withdrew their support when male players came home from the war ready to play again. Obviously, the backers of the women's league didn't want women competing with the men's leagues." She picked up a glass of white wine to sip.

Across the table, Sonia Fancetta began listening to Annie, and Regina, at the head of the table, did the same.

"Surely," said DeBono "because it's not an easy game to master, the women weren't as good as the men."

"Given more time," Annie retorted, "I think they could have been. I played semiprofessional baseball myself, and my team sometimes beat men."

"You, Mrs. Smith?" Clearly, DeBono found it hard to believe that someone as feminine-looking as Annie Smith, in her cloud-blue puffy chiffon, would be able to play a game associated with masculinity. Epstein was silenced.

"Certainly. I once talked to a scholar who said women have been playing since the 1870s. If they'd had any encouragement, they might be playing very well by now. Instead, men have always ridiculed their efforts, just as they once ridiculed the playing of black men in the Negro leagues."

Epstein found his voice. "And now, of course, the black players are being accepted. After many years of separate and unequal experience."

"What fascinating conversation I hear this evening!" exulted Regina.

Sofia Fancetta seemed to shrug off the idea of women's participation in the national game. "I can't imagine any woman wanting to play baseball."

"We all have our special abilities, Mrs. Fancetta. I can't imagine anyone engaging in a business as tempting as one that produces delicious bakery. I'd probably eat all the profits."

Smiles at Annie's end of the table ended the discussion.

Dr. Epstein provided a new twist on the topic: "As for ethnic people entering the popular culture, Professor DeBono, would you say that the Italian Americans are as proud of Sinatra as of Enrico Fermi? And Fiorello LaGuardia?"

"I'm sure of it," DeBono assented. "The Italian American newspapers continually boast about Sinatra, although he keeps some questionable company. Too bad he isn't an opera singer; I myself would admire him more."

At the other end of the table a woman whose name Annie had forgotten but who had been described as teaching writing at Emerson College was speaking highly about the abilities of her ethnic students to a man who had been introduced as an editor from the local publishing house, Houghton Mifflin. The man, whose name Annie hadn't caught, told the writing professor that he'd be waiting to see if her students produced some manuscripts his company would be interested in publishing. Then he turned to Dr. Epstein and mentioned the recent action of Brandeis, the local Jewish-founded university, in erecting three campus chapels, one for Jewish students, another for Catholics, and a third for Protestants. "Can you imagine, Canon McGuire, Holy Cross or Boston College being quite that ecumenical?"

McGuire rose to the occasion: Shrugging, he said, "If Cardinal Cushing stays in his job much longer, I wouldn't be surprised if it happens. Look how the Cardinal excommunicated Father Feeney, a Jesuit, when he continued to express such terrible bigotry against our brothers the Jews. Believe me, things are looking up for Catholics who want to get along with members of other faiths."

"On that positive note, shall we retire to the living room for coffee?" Regina rose, and the others followed.

Charlie Jones, perhaps intimidated by all the learned older people at the dining table, participated in the conversation only with banalities. In the living room he handed around a plate of cookies, then sat down next to Annie to speak privately. "I certainly admired your contributions to the evening, Mrs. Smith. My mother will want you to come often. After coffee, let me know when you are ready to leave. Some of these people will start on whiskey after the coffee; that only gives me a headache."

Annie took that as a hint, and in a few minutes she rose to thank her hostess and say goodbye to the guests. Smiles of approval, except from Mrs. Fancetta, followed her.

In the Rolls, Charley asked if she had been to the North End, where Little Italy was located, and said he'd be willing to show her around. "Thank you, but I think I'd rather discover it myself. I'll take Johnny to one of the Feast Day celebrations. But I believe I'll avoid any of Mrs. Fancetta's shops! I'm sure she disapproves of me."

Smiling, he commented, "She is quite straitlaced and has somehow allied herself with the very Protestant Proper Bostonians of the past. One wouldn't know that she is the daughter of a North End barber. Of course the barber became very successful and owned several shops."

"Speaking of background: I know nothing of yours or your mother's."

"Here we are, so I'll leave all that for our next meeting. Thank you for coming and enlivening the occasion."

Annie lay back on the bed, reeling from the words she'd just heard on the Tel-Magnet machine in her room. Finding that her hotel had installed this new device in its guest rooms, she'd experimented with the one by her phone and found Rick's message. It was this terse sentence: "Vin has been detained in Chicago for the murder of your husband."

23

ANNIE NEEDED TO UNDERSTAND more about Vin's being detained for murdering John. How much is known about that event? Who knows it? If Vin is detained, what about me?

She couldn't reach Rick right away, so she began pacing the floor. Finally he called. "It's not really an arrest, just a hearing to find out whether there's any evidence against him."

She sat down at her desk. "How did this happen?"

"It's the result of that Apalachin meeting, when about sixty members of the various Families were questioned about crimes, especially murders. One of those questioned, a man named Luigi Primo, declared he knew of one murder: Of John Smith by Vincenzo del Vecchio, because Vin had boasted of it to him."

She sat back suddenly. "Do you think that's possible?"

"I don't know. I think you can forget that part. But you will be asked to come to the hearing. Don't worry; just say what happened in Sicily: That you saw John fall over the railing because he was leaning over too far. Understand?"

"Yes," she replied shakily.

"And explain that it was the manager of the hotel that introduced you to Vin, so that he could help you with all the paper work involved and so that he in turn would benefit by fulfilling his desire to come to America. As for the hearing, it won't happen for a couple of weeks. You'll get a notice soon. Meanwhile, keep busy with the things you usually do. Don't stay home and mope. Don't do anything crazy. Just keep busy with your normal life."

That's when Annie decided to start volunteering. She called the hospital that Dr. Epstein had mentioned and asked for the volunteer office, where she was invited to report to Mrs. Stewart on Monday at nine o'clock.

On Sunday morning, while she dawdled over coffee and a freshly-baked muffin, a call arrived from Carl Morris. "I miss you, Annie. I'll be on spring break next week. May I visit you in Boston for a few days?"

She paused. I'd love to see Carl, but I'll have to tell him that very soon I must go to Chicago in order to confront a member of the Mafia.

"Don't answer yet if you're unsure. I'll call back tomorrow night."

On Monday Annie put on a woolen dress, a cloth coat, and galoshes. Mrs. Kane explained how to get to Brigham and Women's Hospital by subway, but Annie thought the directions sounded complicated and ordered a cab instead.

At the hospital, the cabbie asked, "Main entrance?" She nodded. Inside, she asked at the Information Desk for Mrs. Stewart in the Volunteers Office and found it quickly. At the desk where volunteers registered sat a woman who looked vaguely familiar. As soon as she began to speak, Annie became frightened.

"Hello, I'm Jean Stewart. Thank you for volunteering, Mrs. Smith. You've been with us before, haven't you? I'm sure I've seen you."

Stricken, Annie replied, "No. I've never volunteered before."

"But I recognize you."

"Impossible. I don't know you."

"Really. Well... We can think about that later. What kind of volunteering would you be interested in? I can list our openings for you..."

"On second thought, I believe I've changed my mind. I don't feel strong enough to help. I'm sorry. Thanks anyway." She turned around and left. Feeling wobbly, she sat down in a chair near the Information Desk, where a white-haired volunteer manning the desk noticed her stricken face and asked if he could help. She told him she needed a cab to go home, and he called one.

In the cab, she closed her eyes and visualized the face of the woman she knew as Jean, who had been at a desk in St. Luke's when she was trying to find out the room number for Kenesaw Landis, the commissioner of baseball. Her breathing came fast, and her heart pounded.

Too much is happening, she thought; too much. All my terrible moments are returning. If only I hadn't done those things...

She put her hand in her purse and began smoothing some of the talismans her mother had given her.

At home, Mrs. Kane took one look at her and said, "You need some bed rest, Mrs. Smith. How about some soup and a nice nap? I think you're trying to do too much. Let me help you..."

When she awakened it was three o'clock, and Mrs. Kane had put the mail on a tray in her bedroom. It included the official request for her presence in Chicago on February 10 at a hearing in the case of Vincent del Vecchio. She would be asked for any evidence she might offer either for against an indictment of Vincent del Vecchio in the murder of her husband, John Smith.

When Annie's picture appeared in the *Boston Globe* under the headline, "Newton Woman to Testify in Husband's Death," the boys at Braithwaite began ragging Johnny.

"What's this about your mom and the Mafia, Cardello?"

"Aw, nothing. She's just got to tell what happened to my dad. C'mon, let's go to the pool."

"Your mom in the Mafia, Card?"

"Get outta here."

"So did the Mafia kill your dad, Card?"

"Don't be silly. It was an accident. Out of my way."

"Sounds bad to me. What do you say we give Cardello a wedgie, fellas?"

"Yeah. Good idea."

Johnny whirled around,. "You try it and I'll use my steel brace on you." He stood his ground, his eyes fiercely combative, his strong shoulders stiffened, fists ready.

"Okay, okay. Take it easy. How'd your dad die?"

"Fell off a low balcony."

"Where?"

"In Sicily."

"You see it happen?"

"I wasn't there. I wasn't even born yet. C'mon, let's go."

Mrs. Kane saw Annie's nervousness and suffering. "Now, how can they put you through this, Mrs. Smith? Cruel, it is. Enough that you should have been made such a young widow. Come, now, have some lunch. You'll need your strength for the ordeal of speaking in public about something that painful. I mind when my sister..." Annie stopped listening. She decided to phone the Cleveland lawyer who had prepared the document for Martino, asking him to meet her in Chicago and sit in at the hearing in case she needed some legal support or protection. He pointed out that he was not himself a trial lawyer but his firm, Romano and Tesoro, would furnish one to be there for her.

When Bianca called her daughter to commiserate, she also offered to travel to Chicago and be there for support during the hearing. "You need someone with you."

"Mom, I know you hate travel. I wouldn't put you through that."

"I could ask your Uncle Paolo."

"No, Mom, I can't ask him to do that, either. He wouldn't want to, anyway. I'll manage. I have to be strong enough to fight my own battles, or at least to explain my own experiences. I'll be okay. A lawyer I know will be there. I'll phone you from Chicago."

Isabel offered to be Annie's travel companion, but Annie knew her sister-in-law had a golf tournament in Bermuda to attend. "I can always play golf, Annie. I'll come with you."

"Please, no, Isabel. I want to handle this myself. I appreciate your willingness, but I feel as though I must go alone."

The most welcome call came from Carl. "Annie, what can I do to help?" She knew she would love to have him there to depend on, but she decided against it. "It's about time I stood on my own two feet. Thank you for asking." Afterwards, she was a little sorry she hadn't accepted. She realized that she longed to see Carl again, to let him hold her and soothe her. He ended his call with "I'm going to be with you again as soon as I can." That promise gave her a brief glow of pleasure.

Rick did not offer to appear in Chicago, knowing that his own perceived connection with Organized Crime might hurt her presentation at the hearing.

She heard nothing from Charlie Jones or his mother.

On February 9 Annie packed an overnight case, took a cab to South Station, and boarded a Chicago train. For the fifth time she rehearsed to herself the story she was about to tell concerning her husband's death.

She pushed from her mind the blurred mental picture of a figure rushing from behind who picked him up and tossed him to the wind, the sound of her own scream, the feeling of vertigo, the realization that she had fainted, the cool hand of the maid on her forehead as she came to herself, the memory of what she had seen, and the understanding that she had been its cause.

Now she must think only of the revised version of events, the version she would give to the public.

The lies.

Would they sound convincing?

Joe Martino sat back in his living room chair. "So, Cardello, your sister came through with the Andorran account." Rick nodded. "But there's not much left in it."

Rick acted surprised. "Maybe her husband spent it."

"How?"

Rick drank from his glass of light beer. "He gambled. My sister told me he spent a lot of time in Cleveland gambling joints, and when they were in Europe on their honeymoon, instead of seeing the sights he went to all the big casinos, came back with empty pockets."

"Did your sister go, too?" Martino finished a glass of red wine.

"Nah, she can't stand gambling. To her, that's throwing money away. We were brought up to save, not spend." He picked at a lace doily under his arm.

He nodded slowly. "Maybe you're right. He could have lost millions by gambling it away. Well, it's not important. I got plenty of money to retire to one of my houses. The one in Arizona."

"Retire, Boss?"

"Yeah, that last heart attack got my wife scared. I'm thinking of dropping out. Go legit. Make one last visit to Sicily, then hang it up."

"What'll we do then, Boss?" Rick finished his beer.

"Find another Family to hook on with. Maybe you like Tommy Lucchese," he suggested slyly.

Rick Cardello grinned. "Maybe I'll leave New York, go to Florida. I've been thinking about fishing. I like to fish. Used to get perch in Lake Erie, bass in the rivers around Cleveland. I'd like to try deep-sea fishing, maybe strike out on my own, start a business. Connect a fishing camp with a fish restaurant..."

"You have ideas, Cardello. Sure you won't be bored?"

He shook his head. "I hear the Florida women are good-looking." He stopped and grinned. "Besides, I like trying new things. I remember when I tried farming. I learned things that way. I keep my eyes open for opportunities."

"Good for you, Cardello. Good for you."

"Guess I'll take the Long Island train back to the city, Boss. You don't need me, right?"

"Okay. I'll phone if I do."

"We'll have to make a going-away party. Eat a lot of good Sicilian food, drink a lot of red."

"Yeah."

When he got on the train, Rick sighed with relief: I think I'm just about done with Joe Martino. And Annie's off the hook for the rest of the Andorran money.

Now I want to see how she does at the Chicago hearing. If only she doesn't fall apart, go off the deep end as she did once, when she started talking about music and baseball and her Sicilian ancestors.

As Annie approached the hearing room, a man in a dark suit and vest stood up. "Mrs. Smith? I am Robert Romano, the attorney from Cleveland. How are you doing?"

She nodded. "Thank you for coming." She liked his earnest countenance. He was obviously concerned for her well-being.

"I will be in the hearing room at all times, listening to what goes on and giving you any legal support I think necessary. I've already informed Judge Grogan that I will be present to observe the hearing."

"Good. I'm pretty sure what I will be asked, and I've prepared myself with the answers."

"That was wise. I will jump in if I think there is any legal need to do so, or even if I believe you are being taken advantage of in any way."

"Thank you, Mr. Romano."

They entered together, Annie being seated in a front row and Romano behind. About twenty persons sat in the room. Vin was there, and several men who looked as though they belonged to the mob. Annie looked at the judge: He had a prominent lower jaw that made him look pugnacious. But he had intelligent eyes. To Annie, he inspired trust.

The session began with the testimony of the person who had accused Vincent del Vecchio of murdering John Smith.

"Mr. Primo, what did Mr. del Vecchio say to you about the death of Mr. Smith? When and where did he say it?"

Primo's head moved around on a skinny neck. "Oh, we was drinking at Carney's in Chicago last summer. He said in Sicily he killed a rich guy named John Smith."

Annie flinched. Her breath came faster. "Exactly what words did he use?"

"He said something like, 'I knocked that snooty rich guy off his high perch.' Or maybe he said 'snotty.' I don't remember." Primo shrugged.

"And did he give a reason for his action?"

"Not exactly. He just said it had to be done." Annie's eyes dropped, then focused again at Primo.

"How did you interpret those words?"

"Huh?"

"What do you think he meant?"

"I guess he meant that the hit was ordered by his boss, or maybe he thought his boss wanted it done."

"Did you believe him?"

"I don't know. Sometimes Vin kind of exaggerated." Annie could not help glancing sideways at Vin. He looked sleepy.

"How did he exaggerate? Give an example."

"Well, he told me his family owned a lot of land in Sicily. They owned horses and stuff. He tried to make me think they was rich."

"You think his family was not rich?"

"Nah. He had no money, just what that woman—Mrs. Smith gave him when he helped her out." Annie saw, by Vin's reaction, that Primo's remarks didn't sit well with him.

"Why do you think he said things that were untrue?"

Primo shrugged one shoulder and grimaced. "He was probably jealous. I guess the Smiths were rich. Vin said they stayed at a fancy resort in Sicily. And the guy wasn't Italian, but he had just married a pretty Italian wife. I think that bothered Vin." Now Vin moved around in his seat.

"An Italian wife?"

"Well, an Italian American wife. I got the idea that Vin thought the guy should have stuck to his own kind, you know what I mean?"

Judge Grogan retorted sharply, "I'll ask the questions, Mr. Primo. Did Mr. del Vecchio give any details about how he murdered Mr. Smith?"

"Just said he came down off a balcony."

"Do you think Mr. del Vecchio really committed this murder?"

Primo's mouth worked, and his eyes darted here and there. "Maybe. I dunno."

"Thank you, Mr. Primo."

A pause while Judge Grogan consulted his list and then called Vin to the chair.

"Mr. del Vecchio, did you know Mr. Smith?"

"No, Your Honor." Vin sat up straighter. His eyes found Annie's and held there.

"Did you tell Mr. Primo that you had killed Mr. Smith?"

He looked at the judge and squirmed a little. "I dunno. Maybe. We were drinking." He began slouching in his chair, looking around, first at Primo and then back at the judge. Annie saw that his hair gleamed as he turned his head; he must have oiled it in order to achieve his neat appearance.

"Were you jealous of Mr. Smith, of his status in life, of his riches or his pretty wife?"

Vin's face became disdainful. "He was plenty rich, I guess. And he had a pretty wife. But I had a lot of pretty women of my own." He tossed his head, looked sideways, then to the front again. He sat up straight and proud.

"What did you think of Mr. Smith?"

Vin waited. He frowned. "I thought he was stuck up. I thought he looked at me as though I wasn't important. I didn't like that." His nostrils actually flared.

"You observed Mr. Smith when he and his wife were staying at a Sicilian resort?"

"Yeah, they were walking around the town, and they had these big rooms at the hotel where I was working. A whole suite of rooms. They had good dinners in that hotel. He was always taking her arm, as though he owned her. I thought Smith was snooty, nose in the air. I couldn't figure out what she saw in him. What a skinny guy." Vin made a harumphing sound through his nose.

"By 'she,' you mean Mrs. Smith?"

"Yeah."

"Did you decide to kill Mr. Smith because you were jealous of him?"

"Nah. I would like to of killed him, though." Some people in the courtroom could hardly keep from smiling at this remark.

"Did you go into his room and push him off the balcony?" Annie took in her breath sharply.

"I was never in his room. Except later, when the lady asked me to help her."

"Why did she ask you to help her?"

"She couldn't figure out how to ship a dead body, to get the permissions and certificates and things like that, or even who to ask. I got the names of places from the manager and did the telephoning and explained what to do and how much to pay. And she didn't know how to speak Sicilian, or fill out the forms, or how much to give the government guys, or even how to dress right. In Sicily it's important for a widow to look ... modest, they call it. Yeah, modest."

"She didn't speak Italian?" Annie kept he eyes on the brown purse in her lap.

"She knew a few words of Italian, but that's all. No Sicilian. Italian doesn't even sound like Sicilian. It's different."

"So you dealt with the government requirements, and she paid you?"

"Yeah." He corrected himself: "Yes. She was rich, I guess because of her husband." He sounded scornful.

"And you asked to go to America with her?"

He nodded. "I'd heard from somebody about jobs in Chicago, and I wanted a better job." Now Annie was watching Vin again.

"What job did you have with the hotel?"

"I just did things the manager needed, like delivering stuff, ordering some things, picking up food and drinks, phoning people, finding cleaning help, bringing things to people in their rooms, like coffee or their bill—whatever the manager needed to have done."

"And Mrs. Smith agreed to sponsor your entrance into the United States?"

"Yeah. She let me come along. I pretended to be her cousin."

"Once more, Mr. del Vecchio: Did you murder Mr. Smith?"

"No. I didn't need to. He fell off the balcony."

Finally, it was Annie's turn. She walked rather stiffly to the chair and sat down. Then she looked at the judge and answered his first question.

"Mr. del Vecchio could not have murdered my husband. I saw my husband fall. As I was entering my husband's room, he was on the balcony falling over the railing."

"How high was the railing of this balcony?"

"About to my waist."

"And how tall are you, Mrs. Smith?"

"Five feet three inches."

"And your husband?"

"Five feet ten inches."

"So the balcony did not even reach your husband's waist."

"No." She closed her eyes for a moment and held her head with both hands.

"I'm sorry, Mrs. Smith. I know this is hard for you."

"I was on my honeymoon," she added in a shaky voice. "It was terrible."

"Yes. Just a few more questions." She gathered herself and listened. "Is it possible for someone to have pushed your husband and then left before you entered?"

"No. There wouldn't have been time. I would have seen him leave."

"How long have you known Mr. del Vecchio?"

She took a breath. "Since the day after my husband's death, when the hotel manager introduced him to me."

"What reason did the hotel manager give for introducing Mr. del Vecchio to you?"

"The manager said he himself did not have time to help me deal with all the legal matters that I was faced with, that I would have to hire someone to take care of them. He said I would need a person who knew Sicilian laws, customs, and language, and that Mr. del Vecchio, who was Sicilian, could steer me through it all. He recommended Mr. del Vecchio." She looked at Vin. He was watching her, waiting to hear exactly what she would say.

"Did Mr. del Vecchio know your husband?"

"Not that I know of."

"What was Mr. del Vecchio's position at the hotel?"

"The manager said he did odd jobs there, like carrying luggage or picking up people at the station. Sort of a handyman."

"How did Mr. del Vecchio help you?"

Recovering from her earlier panic, she spoke in calm, measured tones, using the words she had written out for herself and practiced saying. "He telephoned the various government departments involved in declaring a death had taken place, and in having my husband's body embalmed and transported. He got permission to have the body shipped on the same carriers as I was traveling on. He arranged for the coffin to be delivered to the nearby town of Catania, then transported on the train from Catania in Sicily to the port of Messina, by boat across the straits of Messina, and then by train up the peninsula to the port of Genoa, and on the ship I was traveling from Genoa to New York, then finally on the train from New York to Cleveland. A van met the train and picked up the body, then took it to the funeral home my in-laws had chosen." She took a deep breath, then went on. "All this took considerable persuasion and some bribery as well, since he knew, and I was already aware, that nothing gets done in Sicily without that."

Judge Grogan was impressed, thinking: She sounds like an intelligent and sensible woman. Reminds me of Claudette Colbert in the movies.

"Is there anything else Mr. del Vecchio handled for you?"

"Yes. He helped me by revealing the customs of the country concerning the behavior of widows."

"What behavior was that?"

"Widows are expected to wear conservative black clothing, and when they go outdoors they wear heavy black veils. I had nothing like that with me, not even a pair of black shoes."

The judge paused while he checked her present clothing: A simple beige woolen dress with a round neck and pearls, matching shoes and purse. Her hair was pinned up in rolls, and she wore little makeup.

"How did Mr. del Vecchio help you with that problem? Surely he didn't take you shopping."

"Objection, Your Honor."

"Mr. Romano, this is not a court case, it is merely a hearing. I will ask all the questions and decide whether the answers are relevant."

"I'm sorry, Your Honor."

Nevertheless, the judge dropped his frivolous tone. "Mrs. Smith, how did you obtain the clothing you were told was needed?"

"Mr. del Vecchio found a dressmaker who could quickly prepare the clothing I needed to wear in Sicily and in Italy proper, including the veil. She also found shoes and a black purse for me."

"How much did you pay Mr. del Vecchio for his services?"

She shook her head. Bewildered, she said, "I don't recall the amount. I paid whatever the hotel manager told me was the going rate. Mr. del Vecchio showed me where the bank was so I could get some Italian lira."

The judge consulted his notes, then went on. "Did you do anything else for Mr. del Vecchio?"

"Yes, I knew he wanted to get to the United States, so I sponsored him as a visitor. He said he had a job offer in Chicago. I was glad to have him accompany me on the trip and help in all the necessary transfers, since I didn't know the language and had never traveled in Europe alone."

"Your husband had managed the trip up to then?"

"Yes. We had been in Europe together for about three weeks. My husband had been there before and knew how to get around."

"On the trip to the United States, did your relationship with Mr. del Vecchio change?"

She shook her head. "Not really. I helped him improve his control of the English language. That was our main contact. I had become pregnant on my honeymoon and got sick on the voyage home, so besides helping him with his English, I didn't see much of Mr. del Vecchio on the ship."

"What happened when you reached your home in Cleveland?"

"As soon as Mr. del Vecchio saw that I was settled comfortably in my Cleveland home, he excused himself and left for Chicago."

"Have you seen him since then?"

"Yes, twice he came to Cleveland."

"Did he stay in your home?"

"Not the first time; he was there only for an afternoon. He was evidently on his way somewhere else. When he arrived a second time, I let him sleep in the room over my garage. He stayed only that one night."

"Is it true that while traveling, you passed him off as your cousin?"

"Yes, I thought it best to use that description for him, so that strangers would accept him as my escort. Passing him off as a family member made him more acceptable." She added earnestly, "Americans don't realize how questionable and even dangerous it is in some parts of Europe for a woman to travel by herself. A male companion can stave off the approaches of petty criminals who try to take advantage of women traveling alone, especially those who don't know the language."

"And what is your relationship with Mr. del Vecchio now?"

"He occasionally phones or writes to ask how I am doing."

"Is that all?"

"Yes."

"Can you think of any reason that Mr. del Vecchio might want to kill your husband?"

She shook her head. "None at all."

"And you believe he had nothing to do with your husband's death?"

"I don't see how he could have. As I've explained, it was an accident, and I saw it happen."

Judge Grogan was thinking of something he wanted to be sure of. "Mrs. Smith, have you remarried?"

"No."

The judge paused. Then he went on. "Do you think Mr. del Vecchio is given to exaggeration?"

She thought for a moment. "Yes."

"Can you cite an example?"

"He told my son that he held an important job in the state government, but he told me that he worked for a man who ran some underworld businesses in Chicago."

"Thank you, Mrs. Smith."

Her knees shook when she stepped down. She walked past Vin. With her peripheral vision she saw his arrogant face and the pose of his body, and she knew that whatever she had felt for him in the past was over. Avoiding a direct look at him, she walked stiffly out of the courtroom, searching for a chair in the hall, and sat down, closing her eyes.

I lied. I just lied in a court of law.

When she opened her eyes, Carl Morris stood before her.

Charlie threw down his fork in disgust and walked to the window, where he watched snowflakes float down slowly into Chestnut Hill. "Oh, Mother, you're impossible. Why not tell Isabel?"

Regina took another forkful of chicken curry. Not all of Charlie's remarks were worth responding to. Finally she made a small sound in her throat.

"What does that mean? Did Trevor Smith get your mother pregnant or didn't he?"

"First of all, I think Isabel already suspects. Telling her would only upset the delicate balance between us."

"What delicate balance?"

"She probably realizes that my mother's sexual proclivities were like Trevor's. After all, when Trevor blew through New London on that Race Day so long ago, he wasn't there for the local fish. It was a day of release, a day to loosen those New England strictures." She took a few sips of her Riesling.

"You mean debauchery."

"A day of fun."

"That's beside the point. You once said that some day you would tell

Isabel exactly who I am. But again you missed a good chance. You should have gone to Cleveland when Emmet died and taken her aside."

"Not a good moment, Charlie. Not at all." She took another bite.

He stopped pacing. "I think you never intended to tell her."

She took a few more sips from her glass.

"Mother, do you intend to tell her? I want her to know. I have a right. I should be getting a lot more Smith money."

"You have no such right. You and I are merely bastards, Charlie. Bastards have no rights."

"Well, if you had pushed for your own rights after your mother told you of sleeping with Trevor, perhaps I wouldn't be one."

She took another bite.

"Weren't there any places in town where your mother could have gotten married after the race?"

"Doubtless there were. She didn't bother finding out. She was having too much fun."

"Fun. I'm the product of fun your mother had with Trevor Smith. And fun that you had with Emmet." He stamped his cane hard on the floor as he walked.

"I meant the race itself, of course. Since she was the winner, many young men wanted her."

"Wanted her for what?"

She sipped her wine. Finally, she said, "Charlie, my mother said she had a lot of fun that day. With more than one young man. Did you think that Trevor was the only one?"

He stopped pacing. "You mean, you're not sure if Trevor Smith is my grandfather?"

"Not exactly, although Trevor certainly got there first. He left town after giving my mother some money and promising to get in touch with her. Which he did, eventually. But the day was still young, and other girls were reveling in the pleasures that followed the annual smock race. Why should my mother not join them?"

Charlie sat down and held his head in his hands. "Good God, this is terrible. Who am I, anyway?"

"Whoever you want to be, of course. When Mother met Joshua Jones in Dutch's Tavern on Green Street, after a few pints she decided that I would be the child of Mr. Jones. Although he smelled of fish and ate fried eels for breakfast, he was a successful whaler, and he wanted her as a wife to return to whenever he was in port. She took a job at the tavern, and they were married in a few days."

"What about Trevor Smith?"

"He visited when Joshua was off on whaling trips. After Joshua was lost at sea, Mother became Mrs. Jones the rich widow, and Trevor set her up in Boston as a sort of wife, where she became richer still through his excellent investments. Whenever Trevor visited us, he patted me on the head and told me I was pretty. Then, after his son Emmet grew up, Trevor introduced us. Emmet and I were attracted to each other..."

She took another sip.

"I enjoyed my relationship with Emmet. I never wanted for anything. Have you ever wanted for anything? No. So be satisfied with your lot, Charlie. And let Isabel alone." She finished her wine. "Leave it at that." She paused and smiled. "I like having the matter vague."

"Oh, Mother, for heaven's sake. You're so impractical. You could have squeezed a lot more out of Emmet."

"Yes, no doubt. But there was no need to get greedy. Don't worry, when I'm gone you won't have to take some kind of job. You'll be on Easy Street." She blotted her mouth with her napkin. "Now I'm going to take a rest."

Charlie sat there thinking. When she's gone I'll be rich. When will that be? Meanwhile, I should have pursued the filthy rich Mrs. Smith. If she survives this hearing in Chicago, I think I will.

Carl took Annie's hand and patted it. "My dear Annie," he said, "you survived another ordeal. And you will recover."

Just behind Carl stood Robert Romano, who stepped forward and said, "Mrs. Smith, you were superlative. Judge Grogan was obviously impressed with you. Mr. Morris, thank you for introducing yourself. I will take my leave of both of you, since Mrs. Smith is now in good hands." He gave a tiny bow of his head and left.

"You'll get his bill, of course," Carl said with a smile.

"It was worth it to hear him tell the Judge to get back in line."

"Although I thought it best not to be in the room, for fear I'd distract you, I heard a lot because the door was not entirely closed. My congratulations on keeping your composure and presenting your case so clearly and convincingly. You came across as sincere and trustworthy."

"It was all a pack of lies."

"We'll talk about that later. You'll be refreshed if you have some lunch now. Let's get a cab." He found her coat on a hook and helped her into it.

After glancing at the menu, Carl recommended the hot soup and some Chicago beefsteak with salad. Then he revealed that he knew what had really happened in Annie's past.

"How do you know?"

"Your brother Rick told me. When I first met you, I startled you by mentioning the Mafia. By your reaction, I knew you'd had some personal experience with the Mafia that frightened you. Eventually, I decided I'd have to take the chance of contacting your brother Rick, who seemed to be close to you, and find out what it was."

"Carl, I had no idea."

"It took a while to gain Rick's confidence, but he finally told me what had happened to you to give you such fear and guilt. Rick shared with me the two experiences that made you so convinced of your own corruption."

"Oh, Carl. I know I'm a bad person."

"I understand why you think that's so. And I learned the original source of your anger: You had been rejected and disparaged as an athlete. You needed support, but you received only discouragement. Then you were exploited and disrespected as a woman. Eventually, your anger built up and made you strike out in ways that you knew were socially unacceptable. Guilt was the result."

She began to cry. "I knew the things I did were wrong. I was so angry I did them anyway."

He soothed her with an arm around her shoulders. "Rick bears some responsibility for your husband's death. It was your concern for your brother that led you to help Rick escape. In that case you started with a good intention, but the way you solved Rick's problem was by making an inappropriate marriage. And remember this: It was Rick who unintentionally recruited del Vecchio's services by revealing to him how unhappy you were."

She sat there wiping away tears. And listening. She felt better already. "I want to believe all that."

"Perhaps if your husband had felt sympathetic to your being rejected by the baseball commissioner, he might have helped you instead of taking advantage of your plight. Unfortunately, he was interested only in himself. That proved to be his undoing."

"You think he was partly to blame for his own death? I never thought of it that way."

"I do. And as for your rejection as an athlete, I can understand how you kept your anger against the baseball administration alive for so long. Historians tell us that when people's legitimate aspirations are frustrated, the result is often an explosion of uncontrollable anger."

"You speak in such lofty terms. And you make what I did sound like something natural, something explainable. Carl, I murdered the commissioner of baseball."

"I doubt that. From Rick's description, I think the commissioner was already at the end of his life when you confronted him."

She was silent. Then she stirred and said, "I'm still guilty. I intended to kill him. And besides, what I did accomplished nothing. How did it help? It didn't. Women are still rejected on their basis of their gender."

"How do you know that?"

"Eleanor Engle's contract with Harrisburg was voided by the head of the minor leagues. That was just a few years ago. Women will never be accepted in the top ranks of the national game. Mine was a useless gesture."

"'Never' is a long time."

"Women don't even have a professional league to aspire to."

"Isn't there something that can be done about that? Can't *you* do something? Think about it: All that money from the Andorran account—surely you don't need it. Could it be used to back a professional league like the one that operated in the forties?"

She was silent, so he went on.

"And what else would you want to spend your time and money on? Anything?"

No response. But her eyes were flicking here and there, as if she were thinking about his idea. She remained quiet for a while. Then she said, "I've never met anyone like you, Carl. You're unsinkable." He laughed. "Besides, I've been wanting to tell you something."

"Is it something I don't already know?"

She smiled. "I believe it is. And now that this hearing is over, I want to tell you. Carl, you're the most wonderful man I've ever met. I've tried to keep my feelings about you submerged below my problems. But they keep bobbing to the surface. Why don't you ask me to marry you?"

"I would, if I thought you were ready to be asked."

"I'm ready. Hurry up."

Epilogue

"YES, IT'S DONE. Need it right now?" John Smith said into his phone. "Sure, I'll have it sent right over. ... Yep. You're welcome... Doug, would you have this—"

"I know, Card. I'll do it right now. Let me wrap it first."

"Thanks, Doug. I'm going to pack up the rest of this work and do it at home." He put on a leather jacket.

"Okay, Card. See you tomorrow."

"Fat chance. Tomorrow's Saturday. I'm taking my grandkids to the ball game."

He limped over to his briefcase and packed it with half-done work and what he called his "idea sketches." When he was gone, the typist turned around and said, "Why do you and the boss always call him Card? Isn't his name John?"

"His middle name is Cardello. Wake up, Susan. Haven't you noticed the C in the middle of his signature?"

"Oh. That's what the C is for. Why Cardello?"

"It's his mother's maiden name. She's Italian American."

"Well, anyway, he's sure a good artist."

"The company's best. I think he's especially good at drawing women. The boss says he's our Drawing Card."

Susan smiled. "Cute."

Doug called the delivery service, then finished wrapping and addressing the package. Soon the Drawing Card's sketch of women playing baseball in short skirts was on its way to the managing editor of the *Chicago Tribune*.

Two days later the *Tribune* published a historical feature about a baseball game that the All-Star All American Girls played on July 2, 1943, at Wrigley field against a team of WAACs.

What made the feature special was the accompanying drawings of some of the women in action. The artist, John Cardello Smith, used snap-

257

shots furnished by the local historical society to produce his drawings, which showed the players as determined, skilled, and attractively athletic.

The feature became a classic, the most admired introduction of the public to the new Women's Professional Baseball League of 2020.

A Note on Sources

The inspiration for this book came from two events in American history, one in 1931 and one in 1952. In both cases, a woman signed a contract to play baseball for a minor league team, but before she could start work her contract was cancelled by the commissioner either of her league or of Organized Baseball. Cancelled for just one reason: The player who signed the contract was a woman.

I have often wondered how these two women felt about being prevented from playing baseball because of their gender. I have never been able to learn whether they protested the cancellation of their contracts or whether their club managers tried to defend them against this treatment. Probably, they acted as women were long supposed to act: Not receiving any support from the managers who signed them, they acquiesced politely and went away quietly. Each woman took her athletic abilities elsewhere, along with her resentfulness.

In this historical novel, a skilled female ballplayer signs a similar contract, and when that contract is cancelled by the commissioner of Organized Baseball, her resentment of this discrimination, along with her personality and her family background, cause her to react angrily instead of accepting her fate supinely.

Writing about such a woman gave me the opportunity to bring in stories about ancient and historical women with athletic ability, positing them as ancestors of my heroine, for I believe that we all not only look like our ancestors, we have similar abilities, and we act much as they do.

Preparing this book also permitted me to use many of my own experiences of growing up in the Collinwood district of Cleveland, where I enjoyed living near Euclid Beach Park and Humphreys' Field, attending Fenn College (now Cleveland State University) and Western Reserve University (now Case-Western), as well as working during college at Halle Brothers Company. My uncle owned the bar and biergarten on the corner of Damon Avenue called Jack's Place.

My personal knowledge of these landmarks was complemented by studies of Cleveland universities like *Fenn College*, prepared by the Cleveland State University Library (Arcadia, 2005) and *Flora Stone Mather: Daughter of Cleveland's Euclid Avenue and Ohio's Western Reserve*, by Gladys Haddad (Kent State University Press, 2007) as well as one about the Halle Brothers Company, *Halle's: Memoirs of a Family Department Store 1891–1982* by James M. Wood (Geranium Press,

1987). I also used a book called *Old Stone Church: In the Heart of the City Since 1820* (Dorning Company, 1994).

My Cleveland experiences were further aided by research in the Cleveland Public Library, the archives of Cleveland State University, and the wonderful material made available online through a site called The Cleveland Memory Project, http://www.clevelandmemory.org/. Helpful books on the early history of Ohio and Cleveland included *Cleveland: Prodigy of the Western Reserve* by George E. Condon (Continental Heritage, 1979); *Cleveland: The Best Kept Secret* (Doubleday, 1967); *Euclid Avenue: Cleveland's Sophisticated Lady, 1920–1970*, by Richard E. Karberg & James A. Toman (Cleveland Landmarks Press, 2002); and even old books like *The Western Reserve: The Story of New Connecticut in Ohio* by Harland Hatcher (Bobbs-Merrill, 1949), which explains the origin of the Society for Savings Bank, a building that is still worth visiting.

For additional background on my favorite place for fun in the Collinwood section of Cleveland I consulted *Euclid Beach Park Is Closed for the Season* by Lee O. Bush, Edward C. Chukayne, Russell Allon Hehr, and Richard F. Hershey, along with its companion film of the same title prepared by Chuck Russell (1991). Although I no longer live in Cleveland, and Euclid Beach Park is closed permanently, I still enjoy Humphreys' popcorn balls, but now I order them online.

Since I have been researching baseball history for sixty years, I have long collected information on the early amateur baseball players, including women players, for the set of three books I prepared with my late husband, Harold Seymour, for Oxford University Press: *Baseball: The Early Years* (1960); *Baseball: The Golden Age* (1971); and *Baseball: The People's Game* (1990). My mother, who was for a time a textile worker in Cleveland, told me about women ball players at her company, too.

A newspaper clipping quoted by James Egan in his book *Base Ball on the Western Reserve* (McFarland, 2008) gave me the idea to present the scene at the game of the Red Stockings, and information about early smock races in *Running through the Ages* by Edward S. Sears (McFarland, 2001) inspired my creation of such an occasion for New London, Connecticut. Stamata Revithi, who ran the 1896 Olympic race on her own, was a real person mentioned in many sources; I merely imagined how her experience might have progressed.

Some readers will realize that I based my character of Joe Martino on the real-life gangster Joe Bonanno. For this aspect of American life I read many books on the Mafia, like Thomas Repetto's *American Mafia: A History of Its Rise to Power* (Henry Holt, 2004) and Tim Newark's *Lucky Luciano; The Real and the Fake Gangster*, but for Cleveland I found Rick Porrello's *The Rise and Fall of the Cleveland Mafia* (Barricade, 1995) most helpful. I also read Paul W. Heimel's *Eliot Ness: The Real Story* (Cumberland, 2000).

A lot of fine studies of the ancient Olympics were consulted, but my favorite is Tony Perrottet's *The Naked Olympics* (Random, 2004); I was glad to learn from Barry Strauss, head of Cornell's history department, that the Perrottet book is his choice, too. I read several versions of a hymn to the ancient goddess Demeter, then finally wrote my own; the one that inspired me most was the translation by Prof. Gregory Nagy of Harvard, which I read at www.stos.org.diotima. Descriptions of Boston, New York City, and upstate New York come from my experiences while living there, and my vacations in the Gravenhurst area of Ontario provided the background for describing it.

The history of Italy and particularly of Sicily makes for colorful reading, and I've collected a shelf full of wonderful books on these subjects. I selected Sicily as the background for my main character after a Sicilian dancer came to Naples, Florida, and presented a program of dance and song that entranced the entire audience. I became interested in Sicilian sulfur mines after reading in my local newspaper, the *Naples Daily News*, about a resident who had worked in one, so I interviewed him and then began researching those mines, surprised to find so much information about them online. My two favorite books on Sicily are Sandra Benjamin's *Sicily: Three Thousand Years of Human History* (Steerforth, 2006), and a huge but gorgeous coffee-table book called *Sicily: Art, History and Culture*, by Giovanni Francesio, Enzo Russo, and Melo Minnella (Arsenale Editrice, 2007).

For much of the information about Judge Landis I depended on the excellent biography by David Pietrusza, *Judge and Jury: The Life and Times of Judge Kenesaw Mountain Landis* (Diamond Communications, 1998).

Baseball and other athletic games as engaged in by women of the past deserves more attention; it's a mostly-hidden aspect of women's history, especially women's frustrating attempts to engage in successful participation in the American national game at a high level of competence. Over the last few years I have frequently read women's comments in articles and in blogs describing their childhood in which they reminisced about how much they wanted to grow up to play baseball for a particular big-league team and were dismayed to learn that it would never be possible because of their gender.

I prepared this book as a historical novel because I thought fiction would enable readers to empathize with some women's joy in intense sporting experiences. I want Americans to realize that rejection because of gender permeates many aspects of women's lives, including their desire to play baseball.

I dedicate this book to all those women of the past who were prevented from realizing their dreams of becoming professional baseball players.